CITY OF CHAMPIONS

A GATEWAY TO LOVE NOVEL

CHLOE T. BARLOW

CITY OF CHAMPIONS- A GATEWAY TO LOVE NOVEL
http://chloetbarlow.com/
All Rights Reserved
Original Copyright © 2013-2014 by Chloe T. Barlow

ISBN-13: 978-1502430526
ISBN-10: 1502430525
First Edition Published November 2014

Cover art by Complete Pixels and Eisley Jacobs

Edited by Marilyn Medina of Eagle Eye Reads Editing Service

All rights reserved. Except as permitted under the U.S. Copyright Act of 1976, no part of this publication may be reproduced, distributed, or transmitted in any form or by any means, whether electronic, mechanical, photocopying, recording, or otherwise, or stored in a database or retrieval system, without the prior written permission of the author. No patent liability is assumed with respect to the use of the information contained herein.

Please do not participate in or encourage piracy of copyrighted materials in violation of the author's rights. Purchase only authorized editions.

This is a work of fiction. Names, characters, places, brands, media, and incidents are either products of the author's imagination or are used fictitiously. Any resemblance to actual events, locales or persons, living or dead, is entirely coincidental.

The author acknowledges the copyrighted or trademarked status and trademark owners of various trademarks, wordmarks, products, individuals and entities referenced in this work of fiction, which have been used without permission. The publication/use of these trademarks is not authorized, associated with, or sponsored by the trademark or wordmark owners.

DEDICATION

To my beloved husband,
I don't know what I did along the way to end up with such a loving, supportive, and incredibly sexy man like you. Whatever it was, I'm grateful for it.

And, to Jess,
You've always been a heroine in my eyes. Now I am finally getting to let the world see it, too. Thank you for sassing me on a regular basis, and for teaching me so much about sisterhood, life, love, and the appropriate fit of a lab coat.

PROLOGUE

"Baby girl."

"Yes, Daddy?" Jenna asked, looking up at her father's face. She forced herself to smile at him as big as she could — a grin so wide it made her ears hurt.

She knew he was sad — had been for a long time now. Her biggest smile always made him happier. Yet it didn't work this time. He didn't pick her up and swing her around. He didn't tell her he loved her.

No — instead, he put his hand out to her and said, "I need you to come with me."

There were tears in his light blue eyes. That was the only feature they clearly shared, because every other part of her was all her momma's.

"Why, Daddy?"

He paused and swallowed roughly and Jenna swung her legs underneath her chair as the rush of fear hit her.

"Because, it's time to say good-bye."

His hand hovered near hers, waiting for her to take it. She loved holding her daddy's hand, it was always so big and rough, just like the footballs that were scattered everywhere around their yard at home. Yet, as much as she wanted to reach for him, Jenna didn't budge.

She felt her smile curl into itself, twisting into a nasty frown. Her stomach turned over so many times she thought she may get sick, but no matter how hard she tried, she couldn't find her words.

"Jenna?"

"I don't want to, Daddy," she finally whispered, looking down at her lap.

He crouched down in front of her and stroked her hair with one hand, while the other rested on his knee, clutched into a tight ball.

"I know," he said to her softly, his voice cracking around the words.

Jenna kept looking down, focusing on the gray linoleum floor beneath them. Maybe if she never looked up again she wouldn't have to stand up and say good-bye. Maybe everything would go back to the way it had been before.

She swallowed around the fist squeezing at her throat and picked at the golden hair of the dolly her mother had given her on her birthday the last spring. That had been right before she'd gotten so tired all the time — back when everyone was still happy and Jenna got to be at home with both her momma and daddy every day.

But then her momma started to feel really poorly until she couldn't get out of bed at all. The days became a blur of doctor visits and grown-ups talking in hushed, worried tones.

One person after another would stop by the house with a casserole or fried chicken. Sometimes they had a new toy for Jenna, but she never wanted to play with them. She would rather sit in the corner quietly holding her dolly until everyone went away again.

Momma and Daddy had just looked so scared all the time, and people kept coming by with sad words and tears. Then one day Daddy had said they all needed to go to Atlanta to be with Grandma, so Momma could go to the big hospital for a long time.

It was almost Christmas and her mother was worse than she'd ever been. Daddy said Momma had gotten a bug. It had made her really sick because she was so weak already. Jenna was starting to get worried they'd never get to go back home.

"Daddy, I want to stay here," Jenna said. She thought maybe if she could hold onto the perfect little doll from her mother and never look up, then maybe the bad dream would end and everything would be better.

It seemed like their whole world had been bad since Momma had gotten sick. Even though Jenna was still little, she understood life might never be okay for them — not ever again.

"Jenna," her father whispered again, sliding his hand to her chin and tilting Jenna's face up to look into his eyes, "we need to go."

"No, Daddy, I won't do it," she said, shaking her face out of his hand.

"Baby girl, please," he pleaded gently, smoothing out the skirt of her brand-new fancy, crinkly dress that Grandma had made her wear.

She just kept whispering, "No, Daddy, no, Daddy," over and over again, as the perfectly curled ringlets her grandma had painstakingly forced her hair into were hitting her wet cheeks with each increasingly violent turn of her head. The stiff lace of the dress — along with the multiple *Band-Aids* Grandma had used to cover Jenna's always-skinned knees — made sitting in her plastic chair uncomfortable. Even so, Jenna wouldn't move from her seat.

She knew her grandma could hear her — almost feeling the heat of her disapproving glare through the back of her head — and it made Jenna nervous for a moment.

Grandma probably thought she was being rude enough to warrant a switch across her rear end. Even though she'd never actually followed through on this repeated threat, the words always made Jenna behave, just the same. Even so, no matter how scared that woman made her, she couldn't get up — her body was glued to its spot.

All she could do was look down again and whisper, "I don't want to say good-bye, Daddy. I'm not ready."

She wanted to stay seated in an ugly chair in that enormous Atlanta hospital with her favorite dolly. If she were just patient enough, Momma would get better. Then they would all go home and they could spend Christmas together. As long as they didn't give up, then they wouldn't *ever* have to say good-bye to her.

Jenna felt her father's large, warm hands wipe away the hot tears that wouldn't stop streaming from her eyes, until he finally turned up her face to make her look at him again.

"I don't want to say good-bye, either, baby girl, but your momma asked us to, and you know I can't ever say no to her. Will you please come with me so I can be strong enough to do it? I need you to be there with me, Jenna."

"You do?" she asked through sniffles, confusion filling her brain. "But you don't need anyone, Daddy."

"Everybody needs someone, baby girl, and your mother and I need you."

She looked up into her daddy's watery blue eyes and felt her spine stiffen. Wiping the backs of her hands roughly across her tearstained cheeks, she breathed deeply and slid from her chair. She stood to her fullest height — already impressive for a girl that was only six-years-old — and held her head up proudly.

Jenna knew she could be a big girl — if even for just a couple of hours.

Her father put out his hand to her again, and this time, she slid her much smaller one into his.

"I'll help you, Daddy."

"Of course you will, baby girl. I knew you would."

They began walking together, but Jenna stopped short and turned to Auntie Cheryl, her mother's best friend. Even though she wasn't a blood relative, to Jenna she'd always been family. She looked so sad, too, with tears streaming down her pretty, dark cocoa skin as she leaned against the wall, watching them.

Jenna wanted so badly to make her feel better, but her hands were full. She looked down at her pretty, blonde dolly, with its soft smile and happy face. As much as she wanted to hold her little doll, she knew there was no time for playing anymore, not with so much else for her to do. So Jenna placed her doll down on her now empty seat and held her hand up to Cheryl, so they could see her mother together.

"Auntie Cheryl, will you please come with us, too?"

"Are you sure, honey?"

"Mm-hmm. Momma needs you. We need you, too. Don't we, Daddy?"

"We sure do."

Jenna didn't move her hand until Cheryl took it into hers and held it tightly.

"So now we go and say good-bye?" Jenna asked Cheryl softly. Cheryl nodded, choking back a harsh cry.

"That's right, honey, you know your momma hates to wait, right?" Cheryl asked, with a squeeze of Jenna's hand. "Kevin, are you ready?"

"I'll never be ready, Cheryl, so might as well just go," he answered, his eyes rimmed in red and swollen.

And with that, the three of them walked slowly down the cold hall. None of them spoke, there were only the sounds of their breaths and Jenna's brand-new dress crunching against her skin while her fancy shoes slid and squeaked on the linoleum floor.

Momma's hospital room wasn't far, but it felt like years that they'd walked. Jenna knew with each of those little steps, she was growing ever that much older.

Despite all her bravado of only moments before, Jenna hung back slightly as Cheryl quietly opened the door to Jenna's mother's now all too familiar sterile hospital room.

Jenna hated everything about this room — the whole hospital really. Every part of it was so gray and depressing, and always stunk like a drawer full of *Band-Aids* and *Lysol*. It was nothing like home, where everything smelled like sunshine, grass, and Momma's *White Shoulders* perfume.

Just the sight of her mother in this ugly place made Jenna's palms sweaty and her legs feel weak. Today was no different — it was actually even worse, if that were possible.

The curtains were drawn open so that a sliver of wan December sun could peek through. It didn't brighten the room, instead, it made it feel that much more empty — hopeless. It took a moment for her eyes to adjust to the dim light and finally see her mother, whose frail body was almost lost in the stiff sheets and coarse blanket of her narrow bed.

Cheryl released Jenna's hand and walked to the side of the

bed so she could fuss with the pillows and blanket. Auntie Cheryl always seemed to be moving things and Jenna was grateful for the distraction as she stared at her hands moving quickly across the bedding, until Momma swatted at her and released a soft laugh. No matter how dismal a day seemed, that bubbling laugh always made Jenna feel better, giving her the strength to move her legs again and walk farther into the room.

"Cheryl, I know you like to always be doing something, but I think you've fluffed my pillows enough for one day. Just relax, sweetie, please, and let's visit for a bit. Maybe water my little Christmas tree? You know that makes me happy."

"Sure thing, Sara," Cheryl choked out, as tears started to appear in her eyes again. She rushed to the bathroom to get water for the tree. Jenna didn't really see why she would go to all that trouble, though. The pathetic little set of twigs was so tiny and really looked like it would die any second. Yet, Jenna was glad it was there, if only because it made her momma happy.

Jenna's mother looked over to her, her eyes hazy with pain and exhaustion but she still managed to twist her pretty face into a smile.

"Hey, baby girl, there you are. Come here, climb on up and sit with me. Can you bring her to me, Kevin, honey?" she asked Jenna's father, who was still clutching Jenna's hand so hard she was worried it would be sore the next day.

"Sure thing, beautiful," he said, with a catch in his throat. He walked slowly across the room until they were at the edge of the small, stiff bed that had been her mother's home for what seemed like an eternity.

Jenna looked up at her daddy and released his hand so that she could grab a hold of the scratchy hospital sheets and crawled up them like a monkey. After she lay down, her mother began to stroke her hair gently.

"It looks like Maw-Maw did your hair, huh?"

"Yes, Momma. She messed around with it forever. I think she burned my neck, too," Jenna pouted out.

"Everyone has things that make them feel better, and that does it for her. I think it's very pretty."

"Thank you, Momma," Jenna whispered.

"You hate it, though, don't you, Jenna?" her mother asked, with that light laugh again.

"Yep," Jenna answered, nodding hard, "I hate it so much, Momma."

"Here, let me pull it back for you. Kevin, hand me a hair tie. Thanks, honey."

Her mother took the elastic band from him and tried to put Jenna's hair in a ponytail but grunted in frustration when her arms were too weak to finish it.

As she fell heavily against her pillows, Jenna couldn't deny that her mother's once tanned skin was now almost entirely gray. Her eyes were sunken deeply into her face, and every time she breathed or coughed it sounded like something had broken inside of her and was shaking and rattling in her chest.

"Damn, Cheryl, I guess I did too much yesterday, can you come in here and help me out?"

"Of course," Cheryl said, leaving the tiny Christmas tree plant to come to the rescue of Jenna's hair. Cheryl's hands were shaking as she looked down at Jenna and her momma, only to start crying again and look away. "Darn it, Sara, are you trying to wreck me?"

"Hey, calm down, honey. It's just a ponytail, it's not the end of the world."

"You know that's not what I mean," she huffed out, dropping her hands.

Momma took Cheryl's hands in her own and said, "It'll be okay, Cheryl. Let's just do what's in front of us and figure it out from there. Right now, all I need is a ponytail and a smile, okay? Besides, you still owe me for driving you to Alabama to meet Ben all those years ago," she teased, releasing Cheryl's hands.

"Sara..." Cheryl said, as she gently pulled Jenna's hair back. Jenna tried to look at her but the movement tugged at her hair too much, and somehow she sensed this was *their* moment.

"No crying, Cheryl. That's the deal. I've already let you get away with too much of that. Come on, fix my baby's hair and remind me of that trip... Please, just give me that, okay?" Jenna's mother looked into her friend's eyes intensely, even as her head rested heavily on the pillow. She only had a slight dusting of fuzzy hair on her head and her body was very weak. It hurt Jenna somewhere inside to look at her.

"Okay, of course, Sara. Um, we-ell, you drove, and it was after finals, and you stuck your left foot out of the car window, because you're so crazy." Cheryl stopped for a moment and wiped her eyes.

Seeing that everyone was so upset, Daddy came over and put a comforting hand on Cheryl's shoulder. He then let her go to put one arm around Momma and the other around Jenna. She felt as though she were wrapped in a warm, safe cocoon and she wanted desperately not to let it get away from her.

Cheryl took a deep breath before continuing to speak, "And I took pictures of you, and you made me laugh the whole way, and... Oh God, Sara, I can't do this..."

"There, now doesn't Jenna look pretty, and so much more comfortable — wouldn't you say, Cheryl?"

"Yes, she's so beautiful, just like her momma. Sara,

please…"

"Kevin, Cheryl, can you let me and Jenna visit for a minute? Just us? Tell Maw-Maw I need a moment, too. Okay? I know she wants to come by right now, but Jenna and I have to talk about something." She looked away sharply and breathed in so hard that Jenna curled up closer. "It's okay, baby girl. I just had a long day. It's all gonna be okay. I promise."

"Of course, honey," Cheryl said, through tears. It was ugly, the way Cheryl was sniffling and snorting, but to Jenna, it was the most beautiful and comforting thing in the world — to know Momma's friend was just as heartbroken as she and Daddy were.

"Cheryl, there you go again, you better go get some water so you don't dehydrate yourself."

"Yes, Sara, you tough cookie. Come on, Kevin, I think I need some *Jell-O*."

Cheryl started to walk toward the door, wiping her face with one hand, while gesturing for Daddy to leave with other. Yet, Daddy wouldn't leave Momma's bedside.

"Sara, I don't want to leave you," Daddy said with a gravelly voice.

"Kevin, it'll be all right. I'll be here when you get back. Please, I need this, okay? I love you."

"Okay. I love you both…so much."

He leaned forward to kiss Momma's lips and then Jenna's forehead, before following Cheryl out of the room.

When they were gone, Jenna placed her hand on her mother's chest, feeling its ragged rise and fall, hoping somehow that the press of her cool flesh could make her mother better. She wanted to reach into her body and take away the sickness. She wanted to be able to make the world better for her mother — to *heal* her.

Maybe it would take them all back to that place in time when they were happy. She hated herself for not being able to make everything the way it had been before.

What did I do wrong? she wondered, suddenly feeling like such a failure as fat tears slid down her cheeks.

Jenna's mother looked into her eyes and grabbed her hand from her chest. Even as thin and papery as it had become, Jenna still loved the feeling of that perfect, soft hand.

"It's okay, baby girl. I need you to breathe, and to know this isn't your fault."

"But it's not fair, Momma!"

"That's because this is life, and sometimes life is *so* unfair. You will drive yourself nuts trying to make life be fair. Instead, you just have to take from life what it's willing to give you, and accept the things it takes away from you. Because I love you so much, baby girl, but life is being a real bastard right now."

"Momma, you said a bad word."

"I know. And you better not ever say that word, I'll know if you do." Her mother tried to laugh but started to cough and shake and Jenna held her so tightly until she couldn't fight it anymore. She just let go, crying into her mother's thin, cotton gown until it felt like her whole world had shaken and fallen apart.

"Oh no, baby, don't do that. That's not what this is about. I don't want you to be sad. I want you to be strong. We don't have too much longer. I have so much I want to tell you, to show you, to teach you. But that all takes time…and time is the one thing I can't give you. So I need to try to capture a lifetime's worth of love and lessons for you in this little moment."

Jenna listened to her words as she squeezed even more tightly against her mother's thin frame. She wanted to make her mother feel calm and happy. Maybe then she'd get better and wouldn't leave her and Daddy alone.

After a deep breath, she said, "All right, baby girl, enough of that. Come on, Jenna, help me get my locket off, please." Jenna sat up and obliged, her fingers trembling around the small, delicate golden clasp. "I want you to have this. There are lots of my things at home that are yours now, but I wanted to give you this one myself."

Jenna opened the locket as she'd done so many times when poking around her mother's jewelry box, but this time, all she saw was bright gold.

"Momma, where are the pictures of you and Daddy?"

"I took them out."

"Why?"

"My momma gave this to me back when I was your age. She told me to fill it with a lifetime of love and memories. I had my time. Now it's yours."

"No. I don't want it. It's still yours. I won't take it. You're gonna need it when you get better and come home."

"Shh, sweetie. I've never lied to you, have I?"

"No, Momma."

"And I won't do it now. I need you to understand that I'm not gonna get better, baby girl."

Jenna tried to struggle and squirm away from the locket, from those terrible words...from *everything*.

"Yes, you *are* gonna get better, Momma, you have to." Jenna's voice had grown loud through all her distress until she couldn't help but let it turn to a whisper. "We need you. Why won't these doctors make you better, Momma? Why won't they fix you?"

"They tried, baby girl, but some things just can't be fixed."

"They *should* fix you. If I were a doctor, I would save you.

If I knew how, I would make it all better."

"I know you would, baby girl," she said, in short gasps, as her teeth clenched in pain. Her brown eyes filled with tears until they finally spilled forth onto her sunken cheeks, and she had to wipe them away with a shaky hand.

"I wish it were that simple, baby girl. Please know that all I've ever wanted in my life was to be at home with you and your daddy. But sometimes we don't get everything in life that we want. And fighting just makes it hurt more. Please take the locket. It would make me so happy for you to have it. And you'd better say yes because I'm getting tired." She managed to chuckle only to start coughing and breathing in tiny, choking gasps.

"Okay, Momma, I'll take it," Jenna said, once her mother's body had calmed down again.

"And I want you to wear it, okay? Don't hide it away in a jewelry box. Please wear it and love it. And when you find something great that life is willing to give you, please promise me you'll accept that great thing. Honor it by putting a picture of it in this locket and — believe me — I will know that you did. I don't know how, but I swear that somehow I will. Do you promise me you'll do that?"

"I promise, Momma."

"Thank you, baby girl," she answered, as she watched Jenna close her hand around the necklace.

Momma didn't speak for a while. Her breaths were short and the rattling sound coming from her chest seemed to get louder with ever gasp of air she tried to take.

"I'm also gonna need you to look after your daddy," she continued, speaking in bursts. "He is gonna be really sad and I will need you to be strong for him. You'll also have to be strong for yourself. Don't ever give up when you want something. Life is hard for girls, and I won't be here to look after you…"

"Stop saying that, Momma," Jenna interrupted, but her mother just patted her hand and shushed her.

"Jenna you're going to have to be tough and rely on yourself. Try not to let anyone hurt you or take advantage of you."

Her mother paused trying to catch her breath again, before continuing to speak.

"Jenna, folks are gonna…gonna try to get the best of you, but I want you to work really hard not to let them. You also need to take care of the ones you love, because that's the most important part of this crazy life. You got that?"

"Yes, Momma."

"I love you so much, Jenna," she added softly, holding Jenna in a close hug, before releasing her and grasping at her chest with a tense hand.

"Momma, what's wrong?"

"Baby, I can't…" She was trying to take a breath, but she couldn't. Her face was turning from slightly gray to the oddest shade of blue. Suddenly Jenna's mother's weak body started to shake and flop on the bed like a bass they'd caught, after her father had thrown it in the bottom of the boat on their last fishing trip.

"Momma!" Jenna was screaming now, crouching on the bed on all fours. She was desperately trying to get her mother to look at her, moving her own head and body to get closer to her face. Yet, it seemed that each time her mother's delicate frame twisted and jerked on the bed, her eyes began to look emptier, so much so, that Jenna could barely recognize her.

Footsteps approached and voices quickly surrounded them. Jenna continued to scream for her mother, trying to be heard over the loud beeping from all the machines connected to her shaking and twitching body.

Beep...beep...beep.

Hands suddenly dragged Jenna off the bed.

"Oh God, Jenna, you need to come with me," she heard Cheryl say, with fear in her voice.

"Auntie Cheryl, no! Let me go. Momma's in trouble. She needs me," Jenna shouted to her.

Her father ran in the room behind the army of doctors and nurses that were wheeling in more scary machines. Everyone was rushing around and saying words to each other that she didn't understand. All Jenna could do was reach for her mother.

"Momma, please, it's me, Jenna. *Momma!*"

Yet, no one could hear her shouting over the constant: *beep...beep...beep.*

Cheryl rushed out of the room, clutching Jenna in her arms. Jenna held the locket in one tight fist, reaching toward her mother with her other hand, frantically kicking her legs to try and get away.

"Shh, Jenna, please stop screaming, sweetie. *Oh Lord, please.*"

"I'll be good, Auntie Cheryl. I won't scream anymore, just let me go back in. Please. I'll be good. *I promise.* I can be good. I know I can."

The door closed swiftly behind them and Jenna wiggled free to the ground. She couldn't get through the door to her mother. Instead, all she could do was stand there in that horrible hallway.

She could feel tears coating her face and snot dripping from her nose and choking the back of her throat. Her stomach became twisted and sick feeling, like when she ate too much candy after trick-or-treating.

Beep...beep...beep.

Cheryl tried to hug her but Jenna shook her off. Her tiny legs were so tired and she let herself slump down in a heap on the linoleum floor beneath her. She took the skirt of her fancy dress to wipe her face, but more tears fell.

Jenna stared at the locket in her tiny fist, wrapped up now with the pleated lace and silk covering her lap.

With a deep breath, she looked at that evil door. It was keeping her from her mother, and she hated it. Jenna could feel Cheryl hugging her from behind.

"Momma's leaving. She's going away forever now, isn't she?"

Cheryl started sobbing in reply.

Jenna looked down and choked out to her in the softest whisper, "But I never said good-bye."

The only answer she received in return for her plea was one last *beep*. This one was never-ending. The sound sliced through the metal of her mother's hospital room door, and straight into Jenna's heart, until all that was left in the world was that brutally vicious echoing. *"Beeeeeeeep."*

CHAPTER ONE

Almost Twenty-Four Years Later

Beep...beep...beep.

"Hey, Dr. Sutherland, can you sign this?"

"What?"

Jenna jumped slightly at her name. She'd allowed herself to become almost hypnotized by the sound of a new patient's EKG. Her nerves were ragged today, she supposed. She found a smile for the nurse waiting in front of her with a patient's chart and pen in hand.

"Sure, Diana," she answered quickly.

"Are you okay, Dr. Sutherland?"

"Oh, yes, of course. I was just distracted by something. Come on, I'll sign it over here."

Jenna walked to the nurse's station, and away from the beeping noise. It was still offensive to her, but it was a part of the job, and there was no room in her life to let it bother her.

"So, Dr. Sutherland, are yinz headin' over to Dr. West's office?" Diana asked in a hushed, conspiratorial tone.

"Yep. Do you need me to ask him something for you?"

"Oh, no, I was just wondering if you were going to ask

him about going up for one of the sports medicine and orthopedic surgery fellowships everyone's talking about.

"Guilty," Jenna said, with a chuckle.

"We're all pulling for ya to get it."

"Seriously? Wow, thanks. Y'all are so sweet," Jenna answered, letting her words drawl a little through her pleasure, even while blushing at the attention.

"Sure thing, hon. Yinz is so nice to us. Plus, it's always great when we get to see a lady get some appreciation around 'ere."

Jenna finished signing the forms and handed Diana back her pen with a grin.

"Well then, fingers crossed. Thanks again," she said cheerily, before turning around and fighting the wash of nerves taking hold in her belly as she knocked on the door.

She tried to ignore the disconcerting nameplate announcing it as the office of the "Head of Orthopedic Surgery." She was worried it didn't bode well that her boss's title could possibly make her lose her nerve and skip this appointment altogether.

"Come in," she heard, and opened the door just as he looked up. "Hi, Jenna."

"Hi, Richard. Thanks for agreeing to see me," she said, before smoothing down her lab coat and sitting down in front of his desk.

"Of course, happy to. In fact, I figured you'd be finding your way into my office soon. I have a calendar reminder for when you eager beavers realize it's finally time for you to be considered for a fellowship."

"Oh darn, and I thought I was so original," she said, over her own bubble of nervous laughter.

She could kick herself. Though she strove always to appear

composed and generally as though she had her shit together, Jenna still felt like the shy, awkward little girl she had been growing up was always just one uncomfortable situation away from bursting right back out of her.

"It's no problem. You have to go after what you want in this profession, or you'll get left behind."

"Right, that's what I was thinking," she mumbled out, hating herself for not having a better response.

"The department still has a few months before we need to decide, so you have time to address my concerns."

"Your concerns?" she asked.

"For one, you're still pretty young."

"I'm turning thirty-one this spring," Jenna blurted out, with what unfortunately sounded too much like the tone of a little girl trying to sound impressive while she held up her fingers to show she was *"this many."* Jenna had to fight back a cringe as she deliberately steadied her voice and continued, "Richard, I'm only a year or two younger than the other people being considered. I've been out of med school as long as them, and I'm just as seasoned. Plus, I've had some of the most challenging patients."

"You know I think you're great, Jenna," Richard answered calmly, walking around the desk and leaning on the edge, in an apparent attempt to make her more comfortable. "You're bright and hard-working, but all our orthopedic surgical residents are. It's your upbringing that really delivers a different dimension to our sports medicine department. The way you grew up, helping your dad with his high school football teams and skills camps? And that you started out as an undergrad college basketball star, yourself? That's the kind of knowledge you can't learn on the hospital floor or in books."

"Thank you Richard. I also have my own personal

experience with sports injuries. Blowing out my ACL and MCL my junior year forced me to."

The thought of the moment sent an acidic wash of painful memories through her brain. She could still remember the fear that she wouldn't be able to finish college and go to med school if Duke rescinded her scholarship.

Her dream of helping people as a doctor someday had been in real jeopardy. Yet, fortunately she'd managed to make it work, even sticking around to attend Duke Med. Yet none of that changed the fact that she had so many more hurdles left to jump before her career was really established.

"Exactly," Richard continued. "And we love your commitment to the community through your charity work at local clinics and after-school programs. But that's why your apparent limitations are all the more baffling to me."

"Excuse me?" Jenna blurted, immediately trying to put on the best poker face she could muster.

"It's rare to have anyone with your knowledge about the inner workings of a team from every angle on our crew, and that's great. Really special. You know physical therapy techniques. You don't look down on the nitty-gritty of improving your patient's training regimen, or how they approach the game after recovery."

"Isn't that what you're looking for?"

"Of course we want that, Jenna. But otherwise you're still so distant with your patients, particularly the professional athletes. And that is disappointing, especially when our department's relationship with the local teams is a cornerstone of its success. Hell, it's a major focus of the fellowship you're trying to get. Being professional is one thing, but with you, well, it seems you treat the whole athlete, but you don't treat the *person*. And in a competitive field like this, that can be devastating."

"So it's my bedside manner?"

"No, the patients like you well enough." Jenna fought back a grimace. "It's just that you have a tendency to keep your cool demeanor and only see them as a condition. We are dealing with everyone from weekend warriors, to ballerinas, to NFL wide receivers. One size does *not* fit all. Maybe if you had more patients under your belt, another year or two of practicing…"

"I understand," she answered seriously, not quite understanding at all.

"Jenna, come on, buck up. It's not the end of the world. I'm pulling for you, but to give you such a high-profile position at this stage of your career means we need to be sure we're doing the right thing. Take these next couple of months to show us you really do appreciate our mission to stay at the top, while still connecting with every patient. I'll try to get you some more high-profile assignments, too. Make some calls to the local teams, see what we can get on your plate to show how you've grown."

"I would appreciate that," she said, as calmly as she could manage. Part of her wanted to scream, to tell him he was wrong — she *was* ready, no matter what nonsense he'd been spewing. Instead, she breathed deeply and regained her composure. She stood, looking him square in the eye while keeping herself perfectly steady and even, just as she always did. Finally, she added, "Thank you, Richard."

"Sure thing, Jenna. Have a great night."

"You, too," she answered, mindlessly walking out the door and waving at Diana while faking the best smile she could in response to her gleeful thumbs up from down the hallway. Every step down the sanitized hospital hallway made her feel more like a failure — a child playing dress up in some strange grown-up's lab coat.

Jenna snatched her purse out of her locker and put her lab coat away, numbly walking out to her car, grateful that no one tried to stop her to chat.

Finally in the sanctuary of her car Jenna let the sheer frustration hit her, as she slammed her door shut and threw the car into drive. She smacked her hand against the steering wheel, cursing aloud, screaming in the refuge of her metal cocoon.

Jenna was about to turn toward home when her cellphone rang, almost making her jump out of her seat. It also jarred her back to reality and reminded her that she'd promised to meet up with her friends for the Pittsburgh Roughnecks game against Denver.

"Hello," she said, answering the phone through her *Bluetooth*.

"Hi, sweetie, how're you doin'?"

"Aunt Cheryl, hi…how's it going?" Jenna asked with a sigh, as she turned her car onto the Hot Metal Bridge, to make her way to the football stadium.

"Pretty well. Dang, girl, you sound downright miserable. Did someone go and steal your bike?" she asked, in that way that always made Jenna feel better.

Physically they couldn't have looked more different, what with Cheryl's dark cocoa skin, beautiful almost amber eyes and ebony hair. But she'd always loved Jenna like she was her very own. At home with her dad, Jenna's focus was on perfection and doing all she could to ease the lingering sadness in his eyes after her mother's death. But with Cheryl, she could be herself, complete with all her worries and insecurities.

Jenna took a breath and unloaded the whole conversation, feeling at least relieved that the words were no longer burning a hole in her own throat.

"Well, he sounds like an idiot. How could you be distant? You're nice to everyone!"

"You're kind of biased, Cheryl."

"That's my job. I'm here to blindly take your side, sweetie. It sounds to me like your boss is wrong about you."

"Thanks. Unfortunately he's a guy that has a lot of power over my career."

"Ain't that how it always is, baby?"

"I know. I'll figure it out. I've worked so hard for this. It's all I know. I can fix it, I suppose. But, how do I change who I am?"

"Don't you change a thing about yourself. Maybe you just need to show them how open you can be to the challenge. You go out there and give your patients all the thoughtfulness that I know you have in you. And maybe you should also think about having something else in your life besides joints and muscles."

"Cheryl…"

"Oh come on. How about we talk about something more fun. Are you seeing anyone?"

"Ugh, that question is never fun. Talking about a root canal — or that crappy meeting I just had — would be more fun. How'd I know that was where you were headed with this?"

"Because I love you, and I want to see you happy and holding more than a medical chart. Look at how happy Tea is now."

It *was* inspiring to see her friend Tea take a chance on love again after losing her husband, Jack, years before. Especially considering how she and her boyfriend, Griffen, had something so real and passionate together. Their relationship was also a daily reminder that Jenna couldn't force herself to feel strongly about any of the men she'd been allowing herself to go out with.

UPMC was a top five hospital nationwide, year after year. It had been a great move career-wise to transfer there and be near her best friend, Tea. After Tea's husband passed away, she'd been struggling to raise their baby on her own. Plus, once Aubrey moved from L.A. to join them in Pittsburgh, Jenna got to have the rare joy of being around both of her best friends from college all the time. Despite these benefits, the romantic side of Jenna's life in Pittsburgh had been pretty lackluster.

"Oh, stop that. You're so pretty and smart — you probably have more dates than you can count."

Jenna groaned inwardly at the unwelcome question. "Ugh, Cheryl. Well other than a few repeat dates here and there and a handful of lukewarm flings, nothing has happened worth writing home about. Nothing with any future, that is."

"Oh so it's more that you don't like your options?"

"I'm looking for a nice, stable guy…"

"And what you're finding is ones that are boring the hell out of you?"

"That sounds about right. I've decided to take a little break from dating the last couple of weeks. Maybe I'll get a taste back for…"

"You'll never develop a taste for dull, sweetie, because *you* are not dull. No matter how much you try to pretend to yourself that you are. Maybe you should branch out a little. Try something other than those boring doctors and whomever else you keep dating. Have a little fun. You know, like Tea."

"Yeah, well that was crazy. The first guy she hooks up with in the almost six years since her husband's death…and boom, he's the one. I've never really been one to have 'boom.'"

"Only because you date guys you have no fireworks with.

You should take some risks."

Jenna swallowed a bitter laugh. "Risks are poison for the Sutherlands, you know that."

"Aren't you just a negative Nelly? All right, I'll leave it be for now. So, speaking of the other half of your Sutherland family…"

Jenna's heart dropped. Cheryl had been regularly sending Jenna updates on her father and none of them had been particularly heartening.

"I saw your dad last week and he really misses you. He's been working himself like crazy over this year's team. Maybe you can come home for Christmas?"

"We'll see. Thanks for letting me know. Cheryl, you've got enough on your plate, I feel bad about you worrying about us so much."

"No. I promised your momma I'd help look after you and your dad, and I will keep doing that till I ain't got a breath left in me. You'll call your dad though, right?"

"Of course, I promise." Jenna ran the fingers of her right hand through her long, blonde hair and glanced at the clock on her radio.

"Dammit! I didn't realize it was so late. I better focus on my driving if I want to make it to the football game in time."

"Business or pleasure?"

"Pleasure, I think."

"You think?"

"Tea's boyfriend is taking us all to the Pittsburgh game against Denver tonight, but I'd rather just curl up in bed and feel sorry for myself."

"Oh, stop it. He didn't say you definitely weren't going to get the fellowship. Don't be so pessimistic. And I wasn't trying to make you upset about your dad."

"I know. I really appreciate you being there for him. He gets really sad when the anniversary of Momma's death knocks on the door. But you have so much of your own to worry about, you know, everything you have going on and all."

"You are sweet, Jenna, but it's been over a year since I lost Ben, and honestly, I need something to keep my mind off being a widow. Fussing over you and your dad has always made me happy, so why stop now, right?"

"Thanks Cheryl. Anything else you need to tell me?"

"Well, since you mention it…um…I don't want you to get worried, but your dad knows you put money in his account. He was *not* happy."

"Dammit. What else am I supposed to do? Those budget cuts at the high school were brutal, and attendance is down at his camps. I hate to ask more of you, Cheryl…"

"Don't be silly. I'll just head over and feed him more often, and sneak him your money any way that I can."

"Thank you so much. Bye. I love you."

"I love you, too. Bye, sweetie."

Center spikes the ball to McCoy.

McCoy drops back for 1…2…3…4…seconds. He's still taking too long.

Ooh, there's that great leg agility he's got. That's right, slip that tackle, use your height, see your man down the field and…

He throws another dump-off pass to the tailback. What in the hell? That's not even enough for a first down. Why didn't he throw it to the wide out? He was totally open. McCoy had to have seen him. He's completed that throw with his eyes closed thousands of times… Jenna wondered with confusion.

She'd been tracking Wyatt McCoy's every movement since the start of the game — never taking her eyes off him for a second that he was on the field.

His style of play had fascinated her for almost a decade now — both his dazzling strengths, as well as his mind-boggling weaknesses. Gifted with remarkable genes passed down from his incredibly renowned quarterback father, he'd been on the radar of everyone interested in football since he was a child.

But what intrigued Jenna was the unique ability he brought to the game all on his own. "Gunslinger" McCoy had a lithe body that was as acrobatic as it was strong. That natural athletic prowess, combined with his seemingly instinctive ability to identify passing opportunities almost anywhere on the field, made him a truly unique talent. In fact, for as long as Jenna had been watching him compete over the years, it seemed he could extend any play, when everyone else on the field, or watching from the sidelines, thought it was already dead.

Even in this disappointing outing, in which he'd already been sacked twice and his team had been outplayed most of the time, he'd still managed to keep the Pittsburgh Roughnecks in the game. He'd orchestrated two breathtaking touchdown drives to tie it up and send the game into overtime.

Studying him over the last few hours had actually been a treat for Jenna — anything to take her mind off her annoying afternoon, though she had admittedly not been the life of the party in the luxury suite.

"You know you can take the night off and just enjoy the game, right?" Aubrey asked from behind her, making Jenna jump a little after being so focused on the field.

"This *is* how I enjoy it, Aubrey. Maybe it's an occupational hazard, or something," Jenna answered, with a distracted tone before turning her attention back to the next play. She was far too fixated on the game — well, really just on Wyatt McCoy, to deliver a better answer.

Jenna was also still racking her brain to process the reasoning behind Wyatt McCoy's decision making and the Roughnecks' play calling on offense when Aubrey continued talking.

"Or is it a 'Jenna Sutherland football strategy obsessed' hazard?" Aubrey countered.

"What?" Jenna looked over to Aubrey for a second before turning back around yet again. "Yeah, that too. But look at him on this play. I've been watching Wyatt McCoy play quarterback since he was at the University of Texas, then after Dallas drafted him, and now here, this last year and a half. He's always taken a long time to drop back, but this is ridiculous. Plus, he's not evading tackles in the same way he used to. Everything is…I don't know, slower somehow."

"I'm glad he's sucking today, because this Denver girl wants a win for her team."

"Sucking is a bit strong of a word. That comeback was incredible, but I'm sorry to say, I don't think it was enough. I'm gonna bet you'll get your win."

"You're sorry to say, are you? Feeling bad that your quarterback crush is going to lose?"

"He's not my crush, jeez."

"That's exactly what a girl with a crush would say! Though I can't say I blame you. I'm not sure which part of his background is hotter, his famous quarterback father, or his beautiful Mexican mother. I've seen some of her old modeling shots from back in the day — a photographer's dream."

"She was, and stop changing the subject. I know I'm in the

minority, but I've always thought he had more raw skill and talent than his dad. Problem is he's not playing up to it lately. I can't be sure from this angle, but I think he's unknowingly telegraphing his throws to the defense. There's something going on with him. I think his shoulder is bothering him? I feel like I have it almost figured out."

Jenna was leaning over the railing that ran along the edge of the luxury box to which Griffen had managed to get them all invited. The entire setting was beautiful and the view was spectacular, but her quick little mind couldn't shake the desire to be down on the fifty-yard line looking at game pictures and barking out ideas, like she used to do for her father so many years ago.

"It's always good to watch a game with you now and again, Jenna, so I can remember what a freak you are," Aubrey said. "You aren't watching any of the other players? Just the gorgeous 'Gunslinger' McCoy?" Her caramel colored eyes were dancing with her signature mischief as she teased Jenna. Aubrey's impressive height made it easy for her to peek around Jenna's shoulder to catch a glimpse of the famous quarterback that was holding Jenna's attention so strongly.

"So? What about it?" Jenna looked at her sideways. With her short dark hair and quirky sense of style befitting a freelance photographer, such as herself, Aubrey had the look of a pixie. It went perfectly with the scheming look on her face in that moment. "Where are you going with this, Aubrey?"

"Nowhere. I just love seeing you take such a passionate interest in an athlete. Watched him since he was in college, did you?"

Jenna rolled her eyes dramatically at her friend and roommate.

"Oh, stop, Brey. It's not like I've ever met him or anything.

I've just been fascinated by his potential for a while now. Okay, watch this third down play — McCoy's taken the snap, faking a hand-off to the running back, and now he's dropping back for the play action pass. There, he's taken too long, again. He's not going to avoid this blitz. Dammit, they've got him."

Jenna watched with a feeling of dread as the inside linebacker slammed into Wyatt McCoy, sacking him and throwing him to the ground.

"Wow, what would I do without you here to tell me what I'm seeing with my own eyes," Aubrey deadpanned sarcastically at her.

"Fine, I'll go back to thinking it all to myself," Jenna said, with a grumble, staring at McCoy as he shook off the trainers and worked his right arm back and forth on the sidelines, staring at the punter returning the ball to Denver's possession.

Aubrey laughed and hugged her from behind.

"Oh, stop it, you big baby. I like seeing you obsessed with a hot man. Especially because Griffen tells me we'll be meeting him after the game. You're going to love that. Maybe you can get some private time with him. You can look at that shoulder a bit more closely."

"*What?*" Jenna asked, straightening up away from the railing in a flash, and knocking Aubrey back. "That guy is notorious."

"Is he? I don't remember hearing about him being *that* much of a player."

"No, being a womanizer comes with the territory. I mean he's known for doing *anything* to get ahead on a team. That is way more dangerous, as far as I'm concerned. Remember when he refused to groom the quarterback Dallas drafted a few years ago? He was so threatened he would take his starting spot that he barely acknowledged him, and Dallas ended up trading

McCoy anyway. Why would I want to be alone with someone that cold-blooded?" Jenna felt a nervous twitching in her stomach at the mere thought of it.

"I wasn't suggesting you join the Roughnecks practice squad and become his throwing partner. You've been apparently staring at him in tight pants for ten years, so you'll appreciate some one-on-one time with him. You won't have to wait too long, either. It's sudden death overtime and I'm pretty sure Denver's going to score on this drive. It's safe to say we can start planning our post-game activities, and I already know what yours will be."

"Aubrey, not everything has to end in sex."

"Whoa, who said anything about sex? How scandalous of you to bring that up," Aubrey said, with feigned shock. "You're the one who mentioned sex. We haven't even met him yet, maybe you should focus on dinner first."

"I'm not focusing on anything with him but his game."

"Oh boy, my wheels are really turning now. I'm going to get you in a room with the Gunslinger, if it's the last thing I do."

"Aubrey, please don't embarrass me," Jenna pleaded. "It's like I'm at work right now. If you put me in a bad spot, it could make me look bad."

"Stop being so dramatic. It'll be fun, and that's what you need more than anything else. You've been too mopey lately. Besides the idea is already planted in my brain. You can't dig it out. Just let the magic happen."

Jenna frowned at her before turning back to the game. Aubrey screamed in delight at the sight of Denver's running back pushing his body into the end zone and winning the game.

A few moments later McCoy walked into the tunnel in

defeat. His frustrated face filled the multiple TV screens in the box, as he stopped to sign a few autographs. Then he disappeared, his head hanging low. Jenna felt a peculiar sensation of sadness and disappointment on his behalf that she couldn't seem to shake.

"Griffen! What's up? Did you guys enjoy the box?" Griffen's friend, Tom Wilkins, the Assistant GM of the Pittsburgh Roughnecks, asked, his voice booming from the front of the luxury stadium suite and jarring Jenna back into the moment.

"It was great, Tom. Thanks so much for setting this up for us," Griffen answered cheerfully.

"I wish I could've also provided a win for you guys. That loss was brutal."

"So true. It seemed like McCoy spent more time on his butt than actually throwing the ball."

"Don't remind me. If you weren't a journalist I'd really loosen my lips on that."

"Oh, come on, I'm more of a writer than a journalist these days."

"Still too much of a reporter for my taste," Tom said, with a laugh.

"Guilty as charged. Well, thanks for the box either way," Griffen responded.

"No, thank *you*," Tom answered, with a smile. "The second I heard Nicky, I mean *Griffen* Tate, of all people, was back in Pittsburgh and settled down, I moved heaven and earth to get you in here."

"Yeah, I have so many people I need to catch up with, but you moved way up in priority with this spread, Tom," Griffen said, smacking his friend's shoulder with his open right hand in that ridiculous way that men do.

"Yes, thank you, it was so nice of you to let us use it," Tea added.

"Tom, this is Althea, my girlfriend, and her son, Johnny," Griffen said proudly, wrapping one arm around Tea and placing his other hand on Johnny's shoulder.

Jenna lurked back, watching the scene quietly.

"Eavesdrop much, Jenna?" Aubrey whispered in her ear, making her jump.

"It's not really eavesdropping if nobody minds you listening, Brey," Jenna answered.

"I guess that's true enough. It's still weird to hear Griffen call Tea his girlfriend, isn't it?"

"It will definitely take some getting used to, and soon he could be calling her his fiancée…"

They both peeked at the happy little almost family, watching as Griffen pulled Tea close to him. Ever since they took their relationship public, it seemed he always had to be touching her in some way as much as possible.

"If they weren't so deliriously happy and good for each other, it would probably all be pretty nauseating," Jenna mumbled, gasping a little when she realized she'd said it out loud.

Maybe Brey would let that slide? Right, fat chance, she thought.

"Rawr, girl, you *are* in a foul mood. I love it," Aubrey teased, making little claw gestures that Jenna swatted away with more force than the situation likely demanded.

"I can't believe he's going to wait another couple of days until Light Up Night to propose. That ring is burning a hole in his pocket. Is that why you're listening in? To see if he proposes to her next to the bowl of chips over there?"

"No. You're so silly, Brey. I was just hoping for a chance to introduce myself to Tom." Tom was one of the members of the Roughnecks' staff that she hadn't worked with before. He was the Assistant GM and that would certainly mean something to Richard.

"You'll have plenty of chances to talk to Tom on our way to meet Wyatt McCoy."

Jenna gave Aubrey a withering look. She followed Aubrey over to the rest of the group and plastered a great big smile on her face as they finished their conversation.

"I hope you had a nice time, too?" Tom asked Tea.

"I did. Thank you again, Tom," Tea answered, honestly looking happy and relaxed in her own skin in a way that filled Jenna's heart with joy.

"So this little man is your son?" Tom asked, crouching down to be eye to eye with Johnny.

Tea's son was wired for sound after the game and Jenna was shocked that he had been so obediently waiting through this boring adult conversation without interrupting.

"Yes," she answered.

"He's Tea's son with Jack Taylor," Griffen added, looking uneasy for a moment, but quickly returning to his usual confident air.

Tom stood and looked Tea in the eyes.

"Um, I wanted to say…I went to high school with Griffen and Jack back in the day. Jack was a hell of a guy. It is such a shame what happened to him."

"Thank you for saying that. He was," Tea choked out. The sadness flashing suddenly across her previously happy face sent a shot of pain through Jenna.

She couldn't help but reach out to touch Tea's arm when she heard the catch in her throat. Griffen's love and attention may have brought Tea back to life, but Jenna suspected the ghosts of Tea's grief and pain were still waiting in the wings.

Jenna understood the power of that constant pain all too well — from the rare times when she indulged herself to reflect on her own tragic memories.

"I didn't want to upset you. I'm sorry," Tom blurted out, quickly.

"Oh, no, I'm fine, Tom. Don't be silly," Tea took a deep breath and schooled her face into a smile, "let me introduce you to our friends, Aubrey and Jenna."

Griffen quickly spoke up, "Jenna's a resident with *UPMC's* department of orthopedic surgery. She's worked with some of your players. They know her as Dr. Sutherland."

"That's great! What a small world." Tom said with a smile, shaking her hand, then Aubrey's. Jenna made sure to look over at Griffen and mouth a silent thank you to him.

"It's a pleasure to meet you Tom," Jenna said, deliberately hiding her exhaustion from the day behind a professional smile. "This has been a great evening. Johnny especially loved it. He plays quarterback."

"Griffen mentioned it." Tom smiled and glanced at his watch, adding, "In that case, let's get going. I didn't realize so much time has passed. I figure Griffen told you already, that I lined it up so you all can meet a few of the players. They should already be waiting for us. We can use the private elevator over here."

"Come on Jenna," Aubrey whispered to her deviously, "I can't wait to get this tour started." Jenna could only roll her eyes and fall in line with the rest of them.

CHAPTER TWO

Pressing his large left hand against the cool shower tiles, Wyatt allowed his tired eyes to close and gently bent his head, leaning his warm forehead against the smooth porcelain.

Warm jets of water sprayed over his chestnut brown hair, down the contours of his face and along the ridges of the screaming muscles in his chest and arms, before finally traversing the length of his legs, only to disappear in a swirl down the drain near his aching feet.

Every part of his mind and body was suffused with anger and frustration, so intense they rivaled the tangible pain pulsating from his right shoulder. With each new rush of water, he tried to imagine that the last four hours of his life, with all the failures and brutal hits they had entailed, were hitching a ride with that cleansing liquid and leaving him forever.

Yet, he found no such relief.

Instead, every time he let his mind wander, it went right back to replaying each of the three bone-crushing sacks he'd taken during the game. No matter how much he wanted to think of the few plays that went his way, the hulking force of each mistake and delayed movement immediately eclipsed those successes, until Wyatt felt so furious he had to slap his resting hand hard against the wall.

There was no denying — at least not to himself — that his right shoulder was killing him. He'd taken time to ice it down with the trainers, but the pain was still there. In fact, the only thing hurting worse than his body was his pride.

He'd played this game since his hands were barely large enough to pick up a football. Recently he felt like he'd never set foot on a field before, never called a play, and certainly never been able to win a game. His mouth turned up in a sneer as he imagined all the media experts ripping him apart the next day.

Even though his team was still hovering around having as many wins as losses, lately it felt like the day after every game was the same. So much so, Wyatt believed he could write the headlines himself by now.

They would probably go something like:

Monday Night Football — the biggest stage you can have in the season before the play-offs — and Wyatt McCoy fell right off the edge.

A football prodigy, with the DNA to match, McCoy still can't seem to hit his stride in Pittsburgh, even after almost two seasons. By this time in his career, his father, the great Jim McCoy, already had two Super Bowl rings. This second coming of the McCoy line has no championships to show for himself, but he does come with a ton of red flags.

Then, of course, there'd be the commentary on *ESPN*.

SportsCenter would probably try to be clever while they made every effort to tear apart his performance.

The same impulsive behavior and surly attitude that plagued Gunslinger McCoy in Dallas has followed him to the Steel City. This gunslinger looked less Wyatt Earp and a lot more Elmer Fudd. He's far from the success and adoration he enjoyed back in Texas — the site of his childhood home and college glory. After almost two years in a city used to winning — *the City of Champions* — *he's starting to look a little lost.*

Ironically, Wyatt's plan was to eventually become one of those annoying talking heads himself — not for the love of the game or of talking about it, but for the pursuit of his own obsessive need to provide security for him and his family. The career of an NFL quarterback, and the salary that came with it, was just a tiny speed bump in the long road of one's lifetime. When his body was too broken and old to throw a ball or evade a tackle, Wyatt needed to be ready with a Plan B, maybe even a Plan C or D. Hopefully with his brain not too broken and battered after all the pounding years on the gridiron.

Because the sports commentary that scared him the most was the one that tormented him relentlessly in his own mind:

Where do I go from here? What security can I achieve if I can't stay on the field? Every plan I've ever had has relied on being out there playing the game...on being a starting quarterback for a lot longer than these measly nine seasons...on bringing a championship to a team at some point in my life.

With a sigh and admission to himself that he was unable to delay facing reality again for another moment, Wyatt rinsed off the last bit of soap from his body and turned off the water. Stepping out of the shower into the locker room, it seemed that every step he took hurt his aching body that much more.

The nearly empty locker room gave him a small moment of relief. He'd taken time with the trainers and an extra long shower in the hope that he could wait out the press and their annoying questions, and it looked like he'd succeeded.

As Wyatt sat on the wooden bench and awkwardly dried his hair with the towel in his left hand, he gingerly pulled his button-down shirt and slacks out of his locker with his other hand.

He was working on some modeling gigs. The guys ribbed

him constantly about it, but the money was great, and the free clothes were even better. It meant he didn't get to bum around in sweats like some of the other players, but it was worth it — one more step in his plan to take care of his abuela, mother, and sister as long as he could.

Everyone loved his dad, Jim McCoy, or at least the image of him they'd been able to see. They didn't know that the man had blown it all and left his family with nothing. Wyatt would make no such mistake.

Even so, Wyatt was unable to shake the feeling that his whole career was turning into an unforgiving mass of promised triumph. Now in his ninth professional season and on his second team, it was all starting to feel to him like he'd built his career around a whole lot of *"almost was"* and *"never will be."*

The thought caused rage to bubble in Wyatt's stomach and he slammed shut his locker door in frustration. The fleeting emotional release it brought was quickly replaced with another angry rush of pain shooting deeply across his right shoulder. It had already been killing him before the game, but being mauled on the field for a handful of hours didn't do it any favors — in fact, it had left his whole body hurting, and reignited his overwhelming sense of worry about his future.

"*Fuck*," he said angrily under his breath, waiting a moment for the rush of agony to subside before snatching up his bag with his still functioning left arm. Silently, Wyatt began to walk out.

"Hey, Wy — wait, where are you going?" J.J., his go-to wide receiver asked him, jogging up to his side.

"Home. Good night, man."

"Come on, dude, you're kidding, right?" J.J. asked, suddenly losing his cool exterior.

"No. What's the big deal? Game ends. People leave. It

happens. Take it easy, dude," Wyatt answered, with a confused laugh, as he continued toward the door.

J.J. jogged after him and blocked his exit from the locker room.

"Don't you remember?"

"What, that you're a spaz?" Wyatt asked, with a laugh, continuing to the door, barely missing a step.

"No, dumb-ass. We have to meet that VIP author dude and his guests."

"Shit. I forgot," Wyatt answered, stopping to look at his friend. "Wanna cover for me, J.J.? I'm not in the mood for that bullshit right now."

"What else is new? You're never in the mood for this shit, asshole," J.J. said seriously, walking closer to Wyatt so they couldn't be overheard. "You know you're on thin ice with the team right now. This extra 'bullshit' is part of the package and you know it."

"Thanks for reminding me. So you're an expert now?" Wyatt grumbled out.

He'd known J.J. for a couple years and he was his biggest ally on the team, so it didn't do him any good to yell at him. It did make Wyatt feel a little better at that exact moment, though.

Wyatt was fully aware he needed to play nice. Between his shoulder still acting up and three losses in a row, he needed to do all he could to show he deserved to be a starting quarterback — whether it be in Pittsburgh or somewhere else — at least for another few seasons. The only way to do that was to get this season, and his role on the team, back under control.

"Don't take it out on me, Wy. I was on that field when we shit the bed, too, you know," J.J. answered, with a sarcastic tone that might have irritated Wyatt from anyone else.

"You're right, man, but I don't like to be around people after a loss. And definitely not any 'VIPs' — it's probably a bunch of rich, douche bag armchair quarterbacks showing off their connections to their boring wives."

"Well, you do have the right attitude to be an ambassador for the team today," J.J. said, with a laugh. "You'll have to leave all the charming up to me then. And if any of those boring wives are hot, it won't be so bad. I'll let them touch my muscles. They love that shit."

"You're pretty optimistic, J.J. Look, I've done enough of this crap since college to be able to guarantee you they are definitely not going to be hot. So fine by me, you and your muscles can have them all. I just want to get this over with."

"I get it, man. You're a cranky old bastard tonight."

"Twenty-nine makes me old, huh?" he asked, finally cracking a smile. "You're twenty-six, you idiot."

"You know what — you're right, we are still young. So why don't you come out with us after this VIP shit is all over? We're going to the Southside to get a drink — or four — and maybe find some Pittsburghers that aren't totally disgusted with us. It'll be good for you to spend some time with the guys."

"No, I need to call it a night as soon as we're done."

"Old *and* predictable — Christ, Wy, you are one boring guy."

"Looks like I am. Sorry, man."

Wyatt actually was tempted to cut loose instead of hiding out in his big empty house all by himself.

But he knew that it all started with one fun night.

In fact, that was how it began, and, ended for his father — simple nights of entertainment, enjoying the pleasures that came with being a star NFL quarterback. In between those nights came too much partying, too many women and run-ins with the law that got swept under the rug. Then came more folks asking for money, and bad investments taking whatever else he had left. Until he had lost the family's home and his wife couldn't ignore the cheating and long absences for another day. She'd taken Wyatt and the rest of their kids to live with her grandparents, so they could try to start their lives over quietly.

Wyatt realized he may be facing career speed bumps, but at least they were all his own. He would deal with those, while doing whatever it took to avoid the failures of his father and the humiliating fate that came with them.

"Man, you really are a pain in the ass, Wy. Fine. Your loss."

"Don't I know it," he answered.

"Come on, let's get out of here so we can go meet these stiffs."

Wyatt tossed his bag onto the bench and followed J.J. to the vestibule outside the locker room, where the rest of their group was waiting.

"Hell, yeah," J.J. said, under his breath. "I definitely still call the women. Old, boring wives, my ass, Wy."

Wyatt rolled his eyes at J.J. before turning around to get a load of what had J.J. all worked up. His taste was pretty lenient — breasts connected to a willing body were often enough to get him going, but as soon as Wyatt turned around he started to think he'd underestimated J.J.

Tom was leading the group next to a guy about Wyatt's age with a riled up little boy who was so excited, he looked about ready to jump out of his own skin.

Behind them was the sight that had J.J. and Wyatt's full attention. Three beautiful women were pulling up the rear —

one had short, dark hair and a quirky smile, while another had a sweet face and a massive head of light brown hair, almost the color of honey. But it was the serious-looking stacked blonde standing next to her that had Wyatt's heart suddenly pounding. Her blue eyes were penetrating and screamed of a challenge he was ready to take on — because, dammit, he really needed a win, and quickly.

"I call the blonde, J.J.," he said to his friend with a quiet intensity.

"Fuck, you're kidding — she's perfect for me."

Wyatt threw him a look that had managed to make unruly teammates fall in line since he was a kid, and now was no different.

"Fine, if that'll cheer you up, I'll let you give it a shot. I like the look of that crazy brunette, anyway," J.J. answered confidently.

"Perfect. Let the games begin," he whispered to himself.

They want me to play nice? Wyatt thought to himself. *Sure, I can do that. I'll play really nice with this hot blonde.*

"Tea, I'm gonna head home after we meet the players," Jenna whispered to Tea as they followed Tom, who was still chattering almost nonstop several feet ahead of them to Griffen and Johnny.

"What?" Tea whispered back with concern, stopping suddenly until Aubrey barreled into her from behind.

"Jeez, Tea, are you trying to kill me?" Aubrey huffed at her.

"No, but I may kill Jenna. She wants to go home." Tea turned back to Jenna, glaring at her with an amount of frustration in her eyes that surprised her, considering Tea was usually so nice — maybe a little dramatic at times, but always sweet. "You really can't be serious, Jenna. Not after Griffen went to all this trouble."

"I know, and I am so grateful for getting to make that connection with Tom, I had a crappy day and am totally beat. It's not like I blew this off."

"You're blowing it off now," Tea whispered angrily in response. "I can't believe you."

"Calm down, Tea…"

"Tea, ignore Jenna. She's just nervous about spending so much time with Gunslinger McCoy."

Jenna rolled her eyes at Tea but was getting no support from that member of their triad.

Instead, Tea simply glared at her.

"Hey, are you guys coming?" Jenna heard Griffen's deep voice boom back to them. He headed over to their direction and immediately looked at Tea with concern. "Gorgeous, is everything okay?" he asked her softly, as he placed his hand at the small of her back. Tea looked up at him and the two simply stared in each other's eyes. The adoration they shared for each other was almost palpable.

"I'm fine," Tea said reassuringly to Griffen. "It's Jenna, she's got a bad case of the stick-in-the-muds. She's trying to skip the tour."

"No way, Jenna, this is a huge opportunity to spend time with these players and they're expecting all of us to be there. It will look bad if one of us bails. It'll be short, I promise, and I know Johnny will be bummed if you leave. *Please?*"

Griffen shot his best puppy dog eyes at her, bending his head down and letting his longish, dark, wavy hair fall on his forehead.

"Uh-oh, Jenna, he's got you in his blue-eyed clutches, you're toast," Aubrey said, with a giggle, which Tea quickly joined in on with her own snickering.

Griffen wouldn't look away and threw out his bottom lip further. Jenna had to admit that he was devastatingly handsome. Yes, he was madly in love with her best friend, but she was a woman with eyes, after all.

"Fine," Jenna muttered in defeat as she started walking toward Tom and Johnny.

"Sweet," Griffen exclaimed. "Come on, hurry up, ladies, they're waiting for us."

"I win," Aubrey whispered to her.

"Grow up," Jenna said, elbowing her in the ribs.

"All right, folks, are we ready?" Tom asked when they caught up to him. Everyone nodded and proceeded to fall in behind him again like obedient puppies until they made it to the entry area in the NFL team's locker room.

Tom stood next to the three players that were pegged for the meet-and-greet portion of what was rapidly feeling like one of the longest days of Jenna's life. The sight of Wyatt McCoy was unnerving. She worked with athletes every day, but none that had intrigued her for such a long time like he did — plus, he was staring at her with such focus that she began to feel downright overwhelmed.

Only one person had ever stared at her that way, or had that kind of power over her, in her whole life. Jenna wanted nothing to do with anyone who stirred up that memory, no matter how much Wyatt may have fascinated her as a player over the years.

"I have our quarterback, Wyatt, wide receiver, J.J., and safety, Trajan, here to meet you. If you're NFL fans, as I know at least a couple of you are, they won't need much introduction," Tom said, with a smooth tone suffused with authority.

Although Jenna was forcing herself to look at Tom, she was having a difficult time listening to his words. Her chest felt oddly tight and her palms were sweating. She refused to meet Wyatt McCoy's stare or let him see that her breaths were becoming unnaturally short and sharp in her throat.

She tried next to distract herself by watching the happy response of Johnny, whose eyes were wide with excitement. Jenna couldn't help but be amazed at how he was speechless for probably the first time since he was born. She loved to see Johnny so happy and proud, knowing that his "Gwiff" had done all of this for him.

Out of the corner of her eye she could see that each of the three handsome players waiting for them had showered and seemed amiable enough. Though it was surely an annoying task having to meet "VIP Pittsburgher" Griffen Tate and his motley crew entourage after a long game and depressing defeat in overtime.

Jenna could almost feel that Wyatt Alejandro McCoy was still eyeing her like she was a glistening mojito on a hot day at the beach. He was blindingly handsome in person. She could also tell how he'd earned the label of moody, intense, and unpredictable just by looking at him.

Every woman that saw his picture wanted him, but not Jenna, of course. She'd watched him like a hawk throughout the game — and his whole career — but she assured herself that her acute interest was purely due to her love of the game and a small concern for what looked like a subtle issue with his throwing arm.

Yet, with each moment he stared at her, her blood warmed and her ability to ignore the focused gaze of his warm brown eyes became increasingly difficult.

"What do you say, guys?"

"Huh?" Jenna muttered inelegantly. She was completely oblivious to anything in the room but the arrogant grin on Wyatt's face. She couldn't believe her own error. Aubrey had already pounced on the opportunity to torment her.

"It's time for the tour," Aubrey said brightly. "I was thinking maybe we should split up. Mr. McCoy, our friend Jenna here doesn't know much about football, could you possibly..."

"Take her on a private tour for more focused instruction?" he asked, with that same damned leering expression.

"No, that's not necessary," Jenna responded curtly.

"I insist. It would be my pleasure. Though I didn't catch your name," Wyatt inquired.

"Jenna, her name's Jenna," Tea blurted out, knocking her forward with her shoulder. "And you two should definitely split off, what a great idea," Tea crooned with a devilish grin.

"Tea, jeez," Jenna whispered, scowling at her. She should've known that Tea would get in on Aubrey's fun. They all loved messing with each other. Jenna just preferred to be on the giving end of it. "Sorry for the hold up, guys, we just need to chat for a bit," Jenna said, dragging Tea and Aubrey out of earshot of the group of confused men.

"You two have got to be kidding me," Jenna whispered with irritation.

"What?" Tea whispered back innocently and then twisted her face into a scheming sneer. "Are you the only person that can pester her friends into talking to guys?"

Jenna turned to Tea and gave her a full scowl, "Seriously...jerky high-profile athletes? You know the answer to that," Jenna answered back. "I'll just go on the tour with the rest of you guys."

"Now, Jenna, you wouldn't want to look rude after members of such an important part of your growing career have been so gracious to us, would you?" Aubrey teased.

"Dammit, Aubrey," Jenna fumed.

"You know I'm right. Now stop being such a pain in the ass and let that hot guy show you around before you offend him or anyone else here," Aubrey responded calmly.

"Fine," she huffed, turning to face Wyatt. "All right, Mr. McCoy, let's go," Jenna said, walking toward him with her toughest facial expression. It just seemed to make him more amused.

"Please call me Wyatt. How about we start with the locker room, that seems as good a place as any to begin your education," Wyatt drawled at her.

Of all the days to have to deal with a cocky self-impressed jackass... This guy can't be for real, Jenna thought to herself in frustration. *It's official, I will be killing Aubrey and Tea later. But I'm stuck with him now, so my double homicide plans will have to wait.*

Jenna took a steadying breath. She then steeled her nerves and schooled her face into its most confident expression before responding, "Sounds good, Mr. McCoy."

"Oh, come on, now. Don't be so formal. Don't you like me, sugar?"

"I just met you, I have no opinion of you," she answered stiffly, immediately bristling at his ridiculous name for her.

"I don't think you're being honest. I'd say you definitely have an opinion of me, and it doesn't seem good," he responded, leading her into the expansive room lined with cherrywood lockers, benches, and various forms of equipment. Jenna had been in countless locker rooms during her life — including this one — but the nearness of Wyatt McCoy made it feel surreal and claustrophobic.

It was a dream set-up for an athlete like herself, but all she could focus on was the singeing heat coursing through her from merely his fingertips on her lower back.

She turned to him to break the connection, but that only served to plant her back against a locker and her face smack dab in front of his well-built chest.

She was suddenly overcome by a terrible sense of *déjà vu* — the sensation that she'd been in this place before. Yet then it had all ended so very badly. Her prior sense of light irritation and intrigue from the current situation was quickly morphing into an overwhelming sense of almost frantic nerves.

Jenna looked up into his eyes and immediately regretted it. Having spent so many years avoiding any romantic involvements with athletes, her instant attraction to this one was vexing to say the least. It felt like her emotions were changing more rapidly than she could process them.

Wyatt stared down at her and smiled. "Now that I have your attention, maybe we can get to know each other better, you can give me a chance to improve that low opinion you have of me. Did you like the game?"

Jenna was relieved that the conversation had turned to her favorite topic, and she immediately felt control and calm return to her.

"It was a tough loss and you seemed to be having a rough go of it."

"Ouch, that hurts."

"You keep telegraphing your throws like that and you're going to spend the rest of the season on your ass — trust me, that will hurt a lot more. You need to shorten your release," Jenna advised him.

"Um, I'm not sure I heard you right. What was that again?"

"Just critiquing your throwing style is all," she answered.

"So, you were watching me closely?"

"It's an occupational hazard."

He looked confused for a moment but quickly regained his cocky composure. Meanwhile, Jenna kept feeling hers slipping away.

With each unsteady breath she noticed another aspect of him that was intoxicating to her, whether it was the slight golden streaks in his chestnut hair, the matching hint of stubble on his strong jaw, or his broad shoulders — everywhere she rested her eyes on him only served to make her body more consumed with attraction and her brain more furious with that fact.

"For the record, I've never heard any complaints about my release," he said, with a wink, and Jenna rolled her eyes in disgust, which only made him chuckle in amusement. "Though I thought you weren't supposed to know about football, sugar?"

"No. My *ex*-best friends were playing a joke. Now that you know the truth, I'll be moving along, let you get back to your life."

"But I'm having so much fun pretending to educate you. Maybe I can teach you Spanish."

"I already speak Spanish, so you've got nothing to teach me."

"Oh, I wouldn't be so sure of that. How about I teach you to relax?" he whispered in her ear — sending a shot of warmth coursing through her traitorous body.

"I'm plenty relaxed," she huffed. He smirked again, running a finger across her shoulder until she jumped.

"Relaxed, really? Hmm," he added with a cocky drawl and a slow perusal of her body that had her stomach tightening, even as her jaw clenched in irritation.

Wyatt leaned into her until she could smell his freshly-washed hair and count the beads of water on the part of his skin bared by the undone buttons at the top of his crisp Italian shirt. He was insanely attractive and far too close for Jenna's comfort. She cringed a little at her own big mouth, wishing she'd left this bad boy well enough alone. The worst thing you can do with someone like Wyatt is to engage him, and she'd done worse, she'd *challenged* him.

Dammit, Jenna, rookie mistake! she thought, chastising herself.

Jenna shook herself out of her hormonal stupor and stood up straight enough that he backed off a bit, "I have to ask — does this usually work?"

"What do you mean, sugar?"

"I mean this ego the size of Texas routine of yours. Calling me 'sugar' and the double entendres. I mean, come *on*. You want my opinion of you? Here it is. I find your little shtick — *and you* — exhausting and insulting. Please excuse me. I need to get back to my friends."

"I was under the impression my 'little shtick' was working," he teased, raising a hand and placing it alongside her head.

"Please. Working? Hardly," Jenna said, rolling her eyes again theatrically and ignoring the tightening in her belly and her powerful desire to bury her face in his chest and just sniff him for a while.

Pull yourself together, Jenna! she ordered to herself.

"Come on, play nice," Wyatt said, with a devious half-smile, looking down at her smugly. "I mean it, you need to relax."

These simple words shook her to the core. The feel of the locker behind her and his proximity, were all too painfully familiar. Her sense of panic returned.

"Let me go. I need to go," she demanded.

"Is something wrong, sugar?"

"My name is not *sugar*, you jerk!" Jenna shouted, and his laugh in response had her face red in anger and humiliation.

Right at that moment, the rest of her group walked in and Jenna felt sheer mortification at her position — pressed up against Wyatt McCoy of all people, in front of a locker — practically in her place of business — screaming at him.

Everyone looked at Jenna in shock and concern at her outburst, though Aubrey merely looked thrilled at Jenna's current predicament.

"Don't worry, folks, we're fine in here. I'll bring your friend to you soon."

"No, that won't be necessary, I can go now," Jenna said, as calmly as she could muster. She smoothed down her shirt in an effort to regain control of herself. She was about to speak when she heard, "Hey, Doc!"

Jenna looked up quickly, averting her eyes from her nosey companions and saw the kind face of one of her patients.

"Hi, Eloni!" Jenna threw Wyatt a sharp look, but he wouldn't move. He still had his hand placed on the wall next to her head and the fiery effect he had on both her emotions and her sex drive, were quickly replaced with plain raw irritation.

That's more like it, she thought. *Best to remember why you stay away from these types of guys in the first place.*

She began to dart under his arm, but he only lowered it more.

"Doctor?" Wyatt asked, with a cocked eyebrow.

"Yes, Mr. McCoy, they let us little ladies be doctors now. What a world! Now, if you would please move your arm."

"Hey, Wyatt, how ya doin', man? How do you know

Doctor S.?" Eloni asked, with his usual gentle giant charm. He was an offensive lineman from Samoa out of the University of Hawaii, and one of the first NFL players to give her a chance.

"Fine, Eloni," Wyatt gritted out. "I was giving her a tour."

"Oh, yeah? What brings you here, Doctor S.? Visiting a patient?"

"No, I came with some friends." Jenna breathed more easily as she turned her attention away from the incredibly unsettling quarterback. "Griffen over there is buds with your Assistant GM," she answered, jerking a thumb over to her group of friends that were now listening to a speech about on-field safety. "How's the knee, Eloni?" She could feel Wyatt's eyes boring into the side of her face, but she refused to look in his direction.

"My knee feels like a million bucks. You're a miracle worker, Doctor S."

"It's all due to you and your hard work. Maybe they'll start naming the surgery after you, you keep playing so well..."

"Hey, Eloni, I think Coach is looking for you," Wyatt's voice boomed as he turned to his teammate. His nearness still overwhelmed Jenna, and she started to make her escape.

"Well, Eloni, it was good to see you. I'm heading off, too," Jenna said, and started walking toward her friends.

"Hey, where are you going?" Wyatt asked, walking alongside of her. "I wasn't done."

"I was."

"Oh, come on. What are you doing tonight?"

"I have plans," she answered, nearing Tea and Aubrey, finally.

"No, she doesn't," Aubrey blurted out.

"See, looks like you're all cleared to let me keep changing that opinion of yours about me. I won't even call you sugar,

Doc."

"No need," Jenna answered, throwing Aubrey a sharp look before shouting, "Hey, Johnny, get over here." Johnny looked at Griffen and when he nodded, Johnny ran over to her.

"Hey, Johnny, Wyatt here said he'd love to watch you throw."

"Awesome! Let's do it," Johnny said enthusiastically.

"That's great, man, I appreciate it, too. Tom would that be okay?" Griffen asked his friend as he walked over.

"Of course. Come on, Wyatt, let's do it on the field. You guys can come take pictures if you like," Tom added.

"Y'all have fun. I think I learned enough for one day," Jenna said, as she stared in triumph at Wyatt.

He looked back at her with a challenge in his eyes and leaned down to whisper in her ear, "Have a nice night, but know that this ain't over, Doc."

A shiver ran down Jenna's spine as she watched six feet four inches of diabolically gorgeous trouble walk away from her and she struggled to decide whether she wanted to view his words as a threat — or a delicious promise.

Jenna turned and walked away, pulling herself back under control and shaking off the drugging memory of his smell and closeness with each step.

CHAPTER THREE

"Hi Doc. This is Wyatt McCoy...again. I'm not used to being ignored, but I'll let it slide this time. I'm free tonight and am very interested in learning more about what you think about my release. I'll look out for your call."

Wyatt smirked to himself as he imagined the face of the beautiful blonde doctor frowning in frustration at getting his second voicemail.

He ended the call but his mood quickly darkened at the sight of a text on his phone from one of his sister, Claudia's, friends.

Wy – this is Nicole. Claudia had to go to the doctor yesterday. Thought you should know.

His stomach flipped over and he tried not to think the worst.

Claudia was much younger than him, and ever since she was a little baby, he knew he wanted to do everything he could to keep her safe. That hadn't always been easy. It still haunted him to think of the night she became unconscious and collapsed when she was only seven years old.

In the midst of all of Claudia's tests and scary nights, their beloved grandfather had to go in for surgery on his heart...and he never came out of it. They'd been living with his mother's parents for a while by then. Ever since she'd finally given up on his dad after so many years of letting him have "just one more chance."

His father had managed to destroy his off field life in a very spectacular way. Yet, he'd kept most of those personal failings a secret from the public. Wyatt had been fourteen the night Jim McCoy tried to come back into their lives. His father was disgusted with Claudia's illness, calling her weak, and worthless. He had watched his father break his mother's heart enough over the years. He wasn't going to let him do that to Claudia, too.

That was the night Wyatt made a deal with devil. If Jim McCoy promised not to fight a divorce and stay away from them forever, then Wyatt would ensure they didn't tarnish his legacy by letting the world know what scum he really was.

Jim McCoy jumped at the chance without hesitation. All that mattered to him was that he would forever be a legend — one of the best quarterbacks of all time. To the wife and kids he'd left behind in Texas, he was just a selfish idiot. The man more interested in partying all night with nameless women than making sure his flesh and blood were safe.

Claudia could've really used a father, or a grandfather, when the diagnosis of juvenile diabetes came back. Instead, Wyatt became the man of the family the night his grandfather died. That meant that Claudia, his mother, and his abuela only had him, and Wyatt took that role very seriously. He swore to himself he would always be there for them. They needed him, and unlike some other McCoy men, that meant something to him.

Wyatt cursed as his throat tightened around the memories. Making his way to his car, he dialed his sister's number.

He breathed out slowly at hearing her voice answer on the other end of the line. It was freezing, but his temper was running hot enough to keep him warm in a blizzard.

"Hi, Wyatt," she answered breezily, as if she hadn't a care in the world.

"Claudia? Nicole texted me about you. What happened? What are you eating? Have you checked your blood sugar today?"

"Well, hello to you, too, Wy. *How are you, sis? What's up?* Oh, not much, sweet brother of mine, just studying. *Good for you, sis, great talk,*" she responded, doing her best impression of Wyatt's voice for his parts in her play-acted conversation.

"Stop being a smart-ass, Claudia."

"Hmm, that's going to be hard, being that 'smart-ass' is my native tongue," Claudia answered quickly.

"Then stop changing the subject, at least," he said, trying not to smile, but damned if she hadn't been able to lighten his mood ever since she was a tiny baby in his young arms. "Give me a break here, okay? You know this is the busiest part of the season for me, so I can't look after you as well as I'd like right now."

Wyatt winced as he threw his bag from his shoulder into the backseat, right before his stomach knotted at his own frustrated denial of the pain.

"You don't have to look after me, Wy, I'm a grown woman."

"You're twenty-two — that means you're still just a baby and you keep refusing to pay attention to your health..."

"Fine, jeez, lay off already, Wy. It's nothing, really. Nicole has a crush on you and knows you'll only answer her texts if she gets you all worked up about me."

"Come on, Claudia, why'd you go to the doctor?"

"Fucking Nicole. I told her specifically not to tell you that," Claudia cursed under her breath.

"You'd better not be hiding shit like this from me. Damn straight, Nicole was right to tell me." His voice was almost reaching shouting level, echoing in the car around him.

"Chill out, Wyatt, seriously. Fine, I had a big project to finish for my computer engineering major and I just pushed myself a little too hard and got hypoglycemic."

"What about your insulin pump? Isn't it working?"

"It's working. They looked at it while I was with the doc. I'm fine, I just got a little light-headed in front of Nicole and it scared her."

"A little light-headed?"

"Okay, I fainted. I'd forgotten to eat and my blood sugar was out of whack, but it's all under control now."

"Fuck, Claudia!"

"It's okay, the doctor said it's common with type 1 diabetes when your stress level increases to have some adjusting..."

"Screw that stupid doctor, I want you to see another specialist. Come up here for a couple of days. I've found one of the leading endocrinologists in the country, and he's right here in Pittsburgh..."

"No! Stop it, Wyatt. You need to listen to me, okay."

"I'm listening, but all I hear is someone that can't, or won't, take care of herself."

"I'm not even going to dignify that bullshit, Wyatt. I'm an adult whether you like it or not, and I can't miss any more classes," she answered, almost yelling now herself. He could hear her pause and take a deep breath before going on,

"Besides, you need to focus on your playing. I saw your game against Denver a couple days ago, you need to get your own shit together."

"Aren't you a sweetheart?"

"I know, thank you, it's a gift," she teased, clearly trying to lighten the mood, and Wyatt tried to force himself to let her. She was so stubborn and ever since she went to college, it was getting even harder to make sure she was okay.

"I'll see if I can get a specialist to see you down there. I wish you attended a school in a city somewhere closer to me."

"I know, Wy, just focus on practicing, and I'll focus on school. Graduating a semester early has its perks — school will end soon and then there will be no more fretting over me every second that I'm at college."

"Yeah, right, don't try to bullshit me, Claudia. Then you'll go to Quantico for FBI training and you'll push yourself even harder. I wish you would take it easy and just graduate in four years like everyone else."

"I'm not like everyone else Wy. It's bad enough I had to redo first grade after I got so sick. I started life out behind, but I won't stay there forever.

"It's like you're deliberately trying to worry me."

"I don't need to make any effort to do that — you'll manage to get yourself all worked up perfectly fine on your own. Speaking of, is everything okay, Wy? You seem even more annoyingly up my butt than usual," she asked with concern in her voice.

"I'm heading to a meeting with the GM of the team."

"What about?"

"They want to get on my ass about something. I'm pretty sure it's about the latest exam the team physician did of my shoulder."

"The rehab isn't helping?" Claudia asked.

"I think it is. And I've been managing the pain with painkillers. I'm going to try a cortisone shot to my shoulder before the next game, but I did take a lot of hits last week."

"I'll say. The season isn't over, maybe you can still show them you can get better."

"That's my plan. Enough about that shit. Do you have enough money?"

"Yes I do, thank you."

"And you're sure you really want to go to the FBI so soon?"

"It's a huge honor, Wy. Everything will be okay, I promise. And after interning at the Washington headquarters, I think I have a real shot of getting placed there."

"You're going to have to take better care of yourself, though."

"I know. I promise I'll be more careful. I love you, okay?"

"I love you, too. Bye."

"Bye," she answered, and as soon as she hung up, Wyatt felt even more convinced he had to do everything in his power to keep weaving links in his family's safety net. One of the only things he'd ever gotten from Jim McCoy was an ability to make money as a quarterback, and that had to sustain them for a lot longer than just these few paltry years.

"Hello, Coach McGill. How are you?" Wyatt asked in greeting to his head coach as he caught sight of him in the hallway on the way to his meeting.

"Hey, Wyatt. I guess you heard that John and Tom want to talk to you?"

"I did. You aren't going to be there?" Wyatt asked with confusion in his voice. A meeting with the General Manager and Assistant GM was concerning enough on its own, but to know that his own coach wouldn't be there made it downright dismal.

"No, I'm not gonna be at this one, but they know how I feel, Wyatt. And you do, too."

"Coach..." Wyatt began, not quite sure what he would say next, but his coach placed a hand on his shoulder, effectively silencing him.

"Wy, I still believe in you and your potential, you know that. But I can't control what the doctors say about your health or what you do about your own attitude. You know this game isn't just about what happens between the hash marks, it's about what happens in here," he said seriously, poking Wyatt hard in the chest where his heart should be. "It's about what you feel about the game and your team — inside of *you*."

If only it were that simple, Wyatt thought to himself.

"Thanks, Coach. I want to do whatever I can to help the Roughnecks succeed," he responded numbly, yet again saying the words he knew the world expected to hear, even though he wasn't sure what he actually felt in his own heart.

"Then don't be your own worst enemy, boy. You gotta play the game off the field, too, sometimes. Look, I knew your dad better than anyone — the real story most people didn't know, not just his talent. But this is your life, you can't let him be a part of it."

"All I know is that I need to stay on the field, Coach," he answered, and it was the truth.

"Wy, this season isn't over yet. You still have time to show us what you can do — show me that you have what it takes in here, to really succeed out there," Coach stated, with another poke to Wyatt's chest, followed by a jerk of his thumb to gesture out the window to the practice field.

Wyatt nodded, and thanked him before walking on to his meeting, his teeth gritted in his mouth. When Wyatt was younger, his skills had been enough to make up for his workman-like attitude about the game. Yet now, it seemed like all these other X factors were becoming much more important, just as his shoulder was causing him so much trouble on the field.

If Wyatt could somehow make himself feel passionate about this game that had always been merely a job to him — a means to an end — then maybe he wouldn't need to have meetings like this. But that had never been the case for him, and it didn't look like anything would change about that now.

He'd managed to keep his brain mostly free of abuse and had a fair amount of endorsement deals to start building that empire he so coveted. But he couldn't do any of those things without a starting position on a viable team.

It certainly wouldn't help if his story turned into a cautionary tale of yet another first-round draft pick bust. Wyatt could not let that happen. He needed to get through this shoulder issue and get back on top, so he could take control of his life — and career — again. Theoretically, he had several more years left to play, but a sustainable legacy didn't come from being just a journeyman, hopping from team to team or never making it far in the play-offs.

Wyatt needed to stay on the field and get some traction in at least one city before he hung up his cleats forever. One sore shoulder and a handful of annoying team executives weren't going to stand in the way of that plan — not if he could help it.

His mind cleared the moment he came upon his agent

waiting outside the GM's office.

"Gabe, it's good to see you, but you didn't have to come all the way here just for this meeting."

"I'm pretty sure I did, actually. They're really worried about your latest physical. Come on, let's head in and get this over with."

They sat down across from John Davison, the GM, and Tom Wilkins, the Assistant GM, and it felt like being called into the principal's office.

"Thanks for meeting with us. I'll get to the point, Wyatt. The club physician is disappointed in your progress. That shoulder is a big problem. And that Denver game on Monday really did a number on you. He thinks you're going to need surgery after the season is over." John looked at Wyatt, waiting for an answer.

"It felt like that to me, too, but I've been working hard on my rehab. I think it's helping a lot," Wyatt answered evenly.

"The club doc is great," Gabe added, quickly chiming in. "But the collective bargaining agreement lets us get a second opinion, John, you know that."

"I do. We have a recommended list of orthopedic surgeons that we've used before. You can see their names and bios here. Any of these individuals would certainly be qualified to perform the second opinion consultation the CBA allows."

Wyatt took a folder from John and flipped through it silently, his jaw twitching slightly in agitation. It was full of older male surgeons, each with impressive levels of expertise, but it was the image of one young, and very sexy, doctor that jumped out at him.

Dr. Jenna Sutherland caught his eye for more than just her looks. He recognized the blonde beauty from the VIP group immediately. She'd turned him down flat — much to J.J.'s delight, as he'd been tormenting Wyatt about it ever since. But Wyatt knew she was drawn to him, just like he was to her. He felt sure of it...

He needed someone he could sway and influence. Despite her cocky insistence that she wasn't interested in him, he could tell she was attracted. If his life to date had proven anything to Wyatt, it was that he could get women to do what he wanted, especially if they were easily manipulated by his charm. It wasn't something he was proud of, that was for sure. Also, the idea of taking advantage of someone just to better his career made him feel all kinds of shitty, but he had to do everything in his power to get out of this situation.

Besides, Wyatt wasn't sure she was that innocent in all of this, anyway. It irked him that a team-approved orthopedic surgeon was watching him play. She even knew he had an issue with his shoulder. That fact had been kept completely secret. If the team was trying to have her gauge his health from a luxury box, then he was sure as hell going to make her get a more complete impression of how well he was actually doing.

Just let her try to ignore me now, he thought smugly to himself.

"We might want to choose a physician of our own, John, like the..." Gabe chattered on.

"Like the CBA permits you to do? Sure, you can do that. But I'm sure you're also aware that Wyatt's shoulder isn't the only thing giving us pause when his contract is up this year."

John turned his head slightly, pinning Wyatt with a serious stare. "Coach is very worried that you've never taken on leadership in the locker room. You're unfocused in practice, and on the field. You haven't bonded with your teammates in any real way. We tried to overlook your reputation from when you were in Dallas, but I'm not sure if we can anymore. We've got a lot of rookies on the team that could really use the guidance from someone that's been in the league for as many seasons as you have, but you're too isolated. You come in, do your time and leave — that's not how we do things here in Pittsburgh. This is a family institution, and the quarterback needs to be an important part of that family," John rattled off, leaning back in his chair.

Wyatt could feel his hands clenching into fists — desperate to shut this asshole up.

Wyatt didn't need to listen to this bullshit anymore. He had a plan of his own, and it didn't involve listening to Gabe and these team bosses bicker at each other.

"This one. Dr. Sutherland. She'll do," Wyatt stated assuredly, tossing the folder onto the table. Her pretty face was staring up at all of them — glowing like an unsuspecting angel against the manila folder backdrop.

"Jenna Sutherland?" Tom asked, his eyes widening with shock at Wyatt's pronouncement. And it gave Wyatt a strange thrill to see he'd thrown the guy off-balance.

"Absolutely. Is that a problem?"

"Of course not, she's very popular with our players, has been requested several times before...it's just..." Tom sputtered out.

"John put her bio in there. I chose her. I told you I can be a team guy," Wyatt answered, staring Tom dead in the eye.

"I'm glad to see it, Wyatt. It's no problem, of course we like your pick," John said, looking questioningly at Tom. "We'll set it up."

"Wyatt, we don't have to decide now," Gabe whispered to him in a hushed tone.

"Why wait? I've got nothing to hide. I'm ready to move forward. Thanks, Tom, thanks, John."

"You got it," John said, standing and walking them out of

the room. "Wyatt, I like you. You know I believed you could have a lot of success here when we brought you in. I still do."

They'd barely made it out of the building on the way to their cars before Gabe looked at him with utter confusion.

"Why the hell did you choose this surgeon? How can you be so confident? Do you know something I don't?" Gabe asked.

"She's younger...and a woman."

"And you have a way with younger women?"

"Generally, yes. And I'm pretty confident I have a way with this *particular* woman."

"What's that supposed to mean? Why was Tom so hesitant in there? Those are their list of docs, so what was that all about?" Gabe asked.

"Because I've met her before. He saw me ask her out. He's probably terrified I have her in my back pocket already. I will soon though, don't worry."

"You're kidding."

"You know I never kid about my career. Look, it worked with Olivia Hayes from *Fox Sports*. I've gotten a lot of favorable press out of her."

"There's a big difference between flirting with an unscrupulous cleat-chasing reporter and manipulating an actual orthopedic surgeon with a career impressive enough to be included in that folder."

"We'll see about that. Besides, who said anything about manipulating her? I just want to give her the chance to have an open mind about my shoulder."

"And you think she'll just start seeing things your way?"

"I definitely had an effect on her. It's a long shot, but I need to use whatever advantages I can find to stay on the field."

"Wy, I've had plenty of clients that have had to get surgery."

"But none that's this invasive right when their contract is up. Gabe, you know as well as I do that needing to have surgery makes me about as unappealing as a one-eyed skinny pig at the state fair. Look at you, and what happened after your knee injury."

A furious look streaked across Gabe's face and a stream of guilt ran through Wyatt's chest. Gabe had been an incredible running back in college, but a catastrophic knee injury and two surgeries cut his career short.

"Dude, I'm sorry, I shouldn't have…"

"Forget it, Wy. This isn't about me. You've got the possibility of several years left in you if you recover fully."

"Gabe, you know how I feel about surgery. The only time someone's putting me under is when they bury me six feet in the ground."

Wyatt felt a pang of pain in his chest. He remembered feeling weak, defenseless, and powerless when he lost his grandfather. Once he was gone, his absence tortured Wyatt — it still did. If something were to go wrong with this surgery, he'd be leaving behind the family he promised to take care of. He couldn't do that to them — *he wouldn't do that to them.*

"Fine, Wy. Well, you better bring the charm to this pretty, young surgeon because you're gonna need all the help you can get if you won't take my advice or the doctor's either. You know, you're making life very hard for all of us."

"Have a little faith in me, Gabe, and stop stressing so much, I know how much you hate wrinkles, pretty boy."

"Fuck you, Wy. Try to be serious."

"Oh, I'm serious all right. Completely. Ever since Dallas traded me, nothing's gone right."

"It wasn't going that well in Dallas, either."

"True. But if I want to get this two-year contract renewed, I can't be off the map with a surgery for months."

Wyatt knew that he had no intention of ever having surgery, but he wasn't going to tell Gabe that.

"Avoiding surgery alone might not fix it. Word is, they've got their eye on a new backup for you. And he's supposed to be ruthless."

"What the fuck? Who is it?"

"I'm still trying to get his name. Everyone has suddenly clammed up on me, and you know that's never good."

"You think he's really my replacement?"

"Possibly."

"And what if they do end up kicking me off as starting QB here?"

"I'm testing the waters with some other teams, but with your shoulder and it being your third team in however many years, you may need to drop down to back-up somewhere."

"And lose all that money and likely blow my shot of a broadcasting gig. You know that's where the stability is. I've got to think about my family. My mom, Claudia, my abuela...I'm all they have."

"Fine, if that's the way you see it, just be careful. I know you're desperate, but this doesn't seem like you, man."

"No. It's not me. Not, at all. But, you said it yourself, man, I'm desperate." And Wyatt couldn't deny that he was. This wasn't just about his career; it was about the livelihood of everyone that mattered to him. As guilty as he felt for what he was about to do, sometimes you have to do something you hate to protect the people that you love. If it were just about his career, then he would be just like his father — and other than his playing abilities, he was nothing like that piece of shit.

This was about keeping promises and seeing things through, no matter how hard or uncomfortable the situation.

"Besides," Wyatt continued as he pulled open the door of his Range Rover, "I've got my dad's blood running through my veins. There must be some of his son-of-a-bitch gene in there to go with all that football DNA. I know I'm as good a player as him."

Wyatt climbed in and started his engine, deliberately avoiding Gabe's disappointed gaze.

As he drove away, a self-loathing grimace marked his lips, but he quickly schooled his face. He let out a deep breath and smiled to himself, planning the delightful text message that he would send to the lovely Dr. Sutherland to share the good news about their upcoming second meeting.

CHAPTER FOUR

"Jenna?" Wyatt called to her softly, his breath fanning across her cheek. "Can you hear me, Jenna?" he added, letting his lips brush against the curves of her ear before leaning back away from her.

"Yes," Jenna answered, shocked to hear that he was using her actual name — no "sugar," no "Doc," just Jenna. It was unnerving.

She looked up at him and her breath caught like a wayward feather in her throat.

He was just so beautiful, with his brown eyes, just barely flecked with hints of gold. His lips were curled into a smile, momentarily hiding how they were almost too full and soft-looking for a man — almost.

His hair was tousled and messy, making her want to run her fingers through it, perhaps to smooth it, or maybe to send it into further disarray. She hadn't yet decided.

"I need you to climb up on this examining table for me," he said, still ever so quietly.

"Okay," she whispered, moving her hands to rest on the edge of the barely cushioned bed. She was ready to hoist herself up, yet she hesitated suddenly, immobilized with surprise — and slight embarrassment — to glance down and see that her body was barely covered by the thin slip of a hospital gown.

"It's okay, I'll take good care of you," he reassured her, gliding the hard, hot knuckles of one hand against the almost see-through cotton covering her chest. She was naked underneath the gown and the jolt of contact on her nipple caused it to tighten and harden in immediate response. She so wanted to do what he'd asked, but his touch had paralyzed her with want, her breaths shortening and quickening in her lungs.

"I can't mo-ove, Wyatt."

"I've got you," he answered, grasping her waist in both of his large hands and sliding her onto the examining table. Her eyes were even with his chest now. He was wearing a crisp white lab coat and it only made her want to see his hard, muscular body underneath that much more. She felt movement return to her body and she reached for him, undoing the top two buttons of the thick, starched material of his coat.

"Oh, no, you don't," he said sharply, pulling his hands up from her waist and wrapping them gently around the soft flesh of her jaw, tilting her face backward, forcing her to look in his eyes. "I'm here to examine *you*. That means you need to stay still."

"But I don't want to stay still. I want to see you," she said petulantly, her bottom lip pouting in protest.

"You will see me soon enough. You will have all of me before you know it, Jenna," he whispered, then gently kissed her cheek until her eyes fluttered shut. The feel of his lips against her skin had her clutching at his coat in excitement.

With a grunt, he pulled away, dropping his hands from her

neck.

Jenna opened her eyes quickly to see that his were flashing with reprimand. Suddenly, she heard a loud ripping of fabric. With a gasp, Jenna realized she was completely bare in front of him, her destroyed gown now in several strips in his hands.

Feeling shy, Jenna tried to cover herself, but he grabbed her hands in his, throwing her back on the table. Wyatt quickly tied her arms behind her. He began gripping, and then pressing down on her ankles so that she was completely exposed on the table. She struggled against her restraints, staring at him in anticipation, only to lose all vision when he took the last strip of cotton and secured it over her eyes.

Jenna's bottom rose off the table, fighting to get up, but it did her no good. He was stronger than her, and his hold was intense. She quickly settled when she felt his calloused hands moving slowly up each of her legs, gently stroking the skin of her inner thighs until she was moaning in excitement.

"Don't move your legs, Jenna. Keep them wide open. Can you do that for me?"

Jenna moaned in reply.

Up and down, his hands moved on her flesh until Jenna was so aroused, it was almost painful.

"Please," she begged, not even embarrassed anymore, so desperate for his touch.

And then, his mouth was on her, his hair brushing the flesh of her mound and his tongue licking the soft folds between her thighs. Two of his hard fingers entered her body. They felt hard and insistent inside of her, but his tongue was soft and fast, almost reassuring.

Jenna could barely move, the cotton wrapped around her was too tight, and she didn't dare close her legs. Each stroke of his fingers and incredible swipes of his flattened tongue against her wet pussy was at once maddening and calming.

Moans escaped from her throat, and she could feel the pleasure he was giving her all the way down to her toes. She was so incredibly close to release, begging for him to take her there, when a loud voice broke through her stupor.

"A water main break has shut down Banksville Road."

"What did you say, Wyatt?" she asked, deeply confused by his words.

"The water is freezing rapidly in these cold temperatures, so you're going to have to find an alternate route."

Jenna's eyes flashed open. There was no examining table underneath her. Her wrists were free of restraint, but her cotton bed sheets had almost mummified her body during her nighttime bout of writhing beneath them.

She looked down and saw there was no masculine head between her thighs — only her own pajama bottoms, slightly damp from her arousal, matching the sweat that had collected across her face and throughout her hair.

She slapped the alarm clock off and threw her head back against her pillows with a huff.

It was the Monday after Wyatt had shocked her with a text message saying that he'd tapped her to perform a follow-up consultation on his shoulder. She'd gotten the text during Light Up Night, right after Griffen proposed to Tea, and it had taken all of her self-control not to let her upset show too strongly on her face. There was no way she was going to let her own personal drama distract from Tea's special night.

Jenna had spent the weekend trying to convince herself she could face this consultation as though Wyatt were any other person. But her dream proved that was very far from the truth. The appointment was mere hours away, and unless she could convince her boss to get her out of it, she was going to be smack-dab in front of the man that had been occupying her thoughts and nighttime fantasies for a week now.

She'd tried to forget about him — told herself it was merely sexual frustration and boredom after so many wasted dates with boring men. Yet, no matter what she did, her mind kept wandering back to the sound of his recorded voice on her phone, or his eyes, boring into hers as he leaned into her body…training his eyes on her lips…

Enough! She ordered to herself.

The only solution was to avoid ever seeing him again. Keep him out of her life until his memory flushed itself out of her bloodstream like a mind-altering drug.

She could only hope Richard would see things her way. Which meant she needed to get her act in gear, and to work — fast.

Jenna had made it to the hospital in record time — even with the delay Aubrey caused by relentlessly teasing her about the incessant moaning that had emanated from her bedroom most of the previous night. Apparently Jenna had sounded like a cat in heat during her erotic nighttime torment. That was certainly mortifying, but thankfully Aubrey hadn't made out anyone's name through the thin wall separating their bedrooms.

Her roommate and dear friend was loyal and loving to the end, but she was also like a bloodhound after a scent when she suspected something interesting — particularly something sexual — was going on within her vicinity.

The mortification she experienced was intense, but blessedly brief. Nothing would arouse Aubrey's curiosity more than knowing Jenna had been dreaming nightly about Wyatt. He was a man whom some dark force had apparently crafted in a black-market-laboratory hot-man workshop, with the sole purpose of including every trait Jenna had tried to avoid her entire adult life, all wrapped up into one spectacularly sexy Mexican-Irish package.

Aubrey had just begun inquiring after the identity of Jenna's "dream man" when Jenna stuffed a piece of toast in her mouth and hightailed it out of their apartment. She felt compelled to escape Aubrey's eagle-eyed presence quickly, as she mumbled through a full mouth about a meeting with Richard.

It wasn't a lie — she did have one with him, even if he didn't know it yet.

Jenna didn't even stop by her office as she rushed to meet with Richard, still in her heavy winter coat. Time was of the essence if she was going to get out of this assignment.

With her heart pounding in her chest, Jenna lifted her fist to knock on Richard's door, but she let it fall to her waist before making contact.

Reality quickly took hold of her as she admitted to herself that this consult was exactly the kind of high-profile opportunity she needed to show Richard that she deserved the fellowship. No matter how much the thought of being near Wyatt McCoy again bothered her, she had no choice but to do it.

Just as the adrenaline ebbed away, Richard opened the door and he jumped a bit at the sight of her.

"Hi Jenna, you're just the person I was coming to see. I have good news."

"I'm going to do a follow-up consultation on Wyatt McCoy today."

"That's right, you must be psychic."

"I just wanted to tell you that I am so grateful for the opportunity. I know you must have pulled strings to get me on the list of options for him. I won't let you down."

"That's great to hear, because he'll be here in an hour."

"What?" she gasped out, then recovering quickly. "That's wonderful, then I can dive right in. Thanks," she said forcing a smile before heading to her office.

Dammit! Jenna thought to herself, throwing her purse and coat down on the spare chair in her office, with a huff. She took a breath and smoothed some stray hairs off her hot forehead with a hand quivering from an overwhelming sense of frustration.

Jenna swallowed hard and sat at her desk. She didn't have much time to collect her composure before Wyatt would be in her fully equipped office, so she reviewed Wyatt's chart that had been left in her in-box.

It was quickly clear to her that her instinct after watching him play had been correct. This was certainly more than a simple impingement in the right shoulder joint.

God, he must be in serious pain, she thought.

With her review of his chart complete, Jenna was left with far too many empty minutes. She tried cleansing breaths, reviewing old emails, and filing away documents, but she couldn't shake her restlessness. Every moment her brain kept desperately rushing back to the memories she'd done such a good job of pushing down for so many years — ones she'd almost convinced herself were gone.

But she'd been kidding herself. The specter of Chase

Matthews — and everything he represented in her life — would never leave her.

No boys had ever shown any interest in her growing up. She'd always just been Coach Sutherland's awkward, motherless, tomboy daughter. She had a head full of frizzy hair and dressed like a guy, because she didn't know how to be a girl. Her life had been football season on the sidelines with her dad, then her own basketball season, and always loads of studying. It was as though no one even knew she existed.

Chase must've sensed her loneliness, because when he zeroed his attention on her at preseason training before the beginning of her junior year of high school, she'd been a goner. As the backup quarterback on her father's team, he had plenty of time to chat with her — he made her feel special and beautiful, despite her baggy tee shirts and profound lack of experience with boys.

Every moment they were together were blurs of excitement and happiness. She never questioned why he never spent time in public with her, or why he seemed always so eager to talk about the team, her father, and how much he wanted to be the starting quarterback for his final high school season. There was no room for doubt when he single-handedly was so many of her firsts — first crush, first kiss, and one hot Georgia night — the biggest first of all.

She wanted him to be happy, and he really did have a lot of potential. So when he asked her to persuade her father to give him a chance at starting quarterback, it seemed completely natural.

For a brief time there, Jenna had been so happy. She actually thought that the life all those normal girls she saw in the halls at school got to live could be hers, too.

Chase had said he loved her and she believed it with all the exuberant glee imaginable in her young heart. That glorious happiness made the crushing realization of the truth all the more disturbing when she came upon Chase talking to a cheerleader in a darkened corner, only weeks into school.

"Brittany, come on, of course I'm not really with her. Are you fucking kidding me? I have the starting position now, I just need to string her along until the end of the season."

And then, he kissed her, and the sight of it knocked the wind out of Jenna. She dropped her backpack and ran as hard and as fast as she could, anything to get away from this horrible moment. She rushed to the boys' locker room, desperate to make it to her father's office, when Chase was upon her.

He leaned against her, caging her in with his body, as he placed one hand on the metal of the locker above her head and stared hard into her eyes.

"Let me go," she said with a quivering voice.

"Calm down, Jenna. You know I love you."

"No you don't, I heard what you said. I saw what you did." She looked down and whispered out, "You never really liked me. I'm so stupid, you just used me, and you were ashamed of me this whole time."

"Fine," he answered roughly, grabbing the tops of her arms with clenched fists.

"Chase, you're hurting me, let me go."

"I'm not hurting you, Jenna...yet," he said, with a twisted smile on his face, lifting a hand up and placing it loosely around her throat, sending her insides into a panic that she willed herself to control. He used his hand to push her harder against the locker behind her. "I'm not letting you go anywhere until you listen to me."

Chase squeezed her throat with his hand, until stars appeared in front of her eyes.

"Chase, stop, please."

He pushed her back hard until her head bounced hard on the metal of the locker.

"I mean it, you need to relax," *he said to her coldly.*

"I-I can't..." *she gasped out roughly.*

"I wanted to just do this the nice way — the fun way," *Chase added. He loosened the grip on her throat and she gasped for air. With a leer he looked down at her breasts, sending her stomach into a twisting battle against itself.*

"But now you're gonna cry like a spoiled brat and run to Daddy."

"I will tell him what you did," *she whispered.*

"You do that and I'll ruin him."

"What?"

"Your dad likes to gamble, doesn't he?"

"You know about that?"

Fear gripped Jenna's heart. Her father did like to gamble, especially on sports. She believed it helped him deal with the pain of losing her mother, but she mainly just tried to ignore it.

"I do. And I have proof he bet on football games."

"He never bet on ours, that's insane."

"All it takes is the suspicion, Jenna. And I have enough dirt on him, pictures, too, to create that suspicion. Do you want to see him lose everything?"

Her shoulders slumped. Coaching was all her father had. The mere thought of him losing that would destroy him.

"No, of course, I don't," *she whispered.*

"Good, then you're going to leave me alone to do whatever the fuck I want to do and you'll keep your mouth shut. Right?" *he asked, moving his hands away from her neck to squeeze the top of her arms again.*

Jenna couldn't find the words to speak until he shook her and shoved her against the locker behind her, sending a clatter of clanging metal echoing through the room, as pain shot across her back.

"Right, Chase. Right," *she answered, tears suddenly sprouting from her eyes.*

"Good, glad you understand me. And stop crying. You weren't too terrible when I fucked you. You should be thanking me for doing you the favor," he sneered out, releasing her roughly.

He walked away and Jenna slid down the cool metal until she was sitting on the floor of the empty locker room and cried by herself. She wrapped her arms around her knees and allowed herself a moment of sheer painful sadness before collecting her emotions so she could be prepared to act as though nothing had happened.

Jenna did a great job of pretending that everything was fine for that whole school year, even if she was hurting and terrified inside. Chase got his scholarship to the University of Georgia, after making sure Jenna got her dad to put in a good word for him.

No one but she and Chase knew what he'd done to her. She'd worked as hard as she could to take the opportunity to graduate early and go to Duke. Her father didn't understand why she wanted to leave him so quickly. Why she wouldn't go to the University of Georgia and stay nearby. Yet, the mere idea of another year at the site of her ultimate humiliation, or of going to the same college as Chase, made her feel sick to her stomach. So she ran the first chance she got.

Jenna had let herself down, but more than that, she was horrified to know that she'd failed to honor the words of guidance her mother had given her.

Sitting there in her office so many years later, Jenna could still feel the moist dirt seeping through her jeans and chilling her knees when she had knelt on the ground to say good-bye to her mother's grave the day before she left for college at just seventeen years old.

"Momma, I'm so so-rry," she had said to the tombstone she'd visited so many times before. "I know you want me to stay here and watch after Dad...but I just ca-an't. I failed, momma. I screwed up. I got fooled, and

now I have to leave. I just do."

Jenna did disappear, but Chase Matthews didn't. He popped up in her life again, like a mean and hateful penny. Nine years had passed by the time he came to visit her in Atlanta. Her stomach twisted at the memory of seeing him again.

Jenna had only recently begun her internship at Emory after wrapping up medical school at Duke. Somehow, Chase knew she had connections at the Atlanta Falcons, and he got her to use them on his behalf to get a leg up toward a position as their backup quarterback.

Part of her wanted to say no to him. She felt confident that her father had shaken his bad gambling habit, but she couldn't bear the idea of risking his career, no matter how slight that chance may be. On top of that, there was the terror of letting her father know of her failure in trusting a creep like Chase, and keeping so many secrets from him for so long. It was wiser — and easier — to just oblige Chase again.

Just the thought of being near him made Jenna feel sick with fear. She had to run and begin a new life again. This time she fled to Pittsburgh to help Tea after transferring to *UPMC*. All she wanted was to try to build something great for herself that would make her mother proud. She felt like she was finally close to making that happen.

This plan left no room for dreaming about a man like Wyatt McCoy. Because, it wasn't him or the rest of the stream of athletes she ran into over the years that she didn't trust — it was *herself.*

She'd been fortunate enough not to hear from Chase for several years. Part of her worried he would find her and torment her again, but she ignored those thoughts.

Instead she preferred to believe that her life was now her

own — and she wanted to keep it that way. Yet, she had no control of her mind where Wyatt Alejandro McCoy was concerned.

She kept thinking about him and it was infuriating to her. Jenna didn't even know him. So how was it that with one meeting and a few attempts to contact her he had completely recalibrated her life's magnet — leaving her with a mindlessly spinning arrow and no true north, except for perhaps a constant nagging need to constantly point her thoughts toward him?

And to make it worse, now he was invading her *professional* life. It made her furious — spitting mad, to be precise. Mainly at herself, if she were being honest. After all she'd been through — the shame and humiliation Chase had caused her — and here she was drawn to someone who could very well be just like him.

Just who the hell does Wyatt think he is? she asked herself.

He's nobody to me, that's who, she answered confidently.

No one is allowed to do that to me. No one. I can't let someone have this power over me — take advantage of me, get the best of me. Not again.

She needed to orient herself back to who she was before, or else she'd be lost in the woods. Wyatt was just another patient, and if she couldn't get over the discomfort he caused her, then she'd never be able to make this career a success.

A knock on her office door jarred her to life. Jenna realized it was Wyatt on the other side of the wooden barrier and she quickly steeled her nerves for the unavoidable meeting.

She stood up straight, thrust her shoulders back, and smoothed down the front lapels of her lab coat. After a long and slow breath, she felt like she could appear strong and calm again.

It was just a one-hour consult. She could get through that and then she would never have to see Gunslinger McCoy ever again.

CHAPTER FIVE

Wyatt swallowed hard as he stared at Doctor Jenna Sutherland's office door, waiting for a response to his knock. He couldn't remember the last time he'd felt this nervous about anything. He chalked it up to the stakes being high.

He'd become almost fixated on getting her to back up his plan to avoid surgery. Yet his mind had also repeatedly gone back to thinking about her for a totally different reason over the last few days. When she opened the door to him that reason took over again and a potent rush began to course through his bloodstream.

She stood in front of him with her left hand cradling the doorframe, pulling the virginal white lab coat snugly across her ample breasts. A simple gold locket with what looked like a woman's face on it nestled in her cleavage. Her silky blonde centerfold hair was pulled into a bun with reading glasses perched delicately on her straight nose.

This woman was a constantly overlapping set of apparent inconsistencies — sexy but demure, tough but sweet, strong but vulnerable. The combinations made her seem like a mirage from a wet dream to Wyatt, and he couldn't wait to make it a reality.

Yes, he needed her help, but that didn't mean he couldn't have some fun with her in the process.

"Mr. McCoy. Hello. Please come in." She stepped aside to let him in, and he made sure to let his right arm brush across her chest until she jumped slightly back, with the slightest bit of a mortified breath escaping from her parted lips.

"I thought I told you to call me Wyatt," he said, leaning his head toward her, until she stepped a full pace back and closed the door behind them.

This is almost too easy, he thought happily to himself.

"You did tell me that, *Mr. McCoy*."

Oh, she's gonna dig in. Fine, then so can I.

She walked across the room with him alongside her, then turned and held out her hand. He took it and only briefly shook it, instead, pulling her closer and stroking her palm with a familiarity he knew was inappropriate.

She looked into his eyes crossly and yanked her hand away, only turning him on more. She spun around with a huff and walked to her desk to sit with a clear attempt at authority.

"It's my understanding you requested me specifically," she said smoothly, but he could see that she kept moving things on her desk with her busy hands.

"That's right, Doc."

"I hope that means you plan to be serious about this consult, Mr. McCoy," she said carefully, catching him staring at her chest. And Wyatt couldn't hold back the smile that spread across his face.

"I'm willing to do anything for my NFL career, Doc. Besides, cut me some slack, you're the one that wore that sexy lab coat."

She practically growled in frustration and he loved it. He

needed her off-balance for what he had in mind, but damned if he hadn't guessed he'd enjoy it this much.

Time to push her a little more, he thought.

As he leaned across her desk and perused her body up and down, he whispered, "Though I do wish it were tighter."

"Right. Because I sit around in a lab coat to be sexy. Like I'm in *Hustler* magazine or something." She suddenly started to coo in a Marilyn Monroe breathy voice. "*Oh, no. This microscope is so heavy. Guess I should bend down to relieve the weight of this massive tool. Oh, what's here between my legs? Oh, it's so warm down there. Maybe I should investigate?* Please. So ridiculous," she said to herself with annoyance. "Excuse me, are you okay, Mr. McCoy?"

He was definitely *not* okay. His mouth had fallen open slightly and all the blood had rushed to his lap. Wyatt was so hard he was practically in pain. He realized he may have underestimated this woman. *Maybe.* Her voice broke through his lust-filled fog.

"I thought it was your shoulder that had the issue. Do you have a head injury too?" she asked with concern, replacing her previously sultry voice.

"Um. Yeah. I mean no. Just my shoulder. You're the second opinion on my shoulder injury, and my coach also said maybe you could help my game. I'm not sure how though."

"It may be hard for you to imagine that you could need help from anyone, but I've certainly been able to assist some of your teammates to use their bodies more effectively."

Wyatt raised an eyebrow and smirked. "Now that's more like what I had in mind."

She rolled her eyes impatiently at him.

"Please, Mr. McCoy. Trust me, me using your body is most definitely not part of the treatment. What I mean is, that I try to help my patients use their bodies more effectively and in a way that can avoid future injuries. It's easy to develop bad habits in this game, especially after playing for so long, as you have. And a professional athlete's muscles need more care and attention. They can often benefit from a better approach to their movements. In your case, if you want to keep your career going for several more years, I think you will need to make some changes. That *is* what you want, isn't it?"

"Yes, absolutely. This makes me feel even better about picking you."

Wyatt began running his finger slowly in a circle on her desk, not even realizing he was making the motion until he noticed her staring at it, and it felt like a triumph.

"Well, it appears that your finger works. Let's get back to the consultation, okay?"

"My fingers work very well. Want to see?"

"Enough. *Please*. Are you always this cocky and unserious?"

"Actually, if you asked most people that know me, they'd probably say I'm generally more of a grumpy asshole."

"So this is a rare treat you reserve for me?"

"What can I say, Doc? You bring out the best in me," he answered, with a smirk. He caught the slightest hint of a smile on her face, confirming to him that, at least in some way, he was getting to her — he could swear by it.

"Lucky me. Now, Mr. McCoy, back to your shoulder."

"You keep calling me Mr. McCoy. I really do prefer Wyatt."

"I prefer Mr. McCoy. You have what looks like a serious shoulder injury that is being exacerbated with every game you play in, so hopefully we can make some headway today."

"I'd like that," he said seriously. Her eyes were earnest and it looked as though maybe she really did care about his well-being. It made his chest feel tight in the oddest way. "Hey, Doc?"

"Yes?" She took her glasses off and placed them on her desk, looking directly at him intently. It was distracting how big and blue her eyes were — huge almost, and rimmed with long, soft lashes. She was so unlike the women who had thrown themselves at him most of his life. Even her physical appearance was a breath of fresh air. It looked like she didn't seem to wear much, if any, makeup. She blinked patiently at him and he remembered it was his turn to talk.

"How'd you know my shoulder was hurting when we met? The team and I have worked hard to keep it out of the press."

"It's my job."

"I've met other people whose job it was also, and they couldn't tell. Was it because you were looking very closely at me while I played?"

"I was, but only out of professional curiosity."

"Come on, Doc. I really want to know."

She sighed, "Fine. Right before you throw, you twitch your right shoulder and glance slightly sideways. I noticed it first when you were a QB at UT, especially in the Orange Bowl. Then when you turned pro and played in Dallas, it was there as well. And it looked like you still had it when you were traded to Pittsburgh."

Wyatt let out a dry, mirthless laugh that didn't meet his eyes.

"You're the one that asked," she huffed out, scribbling a note angrily on her pad, refusing to look at him.

"I'm not laughing at *you*. Trust me. No, I'm just impressed you noticed so much about me over the years. I'm also trying to count all the different coaches I've had since I was barely out of the crib, and wondering why not a single one of them picked up on that."

"Well, it's subtle. Those D-linemen probably register it on some level, too. Even if they don't consciously realize it, they sense it. And all those coaches? Your talent when you are hitting on all cylinders really is remarkable — good enough to overcome that idiosyncrasy in your throw, so they probably weren't looking for it."

"And you were?"

"I have a gift for recognizing things no one else wants to see."

"And how could you tell I was injured?"

"When I saw you play in person, I noticed your tic is even more pronounced than usual and that your release is markedly slower. You've always held the ball longer than most QBs in the pros, but now, you're also dropping that shoulder a bit. And you're often ending up with more dirt on your jersey than on the field. Point is — the injury and repeated trauma you've endured make your habit more obvious. That makes it easier for the linemen to see and figure out what your next move will be when you play. That's why you're getting sacked more, picked off more, you name it."

"So this is the part where you fix my game to prevent further injury? I'm on board with that."

"Hold up, it's true that as surgeons go, I'm generally not as eager to resort to a quick slice and dice, but you have serious repeated trauma to your throwing shoulder, and it's affecting your whole game. Let's start by taking a look at that shoulder. Hop up here on the bed…" She suddenly blushed and looked away from him, causing him to raise an eyebrow and fight the smile breaking out fully on his face. She quickly cleared her throat and blurted out, "I mean the examining table. I need to manipulate your shoulder."

"You got it. I like an assertive woman that knows what she wants." She rolled her eyes, but he noticed her cheeks turning slightly pink. He could see he wasn't imagining it when he remembered she wasn't impervious to him.

Wyatt felt a little shitty about deliberately keeping her off-balance, especially when he thought about his real reason for selecting her as his consult physician. Part of that plan required that he make the most of the attraction she had for him. Even if she didn't want to admit it to herself, he knew it was there, and damned if he didn't really like those moments when her breath quickened and her lips parted.

"Do you want me…"

"What? I don't want you," she squeaked out.

"I meant, do you want me to take my shirt off?" he asked, standing up from his chair and stepping closer to her.

"Oh, um, yes, that would be best, sorry."

He yanked off his tee shirt and she looked away from him just as he started to jump onto the examining table. And he couldn't help but wish that he were taking off a piece of her clothing in return.

"You're going to have trouble examining me from all the way over there, aren't you, Doc?" he asked with a low voice, trying to overcome his own desire that was threatening to throw his whole plan off course.

She turned and laughed with a soft hint of embarrassment that brought back that stupid, tight feeling in his chest as she walked over to him — close enough that he caught the scent of her hair. It smelled like fresh air and that first moment when you see your home come into view after being gone for far too long.

It was nice.

Snap out of it, you idiot! he mentally shouted to himself.

Wyatt tried to bring himself back under control of the situation. These moments of kindness from her, and her sharp eye for his game were no excuse for him to forget why he was there. It didn't matter that the sharp eye in question was part of a set of the prettiest blue ones he'd ever seen.

Oh, why didn't I tell him to leave his shirt on? Maybe I could've had him put on more clothes before I had to touch him. I can't just keep looking at his naked chest and stroking it — I might fry my brain... Jenna thought worriedly to herself.

She was putting all her energy into keeping calm and focusing on performing a relatively simple examination she'd done numerous times before. Yet nothing about Wyatt was simple for her. In fact, she felt like she deserved a medal — or at least a participation trophy — for her efforts in keeping some kind of cool with this man. Regardless of whatever personal issues she had with dating an athlete, her stepping in to perform a consult on him meant that he was, for all intents and purposes, her patient, at least until the assignment was complete, meaning, she needed to be completely professional with him.

That ethical "out" was almost a relief to her confused emotions — forcing her to stick to her guns and avoid this man on a sexual level. Unfortunately though, when he took off his tee shirt, revealing his smooth, olive skin and muscles developed over a lifetime of rigorous physical conditioning, Jenna became sincerely worried she may have swallowed her tongue and would need to find someone to extract it out of her throat for her.

Her only solution was to commit herself to focus on his

shoulder and its marked reduction in range of motion. His chart was concerning enough, but at every stage of the examination, it was becoming clear to her the trauma to his shoulder was far worse than she had hoped.

"You definitely have inflammation in this joint. In fact, it's warm to the touch — which is a good sign of inflammatory activity, though that's not terribly surprising based on the MRI images in your chart. Is this tender?" she asked him as she pressed lightly against his shoulder joint.

He turned his face toward hers at the question and said, "A little tender, but not too bad. You have a gentle touch, Doc. I like it. I hope you don't show the same attention with all your patients. I may get jealous."

"Mr. McCoy, please focus," she answered, but his teasing was getting to her and part of her couldn't help but want to giggle a little bit — if only to release the tension building in her stomach.

"I'm very focused. I'm still trying to process all the great input you gave me on my release and throwing technique. I'm so impressed, I may need to tie you up and keep you all to myself," he said, letting his mouth slip into a sideways grin, as he moved his hand off his lap and onto the examining table, lightly brushing her waist in the process.

"What?" Jenna squeaked out, feeling her cheeks suddenly burning with heat.

He couldn't know about my dream, could he? she pondered with fear. The memory of what she'd imagined him doing to her — touching her, pleasing her...

"Ow! Jesus, Doc, I was just kidding," he answered, jerking his arm back. Jenna realized she'd accidentally squeezed his shoulder in her mortification at the memory of her dream.

"Oh my God, I am so sorry, I didn't mean to hurt you,"

she quickly mumbled out, before dropping her hands and turning to her desk to make a note. "Well, um, I will make a record in your chart that you have tenderness and inflammation in the rotator cuff..." she continued, wanting to punch herself at the realization that she'd let her control get away from her at the worst of times.

If there were ever a reason to make it through an appointment quickly, this was it. I might break him before he escapes from me.

"Do you need to take a moment, Doc?" he teased, and she forced herself to glare at him — anything to stabilize her fraying nerves.

"I thought you said you were going to take this seriously?"

"I am. I'm just also making the most of my time with you. You don't make it easy on a guy."

"Easy on *a* guy or just not easy on you?"

"Let's focus on me right now."

"That's what I'm trying to do, or at least this examination, Mr. McCoy. And you can put your shirt back on and have a seat. The physical portion of the exam is over now."

"Speaking of this appointment, did you get my text and voicemails? I never heard back from you. Maybe I need to call my cellphone carrier and complain," he mused, though his eyes were scanning her face intently.

"I got them. I must say, I felt that was pretty inappropriate of you — to contact me like that. How'd you get my number?"

"Eloni was nice enough to give it to me. I told him you left something in the locker room."

"Oh, did I? And what was it that I left there?"

"My number," he answered with a smile, and Jenna couldn't stop the laugh that escaped her mouth, though she did quickly recover and straightened her face before Wyatt continued speaking. "I wanted to give it to you, but you ran off before I could."

"I guess that makes me some kind of cyber Dr. Cinderella?"

"Phone numbers are much more efficient than glass slippers, but *that* Cinderella was more receptive."

"*He* was a charming prince."

"And I'm not?"

"Oh no, not going there, Mr. McCoy. But I appreciate the information. I will be sure to, um, thank, Eloni when I see him for his next appointment."

"Don't be mad at him. I tricked him."

"I'm not mad. Actually, I'm a little flattered."

"I knew you had it in you, Doc."

"But flattered or not, I am seriously concerned about your shoulder, Mr. McCoy," she said, sitting down at her desk and taking the MRI results out of his chart. "Look at these images, particularly right here. These are from the MRI that your team had done after the Denver game. We aren't just looking at impingement and tearing, we have evidence of serious and repeated damage to that right shoulder. Basically, you had a sudden trauma during a prior game. From the notes here it was a few weeks before the Denver game. Your arm bone was forced hard into the shoulder socket. Add onto that, the repeated trauma you are seeing in other games, and the damage is simply not healing on its own. That is quite serious."

"I've been doing physical therapy."

"I saw that in the notes. I had hoped the physical examination would show some progress from it, but it doesn't look that way."

"I can get a cortisone shot to my shoulder before games."

"Cortisone shots are great. But, they need to be used sparingly, and you can't rely on them.

"I'll do more PT."

"Physical therapy hasn't been enough, so far. A treatment course based solely on PT could be a possibility, if you were a pharmacist that happened to enjoy playing softball on the weekends. But you're not. You're an elite professional athlete. Your performance will never improve and that pain won't go away, unless you have this surgery. The good news is that as long as you don't re-injure that shoulder more seriously, you *should* be able to make it through the last few games of the season. Then I recommend you have surgery immediately at the beginning of the off-season."

"There's got to be another way, Doc. Eloni said you had other advice for him, too. Gave him relaxation exercises or something."

"That's true. I treat the whole athlete."

"I'm not just an athlete, though. I'm a person."

His words jarred her back to her meeting with Richard.

Am I doing it again? she asked herself. *Treating the athlete and not the person? Only seeing a chart and not a human being? If it truly is a barrier to my success, then maybe I need to step back and listen to this man.*

"That's very true, Mr. McCoy. I do try to take that into account — to understand the emotional strain you face. The accommodations athletes need to make to address those challenges. Your body is your life and your livelihood… I get that."

"Because you were an athlete?"

"Excuse me?"

"Eloni told me you played basketball, blew out one of your knees."

"Um, yes. I just don't talk about it much. Most of my patients know it, though, that's true." Jenna looked down at her notepad and tried to regain her composure. The memory of that injury was still fresh and sharing it with Wyatt felt incredibly intimate.

"But I'm not a patient. I'm a consult."

"What? That's true," she said, looking up and focusing on Wyatt again. "I take it just as seriously, though. Yes, I do try to bring my experience as an athlete to bear in all I do. The benefit is that I understand the strain of being at least a collegiate scholarship athlete. To have all those responsibilities."

"And you know football? I played with a guy at UT your dad coached in high school. They don't get much better than him apparently. He even used to coach at Georgia."

"Wow, you really did your homework, Wyatt."

"I told you I take my career very seriously. Georgia's a pretty good gig. You don't see a lot of assistant coaches step down voluntarily."

"True, but that's a hard life to have as a solo parent with a young child."

"My mother would agree with you on that point," Wyatt said darkly.

Jenna paused, wanting to pry so much into his life, but knowing it was wrong.

Instead she simply said, "Yes, I read once that your parents are divorced. Being married to an NFL player can't be easy."

Wyatt's face creased in what looked almost like anger, but it wasn't aimed at her, she could tell that. It looked more like the face of someone with an old hurt — an unhealed wound. It was an expression Jenna had seen on her own face more than once.

"So, your dad decided to become the king of high school football and summer quarterback camps, instead?" Wyatt went on quickly, changing the subject back to Jenna's personal life.

"Yep. And he's really great at it. I hate to be rude, but we should really get back to talking about your shoulder." Jenna definitely felt off-kilter when she was around Wyatt, and all this talk about her dad was all the more unsettling. This guy had a knack for getting under her skin and she couldn't let that happen anymore. She'd already relaxed too much around him.

"Right. We're here to talk about my shoulder. Eloni swears by the extra advice you offer, so bring it on."

Jenna had to fight back a little laugh.

"Eloni had serious stress issues. And his stretching was atrocious. Yoga and sewing with his wife turned out to be very effective."

"You're suggesting I do yoga?"

"You'd have to be careful not to strain your injury, but it could have some benefits to your overall awareness of your body and its cues. It doesn't have to be that. It can be anything you find which makes you feel centered and calm — able to refocus on your body and then, hopefully, your playing style and goals. Have you ever found something that had that effect?"

"Yes."

"That's great, what is it?"

"Oh nothing you'd care about," he mumbled out, a slight blush briefly streaking his cheeks and making her all the more intrigued by him all over again.

"Whatever you end up choosing on that end, unfortunately, I don't think it will be enough. Sometimes surgery is the only option. That was the case for Eloni and his knee."

"No surgeries for me. No hospitals," he said simply, but she noticed him swallowing hard.

"Look, Mr. McCoy…"

"I really mean it," he answered sternly, silencing her. "I mean that I'd like you to call me Wyatt," he continued, softening his tone and forcing a smile. For the first time, Jenna saw something in his eyes that wasn't pure cockiness and bravado. Could it be…fear? That seemed impossible. Yet, even though his flash of vulnerability was gone even more quickly than it appeared, she felt her disloyal heart soften, just a bit.

"All right. I'll call you Wyatt," she said, smiling gently.

He grinned in response, and her whole body seemed to flip over. Jenna hated what he did to her.

She realized she couldn't deny that she was attracted to him. He was like a multiplying virus — overtaking her sense of resolve with each continuing moment, and for all her years of fighting off men like him successfully, Jenna worried there would be no vaccine or cure to avoid the impact of this particular one.

"Thanks. You know my friends actually call me Wy."

"I'm not calling you that. Wyatt is all you're going to get from me."

"Are you sure about that?" he asked teasingly, but his stare directly into her eyes was too penetrating. She decided instead to peer at the chart in front of her. That was much safer than this man.

"I'm very sure…*Wyatt*. Now, I must say, your resistance to surgery is really problematic. Yes, there are risks…"

"I'm not a fan of risks."

"Oh, well, I can certainly understand that." And she could. That was Jenna's life mantra, but it surprised her Wyatt shared that view. She'd assumed he had the kind of confidence and courage to take chances that only came from having everything in life handed to you. That was not consistent with the suddenly cautious and guarded man before her.

"Doc? Are you still with me?"

"Sorry. I was just thinking for a moment."

"Okay. So what else can I do?"

"Fact is, I really don't see how your regimen has made the improvements you need. And with all your emphasis on physical therapy over surgery — to not see marked improvement by this point — it's deeply concerning."

"I *am* making progress though. Let me show you. You have a fresh pair of eyes. I've really been committed to the therapy, and adjusting my game. I think it's helping."

"Has it? The notes from the team physician say your coaches feel you have a problem bringing passion and inspiration to your game. From what I have seen, that makes sense. Your approach is very clinical. Maybe that can work at some stages of your career, but you're almost thirty now, that is a key juncture in the trajectory of your professional life. Passion needs to be in every part of your life — in practice and in PT. That, taken with your resistance to surgery... Simply put, it's counter-productive."

"Wow, I knew you didn't want to like me, but come on."

"This has nothing to do with liking you or not liking you."

"Then give me a chance."

"What?"

"Let me show you what the other doctors are missing. I can do this without surgery."

"Oh, *that* chance. Of course." The flicker of disappointment in her belly made Jenna feel sick. She didn't need to be giving this guy chances of any kind. She needed to get him out of her office and out of her life.

"What did you think I meant?" he asked, a small smile quirking at the corners of his mouth.

"Nothing, um, I think I have my opinion."

"Come on, please."

Dammit, big ole sad eyes, really? she thought grumpily. *Low blow.*

"What do you propose I see?"

"How about you watch me play again?"

"I saw you play a week ago."

"I know, but I think the PT is paying off, and I've been working on my release after you mentioned it last week. I listened."

"Oh, that's great. I did notice your performance was improved in Sunday's game."

"See, I'm not totally a lost cause."

Jenna's instincts were telling her to run and move on from this deeply confusing man. Yet she knew this was a great opportunity, coming at the perfect time in her career. She'd be crazy to say no.

"All right, Wyatt, one more game."

"Great. Then you'll come with us to New Orleans. We leave Friday. I can tell the staff you're joining the rest of the med crew."

"Right, well, I suppose that covers it. I will see you for your next game."

Jenna stood and walked to the door of her office, desperately trying to ignore the tingling in her fingertips and intense nerves she felt with each moment she was near him.

Just a couple more days and then he's out of my life. I can do this.

She reached for the doorknob to open it and suddenly felt his warm, strong hand over hers. Breathing deeply she looked up and tried to pull her hand back, but he simply tightened his grip and looked into her eyes with such passion that Jenna was almost transfixed. The air around her was suffused with him and it occurred to her it should be a crime to smell that good.

"Thanks for listening to me and giving me a chance to show you what I can do. It's very important to me that I can stay on the field."

"I understand, Wyatt," Jenna responded quietly.

Wyatt leaned forward so that his lips were very close to her ear, and whispered, "I think you do."

Jenna willed herself not to look up into his eyes, but her body had a mind of its own, as she felt her chin raise and her face become so close to his. Every muscle inside of her clenched at his nearness and his scent enveloped her. The heat coming off his body was so much more real and powerful than in her dream and she wished she could just lean forward closer to him.

Yet, that was impossible. Nothing about the two of them together made sense — consultation or not, and she needed to remember it. Quickly she took a breath and regained some of her sanity before opening the door and gesturing for him to leave.

"Good-bye, Wyatt," she said, staring past him, afraid of what she would do if she looked at him again.

"See you soon, Doc," he answered.

She nodded, and then he was gone.

Jenna closed the door and fell backwards against the cool, painted wood, allowing some of her heat to seep away against its inanimate strength, as she wondered just how she would survive another run-in with this man.

CHAPTER SIX

Wyatt kicked his feet against the side of the hotel's indoor pool and used the force to dive back underneath the cool water for another lap. He gently moved his arms through the water, being careful to use the stroke his physical therapist had selected for him — the one that promised to loosen his shoulder joint while keeping the strength in his upper torso.

He hated having to limit what he did with his body — another cruel reminder he couldn't control everything in his own world. There was no time for that frustration though, because he needed to have the greatest shot at showing the good doctor what he was capable of during that night's game.

Movement in the water near him registered against his body and he pulled his head above it to see a blonde figure had jumped into the pool with him and was beginning to swim laps of her own. As she turned her head to take in some air he saw it was Jenna. Never having felt particularly lucky during his life, Wyatt couldn't believe his good fortune in that moment.

Ever since they'd arrived in New Orleans, she'd appeared intent on keeping a marked distance from him. Even though she'd watched his practice with the team the day before, she had eaten with the staff and barely said "hi" to him. He actually felt like he'd made some headway with her during her examination of him — especially during the portion when she was touching him.

Lord knew he'd liked that part. Though it wasn't just their physical attraction that he believed made her susceptible to him. He also felt like he was breaking through with her on another level — all of which had left him feeling optimistic that he'd been smart to select her for his second opinion, after all. He just needed to keep that influence going so she would be swayed enough to acknowledge his shoulder would be fine without surgery, such that the Roughnecks would re-sign him as a starting quarterback and everything could get back to normal.

Unfortunately, she seemed to have used their days apart before this away game to seal him off from her all over again. She was proving a bigger challenge than he'd bargained for, but Wyatt wouldn't be discouraged. Especially now that she was a mere few feet from him while most of the world was still sleeping — the sun only having risen a mere hour before.

He was impressed she hadn't hightailed it out of there at the mere sight of him in the pool. After allowing Jenna a couple of laps in peace, he made his way over to her. Wyatt leaned his back against the concrete wall as he waited for her submerged body to swim blindly to him.

Her strokes were smooth and strong, pulling her long, lean body through the water and showing how much effort she put into everything she did. As her blonde head approached him, he realized she was so engrossed in her movements she hadn't noticed he was now directly in her path.

Smiling to himself, Wyatt crossed his arms and watched with wicked anticipation as her right arm lifted out of the water. It arched beautifully, allowing her hand to curl into the water, where it proceeded to smack him fully on his cock. His eager appendage twitched at the attention from her.

Stifling a laugh, Wyatt took immense pleasure in watching her jerk back. She sputtered water from her mouth, before standing up and glaring at him through swim goggles.

In spite of her obvious mortification, Wyatt didn't bother to hide the smug smirk that took over half his face, as he said, "I was going to say good morning, Doc, but I'm pretty sure I like your greeting much better."

Ripping off her goggles, she exclaimed quickly, "What the hell are you doing there, Wyatt? Are you trying to give me a heart attack? Or drown me?" Her cheeks were bright red. From the way she refused to meet his eyes, he felt confident it was due to embarrassment, rather than exertion.

"Easy, Doc, I thought you saw I was in here."

"In here swimming laps, not coming up on me like some extra from a shark week made-for-TV movie." She smoothed her wet hair back and turned away from him, apparently ready to get back to her workout.

"Hey, where are you going, Doc?"

"It's a pool. I'm swimming."

"Well, let your heart rate slow down for a minute. If I really did frighten you that badly, why don't you take a breather and talk to me...unless you're scared."

"Oh, don't be so predictable," she huffed out. "Of course, I'm not scared of you."

"Then it's settled. Good morning, how are you doing? Now, your turn."

"Fine, I guess my heart is still skittering a bit." She crossed her arms, unwittingly emphasizing that beautiful cleavage of hers that he hadn't been able to stop thinking about for days, and leaned back against the other pool wall. Her wet hair and flushed face were lovely, even if she was still looking wonderfully annoyed with him.

"I liked your stroke."

"My *what*? That was an accident! I didn't even know..." she stammered out quickly.

"Through the water. Get your mind out of the gutter, Doc," he said, with a smile, loving the bright pink that quickly returned to her face.

"Oh, um, then thanks. Ever since I blew out my knee, I try to swim regularly to ease the strain on it that my other exercises can cause. What about you? How does your shoulder tolerate swimming?"

"Pretty well. I worked on this regimen with my physical therapist. It's really helped my range of motion before games. You'll see that tonight, I think."

"I hope so. I must say, I'm really impressed by your hard work. You seemed really intent at practice, too. Nothing like what the club physician had put in his notes in your chart."

"I told you that you're smarter than all those old dudes."

"Are you trying to flatter me, Wyatt?"

"Just telling the truth as I see it. You really do have a great eye," he replied as he leaned in more closely to her, examining her face. Water had beaded on her straight nose and her blue eyes were sparkling behind wet lashes. "*Two* great eyes, actually."

She laughed and glanced away briefly before turning back to him with a cool look that seemed a bit too practiced.

"I'm glad to see you're taking this seriously...staying focused. It will take hard work and dedication from you to come back from this injury, no matter what path you end up taking."

"You're judged by what you do, not by what you have, Doc," he replied blankly.

"That's very true, I hadn't expected you to see things that way, though. Oh God, I'm sorry I said that, it's not…"

"I get it. You mean someone born of *the* Jim McCoy, one of the greatest quarterbacks ever, couldn't have a real work ethic? Appearances can be deceiving, especially when it comes to the McCoy part of my lineage."

"Oh, well, I heard rumors, but…"

"About my dad blowing it all on parties and women and bad investments? Those rumors?"

"Yes, those. I didn't believe them, though. I mean Jim McCoy was a legend, his face was everywhere."

"Oh yeah, his face was in too many places, and so was his money. For once, bad rumors turned out to be true. My view of the game may be clinical, Doc, but that's better than being so absorbed in all the trappings of pro-football you let its world suck you under so far you can never come up for air. That's how you screw over everyone in your life. *That's* the Jim McCoy I knew."

"But, what about your mom? I thought she was really successful."

"My dad made her quit all that when they got married. No more modeling money, no more fame, nothing to fall back on."

"Oh God, how awful."

"When he blew all his money and didn't even pretend to want to be around anymore, we moved in with my grandparents. When my grandfather died, all our hopes were on my football career. So, yeah, things aren't always as they seem."

"I'm sorry."

"Don't be. My family has me. And I'll do whatever it takes to make sure they're taken care of. My sister will be done with school soon. I bought my mom a nice *hacienda* on Lake Travis by Austin. It's nothing like the huge place my dad never made the payments on, but she still loves it. My abuela lives there with her. And *I* got it for her."

"They all rely on you financially?"

"Yes, though my baby brother would rather go off and fuck up his own life. Claudia is the youngest, and she can't wait to be independent. Gives me nightmares."

"Are you a tough big brother?" Jenna asked teasingly.

"The toughest."

"I didn't know your dad put you guys through all that."

"How could you know? One of the negatives of keeping a secret well is no one knows the full real you. You understand?"

"Yes. I definitely do."

"Oh, yeah? I gave you the dirt, it's your turn to spill, Doc."

"Never mind. There's nothing to tell. I'm pretty boring."

"I don't believe that. You know, I like this side of you. All vulnerable and sweet — like my very own little wet kitten."

"Don't get used to it," she bristled out petulantly.

"Oh, and there's those claws I like even more." He threw his head back and let out a deep chuckle.

She looked back and forth and her face showed marked discomfort.

"Um, I better get going, Wyatt, I'll see you at the game tonight."

He'd pushed too hard, he could tell, so he decided to step back and let all the information he'd given her sink in for a while.

"Okay, well, I hope you enjoy the game and see how much progress I've made."

"I hope so, too, Wyatt. But I also want you to give surgery some serious thought. If it goes the way I think it will, you could be back on the field in time for training camp."

"True, but there are just as many guys that never play again. Or they get cut and no one wants them. I can't risk it."

"You're still young, Wyatt."

"Youth is a temporary condition. You should know that, Doc."

"A lot of QBs don't even hit their prime until thirty. Your dad was amazing well after that. Despite the many faults it sounds like he had, he did give you a remarkable talent. I've always thought you could be much better than him, in fact."

Wyatt rubbed the back of his neck and stared over her head, suddenly uncomfortable with the glow of happiness that filled his heart at her compliment. After setting his jaw, he met her eyes again.

"Those notes in my chart? They may have been right about one thing. I don't play out of passion. I know that this game is anything but that — it's a business, not a love."

"My father would tell you the love is what makes for greatness, and the greatness is what gives you the best security."

"They don't get much greater than Jim McCoy, Doc. That's not a path that'll keep my family safe for each of their lifetimes."

"Go ahead and tell yourself that if you have to, Wyatt, but mercenaries rarely win any wars. I'll see you tonight. Goodbye."

Before he could challenge her statement, she boosted herself out of the pool by her arms swiftly, allowing streams of water to rush down her beautiful body.

For someone so athletic, she had delicious looking curves

and Wyatt had to remind himself that all this attention he was focusing onto her had a very specific purpose. It didn't involve him letting his brain turn off and the rest of his body to take over all of his decision-making. Before he could get himself under control, she had grabbed a towel and was wrapping herself in it quickly as she walked away.

"Good-bye to you, too, Doc," he shouted after her, before diving back under the water with the hopes that another round of laps would bring him some much needed clarity.

Wyatt couldn't believe how great he was playing, though he wasn't sure what caused it. He assumed it was from deliberately trying to resolve the issues Jenna raised about his release and shoulder tic, combined with his need to show her he could still play this game without having his body cut open.

Whatever it was — he couldn't seem to make a mistake.

Zero sacks, zero interceptions, and he'd thrown for three touchdowns — Wyatt hadn't had that kind of success on the field in over a year. It was as though he could read the minds of every defensive player on the other side of the ball and knew everything they planned to do to him. He'd evaded every tackle and it felt like every move he made was perfect.

With a warm rush of pride invading his chest, he kneeled in front of the ball to run the last few seconds off the clock. He stood and quickly looked to the sidelines for Jenna, already planning a sarcastic and suggestive comment about his "performance" that would make her blush.

Yet before he even had his helmet off, he realized she was nowhere in sight. He felt his teeth grind and his temper rising, hot enough to blow the lid off the dome that covered the stadium.

"Why no smile, Wy? That was an amazing game you played, you must be thrilled." Wyatt heard a nosy voice ask from behind him, as the well-manicured hand it was attached to thrust a microphone into his face. Suddenly his euphoria began to morph into a bubbling cauldron of bile in his stomach.

Olivia Hayes, the most helpful and cloying sports reporter he knew, was apparently eager for a scoop — obviously confused and intrigued by his hostile demeanor.

"I'm tired," he grunted out through gritted teeth. He caught Jenna's eye for a moment. She stared seriously at him and Olivia, before she turned quickly. Leaving only a view of her retreating figure as she briskly left the sideline and entered the tunnel to take her out of the stadium.

Fuck, he thought. He could punch a wall right now. He thought for sure she'd want to talk about how great he'd done, especially after she'd seemed to care so much about how he was playing. She must've seen the improvements he'd made.

"You *have* to be tired, Wy. Do you feel like you put the team on your shoulders out there?"

Wyatt realized a camera was on him and Olivia wouldn't let him go if he didn't indulge her at least a little bit.

"No, I think everyone pulled together and did a great job. This is a great team and I strongly believe we will still make the play-offs."

Olivia continued to bat her eyelashes at him and ask a series of inane questions, before finally ending the interview so he could have some relief and not have to spout out any more tired clichés for her station's coverage. She was with a national sports network but had been assigned to the Roughnecks' division for over two years. She'd provided him some valuable support since he'd been traded to Pittsburgh. In exchange, he gave her some exclusives, and more attention than most women ever got from him.

She was pretty hot, and it hadn't been a hardship, until that moment. Suddenly, he couldn't get away from her fast enough. He made sure the recording light was off on her assistant's camera and he was preoccupied with his equipment before he continued speaking to her.

"I need to get going, Liv. Have a great night."

"Why? Are you trying to catch up with that pretty surgeon you brought along with you?"

"What are you talking about, Olivia?"

"Oh, come on. Don't act stupid, Wy, or at least don't act like I'm stupid," she said, with a high-pitched giggle that he couldn't believe hadn't driven him crazy more before. She flipped her dyed-red hair over her shoulder and asked, "That blonde doctor you selected for your consult. You're into her, aren't you?"

"How do you know I selected her?"

"You're not the only Roughneck I get information from, Wy."

"And I can guess I don't want to know how you do that."

"Oh, are you finally jealous over me, Wy?" she asked with a practiced pout. Then she touched his arm lightly, using her body to hide her familiarity from the curious eyes around them. He willed himself not to pull away from her. He'd mistakenly let his mutually beneficial professional understanding with Olivia develop into something more physical, but now, he felt almost repulsed by her nearness.

"Liv, I'm not jealous, but this game playing shit on your part is getting pretty old. You know that when you and I hooked up, it was only physical. That's how it is with everyone

I'm with, right? You said you understood that."

"Are you being *just physical* with that doctor now, is that it?"

"No. She can help me a lot. I need to keep her happy."

"Well, she didn't look too happy when she ran off into that tunnel. Maybe you aren't doing something right. Though, you did most things right with me."

"Enough, Liv. Look, thanks for the interview, but I really need to get going. And it's probably best if we don't get together anymore. It's a very sensitive part of my career."

He was ready to throttle her already, and what he was working on with Jenna left no room for another woman at that moment.

"So, is your doctor going to help you with your sensitive parts?"

"I don't know what you mean, Liv."

"Come on, Wy. You know exactly what I'm talking about. I heard she gave you a consult, and I saw you staring at her just now. Are you trying to consult with her on other things? Work your magic?"

"Olivia, I don't know if you're nosy or jealous, but I'm not in the mood. It's none of your business, and I do really need to get going."

"I'm *the press*, everything is my business."

"Then I definitely don't want to talk about it."

"Of course, Wy, I'm just trying to be a caring friend."

"Right, well, I'm going to need your caring to be pretty distant from now on, okay?"

"Of course," she cooed, and Wyatt wondered why he'd ever spent so much time with this harpy.

"But my sources say you need surgery and you may not be on the field for the Roughnecks next year."

"Screw your sources, Liv. I'll be back on the field — without surgery."

"How?" she asked. "You have some tricks up your sleeve? Because word on the street is you'll need them with what folks are saying about your shoulder."

"Sensitive as always, Olivia. I won't insult either of our intelligences by saying this conversation is off-the-record. Just know, I have my ways."

"Could those ways have anything to do with that pretty lady surgeon you won't be straight up with me about?"

"Don't know what you're talking about, Olivia."

"I'm not leaving without an answer, Wy."

Wyatt could barely control his temper. He needed to get rid of her before he really lost it.

"Back off, Liv. She's going to see things my way one way or another, all right?"

"Fine, then you better get going. See you next week, Wy," she said, with a slow smile and small wiggly finger wave that Wyatt definitely didn't return. He quickly rushed off the field and found Jenna jotting down notes on a pad in the tunnel. She hadn't completely run off, and that made Wyatt's heart settle down some.

"Where were you, Doc? I thought you were going to watch the game. You just disappeared."

"I saw you play. That's what I was here to do."

"I thought you would stay after to talk to me is all," his voice sounded pathetic even to himself, and Wyatt tried to put on a hard face.

"You got to talk to Olivia Hayes, so I guess you're okay," she said, in a snarky tone, before shutting her mouth quickly.

"So you *were* sticking around for me after the game, after all. You didn't like seeing me talk to her? Are you jealous,

Doc?"

Now *this* was a woman he liked to think was jealous on his behalf.

"Of course not, I just wanted to get my notes written and get on the bus with the rest of the staff," she said sternly, clicking closed her pen and stuffing her notes into her purse. He heard her take a breath and when she looked back at him, her face had turned unreadable. She put her hand out for him to shake it, and said, "Well, I have all the information I need. That means this is it for us, Wyatt. Good-bye."

Like hell, this was it, he thought.

She had to see how much better he was doing. She couldn't just disappear. How could she be so cold? None of this was going as he'd planned.

He took her hand and jerked her more closely to him, making her eyes widen a bit.

"I'll see you later, Doc," he said, with more of a growl than he'd intended, before dropping her hand and walking away from her to the visitor's locker room.

CHAPTER SEVEN

"Wow, I can't believe it's just us in class today," Jenna said to Aubrey as she rolled out her yoga mat, shocked to see there weren't any other attendees in the class with them. She'd been stressed out ever since she'd returned from New Orleans. Every time she tried to analyze Wyatt's case, her thoughts would focus on *him*, rather than his condition, and it was beyond maddening.

What Jenna really needed was a peaceful hour of twisting her body into positions she hoped would distract her from her stupid hormonal desire to twist-up sheets with the man, who happened to possess the most important shoulder of her career so far.

"I don't know, Christmas is only a few weeks away, maybe everyone is doing a downward facing dog into the bargain bin for gifts tonight," Aubrey answered, as she darted her eyes to the door quickly.

"Are you looking for Tea? I swear, she's been running late so much lately..." Jenna began, but when the door opened Jenna's words caught in her throat at the sight of Wyatt McCoy wearing a pair of basketball shorts and holding a yoga mat still in its packaging in his masculine hands. If he didn't look gorgeous no matter what he did, he would appear completely ridiculous.

"Will you look at that, isn't that Wyatt McCoy? I wonder what he's doing here?" Aubrey said awkwardly, as she took far too long to roll her mat on the floor.

"What did you do, Aubrey? You tell me *right* now because he is almost here and I only have about ten seconds to kill you."

Wyatt grinned and waved to her before walking to the instructor to introduce himself.

"What makes you think I did something? Don't you believe in coincidences? Now be nice, he's coming over."

"Hey, Doc. I'm glad to see you made it home from the airport okay. Not that I would know, seeing as you didn't respond to my very worried text checking up on you."

"Text? Oh my, is there something going on here, Jenna?" Aubrey asked, raising her dark eyebrows intently.

"Yes," Wyatt answered quickly.

"No," Jenna said brusquely, at the same time.

Jenna took a breath and looked at Wyatt as calmly as her roiling emotions would allow her.

"So you're stalking me now?"

"It's only stalking if you're unhappy to see me. And I know you're glad I'm here."

"Oh, so should we add lawyer and mind reader to your list of talents?"

"Nope, just being honest."

"Since we are being honest, tell me, why are you here, Wyatt?"

"You invited me," Wyatt answered.

"I did not."

"I'm pretty sure you did," he corrected her. "You're the one who said going to a yoga class would be good for me."

"I didn't mean *my* yoga class."

"Hmm, that's not the way I heard it."

"Fine, but you do realize this is extremely inappropriate, right? I still have to deliver my opinion to your team."

"So?"

"Nice comeback, Wyatt," Aubrey teased. At least she wasn't on his side completely. Aubrey was generally more on the side of what would entertain her most, but that didn't help assuage how unsettling his presence was to Jenna.

"Fine, then how did you even know I was here?" she asked him.

Aubrey quickly looked away, but her guilty eyes told the tale.

"Aubrey! Seriously?"

"He promised me a photo spread. That's a can't-miss opportunity for me and you know it. Besides," she added on a whisper into Jenna's ear, "it wouldn't hurt you to do your *own* spread with him."

"Now *that* sounds like a great idea," she heard Wyatt say in her other ear.

"Aubrey you are the worst whisperer, ever," Jenna sputtered out. "Both of you, out of my ears, now."

"Is everything okay over there?" Kimberly, their yoga instructor, asked with a soft, tranquil voice.

"Yes, it's fine. Sorry, I'm just trying to sort something out," Jenna said, before turning back to Aubrey and growling out, "like how I am going to make you pay, girly."

"Oh, come on, give her a break. And give me one, too, while you're at it. Why are you always fighting me, Doc? This isn't a competition."

"It's not? I don't buy it. The only people who say something's not a competition are the ones that always win. I've been on the losing end of things enough for one lifetime."

"Oh good, we're learning about each other now. My sister tells me that's important to women."

"See, he's showing he's sensitive, Jenna, or at least that he's genetically related to a smart female, so that's something."

"I already knew he has a sister, Aubrey."

"Then why are you being so pissy? You seem to be old buds now."

"Hey, guys," Tea ran up to them breathlessly. "So sorry I'm late, today was crazy and... What *in the* hell?"

"Tea, you remember Wyatt McCoy from the Denver game, right?" Jenna offered with a resigned tone.

"Of course, but I'm just surprised to see him here is all."

"Well, Aubrey..."

"Oh, that explains it," Tea said, in that easy, goofy way she had with things, before putting her hand out for him to shake it. "How nice of you to join us, Mr. McCoy."

"My pleasure. It's great to see you again. Althea, right?" he asked.

"Oh, Lord, only Griffen calls me that. Please, call me Tea," she said, smoothing her hair back with her left hand.

"Wow, that is some rock you've got there, Tea."

"Oh, thanks. How sweet of you to notice."

"I'd have to get my eyes checked if I missed that," he teased, and Jenna could kick him for being so charming. Instead, she fidgeted with her yoga mat with her big toe, avoiding eye contact.

"I'm still getting used to it myself," Tea answered.

"Congratulations. He's a lucky guy. Well, I better get myself settled in for my first yoga class," he said, winking at

Jenna, until she had to roll her eyes at him to control her own desire to smile.

"Wyatt…"

"Yes, Doc?" he said, turning and looking at her in that intense way that always managed to make her forget all of her words.

"Um, uh…"

"Good point, Jenna."

"Shut up, Aubrey. Wyatt, I meant to say, please be careful with your shoulder, okay? Use some of those blocks and a strap from the back of the room, and if you feel any strain in any position, just ask the instructor for a modification, okay?"

"You got it, Doc," he said, with a sweet smile that made her feel gooey in the worst way. Jenna turned away.

"So, Jenna, does this mean you're finally breaking your no-athletes-ever policy?" Tea asked her quietly.

"Oh, it's a whole no-athletes thing? I get it, so it's not about me?"

"Wyatt, you need to stop eavesdropping," Jenna spun around and said to him sternly.

"It's not my fault. Tea is bad at whispering, too."

"Okay, enough of that, all of you. I assume no one else is coming to class today?"

"That's true," Wyatt answered. "The instructor was nice enough to let me purchase all of the remaining slots, except for you three, of course."

"Of course. Fine. Wyatt, you can join the class, but stay in your area."

Wyatt simply smirked and rolled out his mat directly behind hers, situated perfectly to have an hour-long unobstructed view of her butt.

"This room is almost empty and you put your mat there?

Wyatt, that is not your area."

"But the view from behind you is good for my Zen."

She tried to be furious, but a smile was quirking her lips and she had to hide her face.

"But you realize you're messing with my Zen, right?"

"I've been trying to mess with you for weeks now, I thought I made that clear?"

"Let's begin with Cobbler's Pose today," Kimberly intoned from the front of the room, effectively silencing the four of them.

To his credit, Wyatt took the class very seriously, even though Jenna was pretty sure he was staring at her ass more than was necessary, but it did make her glad she'd worn her tightest yoga pants. Just because she couldn't ever have anything to do with him didn't mean it wasn't nice to know he enjoyed the view she presented in Plow Pose.

As the class ended and they packed up to leave, she turned to give him a polite farewell.

"Did you enjoy it, Wyatt?"

"I did. It was great advice. My shoulder feels better already."

"Did you feel more centered and focused like we discussed?"

"I was very focused on your body. Does that count?"

"That's not the kind of outlet I was talking about when we discussed this part of your recovery."

"Why not? It's an outlet I am very interested in."

"Wyatt, please…"

But he ignored her and leaned closely, and with an *actual* whisper, he gently informed her, "You and me? We're going to happen, Doc. I'm not afraid to wait. I'm pretty sure you'll be worth it." He let his lips brush her earlobe, sending a shock wave through her body. Then, before Jenna could even fight to get her bearings back, he leaned away and stood to his full height. "See you later, Doc. You too, ladies." As he walked out, Jenna clutched her yoga mat and tried to appear under control.

"Well, well. Now *that* was hot," Aubrey said to her, making her jump.

"Oh, he's got you all worked up, girl. I love it," Tea said, clapping her hands together.

"Stop it, you two."

"Why aren't you playing with that bad boy? You deserve to have some fun."

"Even if it weren't everything I don't need right now, it would be inappropriate."

"Aren't you giving your opinion soon? So it won't be an issue after that, right?"

"I will, any day now, and technically no, it won't be an issue then — but it wouldn't look right. I can't risk losing whatever chance I have at that fellowship. It's everything I've ever wanted."

"Not *everything*."

"Shut up, Aubrey."

"Good argument, Jenna," Tea said, with a harsh chuckle.

"Get your mat and let's go or I'll tell you to shut up, too," Jenna teased.

"Ooh, I'm scared!" Tea laughed out, with her hands waving comically by her face.

"I'm going to kill you both. Slowly."

"Oh, come on, *sugar*, oh wait, now he calls you Doc, right?" Tea said, as she and Aubrey both began to laugh hysterically.

"Stop it. At least he doesn't call me "gorgeous" nonstop."

"She's got you there, Tea."

"Hey, Jenna, that's not nice. It's so sweet when Griffen says that."

"For you, maybe," Aubrey responded, as she slipped her yoga mat into her bag. "But for the rest of us — blech."

"All right, Brey. It's not that bad, Tea. I think it's cute," Jenna said gently. She may be annoyed, but she also wanted to let Tea enjoy her new life without torment.

"Anyways... Quit changing the subject, Jenna. You know that Wyatt's yummy," Aubrey cut in. "And you've been so crabby lately. I think you should let yourself have a taste of somebody. If not him, what about Griffen's bud, Trey? He seems to like you."

"Trey is a friend and that's all."

"Man, you have a lot of rejections ready, woman. I think you should try out a 'yes,'" Tea suggested.

"Good point, Tea," Aubrey said. "Especially because Trey is hella hot. He makes me want to break my computer just so I can have him come over and fix it."

"I hate you both," Jenna muttered.

"Oh, stop. You know you really do need to relax, Jenna. You're too wound up."

"I'll find another way that doesn't involve opening those cans of worms. Now I really do need to go."

"Okay, honey, calm down. But this conversation isn't over," Tea said, waving her finger at Jenna.

"It never is," Jenna muttered to herself, as she flung her mat under her arm and made her way to the back of the room where they all collected their coats to bundle up for the blustery walk to their cars.

"Hey, Gabe, what's up?" Wyatt said, as he clicked his cell phone onto speaker mode and placed it on his coffee table, freeing his hands up to wrap one of his sister's Christmas presents.

Wyatt had spent most of his day off like this — trying to distract himself while he waited to hear what Jenna would tell his team. His agent had told him the team was informed her report was coming through today, and he'd been wound up ever since.

He told himself that was why he pulled up the only picture of her he could find on the Internet and stared at it for longer than was probably necessary.

Her hospital biography picture didn't really do her justice, but it was good enough to occupy his attention in his quiet house on Washington's Landing. It was a small cluster of homes and townhomes on an island in the Allegheny River that was once the site of industrial pollution, but now had been revitalized into a clean and stunning private haven complete with wildlife and trees, even though it was deep in the heart of the city.

Usually, its quiet beauty reminded Wyatt of when he was very young growing up on Lake Travis. Right then it just made him feel like a caged animal, desperate to escape and grab his own future in his claws and not let it go. Instead, he could only wait — and talk to his agent.

"It looks like you don't have the kind of irresistible force over women you thought, Wyatt."

"Shit. That doesn't sound good."

"Jenna Sutherland supplied her diagnosis."

"And?" Wyatt asked, even though he had a sick dread in

his stomach that showed he already knew the outcome.

"Surgery, with six to eight months of recovery. And she suggested a change in your playing style to prevent future injury and improve your stats. The GM ate it up. She's some kind of football savant apparently."

"Yeah, she appears to be," he answered morosely, feeling his jaw tightening.

"She's not wrong, you know. Her tips sounded pretty good actually."

"You're just full of good news today, aren't you? I heard some of her ideas, I thought they were good, too. But the only idea that matters is that she said surgery. Do you know anything else?"

"I know that management is definitely on the fence about you. They'll wait until the end of the season to decide what to do with you, but if you go out for surgery — there's really no telling what will happen. I've already gotten calls from other teams."

"A third team in three years?"

"Right. And this transition would be to a backup position. Pittsburgh could kick you down to backup, too."

"Hell, no."

"You could move up to starting QB from there, if you prove yourself — for the Roughnecks, or some other team. Nobody wants to take a chance on you right now, Wy. A pay cut and backup position is much safer for any team that's considering you. Maybe you should think about it, too."

"I'm in my ninth year. That's when I'm supposed to be finally hitting my stride. How would surgery and being second string affect our other plans? My endorsements, modeling, broadcasting?"

"It won't help them. I also talked to my friends at *Fox*

Sports and *ESPN*. They liked your off-season appearances on their NFL shows, but I won't lie — they usually want someone that's gone out with a bang, not a whimper. At least gone to the championships. Play-offs aren't enough. I'll keep hooking you up with modeling gigs and endorsements, but if your plan is to support your family after you retire...I think we need to have another idea — a Plan B."

Wyatt looked at Jenna's *UPMC* biography picture again and then at Claudia's half-wrapped gift. It was a key chain for the car he planned to buy her in honor of the holiday and graduating early. It would be a safe, reliable car that would take care of her for years — just like he wanted to do, for her, and the rest of his family.

He steeled himself for what he had to do. Maybe he hadn't been able to persuade Dr. Sutherland yet, but he could still push harder. Even if he wasn't sure how it would turn out, he had to try — there was nothing else for him to do.

"Are you still there, Wy?"

"I already have a Plan B, Gabe. I'll get started on it now."

"Wyatt, what are you thinking? If it has to do with bothering that surgeon, give it up. You didn't affect her opinion this time. You don't really think you can get her to change it, do you?"

"Don't worry about it. Just keep trying to figure out what Pittsburgh wants to do. If they have anyone else in mind to take my position and who it is, okay?"

"Dammit, Wyatt..."

"Talk to you later, Gabe, bye."

"Fine. Bye."

Wyatt knew Gabe was pissed at him, but he couldn't worry about that now. Instead he dialed Jenna's number, trying his damnedest to ignore the tightening in his stomach that happened as he waited — hoped — she would answer.

    This wasn't about fun — it was all business, he assured himself. It was time to see if Dr. Sutherland was in the mood for a little holiday ice skating. He figured women were into that kind of thing, or at least he was hoping this one was.

CHAPTER EIGHT

Wyatt was wrapping up a lengthy round of photographs and autograph signings with eager young kids, all of whom were clearly ecstatic for a chance to meet their football heroes, when he saw Jenna watching him seriously from the edge of the rink, her gloved hands clutching the railing.

Nestled in the heart of downtown Pittsburgh's Market Square, this holiday ice rink with its centerpiece of a Christmas tree was a perfect scene to melt Dr. Sutherland's icy barrier to him, but it was his own that he felt breaking down. There was no denying he was attracted to her. She was dressed simply, but even in jeans and a winter coat, she was downright distracting.

The kids began to skate around the rink, giving Wyatt a chance to take a break and talk to her.

"Well, well, well, look who we have here. How are you, Doc?"

"Hello, Wyatt. You know you're the one who invited me, right?" she asked with an arched eyebrow.

"I'm just surprised to see you came after all. I figured you'd back out. I think I'm growing on you."

"It appears so — kind of like a fungus."

"All right. I'll take it," he laughed. "I'm glad you came to see me."

"Maybe I agreed to come because I wanted to remove the element of surprise. If you're going to keep popping up in my yoga classes, who's to say you won't appear somewhere else — maybe at the Giant Eagle when I'm out getting groceries?"

"Nah, I'm an Austin, Texas boy, I go to the Whole Foods here. That's my hometown store after all. But if you ever shop there, let me know, I'll meet you at the salad bar."

"Another intriguing offer. But I like this one — who can resist an ice skating rink with a big Christmas tree? And I love kids."

"Good, then I guessed right."

"You did, but I have to say, I'm actually surprised you called. I figured you'd disappear after I submitted my opinion. I'm sorry about that, Wyatt. It wasn't personal, I really did take into account all your worries, but it's what's best for you…"

She looked down at her hands and it seemed like she honestly did regret having to deliver news that was so devastating to him. Though, he couldn't let that mean anything to him except that he might be able to get her to reconsider her decision.

He touched her chin for just a moment and turned her face up to look at him. "Hey, you aren't getting soft on me, are you?" he teased, until she shook her chin out of his hand and released a laugh.

"No, never. I'm tough," she said, with a small smile.

"Look, don't feel bad. You were just doing your job. This is my way of saying there are no hard feelings. Who knows, maybe you'll find out you can even enjoy spending some time with me."

"True, who knows?"

"Pretty good event, huh?"

"It is. But there's really no press here?" she asked, looking around a bit nervously.

"You don't trust me?"

"It's not that, it's just, I hate the idea of a lot of attention. I like to live a pretty private life."

"Then this is perfect. It's just for the kids, no publicity, and it wasn't even announced, so you should be safe with me."

"Thanks. I don't know how you guys do it."

"What, ice skate?" he asked with a half-smile.

"No, silly."

"Hmm, you think I'm silly now, do you? That seems like an improvement…"

"Oh, stop, I just meant how do you deal with all the attention. Never being able to go out for a gallon of milk without people trying to get your autograph or take a picture of you with their phones… Just the thought of it makes me feel so…exposed."

"Now don't go talking about you being exposed, you wouldn't want to get me all worked up in public, would you?"

Jenna rolled her eyes at him, but she smiled before continuing her thought.

"I mean, anyone can find you anywhere."

Wyatt leaned across the railing and said softly, "I'm not worried. I'm tough, too." He leaned back and looked at her, adding, "Besides, that's how my life has always been. You begin almost not to notice the attention anymore. Though I won't lie — I do try to have privacy when I can find it."

"Hey, Wyatt, come here, it's time to skate with the kids," he heard his friend, J.J. yell from the other end of the rink. Wyatt looked back at Jenna apologetically.

"I'll be okay, get out there. I was promised to get to see you guys skate around with kids, you better get to it."

"You got it, Doc," he said confidently, and skated away.

Wyatt spent the next twenty minutes with some of the nicest kids he'd ever met. Each of them was selected for being an "at-risk" youth, and this was clearly the making of a great moment in their lives. He felt a pang of guilt for never doing more of these things. They had always seemed like a distraction from his ultimate goal of "get in and get out" in the NFL, without becoming too emotionally involved. For all Wyatt knew, these events were just another example of the league's rabbit hole that had taken his father.

Yet, he couldn't help but think that there was nothing bad about this — and it didn't hurt that a certain pink-nosed blonde was watching him the whole time.

Taking a quick break, he skated over to her and asked, "What do you think, Doc? Look at what great condition I'm in."

"You do move pretty well out there."

"A compliment? I'm shocked. So you don't completely hate me then?"

"Of course not. Just because I don't want to sleep with you, doesn't mean I hate you."

"Hey, you're the one who brought up sleeping together. Besides, you don't have to sleep with me. That's optional. Though I think you'd enjoy it." She raised an eyebrow at him wearily. "Fine, well admit this, Doc — maybe you don't hate me, but I have to think you refusing to sleep with me isn't a *good* thing."

"It just means that I'm a careful person. Yes, I want to have fun and enjoy my life. But I live a quiet life and I have goals that aren't really conducive to a tryst with a Wyatt McCoy type."

"I'm not asking you to go out with a *'Wyatt McCoy type.'* I'm asking you to *spend time* with *me*."

"Type or not, going out with you is still a bad idea. I have ethical obligations as your doctor."

"Oh, no you don't. Your consult is done. You said so yourself. You aren't my doctor, unless your opinion is subject to change?"

Wyatt cringed a little at his own obviousness.

Don't push too hard, you don't want her to catch on to you, he thought. *Besides, I'm kind of enjoying this time with her. Even when she's giving me a hard time.*

"My opinion won't change, I feel pretty confident in it. Besides, I just don't like you in that way."

His heart sank and desperation started to take root again, but he tried to focus on the appealing side of his personality, wishing it would overcome the panic in his chest. The oddest part was that being with her actually made acting like a charming man extremely easy, seeing as one of the things he'd always relied on was his ability to be a calculating son of a bitch.

The part he had to focus harder on was reminding himself he was just acting. It was surprisingly difficult, seeing as how he was enjoying this time with her way too much.

"In what way *do* you like me, Doc?" Wyatt leaned over Jenna, pressing his waist against the railing surrounding the rink and whispered in her ear, "Let me guess. You had a crush on the captain of the football team and he never noticed you. He was a fool. I would have totally made your 80's movie teen dreams come true."

He felt a surge of pride at seeing a smile quirk at the corners of Jenna's reluctant lips.

"Oh, what's that? Is your face okay? It seems to be cracking..." he said teasingly, and she straightened her expression again. "Don't do that, Doc, I like making you smile."

"That's good because I'm not morally opposed to smiling. I am actually quite a fan of it. Now, about your guess, you're pretty close," she added, erasing the last hint of a faint smile from her face and replacing it with a frown and lines of worry between her suddenly narrowed eyes. "But no — he *wanted* to be the captain of the football team and showed me the wrong kind of attention to get there. Luckily for him, I was stupid enough to let his plan work." She breathed deeply and looked straight into Wyatt's eyes with an almost challenging sense of control. "There you have it. Simple enough."

"What?" he asked angrily, gripping the edge of the railing till his knuckles turned white.

"It's nothing. I was the coach's daughter and a foolish kid. End of story," she said, raising her chin in a show of strength, but Wyatt's chest felt an uncomfortable twinge of conscience at the quick shimmer of pain across her lovely eyes.

"It's not nothing, Doc. I know better than anyone the crap people will do to be a part of this game..."

I'm doing some of that crap myself right now, he thought guiltily.

"Thanks for caring. I really mean that, Wyatt. Anyway, how does the shoulder feel? This kind of exertion shouldn't cause it too much strain."

"You can't say something like that and then change the subject, Doc."

"It's in the past. We all have regrets, and that's one of mine."

Wyatt felt his jaw click and an unexpected anger rolled through him. "I could find him and kick his ass."

"That is strangely touching. Thank you — but no, that's okay. I don't like thinking about it. So I don't. It's simple."

"You've got it all figured out then. Just like that?"

"Just like that." She snapped clumsily with gloved fingers and gave him a small smile.

"Wow. You're so logical and cool about everything. It doesn't stop me from getting pissed about what you just said, though."

"Enough of that. No worrying about me allowed. You'd better get back to showing me your moves, Wyatt."

"Are you flirting with me, Doc?"

"Maybe you're growing on me, after all. Now get out there before I change my mind."

Her words had the weirdest impact on him, as though he was suddenly taller and his chest more puffed out — and her saucy wink almost knocked him onto the ice beneath him.

But he followed her orders and skated away.

"Does it feel good to be back on solid ground again?" Jenna asked as Wyatt stepped onto the concrete beside her.

"Feels awesome. There's a good reason I don't play hockey. How about I walk you to your car?"

"Okay, but I'll warn you — you're making this seem dangerously like a date, Wyatt."

"Is that such a bad thing? Come on, tell me the truth."

"The jury's still out on that. A part of me keeps telling myself we're a bad idea, but another part can't deny I do have a good time with you."

"I suggest you listen to that part — the good time part."

"I might. For now, I'll just keep weighing all the evidence."

"I'll have to make my best case then, I suppose," he answered. They continued to walk the short distance to the parking garage in polite silence, but Jenna couldn't help but feel Wyatt was counting the moments until it was time for him to challenge her again.

A heady cocktail of relief and disappointment hit her hard when she caught sight of her car. She pulled out the key fob and unlocked it before placing it in her pocket and turning back to Wyatt.

"Well, this is me. Thank you for walking me here," she said, as she went to open the door.

"Hey, don't I get a kiss good night? If you're going to weigh all the evidence, then you need to let me present all I have to offer."

"I'm sure you have a lot to offer, but Wyatt, I told you already — you're not my type, okay?" Jenna spoke quickly.

"I'm everyone's type," he responded, and simply laughed at her withering glare. "Come on, it was a joke. Lighten up a bit, Doc."

"Why do people say that? It always has the opposite effect. I feel much less 'light' right now, actually."

"You aren't really mad at me, are you?"

"No. I'm sorry. Maybe you bring out my touchy side."

"How can you be so patient and understanding with everyone, but you won't even give me a chance?"

"Because with this chance, it's me — *my* life — that's at stake. And I can't let myself have any room for error."

"So *I'm* not allowed to have any room for error with you either, then? Or is it that you don't *want* to like me?" he asked as she turned her back to him and opened the door.

"I like to think things through, Wyatt, and taking that kind of step with you...that would be a huge thing for me. Please stop making this so hard for me," she whispered, tossing her purse onto her passenger seat, then unzipping her coat and throwing it on top of her bag. She closed the driver side door, took a deep breath, and turned, only to find that he was standing right in front of her. He was so close she could feel the heat of his body through her thin cardigan.

"You're all twisted up, Doc," Wyatt whispered, as he slid his hands to the front of her sweater, then dragging his fingers up her body.

"Wha-at are you doing, Wyatt?" she asked, suddenly feeling her face heat up and traitorous excitement flooding through every part of her body.

"Your buttons…"

Jenna looked down and felt another rush of blood to her cheeks when she realized she'd buttoned her sweater completely wrong before heading out of her apartment to meet Wyatt. For all her bluster about being so careful, here was physical proof she was full of it.

There was no denying Wyatt McCoy had a mesmerizing sway over her, and now he knew it, too.

"Were you distracted when you got dressed to meet me?" Wyatt asked quietly, forcing her to look up at him. She quickly realized her mistake, because she couldn't look away from his eyes, and was instantly transfixed by the flecks of gold streaking across their warm, brown depths.

His gaze never left hers as his nimble fingers worked their way down the front of her body, unbuttoning each inch of the light wool until there was only a thin tee shirt between her body and the warm flesh of his fingertips. Her breath became labored, turning into tiny, quiet pants. The sensation of his touch even through the fabric was almost too much for her to stand. Her fingers felt itchy, wanting so much to touch him, too — to see if her touch could affect him like his did to her. She clenched her hands in fists, trying to fight back the urge.

He leaned forward and whispered, "I asked you a question, Doc."

"I was in a hurry. I guess I wasn't paying attention," she muttered against his cheek. Her lips were dangerously close to him, but she couldn't find the will to break his powerful hold on her. Instead, she let her back lean heavily against the side of her car as her breaths fanned against his skin. She finally leaned away from his face and looked up at him. Her mind twisted and turned, trying to come up with something sensible to say — a rational thought that would finally explain why the two of them together wasn't a good idea but nothing came to her — she was completely mute.

Instead she could only stare at his handsome face, with its penetrating eyes and full lips that, on him, somehow looked both sensual and masculine. Even his jawline was captivating to her. She always went back to those eyes of his — so full of promise and passion, but also enough risk that she couldn't make herself take that leap and tell him she was ready to let go — at least not out loud.

"Let me take care of it for you," he said gently, and Jenna felt her head nod in acceptance.

Starting at the bottom of the sweater, he gently closed each button in succession — all the way back up to her chest. He didn't touch her body, pulling the sweater away respectfully as he buttoned it, but she could feel the warmth coming off his hands with each gentle movement.

It did feel as though he was taking care of her, and the sensation was beyond unnatural for her, but also completely pleasurable. Letting herself want someone usually terrified her, because that led to need, and needing led to loss.

Jenna didn't think she could bear to lose anything else in her life, but maybe she could indulge herself just once — a brief respite from her own implacable loneliness.

With each flick of his fingers across the material, Jenna could feel the tingling shock wave of pleasure that his touch always seemed to send shooting through her body.

Jenna sighed sadly when he reached the final button and reality sunk back in, she had to accept it was time to leave — return to her normal existence.

Her little break was over. She needed to get back into her car and to a world where she never felt this strange rush of overwhelming pleasure. With all that excitement always came the threat of humiliation and regret, risks she couldn't fathom taking ever again — and it didn't get much riskier than Wyatt McCoy.

But he didn't let her go, instead he moved even closer to her, pressing her firmly against the door of her car with the length of his tall, hard body. It was as though she were paralyzed — completely unable to move her body away from his. Regardless of whether she believed this was wise or stupid, her body had made its decision. When his hands moved up to her neck and into the waves of her hair, she closed her eyes and breathed him in. He filled her senses with his own breath and his scent of masculine sweat, spice, and fresh laundry that always made her want to wrap it around herself like she were slipping into a freshly made bed.

"Look at me, Jenna," he ordered.

The foreign sound of her given name on his lips jarred her back to the moment and she opened her eyes in a flustered frenzy, her heart pounding erratically inside of her.

"I don't want you to hide from me anymore, Jenna. No more excuses, because I've heard all of yours and I don't buy any of them. I want you to open up that margin of error for me. Do you understand me?"

Wyatt's voice was thick, his hot breath tickling her face with each of his words, causing her core to spasm violently. Jenna was becoming wet between her tensing thighs with each of his delicious commands. She tried to stand up straight and collect herself, but she couldn't move her legs.

Her mouth parted but no words came out — the insistent touching and rubbing of his fingers through her hair and against her scalp was too distracting, the flashing of his eyes on hers too hypnotic. All she could do was nod her head again as she looked wordlessly at his face. He was all hard lines and desire and all she wanted was to feel more of him.

What would it be like to taste him? To bring that scent and his breath inside her body — would it overwhelm everything inside her and leave nothing else behind but him?

Hesitantly, Jenna lifted her hands and rested them on his waist — so lightly that her fingertips barely touched the leather of his belt. That was all the encouragement he needed, because he immediately descended onto her mouth.

His lips were so soft against hers, but his kiss was hot and demanding. It was the most powerful combination of gentle and hard she'd ever experienced.

Jenna slid her hands up his sides, underneath his jacket, and rubbed them against the hard ridges of his back until he groaned into her mouth. She slipped her tongue deeply into his mouth, as he pressed his full body against her. The metal of her car door dug into her back and the handle pressed uncomfortably against her butt, yet she couldn't be bothered to care.

In this moment, all she wanted in the world was more of *him*, every part of him. She bit down on his bottom lip, then licked against it with her tongue and he responded with nibbles and licks of his own. He slid his hands down her body, grasping her bottom in his large hands and pulling her roughly against him.

She could tell he was hard through his jeans and it made her feel like a ravenous lioness, desperate for food after seemingly unending deprivation. She wanted to sate that hunger — eager to tear him apart with her teeth, if only to taste him that much more completely.

Jenna's brain knew this temporary insanity was simply the result of a rush of hormones releasing from her brain into her bloodstream. She understood that his enticing body was just a beautiful example of evolution and genetic muscular development, creating his tall body and sinewy limbs — but her body didn't give a shit about all that.

No — her body wanted to take her brain out back and beat it up until it stopped getting in the way of what the rest of her wanted — what she *needed*.

With another press of him against her, he slid his face down to her throat, sucking and nipping delicately at the flesh. He backed up slightly and she groaned in frustration, raising her hands to his head and pushing him harder against her throat. She bent her head, exposing more flesh in complete surrender to him, stroking his soft hair and reveling in each perfect sensation.

Sliding her hands down, she went to unzip his jacket when a strange voice burst through the quiet air around them.

"Holy shit, Donnie! I think that's Wyatt McCoy. Look at where I'm pointing, ya jagoff. He's over there, with that chick!"

"Oh my God," Jenna blurted out, whipping her head around to see two middle-aged guys pointing at them, clearly excited to have spotted the famous quarterback. She was instantly shocked back into reality and totally mortified with herself. She pushed Wyatt back, to see his eyes were full of confusion and desire.

"What the hell? Don't worry about them. They can't really see us," he mumbled against her, kissing her neck again, but she pushed him away quickly.

"I have to go. Crap. What was I thinking?"

Jenna yanked at the door, bumping both of them with it.

"Stop it, right now, Jenna. You're being ridiculous," he said.

Her whole body was shaking, and she couldn't seem to make herself create a single coherent thought other than a powerful impulse to run.

"Sorry, Wyatt. I mean it. Oh, hell."

She threw herself into the car and fished her keys awkwardly out of her pocket, starting the car as quickly as she could. She caught sight of the two men that had interrupted them coming toward them and she moved even more quickly. They really were far away, but not enough for her taste.

"I'm sorry, Wyatt. I have to go and I...I think we shouldn't see each other again, okay? You get that, right? Okay, gotta go." The words just kept babbling out of her mouth like water over stones in a creek, tumbling on top of each other in idiotic succession.

"Jenna, get out of that car and talk to me, now," he ordered, but she pulled out of the spot and drove too quickly around the sharp turns of the parking garage.

She watched Wyatt in her rearview mirror as she tried to hide her face from anyone that may be able to see her. He looked furious, but not nearly as mad as she was with herself.

"And that is why we don't take risks, Jenna," she berated herself out loud, but there was nothing but the steering wheel to hear her, and she couldn't be sure, but it seemed pretty furious with her, too.

CHAPTER NINE

"Hi Laney, thanks for squeezing me in for my annual. I've been swamped lately!"

Jenna gave her friend a hug and then pulled down her flimsy examination gown. The old mantra that doctors made the worst patients was certainly true in her case. The moment she walked into a doctor's office for her own health, she immediately became uncomfortable and jittery. She was grateful that her yearly Pap smear was with one of the first new friends she'd made after moving to Pittsburgh and joining *UPMC*.

"Some things never change, right, Jenna?" Laney said cheerily, her light brown hair smoothed back in a simple ponytail from her cute face and pert nose that still somehow engendered confidence in her patients, even if she was completely adorable. "All right, you know the drill. Into the stirrups. Giddyup," Laney said, with a wicked grin and a slap of the cushioned table.

"Seriously, Laney?"

"What? Come on, I gotta keep it lively."

"I know, but *every* time…"

"Hey, you get to touch sexy injured athletes all day, you don't need humor to keep your life interesting. I, on the other hand, have chosen a life that keeps me up to my neck with lady bits all day. I like to mix it up a bit."

"If I recall correctly, you are perfectly happy with spending your private time with lady bits, too, so how can you complain...?"

Laney washed her hands at the sink and looked back at Jenna over her shoulder, "I never take my work home with me, I keep those particular lady bits separate — thank you very much. Plus, I don't limit myself to ladies, so I have my bases covered. Besides, at least I *have* a personal life. How's your dry spell coming along?"

Jenna blushed and quickly changed the subject back to mundane complaints about hating the cold weather, because she did not want to talk about any spells — dry or wet.

Lying back, she tried to ignore the discomfort going on in her southern hemisphere as Laney went through her series of procedures for the exam.

It had been a handful of days since she'd lost her mind and rubbed herself against Wyatt as if she were trying to test the flammability of their clothing fibers. Yet, she still couldn't sort out her feelings. Besides the fact that he was totally wrong for her, she had only just delivered a consult on his health. It was true that their limited medical relationship was over, but even if the ethical lines in this instance were fuzzy, there was no denying that entering into a relationship would appear highly improper. She was at a stage in her career where she needed to be above reproach.

With each logical consideration she made against pursuing anything with him, a powerful — and impractical — thought popped up in her mind, and that was her intense need to touch him again and explore this draw he had on her. No one had interested her in this way in such a long time, and it was impossible to ignore him. He'd tried to contact her with a couple voicemails and a text, but so far she had ignored them. She didn't know what to say, even though he was occupying her mind every day.

Wyatt wasn't making it easy on her either. Whether it was a funny text or a picture of a restaurant he wanted to take her to, he just wouldn't let up. It was all starting to wear her down, but she'd made it this far without giving up, she could go a little longer.

"Jenna, your pelvic exam looks good. I'm just going to feel your stomach and do a breast exam, and then we'll be done."

"Great, thanks, Laney."

"You're welcome. So how's work? Have you talked to your boss about that fellowship?" Laney asked, as she pressed on Jenna's stomach and made her way to her breasts.

"I did. It didn't go very well. You know Richard, he likes to act like he's everybody's dad. He just said..."

Laney's face turned very serious and Jenna suddenly felt nauseated.

"Laney, what's up?"

"Jenna, have you been doing your home breast self-exams?" Laney asked seriously, moving her hands to the other breast and then to Jenna's armpit.

"Yes," Jenna answered, with a bit more confidence than she felt. "Maybe not for a couple months, but yes, I generally do. Let me think..."

How long has it been? I try to be so good about this. Oh God, it's like when the dentist asks if you've been flossing. You always say yes, but can you really remember every time? And Aubrey loves to hog the bathroom... Dammit, focus Jenna!

Laney started examining Jenna's right breast again, and

then the left...and the crease between her eyebrows worried Jenna.

"Jenna, you've got a few concerning lumps here."

Jenna sat upright and suddenly felt dizzy. All of the humor was gone from Laney's lighthearted demeanor.

"I'm going to refer you to an oncologist. I'll want you to go ahead and have an ultrasound and mammogram, too, but I don't want to take any chances here."

All previous distracting thoughts of Wyatt quickly left Jenna's mind as she started to panic internally. *This cannot be happening to me.*

"Of course. I understand." And she did, all too well.

Laney sat down at her desk and started jotting down information while Jenna yanked the gown down across her suddenly shaky body.

"I'm going to send you to Dr. Raj Kannan. He's the absolute best. He is in pretty high demand, but he should make accommodations for another physician, and he's a friend of mine, so drop my name like it's hot, okay, Jenna?"

"What? Oh yes, I've got it. I appreciate it."

Jenna felt as though she were a mile above the ground. Everything was quiet and hollow — so disorienting.

Laney stood in front of her and went on, her lips moving, though Jenna could only barely hear her.

"Jenna, you know most of these lumps turn out to be benign. Just nature's way of being an asshole and keeping us on our toes...but with your family's history..."

"I know, we can't take any risks."

"Right, come on, hop on down and let me get his information for you."

Jenna nodded and slid her body to the floor, but her feet were numb and she just had to hope she'd find her way home.

Jenna walked into her apartment still on autopilot after her appointment with Laney. She had to get a series of tests done and then wait a couple days to get in to see Dr. Kannan for more poking and prodding. Going to an oncologist right away was aggressive, but no one wanted to take any shortcuts with a doctor, let alone one whose mother died of complications from a catastrophic and particularly challenging form of breast cancer at almost her exact age.

The holiday season made everything slower and more difficult, though Jenna felt like she wanted to put it all off for a while — maybe forever.

She threw her coat and purse down in the living room and made her way to her bed, only to find Tea on it, sprawled on her back, her massive head of hair lying like a beautiful halo across the pillow.

Her body was flopped on top of the duvet, and brochures and bridal magazines were strewn around her like wedding rice.

Jenna rolled her eyes slightly at Tea's position and said sarcastically, "Is it Southern lady drama hour in my apartment? Let me guess, have you 'taken to your bed, Miss Scarlett?'" Jenna teased, invoking the name of the original Southern drama queen. Like many women from the South, Tea had a tendency to be pretty emotional, and it always left Jenna at a bit of a loss.

"No, Jenna, I've taken to *your* bed."

"What happened?"

"I've started to plan the wedding. Griffen got really excited, which was great. Then he said he wanted me to take his name and that he planned to adopt Johnny, too. It was so sweet, but..."

"Wow, he just went for it all right out of the gate, huh?"

"Exactly."

"Did he say why?"

"No, and it was so much to have to digest all at the same time, I just... I wanted a little break. I didn't want to worry him, so I headed over here." Tea closed her eyes until Jenna sighed and flopped down beside her.

"Are you okay, Jenna?"

"I don't want to talk about it."

"What else is new?" Tea grumbled at her.

"What's that supposed to mean?"

"You never want to talk about your own things, Jenna."

"That's not true."

"It sure is. You pushed me to open up and move on with my life. You tell Aubrey to be honest and open about things, but you won't let us ask you anything. You've always been closed off on your own stuff, but you push, push, push everybody else. Maybe we have a diagnosis for you once in a while, Doc."

"Don't call me that," Jenna grunted out at her, unable to deny what she said, but still angry regardless.

Tea and Jenna were lying on the bed with their arms crossed and faces looking bitter and angry when Aubrey bounded into the room.

"Hey, guys, what are we doing?" she asked.

"Tea is being annoying."

"No, I'm not. Jenna is being pissy, but don't ask her about it."

"Thanks for the recap, I think," Aubrey said, with a confused frown.

"Point is," Tea answered, "we have taken to our bed."

"Oh, fun, me too! Let me in." Aubrey leapt in beside them until the bed bounced them up and down.

"What's bothering you?" Tea asked.

"Nothing, I just don't want to be left out." Aubrey bounced on the bed merrily until the whole mattress jostled beneath them. "So... Why do you claim Tea is being annoying, Jenna?"

"*I'm* not being annoying," Tea interrupted. "*Jenna* just doesn't like that I'm trying to make her talk about what's bothering her." Tea sighed deeply before adding, "I am upset, though. That's true."

Jenna softened and patted Tea's hand. Turning to Aubrey, she said, "Griffen is pushing for Tea to change her name to Tate, and he wants to adopt Johnny."

"Oh, yep, that would do it. Griffen can be so dense sometimes," Aubrey said simply.

"Hey, that's not true, Aubrey. Griffen is so sweet," Tea said, quickly jumping to his defense.

"Sweet or not, he needs to remember he parachuted into our lives — er, I mean your life — and you're still dealing with stuff. He can't just change everything right away," Aubrey said.

"He's just excited, Aubrey," Jenna said. "Did you hurt his feelings, Tea?"

"No. That's why I came here. I didn't want to hurt his feelings."

"What did you tell him?" Aubrey asked.

"I thanked him for being so supportive and helpful about the wedding but that I had plans with you two, so I couldn't work on anything today. See? I'm growing."

"Riiight," Jenna said slowly.

"Stop it, Jenna. I just needed some time to think through things. If I take his name, if he adopts Johnny...it feels like

Jack would just...disappear."

"You and Griffen would never let that happen," Jenna said with a softer tone, stroking Tea's hair softly.

"It's just so real now. Do I go and have another wedding with a white dress and cake and all the trimmings? Do I just become a new person? I was 'Tea Taylor' for so long. I'm not sure who 'Althea Tate' is."

"You don't have to know now, do you?" Aubrey asked.

"But she has to deal with it at some point, Aubrey," Jenna answered. "She can't just ignore it and disregard Griffen's feelings."

Jenna felt guilty for being so tough on Tea, but focusing on other people's problems, rather than her own fears, was all she could handle at that moment.

"Oh please, Jenna, that pretty boy is going to be fine." Aubrey turned to Tea and added, "You baby him too much." She laughed softly, and then continued, "Okay, so, we know Tea's issue. Jenna, why are *you* being pissy?"

"I am not being pissy! I just had a bad day and don't want to talk about it."

"Of course you don't. You never want to talk about your shit," Aubrey said.

"Thank you!" Tea responded in a sarcastic tone.

"Oh, stop. Is this pile up on Jenna day?" Jenna said, elbowing Tea, only to get elbowed back, until they were in a full-on cranky pants, mutual hissy fit.

"I like the sound of that! Tea, let's pile up on Jenna!" Aubrey's long, limbed body and Althea's mass of hair suddenly overtook her vision as they tickled her until it hurt.

"Stop! I give, I give."

"Good," Aubrey said, a little breathless from her onslaught. "I say enough, you little babies. You know what you two need?"

"What?" Jenna asked warily. Aubrey's brilliant ideas usually ended…colorfully.

"You both need to go out with me…and get drunk."

"Hmm," Tea answered thoughtfully. "I'm listening."

"I suggest we go to the casino on the North Shore and party like some blue haired old ladies. Though I think we should also get dressed up all sexy and let lame visiting businessmen buy us drinks all night."

"I'm in," Tea said gleefully, dragging Jenna off the bed with her.

"Come on, you, no more moping," Aubrey ordered with a grin, and Jenna decided to give in and have fun for a night, too.

"Okay, I'm bored with the slots. Let's go to that big bar with all the TVs over there," Aubrey ordered to Jenna and Tea.

Jenna's head was already spinning, but it definitely sounded like a great idea. When Jenna was drunk, it always seemed like Aubrey came up with the best ideas.

"Sure, Aubrey. They have alcohol there, right?" Jenna asked.

"Of course! They have alcohol and plenty of opportunities to make bad decisions. It's just right over there," she said in a singsong voice, gesturing and slopping a bit of her candy-colored appletini onto her hand.

"Sounds good to me," Tea answered, toddling over to the huge bar and dragging her barely-covered ass up onto a stool.

"Sold!" Jenna said, following quickly behind her. She was in the market to make some bad decisions.

Jenna had played by every rule, done everything right,

looked after everyone, and delayed every form of self-gratification her whole life.

And for what? she wondered. *To possibly have the same outcome as my mother? To face the promise of a painful, early death?*

"Hey, Jenna, why'd you get so sad looking? Tell us," Aubrey demanded.

"I know what it is," Tea answered.

"You do?" Jenna suddenly felt panicked through her alcohol fog. The last thing she wanted was for her friends to know about those lumps — they didn't need to be scared, too.

"You need to get laid, girl. You are being seriously uptight. If you won't sleep with Wyatt, what about Trey? He's pierced, tattooed, delicious, and he seems interested in you," Tea suggested.

"Ooh, good idea, Tea," Aubrey added. "Trey is like an international bad boy of mystery. I think he was a spy before."

"You're probably right," Tea said seriously. "That does make sense."

"Enough of that, you two. Okay, *One* — I've told you, Trey and I are friends, we like each other, but not that way and — *B, er I mean, Two*...Tea, seriously, you're acting like the expert on getting laid now?" Jenna asked skeptically. "Ms. '*I will keep my vagina on ice for almost six years, thank you very much*' is suddenly the voice of constant sex."

"Hey, if I lived with Griffen 'The Sex Machine,' I'd be a sex-pert, too," Aubrey said in defense of Tea.

"I thought you already were a sex expert, Brey." Tea giggled.

"That's true. Let's go on the road then, Tea. We could do seminars. I'll call my advice, 'Brey Bites.' And you can call your advice something like: 'Cups of Tea' or 'Tea bags.'"

"No way, Brey!" Jenna exclaimed. "You can't do that."

"Man, still no-fun Jenna. We were joking."

"We're supposed to be making Tea feel better," Jenna said. "Tea, do you feel better?"

"I think so, I guess I just got a little overwhelmed..."

"You poor thing. You have a hot millionaire that loves you and can't wait to marry you. Wah-wah, boohoo," Aubrey teased with a biting tone, as she twisted two fists in front of her eyes.

"Stop it," Tea said through laughter, while swatting at Aubrey's hands.

"Do you not want to marry him?" Jenna asked fuzzily, fingering the smooth rim of her martini glass — almost hypnotized by it.

"Of course I want to marry him. I said yes, didn't I?" Tea said sternly.

"I know, but it's okay if you're having regrets now. It's okay if you don't want to," Aubrey said, leaning heavily against Tea on the bar.

"Shut up, Aubrey, you just want her to bang him and then hang out with us all the time. That's not a relationship."

Aubrey just snorted and said, "Sounds like the perfect relationship if you ask me. Have sex with a hot guy who treats me right and then makes himself scarce so I can have time with my favorite ladies."

"And you helped me approve the ring for Griffen, Aubrey — enough with your mixed messages."

"Enough of that, you two. I love having Griffen around. I love Griffen. Everything about him. I never thought I'd even date again, much less marry... Now, I don't picture a day in my life that he's not in it." Tea's eyes got weepy and her voice cracked, and then she hiccupped a little.

"All right, sweetie, we get it. Calm yourself. You're getting all red. God, you are the most emotional drunk ever, Tea!" Jenna shouted out at her, more loudly than she'd intended.

"Ex-cuuuuse me, Doctor Tough Cookie. Keep that temper down, you. It's just a matter of time before you want to go pick a cat fight with some trashy girls, you bad-ass," Tea warned her.

"I got in one fight once in college..."

"And that time we went to the Outer Banks for vacation," Tea added.

"Oh yeah, you remember that. Don't change the subject, we were talking about you being all weepy. So you love Griffen? What's the problem?" Jenna asked.

"I'm crazy about Griffen, but it's all even more real than ever. Jack? That life we had? It's really gone, and that makes it feel like he's died all over again, but then I see Griffen and my whole heart swells. It still gives me a thrill just being near him, and I know it always will. I just need to reconcile that happiness with the knowledge that I had a life before, and it's gone."

"It's only gone if you let it be," Aubrey interrupted.

"Right! It's not gone. You have Johnny, and Griffen loved Jack, too. You need to tell Griffen why this name thing freaks you out. I mean, he's probably scared, too. Why don't you tell Griffen what you're feeling?" Jenna asked.

"Because we *just* got everything sorted out between us. This is *my* thing to get over. I can't risk losing Griffen, so I have to figure it out on my own. I put him through hell for a while there. It'll hurt him too much — he won't get it."

"If you're marrying him, he's gonna have to get it."

"No. I'm not making the same mistake twice. I'm going to protect this relationship at all costs. Even if it's against myself."

"Tea, you've been so focused on the protecting part of

your plan that you forgot about the other mistake you kept making," Aubrey said seriously.

"What do you mean?"

"Communication. If you have worries then you have to tell Griffen about them," Jenna said.

"Did you not hear me? I put Griffen through hell. I don't want to upset him when we're finally together."

"You made him sweat it out for a couple of days. It's not Dr. Zhivago we're talking about here. I think he'll live."

"I don't know, Aubrey. I feel bad. I know my feelings are irrational."

"Of course, they're irrational," Aubrey said, with a dramatic slurping of her appletini. "That's why they're called *'feelings,'* otherwise everyone would just call them *'thoughts.'*" Aubrey continued on, "have faith in what you feel and what you want. That's what feelings are there for. Life is a real asshole. It may give you something nice, but it will make that nice thing hard as fuck to keep. Right, Jenna? Jenna, are you okay? Fuck, you're so quiet."

"What? Oh, yes. Right." Jenna must be drunk because Aubrey was making loads of sense. In fact, it was causing her to rack her brain to collect her thoughts and memories.

She wanted something good and nice. How could she so desperately want to enjoy her feelings with Wyatt without it meaning something?

"Enough picking on me," Tea said. "Jenna's awfully quiet over there. I swear, Jenna, you look so hot in that dress. You need to shake your cookies more often. I mean, you're built like you model for mud flaps, but you keep trying to be serious doctor lady."

"Tea, you're just all about meddling now, aren't you?"

"Yes. I warned you it was my turn."

"And I actually happen to *be* a serious doctor lady."

"Just keep telling yourself that. You're not fooling us, we know you need to get some action, like Tea said," Aubrey said assuredly.

"Why are you picking on me? I'm just having a dry spell. Tea had the whole Sahara desert."

"Yeah, and we should've stepped in sooner. I'm worried you'll end up in some kind of nunnery for hot, delusional doctors. I think we need to nip that in the bud right now."

"I'm glad you waited to push me. It was worth it to wait for Griffen," Tea said dramatically, as she started to get emotional again.

"Ugh, see what you did, Brey? You got the drunk waterworks going again. Give the crybaby a cocktail napkin, would you?"

"You always change the subject, Jenna. Point is, you haven't gotten any in a while."

"And, that's none of your business."

"It *is* my business because I live with you and it's making you be bratty. I don't like it."

"It's not my fault that no one is doing it for me."

"Except Wyatt," Tea said, then immediately started sipping so hard through her cocktail straw that her cheeks had hollowed.

"Shut up about Wyatt."

"I knew it!" Aubrey exclaimed, pointing at Jenna. "Wasn't I right, Tea?"

"Of course, Brey, it's *kind* of obvious."

"What is?"

"That you want to jump Wyatt's Latin-Irish bones, and you're mad at yourself for it," Tea explained.

"She's right Jenna," Aubrey added. "I think you should go

for it with Wyatt. I mean other than your nighttime solo fun, you are practically celibate."

"Nighttime fun?" Tea asked eagerly.

"Oh yeah, Jenna has been having sexy dreams recently. In fact, they started ever since that Denver game."

"Hmm, I wonder what that means," Tea said, with a laugh, and then she swooned a bit before continuing. "Uh-oh, guys I think I'm too drunk, maybe I need to go home."

"Yeah, that sounds like a good idea," Aubrey answered.

"Let's take a cab to my place," Tea said.

"Awesome," Aubrey cheered in agreement. "Are you coming, Jenna?"

"Oh, I'd love that, but I really need to get home. You guys head on without me. I have to take care of stuff there in the morning."

Thank God we're all drunk and they believe me, because my excuses are terrible.

"Are you sure?"

"I'm just going to go to the bathroom and then get my own cab."

"You aren't going to go and be all mopey, are you?"

"No way. I'm wrecked. I think I'll eat some ice cream at home and pass out," she answered, the words slurring from her lips.

"Okay, sweetie," Aubrey said. They put on their coats and kissed her good-bye.

Jenna snuck away to a particularly plush corner of the casino and plopped down heavily on an overstuffed love seat. Her tiny dress was hiked up and she couldn't even be bothered to pull it down to cover more of her thighs.

Jenna didn't care about propriety or doing the right thing. Point was, she was tired of saying no to everything. Maybe it was time to try out "yes" for a change.

She took out her phone and stared at it. The touch screen was a little blurry and wiping it off didn't help. It was no problem. She didn't need to write a sonnet. She just needed to text a booty call. It had been years since she'd done anything so brazen. It wasn't like Jenna had lived the life of a virgin, far from it. She just planned every detail of her life and avoided all risks. Wyatt was like an entire whiskey bottle full of trouble.

I'll probably regret this. What if it all goes badly? But, I don't have all the time in the world. None of us do.

She was ashamed to admit she knew his schedule. He'd had a Thursday night game, so he should be home now.

Is he with someone already? Is he alone and thinking about me? Stop it, woman!

Before she lost her nerve, she typed out a message and hit send.

Wyatt opened the door to his home and helped Jenna stumble on her high heels into his foyer.

"Thanks for picking me up, Wyatt," she said to him, turning and sliding her coat down her arms, revealing her smoking-hot body in a tiny, clingy dress. Letting the coat fall to the floor, she looked at him intently, her eyes smoldering into his. She was clearly wasted, so it was more like a squint alternating with a wide-eyed stare. It didn't lessen how desirable she was, though.

Their kiss by her car had made him want to find her and rip off all her clothes, whether it helped his career or not. He figured it hadn't had the same impact on her because she'd been completely ignoring him for days.

Now, she was standing by his front door and seemed suddenly to have a very different attitude about the wisdom of them becoming physical.

"Of course I came to get you, Doc. I figure if you were asking for *my* help, you must really need it."

"Don't be like that," she slurred out, and he finally heard that thick Georgia accent he'd suspected she'd been hiding underneath her flat, professional tone. Jenna began sauntering closer to him. "I have a lot of people I could've called to help me get home. I didn't want to go home. I wanted to be with you."

"Oh, yeah?" he asked, swallowing deeply and wishing he had something cooler to say.

"Yeah."

"And why's that?"

Damn, this woman makes me stupid.

"Well," she said, crossing the space between them in long, slightly wavering strides, "I've had a lot of shit in my life. A lot of things that felt like shit. But, you make me feel good...when I'm with you...and I want to keep feeling good...with you. Okay?"

"That sounds great. But what happened to you being careful and reviewing all the evidence, or whatever, before taking this step with me?"

"Yeah, right now, that seems like a dumb idea. I think it makes much more sense for you to kiss me again," she said, while leaning toward him, her legs wobbling on the stilts on her feet.

"Doc, maybe you should lie down for a bit."

What am I saying? That dress is so low-cut and so damn short. Her legs are endless. Shut up, asshole, he thought angrily to himself. *I've imagined those legs wrapped around my waist so many times, and now I'm going to say no? Of course, I have to say no. After I've already lied to her so many times, taking advantage of her is just so fucking wrong. So, this is what it feels like to have a conscience? I don't like it. Fuck!*

His anger at himself grew more intense when he watched her beautiful face fall — the curved lines of her brows and cheeks suddenly descending into a look of shame and sadness.

He'd imagined being with Jenna plenty of times, and in each of those fantasies, he never turned her down, which made the words he had just said all the more unbelievable to his own ears.

"Lie down?" she demanded with a stomp of her foot, jarring him from his silence. "You've been chasing after me, *harassing* me all this time. I finally come here...throw myself at you, and *you* tell *me* to '*lie down?*'"

Her face wasn't downturned in sadness now — no, she was blistering with rage, and it was all focused on him.

"Doc, you're drunk, I think a little rest will do you good."

"Oh, you do, do you?" she said. After a moment she lowered her voice and tried a new tactic, this time leaning toward him with pouting lips. She ran one finger back and forth across his chest, making his pulse quicken. "So that's your game, is it? You know what you are, Mr. Wyatt McCoy?"

"No, what's that?"

"You, sir, are...a...tease."

"Me? *I'm* a tease?"

"Yes, you led me on and then when I'm here ready for you, you say 'no.' Is it some power thing for you? Turn the blonde doctor into a begging pile of goo or something? Unless it's that you're chicken? Is that it, Wyatt? You're chickening out?"

Jenna removed her finger from his chest and started to make chicken wing motions with her arms, adding in a loud,

"Bock-ba-ba-bock."

"Wow, you are a charming drunk. I think that's about enough, young lady. You need to go sleep it off."

"I am not going to sleep!" she shouted, stomping her high-heeled foot more firmly, in a completely adorable way. "I'm a grown woman, and I want you to do dirty things to me. Right. Now," she added with another pout, this time poking him in the chest, hard.

"Okay, that does it," Wyatt growled. Leaning forward, he grabbed her waist with both his hands, and then threw her over his left shoulder.

"Put me down, right now, you asshole!" she shouted, kicking her legs and punching at him with her fists.

"You're a scrappy one, Doc. But you need to make up your mind. Am I a tease, a chicken, or an asshole?"

"All of the above, and I'm just going to get more scrappy," she moaned, lifting up his shirt and rubbing her chest against him as she licked his back, and then pinched the top of his butt. Wyatt was close to laughing, but suppressed it. *Is she for real right now?* A man only has so much patience when a woman was close to dry-humping him into blue ball hell.

The little sounds coming out of her were almost his undoing. He had to take a deep breath, fighting back the desire to put her down and flip her on to her back just to shut her up. But he knew what he had to do, hard as it may be. At the heart of it, Jenna seemed pretty emotional and carrying her around like a curvy sack of potatoes was probably enough mortification for her for one night. He made it to his bedroom and laid her down on the bed as carefully as her still-writhing body would allow.

She glared at him, crossing her arms, her hair splayed out across his pillow. He could tell she was trying to fight her exhaustion, but he imagined that last burst of exertion had taken most of the energy out of her. Wyatt came toward her and sat down next to her on the bed.

Ignoring the indignant harrumph that escaped her throat, he gently stroked her hair and watched her eyes flutter shut softly for a moment.

"Mmm, that feels nice," she slurred out quietly.

"That's good, because I'm not being chicken, Jenna. I would love to say yes right now, but I'd rather not give you another reason to hate me tomorrow, okay? So let me do the right thing."

She breathed in slowly and gazed at him through hazy, unfocused eyes. "I don't hate you, Wyatt," she whispered, and curled her warm body into the crook of his arm, almost purring against him as he stroked her silken hair for several more minutes until she fell deeply into sleep.

Wyatt took the chance to study her pretty face. She was so often trying to seem strong or serious, or bust out with a witty quip, that he rarely got the time simply to look at her.

Long eyelashes curled and fanned across her ivory cheeks and her lips were plump and slightly open in sleep. His eyes moved down to her beautiful, full breasts, showcased deliciously in the provocative, silver slip of nothing she was wearing. He was torn between loving the sexy little number and furious that who knows how many other men got to see her in it before he came to collect her from the casino.

He'd put so much effort into trying to win her over and get her on his side, that it seemed like it would never work. Yet, when her defenses were down, she'd come running to him. It did feel powerful, she was right about that. It also made him think he may actually convince her to change her diagnosis — that being around him, hooking up with him, and caring for him would make her come around.

Yes, it sounded awful, he knew, but he was desperate and he really did want to touch her. He could almost convince himself he wasn't doing anything wrong — it wasn't a betrayal to give her more time to reconsider her decision. She would come to see he really could take care of this issue without surgery, and if the morning went as he hoped, she'd have some fun in the process. It was one thing to take advantage while she was drunk, which he would not do, another was to lay her flat on that pretty back of hers in the morning while she was sober.

Wyatt's gaze suddenly landed on the gold locket around her neck. She'd worn it every time he seen her before. It was clearly old and he worried that a drunken night of tossing and turning in her sleep might ruin it. Delicately, he removed his arm from underneath her, smirking at her sleepy grunt of displeasure, and unclasped the necklace, placing it on the bedside table.

Just as carefully, he removed her dress and tried his damnedest not to stare at her in the bra and panties she had on underneath. Instead he turned, laying the dress across the back of a chair and pulling out his favorite old University of Texas Longhorns tee shirt. If he was going to stick to his guns, he needed to cover her up, and fast.

When she was halfway decent, Wyatt leaned forward and removed her bra — a skill he was still proud to have, ever since he learned it in high school. He pulled the tiny lacy garment off her through the tee shirt, careful not to touch her — too much.

Finally finished, he kissed her lightly on her forehead.

"Good night, belleza," he whispered against her warm skin, smiling at her happy answering sigh, before leaving his own bedroom to sleep on the living room couch.

Even though he'd been a gentleman because she was plastered, he had every intention of a very different outcome when she woke up the next morning.

CHAPTER TEN

"Up and at 'em, sleepyhead," Wyatt said cheerfully, as he plopped on the bed beside Jenna, making her lean body bounce up and down on the mattress. He'd been watching her sleep for a while and was sick of waiting — he needed to know if he'd broken through for real, if she was really willing to give him the opening he'd been working toward for weeks.

"What? What's going on?" She opened her bleary eyes. For a moment they flashed something that looked like happiness at seeing him, which quickly contorted into panic. "Oh, hell. What are you doing here?"

"I live here."

"Oh, hell, again. Then what am *I* doing here?" she asked, shooting up to a seated position, only to quickly grasp her head with her right hand and flop back down on the pillow.

"Not a morning person, are you, sunshine?" Wyatt asked mercilessly.

"Not this morning, I'm not. And now you're calling me 'sunshine?' Do you spend your days coming up with annoying things to call me? Jenna is also an acceptable name for me, you know."

"I like that one, too, but that would annoy you less, so that wouldn't be as much fun. I was testing out sunshine, but I think it's a no-go — doesn't seem to fit you today."

"Ugh, of course it doesn't, that's because I think I'm dying."

"You're the doctor, not me, but I'm going to bet you'll be okay."

She grunted deeply and rolled over, pulling the blanket over her head, only to pull it back away with a gasp.

"Why am I just in your shirt and my panties? Where is my dress? Oh God, please tell me we didn't..."

"Christ, woman, I'm not *that* bad a guy. I put you to bed and thought you'd be more comfortable like this. I was a perfect gentleman. I barely even touched you."

"I'm sure you didn't," she snorted out.

"Hey, Doc, news flash — you're the one that demanded I touch you. You were pretty mad at me, too — didn't want to take no for an answer."

"Oh, *hell*...this is getting worse by the second. I think you're trying to torture me."

"I didn't even peek, I promise, well, maybe a little. And I lent you my shirt. That little sparkly thing you had on was hella hot, but didn't look too comfortable."

"Aren't you so chivalrous," her voice broke a little and she made this funny smacking gesture with her lips. With a chuckle, Wyatt handed her a big glass of ice water, which she gulped gratefully, before plunking it on the table beside her. "Thank you. And, I got here, how?"

"You sent me a text me to come get you, so I did."

"Oh, the text. It's all coming back now. Unfortunately. Ugh, I can't even do a booty call right anymore. I really am a disaster." She threw the cover back over her head. "I can't believe I did that. If I didn't feel like I was about to die, I'd run and hide right now."

"Of course, you would, Doc." He smirked and pulled the cover back to hand her a fizzy glass of water.

"What is that? *Alka-Seltzer*?" she croaked out. "Are you eighty years old or something?"

Wyatt couldn't help but chuckle a little. She was clearly trying to keep up her stoic front, but all he saw was an adorably grumpy ball of blonde sexiness curled up in his bed.

"Hey, come on, Doc, don't hate on *Alka-Seltzer*. It's saved my life a couple of times, or at least it felt like it. Drink up."

"Fine," she muttered, sitting up in bed with jerky movements that made Wyatt's mouth go dry at the look of her in his favorite old University of Texas tee shirt. The two horns were touching her breasts and it was really distracting — so much so, he didn't even notice her finish off the glass and place it down on the bedside table with a clank.

"I guess I better get going."

"What? So soon? I mean, I didn't mind taking care of you, but I haven't really gotten the good end of the deal here."

"And this is the good end?"

"Well, you're conscious, so that's an improvement. And you look good in my tee shirt, so I'd say I'm okay with this morning so far. But I have some other ideas about your good end."

"Lovely. So let me get this straight, you apparently turned me down last night? Wow, my self-esteem has had better days."

"Oh, come on, Doc. You know I think you're incredibly hot, but you were practically unconscious. Give me some credit. I mean, I'm an asshole, but I'm not a dick."

Jenna moved her head so her hazy-blue eyes could focus

on his face.

"You're not an asshole or a dick, Wyatt," she said on a deliberate sigh.

"Wow! *Now my* self-esteem is through the roof. Easy with the praise, Doc. I could get used to this."

"Oh, stop it." She halfheartedly threw a pillow at him.

"Oof. Oh, I think you hurt me. I may need you to examine me. Make sure I'm all right."

"You're fine," she huffed out, sitting up. "I mean it, though, I really should go."

"Wait a second. I thought we would discuss your offer from last night a bit more."

"I'm not even entertaining that comment until I brush my teeth and feel half human for the first time this morning."

Wyatt smiled. That wasn't a flat-out rejection, so he had some faith.

She awkwardly hoisted herself out of bed, slapping her bare feet on his hardwood floor as she pulled his threadbare tee shirt further across her curvy, athletic ass.

"Hey, cut it out!" she shouted, turning to glare at him.

"What?" he asked with feigned innocence.

"Stop staring at my ass."

"I'm not staring. I'm just appreciating it…intensely."

"Fine. I'm too tired to fight you. Can you show me to the bathroom? I need some toothpaste."

"Of course, Doc. I will set your mouth up perfectly."

"Right. Charming as ever, Wyatt."

"I aim to please. Follow me."

He stood and began to lead her out when she stopped short.

"What's that? Is that a guitar?"

"Yep."

"You play?"

"I do. I sing, too."

"You're kidding me."

"Don't act so surprised. I'm not half bad, I mean my abuela is a fan. More so of my Spanish guitar playing. That one is in another room. This one's more for my Irish-beer-drinking half."

"Ugh, don't mention beer, I'm still trying to let that *Alka-Seltzer* work its magic. Talking about alcohol could have unpleasant consequences."

"Duly noted. Now, about that toothbrush."

"Yeah, please show me the way," she whispered, still studying the guitar with confused eyes.

Jenna grasped the edge of Wyatt's marble bathroom basin with white-knuckled force, as she tried to fight back the emotions of complete shame and panic rising in her chest. He'd been pleasant enough, especially considering she'd practically jumped him the night before. She'd been so bold only a handful of drunken hours before — ready to put a lifetime of responsible decisions behind her, only to get rebuffed and humiliated. A rational part of her brain appreciated that he'd done the right thing, but the rest of her couldn't get over the feeling of embarrassment and self-disgust.

She looked in the mirror and was shocked to see the same face that had greeted her for the last three decades of her life. Jenna had imagined a different woman would be there, one who handled challenges with grace, but no — it was just her, with some extra mascara streaks on the tops of her cheeks.

"It looks like I don't wear 'dangerous fun' well," she said

out loud, into the cavernous room, which could've swallowed her entire bedroom. She turned around and let herself take it all in. There was a glass shower with a dozen shower heads that her logical eye could tell weren't just for comfort, and an enormous bathtub that ignited a slew of fantasies of sloshing around in there with Wyatt.

"It looks like my sex drive still hasn't learned its lesson. Time to brush my teeth, stop talking to myself, and get out of here."

She turned around and finally noticed there was indeed a brand-new toothbrush already on the sink for her next to his toothbrush and toothpaste. She snorted to herself, assuming he had a hundred of these fresh toothbrushes for his overnight lady friend guests, most likely buying them in bulk.

A pang of guilt struck when she saw the name of his dentist on the handle.

"Okay, maybe I'm being too hard on the guy. And...I'm still talking to myself. Jesus, woman, pull yourself together," she mumbled out loud, right before she shoved the toothpaste-soaked bristles into her mouth.

With her face scrubbed, teeth polished, and dignity slightly more intact, Jenna ventured back into his bedroom. She hadn't gotten much of a chance to explore his home when she'd trampled into it the night before like some kind of a blonde tornado.

She grabbed her bra off the chair, feeling impressed it wasn't thrown on the floor. Looking toward the door to make sure she'd be alone, she quickly lifted the shirt and put the bra on, closing the clasp in the front. She was starting to feel normal again. Yet, all that relief flew away when she realized her neck was bare. She yanked the shirt down and scrambled to the bed, tearing at the covers and pillows, desperate to find that most-prized connection to her mother.

Just when she was beginning to fear it may be lost forever, like so many other things Jenna had once loved, she saw a ray of sunlight out of the corner of her eye, glinting cheerily against the gold heirloom that meant so much to her.

Her locket was resting safely on Wyatt's bedside table. The relief was almost crippling to her in her over-emotional and hungover state. Everything in her life was so confusing and scary, with no telling what the next day or week would bring. Jenna sank heavily into the mattress of Wyatt's now disheveled bed, her still bare legs dangling off the edge, and her heart firmly nestled in her throat. For the life of her, she didn't know what to do next. Time was marching ahead second by second, but Jenna felt like she was standing still with no idea what to do next.

All she knew for sure was that this precious piece of her mother was safe in the bedroom of the last man she ever thought would make her feel looked after and protected. But he'd rushed to her side when she'd asked, and taken the necklace off her when she was too stupid to do it for herself.

It was such a little thing, but it felt huge to her — significant, in fact. The whole morning was so confusing. Everything had been so much easier when she could tell herself Wyatt was nothing but the same jerk she'd met before. It wasn't that simple now.

Whatever the Jenna from the night before had thought, the Jenna of today knew she needed to face her fate alone. She couldn't allow herself to rely on Wyatt — he had already gotten under her skin too much. She worried if she grew to care for him and then found out she was sick, would she be strong enough to say good-bye? The only smart answer was to have the consideration to thank him quickly, but then get the hell out of there, and *fast*.

Breathing deeply she willed herself to put on a neutral face and get this over with quickly. Standing up briskly, she grabbed her dress only to toss it back on the chair after she caught a whiff of the stench of the casino and too many spilled martinis.

"I'll put it on after I say good-bye to him. It's going to be bad enough facing him again without having this funky thing on," she whispered to herself, before grabbing her locket and charging into his kitchen.

His elaborate, beautiful, and *empty* kitchen.

"Going somewhere?" he asked from behind her, with a gentle touch to her back, making her jump. "Whoa, easy, Doc, I've got hot coffee here and I generally try to avoid third-degree burns in my daily life, if I can."

"Oh, yeah, sorry, I wasn't looking at that side of the kitchen and you surprised me. I think I'm a little nervous."

"Just relax. Here, I made this for you," he said, showing her the mug.

"Wow, thanks. I feel like I'm getting the five-star treatment here."

"Well, you're the only woman I've ever given this treatment to, so I guess it's at least exclusive."

"Ooh, now if you go and make me feel special, that might go to my head, you know?"

"Ah, come on. A sensible girl like you? I'm not worried."

"I don't feel too sensible right now. I figure a trip back to my real life will work wonders for me."

"Don't you want your coffee? What do you have there?" he asked, as he placed the coffee mug on the counter behind her.

"What?" she asked.

"Behind your back. Stop being a baby. Show me."

"I'm not being a baby. It's my necklace, that's all. Thanks for taking it off for me."

"Which did you like more, me taking off your dress or your necklace?"

"The necklace, of course. I just mean, well, thanks for doing that when you, um..."

"Very tastefully prepared you for bed?"

"Right. Well put. I would just hate for it to get damaged," she said, stroking her thumb across the locket, "so I appreciate you doing that."

"I don't want anything of yours to be damaged. Especially something that seems to be so special to you. You wear it all the time, Doc."

"Thanks. It was my mother's."

"*Was?*"

"Yeah," she looked away from him and cleared her throat uncomfortably as she fumbled to put the necklace back on with trembling fingers.

"Here, let me," Wyatt said calmly, taking the delicate chain from her hands.

"Are you sure you can do it?"

"I grew up with three generations of women under one roof. Trust me, I can handle putting on a necklace. Come here."

Wyatt reached around her to push the coffee cup farther back on the kitchen counter, gently grazing her waist on the way. The contact quickened her pulse and she could feel her breaths become more rapid in her throat.

"Don't want you to get burned," he said, winking at her. "Turn around," Wyatt whispered against her hair, and she obliged. Jenna felt his fingers against the back of her neck as he moved the tangled mess of her hair across her back and over one shoulder. "Good."

She could feel the full length of his hard body against her back, her legs, her ass — everywhere. *What is it with this guy? He has a way of controlling my body and it refuses to tell him no.* She stood completely still — she wanted to be there with him and no sense of sanity would sway her to move.

Wyatt leaned forward, breathing against her cheek as he slid the locket along her breasts and then pulled it higher, dragging it slowly over his tee shirt — the pressure of the metal teasing her already sensitized skin. Then his heated fingers were at her neck and she could barely process her own passionate desire for him. Each pass of his fingertips against her nape was sending her nerves into a tailspin, but just when she was ready to turn around, he stepped back and all the glorious sensations he provided her were suddenly gone, leaving her feeling completely empty.

"You can turn back around now," he whispered hotly, against her bare ear.

Jenna turned around slowly and looked up into his face. She was shocked that Wyatt looked just as overcome as she was. His brows were slightly furrowed and his eyes were as dark as sweet chocolate, focusing on her lips, then slowly moving down to her chest. He lifted his right hand toward her face, but hesitated, instead taking the weight of the pendant in his hand, stroking the delicately carved face with his thumb.

"Very pretty."

"Thank you," Jenna choked out.

"May I?"

"Open it? Okay, but it's empty. Nothing to see in there."

"An empty locket? Well that's just sad."

"Hey, don't be mean. I just haven't had anything special enough to put in it — yet."

Jenna was shocked by her own candor, and clearly so was Wyatt because his face turned up quickly. He looked into her eyes again, but swiftly dropped his hand from the necklace.

Jenna tried to be relieved, but it was just the same old roller coaster as every other time he was near her — concentrated adrenaline and excitement, immediately replaced with loss and disappointment when his touch was gone.

Jenna didn't even care anymore that he wasn't what she was supposed to want — that he was bound to break her heart and make her feel like an idiot all over again. No, all she wanted was for that euphoria to come back to her, to experience the overwhelming intensity being with him gave to her.

He picked up her coffee mug and placed it in the sink, returning to stand in front of her with a small smile on his face. Just when she almost had the courage to make a move, his large hands were at her waist and he picked her up off the floor, sitting her down on the marble countertop. The stone was cool against the heated bare skin of her legs, only emphasizing how powerfully she responded to this man to whom she'd tried so hard to be immune.

"That's too bad."

"Huh, oh, um, why?" she asked, trying to shake some sense into her still fuzzy brain.

"Because I think you should have lots of special things, Doc."

"You do? Be careful, Wyatt, you might soften me up."

"I'm willing to risk it. I think I'd like the soft parts of you very much."

His right hand slid up from her waist slowly, taking extra time as he grazed some of those soft parts he had referenced, leaving a trail of tingly fire in his wake, until he finally rested his large, rough hand in the curve of her neck, wrapping his fingers around her smooth skin.

"How can you think that? You don't even know me."

"Because you won't let me. I know you well enough that you asked me to pick you up last night."

"I blame the martinis and my itchy texting finger. It was horny and it wouldn't listen to reason."

"Hmm, so that's your story now? In that case, I think I like that finger. Which one is it?" he asked with a turn of his lips that creased one cheek. Wyatt lightly lifted her right hand and held it to his face. With the slightest movement of his tongue, he drew her index finger into his warm mouth and sucked it inside. After a moment, he let it slide slowly off his lower lip.

"Is it that finger? Because I like that one already."

"Sometimes I text with that one, but I was in a hurry, so... You should maybe meet the thumb, too." Jenna's heartbeat seemed so loud in her ears, it was almost embarrassing.

"Oh really? This thumb," he whispered, and then pulled the flesh into his mouth by his teeth and Jenna couldn't help but let her body arch toward his. Her brain was still in that hazy zone somewhere between hungover and maybe still a little tipsy, and every touch of Wyatt's tongue on her flesh was making her feel as though her whole body was quivering.

"Yeah, that thumb."

Wyatt licked a circle along the center of her palm. He was looking up at her and she could sense the excitement in him, but also the hesitance, and that drove her even more crazy.

"Was it only the texting fingers that wanted to see me?" he whispered against her hand, his warm breath making her tingle deeply throughout her body. It was as though each word and every breath from his mouth were pulling a thread on the torn sweater of Jenna's resolve until she was completely unraveled before him. "I asked you a question, belleza."

"Oh it's *belleza* now? I guess that's progress."

Wyatt gripped Jenna's wrist harder and bit the fleshy part of her palm hard until she squealed.

"Hey!" she cried, trying to jerk her hand away, but he just pulled her back and forced her to look in to his eyes.

"I asked you a question. Did *you* want to see *me*?"

She instantly looked away. Her brain wanted to lie — to pretend it was all a drunken mistake — but she knew she couldn't do that, not when she was staring down the prospect that had filled her with terror since she was six years old. The mere idea she could be a frail, helpless woman lying in a hospital bed set her heart to racing and it was just too exhausting to lie about *everything*.

"I'm waiting," he said sternly, and Jenna let herself look into his eyes that were so forceful, yet there was a warmth in there that she couldn't place.

If I just focus on that look, then I don't have to feel so alone — so scared.

"I wanted to see you, Wyatt."

"And why's that?" he whispered, leaning forward and nibbling on the part of her body where her neck met her shoulder, and Jenna was sure her whole body had turned to *Jell-O*.

"Um, because...I wanted to be alone with you," she gasped out, noticing that one of his hands was swirling a tight circle against her bare waist, underneath his tee shirt. "I wanted to look at you. To feel the way I feel when you're near me. I don't know what any of it means, but I know I felt that way."

"And how do you feel now, belleza?" Wyatt's other hand slid its way down the side of her body until it found her hip and gripped her tightly.

"I feel like I want to make good on what I tried to start last night."

Pleased with her answer, he smiled and trailed his tongue across the raised mound of her palm until he reached her thumb again, sucking it firmly into his mouth.

Everything was getting away from her and Jenna knew she needed some kind of control — to stop or go full forward, and it suddenly became so clear to her which one it had to be. She spread her legs wider. Her hot thighs slid across the cool granite, allowing his firm hips to fall heavily between her legs. She could feel his hard muscles, and already firm length pressed hard against her pulsing core.

Wyatt grinned and opened his mouth to speak.

"Don't fuck this up by talking, Wyatt," Jenna said, her eyes locked on his and her thumb still firmly in his mouth. She slowly dragged the thumb out and wrapped the rest of her hand around his chin, and pressed her lips on his.

That was the last moment of control she had before Wyatt quickly took both his hands and grabbed her ass, pressing her roughly against him until she was practically writhing against his body. Jenna moaned and pressed her lips more firmly against his.

His lips were soft and his tongue was insistent, and he tasted so damn good. It was all teeth and lips and delayed gratification — so potent that Jenna felt like her chest would explode. As Wyatt squeezed her bottom and brought her against him again, he thrust just slightly against the cotton of her panties and groaned heavily.

He leaned back and looked in her eyes, and it was only then that Jenna realized she had fistfuls of his hair in each hand. His lips were wet and swollen and all she wanted to do was to kiss him again.

So she did.

But this time it was softer, more sensual, she could feel each little crinkle of his full lips and the scratch of his stubble on her soft skin. Each touch was like gasoline on her already wildfire-level of excitement, and she didn't want it to cool down. If she was going to do this, she was going to be all in, but he leaned back from her and a groan of protest escaped her lips.

"Hey, get back here," she whispered, yanking him toward her, within an inch of her lips.

"Are you sure, Doc?"

"Shh, I told you not to talk," she answered, her lips twisting into a smirk, and he chuckled slightly. He leaned her backward, so her bottom tipped up, and slid her panties down her legs.

Wyatt tore off the tee shirt he'd given her and popped her bra open in one smooth motion and stared at her, looking her up and down, until she suddenly became uncomfortable. Jenna slowly reached her arms up to cover herself, but he grabbed her hands and pinned them back on the counter, covering hers with his own.

"No. That's not happening. I want to look at you. I feel like I've wanted to look at you for forever. Fuck. I think you're going to make me go insane. I may have to lock you up here just so I can keep looking at you."

Jenna started to roll her eyes, but Wyatt took one of her heavy breasts into his hand and licked the flesh softly, then blowing against it until Jenna was groaning and those same eyes rolled back into her head. Her nipples were so hard and tight, that it was almost painful.

She'd spent a large part of her life trying to hide her figure. It's hard to be taken seriously as a surgeon in the sports world when you have blonde hair and big breasts.

No matter how many times Aubrey and Tea pushed her to show off her body, it always felt more like a burden than anything else. Yet, Jenna quietly thanked each stroke of genetic fate and every brutal hour she endured of yoga, swimming, and jogging that created the body and face that now perched on this cool countertop — because nothing felt better than having Wyatt's gorgeous face buried in her cleavage and gripping her tight thighs. Jenna felt at once powerful and overtaken, and it was amazing.

"I need more of you. I want to lay you out in front of me," he growled against her nipple, until it sounded like the best idea she'd ever heard.

"Hurry up, Wyatt, because if I don't feel you inside me soon, I'm going to have to take matters into my own hands."

"As much as I'd like to see you try that..." he said, trailing off before he scooped her up, wrapping her legs around his waist and kissing her mouth and throat while he carried her quickly to his bedroom.

"Wyatt, your shoulder!"

"Fuck my shoulder."

"That wasn't really what I had in mind. I'm more interested in taking advantage of the rest of your body," she teased. "But I don't want you to hurt yourself more."

"I told you, it's not as bad as you think. Ow."

"Dammit, put me down, Wyatt, you're going to hurt yourself."

"Stop it, woman. I just banged my knee on the doorway while you were distracting me. Now, back to bed with you, you're talking too much," he said, with a low chuckle. Wyatt threw her down in the middle of the mound of sheets and covers that once were his relatively tidy bed. She began to compulsively try to smooth down the sheets in some misplaced attempt to be a good guest.

"Um, I was looking for my necklace, sorry about the mess."

"Trust me, I'm not worried about a messy bed right now. You look good there...naked in my bed."

"Good. Then maybe you should get rid of those boxers. I want to see you, too."

"I like that idea," Wyatt answered as he slipped his hands under the waistband of his black boxer briefs, pulling them down to reveal the line of more taut muscles descending on an angle into a thatch of trimmed, dark hair, finally revealing his thick, long erection. He paused and smiled down at her, "You're staring, Doc."

"I'm just appreciating the view — *intensely*," she teased.

Wyatt shook off his boxer briefs and in a swift movement, he descended upon her, stretching his long, naked body over hers.

"Oh, I like this view, too," she muttered, only to have her words silenced by his mouth over hers, as he caressed her lips and teased them apart with his tongue.

Jenna suddenly had an overwhelming need to touch him and feel him, every inch of him. Her hands moved down his shoulders, his rippled arms, over to his chest, down to his stomach, finally finding the soft, velvety skin of his hard cock. She rested one hand on his tight ass, letting the other explore the enticing length of him. He finally groaned into her mouth and pulled away.

"Fuck," he grunted out, before rolling off her and hurrying across the room.

"What are you doing, Wyatt? Is everything okay?" She hated that uncertainty invaded her brain as she felt his newfound absence in a palpable way.

"Finding a condom. I told you, I don't bring women here."

"Oh, wow, so I even get the exclusive 'hidden condom' five-star treatment? I'm feeling pretty honored, Wyatt."

"You should," he answered over his shoulder, in an easy tone that sent shivers down her body and a clench in her stomach. Her hesitancy from a moment ago was gone. All that remained was excitement.

Jenna was hypnotized by his naked ass — so perfectly taut and muscular as he walked away — and Jenna figured she could have a little bit of patience while she enjoyed the view.

"Got it!" he shouted, trotting back to the bad, his erection hitting his leg on the way, making Jenna giggle. He stood beside the bed and cocked an eyebrow at her. "Doc, it's not generally a good idea to laugh at a naked man. You don't want to give me a complex, do you?"

Wyatt crawled back onto the bed, climbing up her body until he was above her again, caging her in with his arms.

"There's nothing funny about you, Wyatt," she whispered seriously, only to gasp at the feel of his fingers inside her, so rough and insistent. Her eyes closed and her head went back hard against the pillow beneath her. She felt his mouth over one breast, nibbling at the nipple until she was writhing beneath him. With a twist of his fingers, Jenna suddenly cried out.

"Look at me, belleza."

Her eyes opened slowly at his command, suddenly gazing at his soft hair and the sexy way it grazed his eyebrows. His stormy eyes were dark and so focused on her that Jenna couldn't look away. She moaned deeply, circling her hips beneath his hand, but when his thumb touched her tight clitoris, a scream unleashed from her throat. She fought to keep her eyes open but the sensation was too intense, so much more than she could ever recall experiencing with a man.

Wyatt's fingers left her body but her brain was still unsteady from the experience when suddenly his body was plastered against her. His hips were between her legs, and his arms tense and flexed around her as he supported himself over her.

She looked up at him but his expression made her pause. He looked oddly worried, with his brows furrowed from some kind of emotion, or could it be guilt? Jenna couldn't tell what it was, but she knew it was concerning to her.

"Wyatt? Are you okay?"

"Yes," he whispered, before the uncertainty left his face and he lowered his mouth to hers. His kiss was soft and reassuring, awakening her senses all over again to the feeling of wonder that happened every time he touched her. While his lips distracted her with that gentle kiss, he entered her body slowly.

He stroked inside of her with shallow thrusts, letting her adjust to the size of him, before pushing deeply into her. She had to break the kiss to cry out again and open her eyes to look at him. His eyes were still trained on her as he began to thrust into her faster and deeper.

"So good," he murmured, finally leaning down to rest his cheek against hers. Grabbing her legs under the knees and lifting her bottom off the bed, he entered her even more deeply. Jenna screamed in response. She vaguely registered that all her usual control was gone, reveling in the blissful release and surrendering to him in this perfect moment.

She let go of herself, allowing the moment to wash over her as another powerful wave of pleasure took over her body, causing every muscle in her body alternately to tense up and then relax.

Jenna wasn't alone. Wyatt suddenly released her legs and drove into her fully several times, finally releasing a long groan. His head descended into the curve of her neck and breathed deeply. She wrapped her arms around his back and sighed as contentment coursed through her body.

Her fingertips trailed up and down the smooth, tan skin of Wyatt's back. Happiness overtook her, and she mused to herself that if this was what taking risks and finally being willing to do the wrong thing looked like, then she was certainly game for more.

After several moments of quiet closeness, Wyatt rolled off Jenna to lie alongside her in the bed. His fingers trailed up and down her naked chest, lingering around her full breasts.

"You have an amazing body, you know that, Doc? I imagined it would be incredible, but I wasn't sure."

"You imagined me naked?" she asked, with a laugh. "How many times?"

"Let's just say, a lot of times, but the reality is so much better than the fantasy."

"Right back at ya, Mr. McCoy."

"I knew it! You've been undressing me with your eyes for weeks."

"Guilty as charged. But I also prefer the reality," she said, running her hand up and down the length of his hard body.

He looked over at her face and said, "You're going to need to give me at least a couple minutes, Doc, but I promise I'll be ready to make the most of your body very soon. In the meantime, I believe I promised you coffee. I'll have to make a new cup, but I'm no welcher."

"Not a welcher, huh? Well, that's good, because I may want more than coffee from you. I think I have to take you up on that promise of being ready again any minute now..." Jenna teased, as she ran her fingers through Wyatt's hair and tugged his face toward hers, only to be jarred to her senses by her phone vibrating and chirping from her purse across the room. "Oh shit," she exclaimed, suddenly realizing that the world thought she'd gone home last night. She rolled over quickly, knocking Wyatt's muscular form over to the edge of the bed.

"Jesus Christ, Doc, you trying to mess up my *other* shoulder?"

But Jenna was too busy rushing to grab her purse, her phone, and her connection to reality.

Looking down at the notifications on her screen, nerves invaded her throat.

"Six texts and two voicemails. Dammit!" She immediately began reading her texts.

"Hello?" There were a couple of those from Aubrey to start.

Then some from Tea:

"Brey's still here. We feel like hell. How about going to brunch? Or just a dark room and a Bloody Mary?"

"Call us, Brey and I are worried, she's going home."

She switched to listening to the voicemails. They were both from Aubrey:

"I'm home. Where are you? Your bed isn't slept in."

"You better answer me or I will dredge the Ohio River for your body so I can beat the shit out of it."

"Shit. Shit," Jenna blurted out in frustration.

Jenna's throat went dry at the realization of all the worry she must have put her friends through after vanishing like she did.

"What's the matter, Doc?"

"I disappeared on my friends last night and they're worried because they don't know where I am."

"It's okay, just tell them you're with me," Wyatt offered, still lying in bed calmly. He moved his hands behind his head and smiled at her lazily.

"Yeah right," she laughed. "I don't think so."

"Hey, what's so bad about being with me?" he bristled, releasing his hands from his head and sitting up. Jenna swallowed hard as he tensed every muscle in his body. Jenna didn't know if she should jump him or run away even faster. Underneath his hostility was something that disturbed her even more — it almost looked like he was hurt. She shook the emotional response as quickly as she could and grimaced at the smelly sparkly dress she needed to put on as part of her escape.

"Wyatt, they'll either think I'm lying, or they'll believe me and check me into a mental institution." She sank heavily on the edge of the bed.

"Because you hooking up with me is insane?"

"For me, it is. I just submitted an opinion to your team. Oh God, this looks so bad." Her heart hurt thinking of never touching him again, but she tried to be realistic. Brushing her hair back from her face she looked at his handsome face and sighed. "Even if I hadn't consulted on you, trust me, Wyatt, you don't want any part of me…or my life right now," she said sadly.

With a sigh she stood and grabbed her dress. Remembering her bra was still in the kitchen, she pulled it over her bare breasts. That part of her body had just been a source of pride, but she quickly remembered they could be her very death knell.

"So this was a one-time thing?"

"What?" Jenna shook away her morbid thoughts and looked at his sweet face and felt a pang in her chest she'd rather not think about too hard. She swallowed hard and stood to her fullest height, searching for the tough girl she'd spent so many years cultivating. The kindest thing she could do for both of them was to end this before that haunting face of his started cutting into her heart any more deeply. "Isn't that what you want, Wyatt? I figured you for a 'Wham-Bam-Thank-You-Ma'am' type."

"Stop this tap dancing bullshit, Jenna, you're officially starting to piss me off."

"*I'm* pissing *you* off?"

"Yeah, what have I ever done to you other than just be someone you wish you didn't like so much?"

"Somebody thinks highly of himself."

"It's hard to do that with the way you run me down all the time."

"All right, you can stop being so dramatic. I'll admit I may have been a bit…insensitive just now."

Wyatt pulled on his boxer briefs and stood directly in front of her. His face wasn't soft anymore. He was all hard edges and penned fury.

"Don't go too far out on a limb or anything, Doc, I wouldn't want you to fall off without your high horse there to catch you."

"Aren't you a gentleman? What the hell do you want from me?"

"Oh, I don't know, maybe treat me like a human being?"

"Come on, Wyatt. Let's bring it down a notch. I'm willing to take some blame for acting like a bitch here, but don't push your luck."

He stepped closer to her until she backed up and felt the hard wall against her flesh.

"If you're trying to stop pissing me off you're doing a really bad job of it, Doc," he grunted out.

"Now *you're* the one not being fair."

"Okay, fine, if we're negotiating, then I'll agree to admit you aren't *that* bad."

"Fine, now tell *me* — what do you really want, Wyatt?" Jenna asked calmly.

"What do you think, Jenna? Turn that big brain of yours on and think about it. And be honest — I know it's hard for you to do when you're with me."

"Okay. I'll take a guess. Maybe you want me to be a little nicer to you and to let you play with my boobies more," she said, with a smirk and a tiny hope that he would say yes.

"That's a start," he said sternly, but a smile was playing at the corner of his lips

"Okay, I'll start with the being nicer part — I'd like to see you again, too, Wyatt. And as for the rest…I'd also like you to play with my boobies again. But for now, I need to call my friends and I think it's best if we don't tell anyone about this or answer any questions about us."

"What's the big deal?"

"Because you and I both know we have no answers to give anyone. Okay? And I consulted on your shoulder only a couple weeks ago. You and I being openly involved wouldn't look right. This is a pivotal point in my career. I know you understand that."

"Right, I get it," he said, with a low and somewhat angry voice.

Jenna walked to him carefully and held his cheek, turning his face to hers. He tried to avoid her eyes, but she stilled his face and kissed him, letting her tongue trail across his bottom lip before releasing him. Cradling his cheek, she smiled at him, enjoying the way his eyes were still slightly hooded from the effect of her caresses.

"I'm sorry," she whispered, her breaths hitting his face so hot, they bounced back against her lip.

His eyes widened, "I never thought I'd hear you say that, Doc."

"Maybe you bring out the best in me, Wyatt," she answered, scraping her nails against the stubble on his face. "Now let me call my friends before they have themselves a couple of heart attacks, okay?"

"Be my guest," he answered, letting his hands slide to her hips and pulling her dress up so he could press himself against the naked bottom half of her body.

Jenna fumbled with her phone, finally managing to call Aubrey through her latest Wyatt-induced lust trance. The phone had barely made it through one ring before Aubrey picked up and scolded her.

"You better be in one piece, girl, because I want to be able to rip you limb from limb," Aubrey said sharply.

"I'm fine, I had to fill in for someone at work. I made my bed before I left," Jenna answered, the lie skipping off her tongue as she studied Wyatt and his hardening face.

"But your car's here," Aubrey challenged in a tone so frustrated it jarred Jenna out of the searing trap of Wyatt's dark stare.

"I took the bus."

"The bus? You're kidding."

"I didn't want to deal with driving and parking. I have a killer headache. Don't worry, Brey, okay? I'll be coming home soon, I promise. But I should've texted, I'm sorry."

"Damn right, you should've. Never again, missy. Man, you've been acting so weird lately."

"I just have a lot going on at work, I really want that fellowship."

Jenna could at least say that part was true.

"Okay, well, I'll see you soon. Bye."

"Bye."

Jenna ended the call, swallowed deeply, and looked back up at Wyatt.

"You always lie to your friends like that?"

"Are you saying you've never lied to anyone?"

His face clouded and his brow crinkled, but Jenna couldn't make out anything from his expression.

"I'm the one that asked the question."

"When the situation requires, I find that withholding information can be the best for everyone." Wyatt looked almost disgusted at the answer, and she quickly added, "I promised to play nice with you though, so let me play nice."

Jenna slipped her fingers into the waistband of his boxer briefs, pulling him flush against her body. She wanted to jump full force into craziness — to do the wrong thing, over and over again, until she could forget about how doing the right thing had never gotten her anywhere.

"That's better," he muttered.

"How about we have some fun with each other?" He nodded in response, his jaw twitching slightly with tension. "So I'll see you soon, Wyatt, but for now, I'm gonna need to borrow some clothes, and maybe a ride, too?" she requested as a nervous laugh escaped her throat.

Wyatt smiled wickedly and squeezed her ass hard.

"I'll get you to where you need to go, Doc. But the ride? That comes first."

Jenna laughed and wiggled out of his grip. She jumped

onto his bed, positioning herself on her knees. After quickly tearing off her stinky dress, she beckoned him to her with one hooked finger.

"Then what are you waiting for, Wyatt? Come and get me."

CHAPTER ELEVEN

"Hey, Jenna, you're awfully quiet today. Is everything okay?" Griffen asked her thoughtfully as he held Tea's left hand.

Griffen and Tea had come to her and Aubrey's apartment for a drink before heading over to Carol's Christmas party that night. Jenna had been looking forward to a chance for all four of them to catch up while Griffen's mom looked after Johnny, though, she hadn't accounted for how uncomfortable even such a mundane question would make her.

Jenna watched Griffen toying absentmindedly with Tea's massive engagement ring as she selected her words carefully.

"Oh, I'm fine. I've just been working a lot — trying to show I deserve that fellowship, you know," Jenna finally answered.

She felt guilty about all the secrets she was keeping from these people who were such an important part of her life, but she didn't know how to tell them about everything on her mind. Between the madness of her health concerns and her brand-new — whatever it was — with Wyatt, she felt keeping everything to herself was the only way to preserve some kind of control over her life.

"That's too bad you've had to work so much," Tea said. "Um, but you two are still going to Carol's Christmas party at *Viola* tonight, right?" Tea asked with a bit of nervousness in her voice. Griffen looked at her sideways, releasing her hand to wrap his arm around her shoulders reassuringly.

Jenna had a feeling the two of them had come over in part because they were desperate for some low-key fun before an evening with Tea's former mother-in-law, Carol. That woman was a permanent pain in the ass, as far as Jenna and Aubrey were concerned.

Aubrey chimed in and said, "Of course, we'll be there. Jenna will down some coffee and I'll drag her there by the hair if I have to. We won't leave you guys alone."

"Thanks so much, you two. I know a Wednesday is a hard day to swing, but it's the easiest night for Carol to be able to shut down the restaurant. I think if we're all there, it will be fun."

"And don't worry, it won't be too late a night," Griffen added. "Tomorrow, Johnny is joining that hockey league I found for him, so we'll want to get him home at a reasonable hour." Griffen was beaming over this news as he refilled everyone's wine glasses.

"Hockey, now, too?" Tea asked with a laugh.

"It's Pittsburgh, gorgeous," he said, winding his fingers in her hair and pulling her gently toward him to plant a kiss on her forehead. "Hockey's a required part of Johnny's development." Griffen moved his arms to her waist, pulling her off of her chair and into his lap, planting a soft kiss on her cheek as he rubbed circles on her knee.

"My hero," Tea said over a smile, kissing his neck lightly. "See, I would've let that poor boy go through his entire adolescence without ever holding a hockey stick. I just need to sort out getting him to practice..."

"Don't worry about that. I'll take him."

"Oh, well, in that case, I'm even more in love with the idea," Tea whispered against his cheek. "You know, you'd make a good kept man, Griffen."

"As long as you're the one doing the keeping, gorgeous," he said, with a smile.

Jenna took a sip of wine and tried to keep her eyes averted as Griffen whispered something to Tea that caused her to blush. Seeing him get Tea so worked up reminded her of Wyatt and his many talents. Instantly, her texting finger started to get twitchy.

"All right, you two. Knock it off. I want to keep this wine in my belly," Aubrey blurted out.

Jenna laughed with everyone else but couldn't help but feel her temperature rising. "Hey. We aren't that bad...are we, Jenna?" Tea asked with a laugh, as she smiled in response to another kiss on the cheek from Griffen.

"It *is* a bit nauseating, but only in the sweetest way," Jenna offered gently.

"Oh. Well, I guess that's okay. Hey, by the way, what happened to you after we went out Friday night? Brey and I were really worried about you."

"I told Brey. I was at rounds."

"I know, but that's why I was confused," Tea said, "I called the hospital to check on you when I couldn't find you, but they said you were off."

"Did they now?" Aubrey asked, her tone dripping with suspicion.

"Why are you still tormenting me about this? I told you I was filling in, maybe that person just looked at the schedule and didn't know. Nothing too exciting happened. The people that were there barely even saw me."

"Okay, fine," Tea said. "But we'll never apologize for worrying about you."

Griffen whispered in Althea's ear again, rubbing his nose against her face lightly and making her giggle. He looked at his watch, and said loudly enough for the rest of the group could hear, "Althea, I think we should get going. My mom is bringing Johnny back to our place in about an hour. If we want to get some time to ourselves before the party…"

"Oh, right, yes, let's get going. Sorry, guys, we need to head out."

"So you guys can grope each other in peace. I get it."

"Aubrey, give them a break," Jenna said, choking on her wine as she laughed.

Tea blushed brightly, as she grabbed her coat and purse and headed to the door.

"Hopefully once we get a bigger place, it'll be easier to have some alone time," Griffen said, following Tea to the door.

"A new place? You guys are moving? Tea, is that right?" Aubrey asked, a bit shocked.

"We *might* be moving, nothing is decided," Tea replied. "Bye, you two, see you tonight."

She gave them each a kiss and grabbed Griffen's hand, leaned into his ear to whisper something. It must've been good, because he groaned out loud.

"Yeah, we gotta go. See you two tonight," Griffen added, whisking Tea out the door so quickly that she squealed as they scurried down the apartment hallway.

Aubrey closed the door firmly and rolled her eyes at Jenna.

"Oh my God, can you believe those two? We get it, they're

in *looove*."

"Very true. Also, it looks like she hasn't put our communication advice into action, yet."

"Yeah, I think the *Griffen Express* is still chugging along at full speed with ten new life-changing stops along the way. Tea will probably just stay silent for each of them."

"It's Tea, you know how she is. This is as much her doing as it is his. She'll let him know what her worries are on her own unique time frame."

"Right, and I know she's got a lot of adjusting to do. Hell, we all do. It's just that..."

"We can't exactly complain. We pushed her into this, Brey, remember."

"I thought we were just trying to get her laid. Now I feel like I'm on a diet where I never eat because I'm always losing my appetite from their PDA or my own shock at all the changes they're making... But I know Griffen makes her really happy."

"He does. I get how you feel, though. Their relationship *has* changed everything. I feel like we barely see her or Johnny anymore."

"Right, that's been really tough for me."

"But he's so good for Johnny. You aren't going to say anything, are you, Brey?"

"Hell, no. I'm not going to be *that* friend that complains to her happy friend about being in a relationship and spending less time with her. You know, the one that mopes all the time — standing in the way of her happiness."

"Oh, you aren't?" Jenna chuckled out. "Then what friend are you?"

"I'm that friend that supports her to her face, and then privately bitches that things are different now."

"Yeah, I've been feeling like that friend, too, lately. Does that make us awful?"

"No way! We both feel that way, so that automatically means it's okay. We can't be awful. Needy...maybe. But never awful."

"Not sure it works that way, Brey."

"Oh, I'm totally sure it does. That's why I love having two best friends. My odds are doubled that one of you will validate my craziness for me."

"We are still going to support her as her friends, though, right?"

"Of course. We're women. We look out for her, but we also need to talk about her and meddle nonstop. You know...for love," Aubrey said confidently. "And I won't let Tea know just how much I miss the little family we had, but it still bugs me how everything is changing. It used to be the three of us hanging out, having sleepovers with Johnny. Now, Johnny's with Griffen all the time."

"I've missed our time with him, too. But I guess we need to give them some space. We do see them, still. It's just different. That's what happens when people fall in love...or so I've heard."

"Can't argue with that."

"Well, Brey, I better go get showered and ready for tonight. And I have some phone calls to make," Jenna said.

"While you're at it, make one to your dad. He called during your rounds yesterday."

"Oh, okay."

"Are you going to call him?"

"Maybe."

"Jenna."

"Back off, Aubrey."

"Why are you acting like that? I think he's a sweetheart."

"Of course he is, and I love him, but he's also exhausting. I swear he's got to be the only parent disappointed their child became a surgeon."

"He just wanted you to follow in his footsteps and stay near him. That's not crazy, girl."

"And, to go to the University of Georgia. Stay with him and run his camps and coach his boys. Now, he wants me to move back there. And none of that is going to happen — he needs to drop it. I don't want to live there again."

He also will want to know about my health and I'm a terrible liar. I need to get through this biopsy, and then I can worry about Dad. It's not fair to him to put him through any of that.

"Easy, Jenna, no need to snap at me."

"Sorry. You're right, I didn't mean to," Jenna said softly, feeling terrible for letting her feelings get the best of her.

"Something's going on with you, girl. I just know it!"

"Relax, Brey, everything is fine," Jenna said over her shoulder, as she went to her room and closed the door.

She'd seen that Wyatt had called her cell phone about a half hour before and she couldn't wait any longer before calling him back. Jenna tried to ignore the butterflies in her stomach as she pressed the contact she'd made for Wyatt. It had been a handful of days since their crazy morning together and her hormones were pinging inside her at the thought of being with him again.

They'd texted and talked some, but both of their schedules over the last couple of days had been packed. She hadn't gotten any time to see him again.

"Hi, Doc," he answered.

"You rang, Wyatt?"

"I did. I'm calling you on your promise. It's time for me to play with your boobies again. You've put me off long enough."

"You've been pretty busy too, you know."

"True, but I'm free now. How about you come by tonight?"

"I'd like that, but I can't make it tonight."

"Why not?" he asked with a skeptical voice. "Are you ignoring me again, Doc?"

"No, it's just that Carol's Christmas party is tonight at her restaurant, *Viola,* on Mt. Washington."

"Who's that?"

"She's Tea's former mother-in-law and Johnny's grandmother. Carol's already really particular about her parties without any added drama, but now that Tea's engaged, things are still a bit tense. Tea will need all the support she can get, so I have to be there."

"Well, that sucks. The team leaves for Oakland tomorrow. It's a Sunday night game, so I won't be back until Monday. I was hoping to see you tonight."

Hearing he wanted to see her sent a shot of warmth through her body, and Jenna could barely suppress a girlish giggle.

"I want to see you, too. We'll have to wait until you get back from Oakland. I'm sorry."

"I understand. You're just going to have to promise to think about me."

"That won't be a problem," she answered, not bothering to hide the laugh of pleasure that escaped her throat. "Good luck on Sunday, Wyatt."

"Thanks, Doc. I'll see you really soon. Good-bye."

"Good-bye," she answered.

After ending the call, she pulled up her calendar and added the appointment she'd scheduled with Dr. Kannan for Friday.

It was the soonest the well-renowned oncologist could squeeze her in and she was dreading every minute she would need to wait to learn the truth.

It was going to be a long and lonely few days. For now, she would focus on what was in front of her — and that was getting dressed for a party.

Wyatt exited his SUV and handed his keys to the *Viola* valet. The kid couldn't have been more than eighteen years old, and was trying his damnedest not to be starstruck at the sight of Pittsburgh's starting quarterback. He smiled and thanked him but Wyatt didn't have time for much else.

It had taken some scrambling after his phone call with Jenna that afternoon to get in touch with Aubrey in time to score an invitation to this Christmas party. After all the progress he'd made with Jenna, he couldn't risk letting so much time go by before he saw her again.

If he was being honest, Wyatt really didn't want to wait any longer. His motives for spending time with her may be murky, but he definitely enjoyed her company, especially the company of her naked body. It was more than that, though. He couldn't remember the last time he'd felt this way about any woman, and he was going to make the most of his chances to have more time with her.

He caught sight of her talking to Aubrey and knew he'd made the right move. Jenna looked stunning, as always, but with her long blonde hair falling in cascading waves down the open back of her fitted navy dress, she was damn near perfect. He crossed the room to her, feeling his fingers itching with the desire to touch that smooth, exposed skin of her back in a way that told everyone in the room she was all his.

"Oh, look who's here," he heard Aubrey say loudly as he approached, snapping him back to reality — reminding him he needed to keep his hands to himself, for now.

Jenna turned and her already large blue eyes widened even further at the sight of him.

"Wyatt? Hi. Aubrey, what the…"

"What? He called me a couple hours ago to thank me for the great photo shoot I did."

"I'm sure he did," Jenna said slowly, looking at Wyatt carefully. He could tell she wanted to appear exasperated, but couldn't quite pull it off, especially once she licked her lips slowly at the sight of him.

"*And* he offered to let me take some follow up shots for the holiday posts on the magazine's blog page. Since I was already set up to handle all of the photographs here for Carol's party, I figured it was no big deal."

"Imagine that? How nice of you to do that for Aubrey, Wyatt."

"It's my pleasure, Doc," he answered. Stepping forward, he placed a hand on the smooth, warm skin of her back, letting his fingers slip beneath the draped material slightly. Then he whispered in her ear, "You look great."

A thrill went through him when he felt her shiver slightly at his touch.

"Thanks," she said, raising her eyes to his. He could tell she was both excited and nervous to be so near him again.

He focused his eyes on her, smiling slightly, just waiting to see if she'd break.

"And you look great, too, Wyatt. But you always do, so that's no surprise," she said, stepping away from his touch to grab her cocktail off the high table next to her.

"He'd better look great," Aubrey exclaimed. "I'm not waiting for long — I'll be tormenting him with that photo shoot any minute now."

"That's the only reason why you're here, Wyatt? For more pictures?"

Wyatt leaned forward, closing the space between him and the peaches and cream skin of her face.

"I must confess, I was wrangling for an invite," he said quietly to her.

"I'm sure we can get some good shots here," Aubrey interrupted. "Though you two really do look good together. I might have to sneak you under the mistletoe and take some pictures of you together."

"Oh, I don't know about that," Jenna muttered out.

"I do. I'm going to get you to hook up someday, I promise," she added, and Wyatt had to hide a chuckle behind his hand at the sight of Jenna choking on her cocktail.

"Are you all right, Doc?"

"Never better. I just don't think it's wise to push two people together."

"It's fine by me. I'm in favor of Aubrey's plan. You can keep it up, Aubrey," he said, carefully monitoring Jenna's response.

"I will! I wish I could harass you both some more right now, but I have to test the lighting and I have some last minute decisions to make on the shot location. That means I'm leaving you crazy kids alone."

"Aubrey, wait. Aren't you worried he'll screw up Carol's party? Wyatt's celebrity status has a way of getting attention."

"Nope. I gave everyone the heads up and asked them to behave. Carol seemed thrilled at the idea of the restaurant getting all this attention."

"You told everyone, but nobody warned *me*?" Jenna asked, with more than a hint of annoyance in her tone.

"What would be the fun in that?" Aubrey asked with innocent looking eyes, that elicited a slow eye roll from Jenna's perfect blue ones. "But I really do have to run and get everything set up. Have fun, you two."

Once Aubrey scurried off, Wyatt moved closer to Jenna.

"You really do look great, Doc. I love this dress."

And he did. On anyone else it might have been conservative, but with its snug fit and her large breasts and small waist, it was practically indecent.

"Thank you, Wyatt."

"But you know how much I like you in…and out…of dresses."

"I thought you liked me in a lab coat, too?"

He stifled a groan at the image of her in a lab coat with nothing else underneath.

"Are you trying to make me hard before I have to go get my picture taken?"

"I'm not putting that much effort in…yet. I could try *harder* if you'd like," she added, whispering against his ear, and he could have sworn she licked his earlobe. It shocked him how much she was teasing him, but he definitely liked it — a lot.

"Do you think she knows about us?" he whispered in to Jenna's ear, then turning to watch Aubrey scurry around with her photography equipment.

"Aubrey? No, she can't know, or else she'd be too busy taking all the credit."

"She likes me, then?"

"She likes that you're hot and you get me all worked up. I'm not sure if her devious plans go much further than that."

"So, Doc, does that mean you aren't mad at me for being here? This party sounded fun, I didn't want to miss it."

"Right, that's why you're here? It's one wild night in here for sure," she said, with a smile that convinced him she might actually be happy to see him.

"I told you I wanted to see you again before I had to leave, so here I am. Though, Aubrey did technically propose the idea when I called."

"Sounds to me like you planted it in her brain…but it's fine. I'm glad to see you. Oh, don't look so surprised. You should know by now I can't hide how much I like to be near you. I just thought we were past you ambushing me at places."

"I never agreed to that. It's too much fun to see you so surprised."

"Right, well, you probably should get those pictures over with."

"Running me off already?"

"No. Just looking out for you. Aubrey can be very insistent about these things."

"All right then, but I'm not giving up on her mistletoe idea."

"We'll see," she said, lifting her drink to her lips as her light blue eyes peered seductively at him over the glass.

"Wyatt, over here!" he heard someone yelling out from behind him.

"That would be Aubrey that's braying at you right now like an old mule. I told you — she's insistent."

"Yeah. It looks like I've asked for it, haven't I?"

"You sure have. You'd better head over there before she comes by and drags you away," she informed him.

She threw him one last sly smile that gave him a bit of a thrill before he walked away.

Wyatt settled in with Aubrey and followed her many orders and incessant picture taking, all the while never losing sight of Jenna from the corner of his eye.

He could tell she was having a field day with his quiet monitoring of Jenna, because she used every chance she could get to mention Jenna's name or tease him about watching her. That was fine with him. Getting closer to Jenna meant winning over her friends and he could do that.

It was no hardship keeping Jenna in his view, either. Whether she was mingling and talking to other people, or playing with young Johnny, she always had the most honest and kind face. He was enjoying spending time with her, even if that hadn't been his original goal.

Yet, all those warm and fuzzy feelings immediately disappeared when he caught sight of Jenna laughing with lighthearted glee with some dark-haired, tattooed asshole. He was leaning over her, whispering in her ear — and she was letting him. Wyatt couldn't be sure, but it looked like he might've touched her bare shoulder. Just the thought of his hands on her was making Wyatt feel hot with irritation. Jenna should be waiting for *him* to come back and talk to her, not letting that jackass hold her attention like that.

"All right, McCoy, I'm gonna need to ask you to lay off this scary, angry thing you've got going on here. This is a feel-good Christmas piece we're going for — so I'm really not looking for shots of you going all 'Hulk smash,' okay?"

"What? Oh, yeah, sure. I'll try."

"What are you looking at anyway?"

She turned to follow his eyes and immediately started laughing.

"Oh, I get it. She's over there talking to our resident mystery man."

"Your what? Who is he?" Wyatt even felt angry at jokes about this guy.

This doesn't mean anything, I just can't have her distracted if she's really going to come around and see how wrong her diagnosis was. That's all.

"That's Trey, Griffen's friend. He's Jenna's friend, too, I guess. At least that's what she keeps swearing to us. Don't worry. I think you're wearing her down. She'll cave sooner or later."

"Thanks."

"Don't thank me, she's been wound so tight recently, I'm hoping she uses you for a little release."

"Uses me?"

"Don't act so shocked. You are *not* Jenna boyfriend material. She'd never let her guard down with a guy like you."

"Are you sure about that?"

"For whatever reason, she won't get involved in relationships with high-profile athletes or hot bad boy types."

"Maybe she's ready for a change."

"I hope so. She's so controlled about her life. It makes for some boring overnight guests on her part. Believe me."

"Who are her overnight guests?" Wyatt couldn't believe how pissed he felt just thinking about Jenna with someone else. First, he wanted to kill tattoo boy, now, he wanted to beat up nameless, faceless guys he knew nothing about.

What's wrong with me? Why the hell am I getting so nuts right now? It must be because the stakes are so high with her diagnosis, that's the only thing that makes sense...

"Argh, there's that *crazy* face again. I'm going to need you to bring it down a notch, dude, or I'll have to Photoshop a puppy into these pictures, or save them to scare people when next Halloween rolls around."

"Sorry. My mind was wandering."

"I bet it was. Don't worry. She hasn't had any overnight guests for a while. Though now I'm not so sure I want to go keep pushing you on her."

"Why not?"

"Well, you're kind of freaking me out with this whole stalker vibe you're giving off right now. Besides, it's bad enough having Griffen here…"

"What?"

She ignored his question and squinted through her viewfinder.

"Look at me. Lean against the window. We want that great view behind you. Perfect. Rest one shoulder on the glass, and look at me. Smile. Good one."

"You don't like Griffen?"

"Huh? Oh, he's fine. All right, he's awesome, but he's changed everything. That's why you're perfect — you won't mess shit up by trying to stick around and be Jenna's boyfriend or something."

"How flattering. What about that tattooed guy over there? Is he around her a lot? Overnight, or whatever?"

"See, now there's that jealousy shit that makes me nervous. You aren't getting soft on me, are you?"

"Never."

"Perfect. Now let's do some shots by the Christmas tree. Maybe hold a present. And don't worry. Trey has never stayed over with her like that. There's the smile I was looking for, Wyatt — much better."

"You guys are really in each other's business?" Wyatt asked.

"We're family. That's what families do."

"I agree. That's how I am with my family, though my baby

sister would likely say she wished I had a different approach."

"Oh, that's a great look when you're talking about your sister. Very sweet. Keep it up, perfect for the holidays."

But Wyatt wasn't thinking about his baby sister.

No, he was still intently focused on his favorite doctor.

Jenna froze when she saw Wyatt walk away from Aubrey toward her. She'd put all her energy into acting casual at seeing him, but he'd completely thrown her for a loop when he walked into *Viola* that night.

She'd finally accepted that she felt disappointed at not being able to see him for several more days when — boom — there he was, in Carol's restaurant.

He was attracting the attention of the whole room with his mere presence. Wyatt was larger than life at a time when Jenna was completely overwhelmed by the implications of her own normal, regular-sized existence.

Being with Wyatt right then shouldn't make even a lick of good sense. Everything about him screamed for her to run, and she'd managed to succeed at that for a while. But now that she'd let herself have a taste, she couldn't stop thinking about him touching her, kissing her, and making her forget everything that was bothering her. He sent her nerves into a tailspin and that was a relief. Having more of that feeling made more sense to her than anything else in the world.

"There you are, Doc, and finally alone, I see," he said, with a tight smile after he reached her.

"Yes, I am. Is everything okay, Wyatt? You look kind of…intense."

"I'm fine. Just glad to be done with the work part of the

evening, I guess."

"Okay, so that means Aubrey released you from photo shoot prison?"

"Yes, but I'm on probation. If she sees another good shot, I'm supposed to immediately report to her."

"Wow, she's strict."

"I'm pretty sure that probation allows me to sneak off somewhere with you, though."

"Oh, yeah? I haven't seen the terms of your release, so I'll have to take your word for it."

"You can trust me," he said tightly, without looking at her in the eyes.

"Um, okay. Why don't you relax a little? I'll get you a drink."

"No. I want to be alone with you. Come on, follow me."

She glanced around quickly and said, "Right now?"

"Yes." He leaned forward and growled into her ear, "It's been days since I was inside you. It'll be several more before I can be again. I'm not missing this chance. Come with me...*now*."

Jenna swallowed and looked up at him, only able to choke out the word, "Okay," before she looked around to be sure no one was looking at them.

He began to walk away and she scurried after him, like a horny little trained duckling.

When they reached the coatroom, he looked at her and winked.

He quickly opened the door and blocked the view of her entering with his frame.

Once inside, he pressed her body firmly against the wall and scanned her eyes in the dim light for a moment.

Before she could try to discern what was running through

his mind, he kissed her deeply. His tongue explored her mouth while one hand grabbed her bottom and the other slid up to stroke her breast through her dress.

She let her head fall back against the wall with a "thump" as he slid a strap of her dress aside and down her arm, baring half of her uncovered chest. He let his tongue glide down from her ear, to her neck, and then to the tight, hard bud of her nipple. He pulled the dress away from the other side, revealing the other breast, which quickly received the same warm, hot treatment as the first.

It was so strange to her that his attention on her breasts made her feel so free and beautiful, even when they were the source of so much worry to her every other moment of that past week.

"Wyatt," she breathed out hard, as she grabbed his hair and yanked his head back so she could look into his eyes. They were dark with eyelids half-closed in arousal and Jenna knew she had to taste him. Sliding down the wall, she crouched in front of him and pressed her back hard against the door so that it couldn't be opened while she indulged in something so incredibly unlike her.

His groan at her position in front of him only spurred her on more, as she scraped her nails up the length of his slacks, slowly reaching the hard bulge in the front. She cupped him and caressed him through his pants, until he leaned forward, pressing both of his hands firmly against the door. Before she lost her nerve, Jenna slid down his zipper, her breath catching in fear at the loud sound it made in the quietness of the coatroom. Neither the racks full of heavy winter fabrics, nor the loud pounding of her own heart, did anything to muffle the sound to her ears.

There was no turning back now, and she didn't want to

anyway.

Sensible Jenna was on vacation. This Jenna was still here in town and she was ready to act crazy. She'd been continuing to caress his length through the cotton of his boxer briefs, but she couldn't wait anymore. Neither apparently could he, because when she pulled him out, he was rock hard and a tiny drop of liquid had escaped from him — a slow and tantalizing promise from the head of his penis.

Looking up at him, she darted her tongue out and licked the salty treat off, eliciting a deep groan from him that made her feel beyond sexy and powerful.

With one hand cradling his balls, she licked up and down his length, then swirled her tongue over the head and took it into her mouth. After letting him experience the warm wetness of her tongue and lips, on a deep breath, she took him more fully into her eager mouth. Jenna moaned lightly, enjoying the earthy taste of him.

She felt his large hands move to her hair, gently guiding her mouth up and down his cock until she could feel him somehow become even harder inside her. He held her face in one place, controlling her every movement. After adjusting to the sensation of him possessing her mouth, she sucked at him with a repeated rhythm and rubbed her tongue against the underside of his velvety length.

"Oh, belleza," he whispered, before pulling out of her mouth. Her sense of loss was short-lived because he brought her up quickly and kissed her hard, pressing her fully against the door as he held her jaw in place with one hand, and used the other to pull her dress up — inch by maddening inch.

When he reached her bottom, he slid his hand around the soft material of her panties. Then he yanked at them until they were ripped free into his hand.

"Wyatt," she whispered. Maybe she meant to tease him for his impatience, or to beg him for more, but she couldn't frame any coherent thoughts as she became aware of her own nakedness from the waist down. The still air of the room settled against the bare skin of her legs and the wet folds that needed his touch. His hands and body were the only thing that quieted her nerves and made her believe it would all be okay — if only for a moment. "Oh, Wyatt, please, touch me."

"You're going to have to be quiet. I love it when you scream, but not now. Okay?"

"Okay, I promise."

"You break that promise, I will *make* you be quiet. You understand?"

"Yes, I do. Please." She didn't even care that she was begging. She couldn't be bothered to let any of this worry her, especially when he spun her around and placed her hands against the door.

He let her go and several moments later, she heard the tear of the foil before she had to wait several excruciating seconds more for him to put on a condom.

Finally, Wyatt reached down and arched her ass toward him and in an instant, was inside her. Her self-control lasted through two powerful thrusts, but it felt too good, she could feel the moans building, the scream lodged in her throat fighting to break through.

Before she even knew she'd made a sound, he said with a deep voice and heavy breaths that heated her ear, "Shh. I told you to be quiet, belleza. You know what this means."

On a deep upward thrust that almost lifted her off the floor, he shoved fabric in her mouth just in time for her to release a muffled cry of pleasure into the satin material of her own panties. She smelled herself on them, but instead of making her uncomfortable, it only aroused her more. She couldn't see him, but she felt him against her back, inside of her, kissing her neck, stroking her thighs. He was everywhere, driving into her from behind. Her own scent emanated from her mouth, but it was drowned out by the hot smell of them together.

Wyatt reached down to stroke her clit until she burst with so much pleasure that she had to dig her nails into the wood of the door. As she came back to reality, he took his other arm to pull her tightly against him, and drove into her fully, staying there until he found his release.

Jenna rested her forehead against the cool, newly scratched wood. Her conscious self was floating above her body, barely registering as Wyatt removed her own panties from her mouth. Out of the corner of her eye, she saw him put them in his pocket, and then he turned her around. With one hand on her cheek and another stroking her hair, he let her dress fall back down over her legs.

Leaning down he kissed her cheek, moving away to say, "Are you about ready to rejoin the party? Maybe we can still catch the Secret Santa gift exchange," he whispered against her ear with a laugh.

Jenna couldn't help but chuckle, too. Yet she quickly caught herself when the noise reverberated through the room.

"Don't make me gag you again, Doc. I'm only looking out for you, I know you don't want to get caught in the coatroom with me."

"I didn't know you could be so resourceful. Though now, I'm feeling awfully exposed down there."

"Only you and I will know, but trust me, I'll be thinking about your bare pussy the rest of the night."

"Oh, you sweet talker, you."

"Hardly, but you know that already." He smoothed her dress down slightly. Then he moved both his hands to her face, turning it gently so their eyes were locked. "But whatever type of person I may be, I know I want to keep having fun with you, Doc."

"I like that idea," she said, with a smile. Jenna searched his face in the darkened room. It was amazing how the dim light only accentuated the unique shadows and lines that made him so handsome.

"What are your Christmas plans, Doc?"

The question caught her off guard, but he simply stared at her, waiting for an answer. She said, "I don't have any. Aubrey's leaving, she's decided to go home to Denver."

"And you're just going to stay here by yourself?"

"Usually we would both spend it with Tea and Johnny, but this year she has Griffen. I think they want their privacy."

"Then it's settled, you're staying with me."

"What? You're kidding, right?"

"No, what's so crazy about that? We're busy people. It's going to be hard to find time for each other. As much fun as this was, I do prefer the privacy of my house over fucking you in a room full of other people's coats."

Jenna looked around the room sheepishly.

"But, what about *your* family?" she asked.

"I definitely don't want to screw you with them nearby."

She slapped his chest and laughed a little.

"Stop it. I mean, aren't you going home to Austin to see them?"

"No, they're pretty busy with their own thing, so they told me to stay here. I'm just going to stick around and focus on the last couple games of the season and work on my shoulder. I think it's already showing improvement. Don't you?"

"You've definitely been playing better recently."

"Thank you," he said, leaning forward closely enough that she felt his breaths tickle her ear.

"Okay," Jenna said. "Then maybe we see each other through the New Year? After that…I don't know what will happen."

Jenna heard the crack in her words and prayed he missed it. A wash of panic was rushing through her body at the realization she had no clue what awaited her after the New Year. She felt like her body could be a ticking bomb and it was easier for her to ignore how terrified she was about the future — if even for just that moment.

"Are you okay, Doc? You seem upset."

"What? No," she squeaked out. "I mean, yes, I'm fine, just thinking about the holidays."

"Okay, then," he said with skepticism, invading every word. "Just through the New Year. Why?"

"No particular reason," she said slowly, desperately trying to sound calm. "I just figured we shouldn't push it. You know, let's just see how it goes and take it from there."

"Fine, I guess. But for now, let's try to get you out of here without anyone seeing." He opened the door slowly, scanned the room outside and whispered, "All clear. Come on."

Jenna walked back into the main area of *Viola* trying to look as calm and composed as possible.

Suddenly, she was shocked to hear raised voices — one of them coming from a very upset Tea. Dread sunk into Jenna's stomach as she started to get an idea of why no one had noticed that she and Wyatt had disappeared.

In the middle of the main dining room, Tea and Griffen were in a heated discussion with Carol, the mother of Tea's deceased husband, and his younger brother, Baxter.

"Who are those people?" Wyatt whispered to her.

"The older woman is Carol, the one I told you about. The good-looking blonde guy is Baxter Taylor, Carol's other son. But last I heard he wasn't able to make it to this party. He's been studying in France..."

Tea's voice broke through Jenna's explanation.

"You didn't tell Baxter about me and Griffen? Carol, you can't be serious?"

"Oh, hell. Wyatt, I have to go in there. I'm sorry," Jenna said quickly.

"Okay. I'll be here if you need me..."

Jenna rushed into the room before he could finish his sentence. She found Aubrey on the fringes of the conversation, holding Johnny's hand. She was silent, but her face was red with fury.

"Jenna, there you are," Aubrey blurted at her. "Where'd you run off to anyway? I was looking for you when Baxter burst in here."

"He what? I, um, I called into the hospital to check on one of my patients. Tell me what's going on," she whispered, inwardly cringing at how easily these lies seemed to spill from her lips.

"The FBI wanted to interview Baxter about Jack's death for their preparations for David's trial, so he came home early from Paris. He decided to come straight to this party. He walks in and sees Griffen here, holding Tea's hand and..."

"And he lost it because Carol never told him those two were together?"

"Exactly. He went nuts. Just listen."

Jenna turned her attention back to the scene that had all the partygoers clearly trying to decide between pretending to ignore what was happening or just giving in and completely eavesdropping.

"Carol, please answer me," Tea pleaded, almost in tears. "Why didn't you tell Baxter about me and Griffen? Or at least warn us he didn't know, so *we* could tell him."

"Warn me is right. This is totally messed up," Baxter grunted out, his fists clenched.

Carol placed a hand on Baxter's shoulder, calming him for at least a moment.

"Well, Tea, sweetie, Baxter was in Paris studying. That's so far away," Carol said, with more confidence than Jenna thought the situation warranted.

It was unreal how much this woman was willing to view the world in her own ridiculous prism. Maybe Tea and Griffen could be patient with her, but Jenna was livid.

"Email, phone, carrier pigeon? Christ, Carol!" Griffen burst out in response to Carol's hemming and hawing.

"Don't talk to her like that," Baxter growled, pushing Griffen's shoulder.

"Bax, you're like a brother to me, too, but I won't hesitate to shut you up if I have to," Griffen responded angrily, his face dangerously close to Baxter's.

"Calm down, you two. I'm sorry Baxter found out this way, but I just couldn't figure out how to tell him. I was worried it would upset him so much. And he was so busy getting admitted to Carnegie Mellon for his business degree, and… Well, I thought there was a chance you guys might break up before he got back."

"Christ, Carol. Why would you think we would break up? Althea and I are engaged!" Griffen said more loudly than anyone expected.

"What the *fu*—" Baxter growled.

"Baxter! Language," Carol exclaimed.

"What the...*heck*, Nicky?"

"He goes by Griffen now," Tea said faintly.

"I don't care."

Jenna understood Baxter's shock. Griffen had been best friends with Carol's son, Jack, growing up, but Griffen's vagabond life after high school meant he'd never met Jack's wife. It was a surprise to everyone when Tea and Griffen's connection was revealed. Either way, the two fell in love so quickly, that even Carol had to accept their relationship.

Unfortunately though, Baxter wasn't present for any of that. All he saw was his dead brother's best friend suddenly in a serious relationship with his widow, without any warning. It was sure to upset even the calmest person. Considering Baxter was a notorious hothead, Jenna was grateful no furniture had been thrown, yet.

Jenna watched with worry as Griffen's jaw clenched and Tea looked completely distressed.

"Don't talk to Althea like that, Bax. She did nothing wrong," Griffen said to him in a rough tone.

"Sorry if I'm not being a gentleman, *Griffen*. Maybe I'm a little off my game, seeing as I'm just finding out you betrayed my brother. I'm kind of thinking I should kick *your* ass."

"Is everything okay?" Wyatt whispered in Jenna's ear, making her jump.

"No, it's *not* okay, Wyatt."

"Fuck right, it's not," Aubrey whispered.

"Auntie Bwey, am I allowed to say that word yet?" Johnny asked, making Jenna and Aubrey's eyes widen. In all the craziness, they'd forgotten he was witnessing all of this mess.

"We need to get Johnny out of here," Jenna said frantically.

"No. I want to stay," Johnny demanded. "Why are Uncle Bax and Gwiff fighting?"

He looked up at Jenna with wide, confused eyes and her heart squeezed in her chest. She loved this little boy like he was her own and always admired his ability to respond to all the changes he'd faced recently. Regardless, him seeing Baxter lose it over Griffen would be a lot for any kid to try to understand.

"It's no big deal, little man. They're just talking loudly," Jenna said lamely. She took Johnny's hand from Aubrey, who immediately headed over to Tea's side.

Jenna started looking around the room frantically for something to distract Johnny.

"How about we check out some of the presents people got you?"

"Here, I'll take him," Wyatt whispered in her ear, as he took Johnny's hand from hers with ease.

"Are you sure?"

"Don't worry. I got this. Your friend needs you."

"Oh, okay," but Jenna had no other words, because she was too lost in the relief of the moment.

It wasn't just nice having someone there for her, it was actually incredible to have this *specific* man stand in front of her and give her peace in a moment that was so disturbing to her.

She couldn't think of a single time in her life when a man had made her life easier. The thought that it was Wyatt McCoy delivering that comfort was downright stunning.

This feeling of happiness I have right now is a tad disconcerting, but not entirely unpleasant, she thought carefully, trying to pull her feelings into order.

"Besides, Johnny and I are old friends, right, buddy?"

Wyatt said smoothly.

"We are!"

Wyatt crouched down to talk to Johnny at his height.

"Have you been practicing the throwing tips I gave you a few weeks ago?"

"I have!" Johnny turned to Jenna. "Auntie Jenna?"

"What?" she stuttered out, completely entranced by Wyatt's kindness to the boy who was so dear to her. "Oh, right, sorry, Johnny. What is it?" Jenna had been staring at Wyatt without even realizing it. He was looking right back at her with an easy smile that rarely graced his face.

"Will everybody be okay if I hang out with Mr. McCoy?" Johnny asked her.

"You are such a good boy, Johnny. We'll be fine." Jenna looked over to Wyatt and quietly said, "Thank you so much. If I don't get over there soon, I'm worried Baxter will get punched."

"Is Griffen like that?"

"Not sure if he is, but Aubrey will cut anybody that makes her friends upset. Tea is beside herself right now — especially after everything Carol put her through since Jack died. I'm worried Aubrey might break Baxter's teeth if he says the wrong thing to Tea right now."

"Then you better head over there. I told you, I've got this."

"Thank you, Wyatt."

"My pleasure." Wyatt leaned toward her like he was going to kiss her cheek, but thought better of it and backed away. Even though she knew secrecy about their physical relationship was the smart idea, it made her feel oddly empty at the lost promise of his touch.

"Bye, Wyatt," she muttered, and rushed to Tea's side, as well. It wasn't a moment too soon, because Aubrey was already yelling at Baxter, her finger wagging in his face.

CHAPTER TWELVE

Aubrey dropped her packed duffel bag and purse beside their apartment door. With a sigh, she turned around to look at Jenna, a frown marring her delicate features.

"What's wrong, Brey? You're going to miss your flight to Denver if you don't get going."

"It just feels weird leaving for Christmas. I mean, we've spent it together every year — you know, with Tea and Johnny, and now…"

"I know. But she's got Griffen this year and it makes sense they want to spend it alone."

"I suppose so. They'll probably have lots of privacy now that Carol will be focused on Baxter."

"That's true. I'm glad everyone was able to wrap up Carol's party without anyone breaking someone's nose…you included, Brey."

"Can you blame me? Baxter's lucky I didn't clock him. I was pissed."

"Me, too, that's for sure."

"And we owe Wyatt one for keeping an eye on Johnny before Tea and Griffen decided to give up and call it a night."

Jenna began to study the woven material of her sweater at the mention of Wyatt — anything to avoid eye contact with Brey.

"Yeah, I guess we do," Jenna mumbled.

"Either way, it's all so weird this year — so different all of a sudden."

"Things couldn't stay the same forever, you know."

"I don't see why not, Jenna. You know I hate change, right?"

"Yes, you've made that clear about a million times," Jenna said, with a laugh, before her voice dropped and became more serious. "But things are always going to change. That's how life is. Everything ends, Aubrey."

"Merry Christmas to you, Scrooge McDuck. Jeez, Jenna. I don't want to leave you with this lack of holiday spirit."

"Oh, stop. I'm not being like Scrooge McDuck. I'm just being honest. Though, I wouldn't mind diving into my own gold coin pool. Look, Brey, if you're worried about my Christmas spirit, don't be. I'm fine."

"Of course I'm going to fret thinking about you. What will you do while I'm gone? You've been all over the place lately, babe. You make me want to nix this trip. Are you going to be okay?"

"Of course. What do you mean?"

"It's Christmas. And you've been acting funky lately. I hate the idea of you being here alone. What about going home to see your dad?"

"No, it's too late to get a flight, and we wouldn't know what to do with each other if I went down there."

Jenna always balked at the idea of returning to Georgia, ever since Chase started playing in Atlanta as a backup quarterback. She told herself it was silly to let him bother her so much — but the thought of being near him always sent a cold trickle of fear down her spine.

Even if Chase weren't in Georgia, visiting her father this particular Christmas was out of the question. The mere idea of seeing her father with the specter of breast cancer looming over her head, made her want to throw up. She hated the thought of putting him through any of that worry and sadness again. So she would just have to delay it as long as it was in her power to do so.

"Because you aren't even trying. I know it makes you sad to see your dad at Christmas. You know, what with it being the same time of year your mom died. But Jenna, at some point you both are going to need to learn how to deal with each other."

"At some point, is right. That point is not this year."

"Fine. Then why don't you come home with me to Denver? We can go skiing. Maybe invade some five-star snotty resort in our snow boots and pretend we're aliens that only learned the Finnish language before crashing here on earth."

"And we can clomp around the lobby asking for herring and a flux capacitor?"

"Ooh, nice. *Time-traveling*, Finnish-speaking aliens. Even better!" Aubrey said, jumping up and down, clearly very excited at the idea. "Just come home with me, Jenna. I'm worried about you."

"Oh please, you're not really." Yet, Jenna felt like her protest was halfhearted. Heck — it wasn't even a quarter-hearted.

Jenna knew Aubrey well enough to recognize when she was truly worried about her, and it made her feel terrible.

"Thank you for inviting me, Aubrey. It does sound like fun, but really, I'm okay. You never get to see your family. I know you're excited to see you parents and your brothers, please don't let me interfere with that."

"I don't want you to be by yourself."

"I won't be... I mean...I'll be fine."

Jenna suddenly felt her heart clench. God, how she hated secrets, and keeping so many from her best friend was terrible.

Why don't I tell her? she wondered. *Why don't I say, I just had my biopsy and a slew of other tests. Now I'm waiting for the results. I'm worried I may die in the same terrible way my mother did.*

I won't be alone because I've wrapped myself in the madness that is Wyatt McCoy. I don't want to tell anyone about any of what's going on, because I'm scared and confused and I don't know what to do with this odd — but good — feeling that keeps bubbling up inside of me when I'm near him. No matter how much I may be terrified right now, that man makes me feel alive. I don't know how to tell you because I don't understand any of this myself.

But those words didn't come. Instead, Jenna merely swallowed hard and put on her best sensible façade and said, "Aubrey, things have been nuts the last few months with everything going on with Tea and the investigation, and all these changes... I think it will be nice to just chill out by myself. I may binge watch a series or two on *Netflix*."

"That sounds so depressing. Promise you'll call me if you get lonely?"

"I promise, but I mean it, I'll be fine. Go home, spend Christmas with your huge family and all your hot mountain men brothers."

"Gross, don't talk about them that way. Ick. Though if you come with me, I will avert my eyes if you want to hook up with Kyle again."

"One time! One time, I hook up with a brother of yours, and you never let me forget it."

"Of course not. That's your punishment."

"It was eight years ago!"

"I'll reconsider after two more."

"I'll hold you to that. All your brothers are hot and I was young. You're not being fair."

"I think it's totally fair to torment you about this."

"Fine, I'll just keep waiting you out. All right, now get out of here, you. I can't start missing you if you won't leave."

"All right, all right, I'm leaving," Aubrey answered, turning to pull Jenna into her arms and kissing her cheek. This soft side of Aubrey always tugged at Jenna's emotions, and today it was even more powerful.

Jenna let the hug continue a little longer than usual. Finally, with a hard squeeze she released her and fought back the tears that wanted to break through her composure.

"Bye, Brey. I love you."

"I love you, too. I'll call you when I land, and on Christmas...and whenever else I feel like it."

"Okay, Brey. I'll be waiting."

Jenna watched as Aubrey grabbed her things and left their apartment.

Suddenly, she was completely alone, with nothing but the twinkling of their small, brightly decorated artificial tree to keep her company.

Jenna waited a moment to make sure Aubrey was really gone before heading into their kitchen to face her daunting mental to-do list.

Some list, she thought.

Go to the grocery store? Check.

Do laundry? Check.

Help Aubrey pack and get out of town? Check.
Contact doctor for results of invasive biopsy? Still not yet checked.

She'd be leaving to meet Wyatt at his place in about an hour, which didn't leave her much time. As scared and confused as she was, it gave her a surprising sense of peace to know she would soon be enjoying the distraction he always seemed to provide her.

They'd texted back and forth over the last couple of days. Those little stolen moments of communication had been the only thing that seemed to take her mind off her worry. She'd even let herself get a bit brazen — sending him a shot of her cleavage, with no face, of course, and the message:

Would you like these wrapped or unwrapped for Christmas?

That was the last text she'd sent him before he got on his plane ride back from Oakland, and she hoped it set the tone for lots more fun to happen between them.

Jenna had never talked or acted that way with a guy before. Yet, it came naturally to her with Wyatt. Above all, freeing herself from her own self-imposed rules and shackles at such a terrifying time seemed so important, that she couldn't imagine behaving any other way.

But until then, she had no choice but to make the call. She put on her glasses to read his phone number. When Dr. Kannan answered his direct line, it took Jenna a moment to speak.

"Hello, Dr. Kannan. It's Jenna Sutherland returning your call."

"Yes, Jenna, thank you. And I already told you — please call me Raj."

"Of course, Raj, sorry, I forgot," she answered, bouncing back and forth on her feet in agitation.

"I completely understand. I'm sure the last couple days

have been stressful for you. How are you feeling after the biopsy? Any tenderness?"

"A bit, but it's much better today."

"Good. Well, I have the results. I appreciate your patience. I'm sorry to have to deliver results over the phone, but..."

"It's no problem. I know you squeezed me in... Sorry, I didn't mean to interrupt you."

"It's fine. Well, Jenna, my initial thought was correct. We are dealing with fast growing phyllode tumors. At your age, that was a likely culprit. From the biopsy, ultrasound, and MRI, it appears we are looking at borderline phyllode tumors, meaning the cells are exhibiting both benign and malignant mutations."

"Oh," Jenna said softly. His words were floating in her head, as if suspended in a series of delicate bubbles that gently bumped each other, before coasting over to another corner of her brain.

This must have been how it began for my mother, she thought. *It would've started with just a series of words for her, too: aggressive, malignant, borderline, radiation.*

These words are no different than any other — a collection of consonants and vowels, pushed together to communicate something to another person. But there is nothing innocent about them. They just lead to even worse words, until the only one that had been left for my mother was the most viciously brutal one of all: death.

"Jenna, are you still there?"

"Yes, Raj. I'm sorry. Please go on."

"The good news is they are not clearly malignant. However, since they are borderline, we still have a lot to be worried about. We can't be certain what we're dealing with until they're removed through a lumpectomy. I will want to do that very soon. Followed by radiation to be sure we've gotten everything. It's very targeted, so you shouldn't have hair loss beyond the sight where we conduct the focused treatments. We do need to be vigilant though, Jenna. There's a chance with borderline phyllode tumors that they can metastasize, spreading cancer and malignancy throughout your body. Even if that doesn't occur, they can come back after surgery if we haven't effectively addressed the problem. These tumors can be very aggressive. I don't want to take any chances here..."

"Malignant phyllodes are what my mother had," she answered, her voice sounding distant to her own ears.

"I know. Your gynecologist, Laney, told me."

"And you think a lumpectomy is the way to go for me?"

"That is up to you. Lumpectomies with targeted radiation have been very successful, though a double mastectomy is the most powerful weapon I have."

She sat down, waiting for a moment in silence, before deciding.

"I'd like to try and keep my breasts. If this doesn't work, we can go from there," she whispered, the words seeming like they were coming from someone else, who was very far away.

It felt to Jenna as though she were watching a movie — seeing and hearing the conversation. She was judging the scene from the comfort of her theater seat. All the while having the safety of knowing she could leave when this horrible film was finally over.

But it wasn't going to end. The credits weren't going to run across any screen. She wouldn't watch the lights come back up.

Because this was *her* life, *her* story, and there was no guarantee of a happy ending.

"Very well, Jenna. A lot of women make that choice. I understand. However, it means the radiation course I mentioned is vital after the lumpectomy. The size of your available breast tissue will actually increase the chances I can remove a sufficient amount of the area surrounding the tumors, too."

"Finally having huge boobs will make my life easier," she said, with a dry laugh.

"I can't promise that, Jenna, but we'll get to the bottom of this. I wish I could've told you they were definitely benign and that we'll be out of the woods soon. But we're just going to have to fight some more, is all."

"Fight? I can do that," she said.

"Good. Now, I'd really like to get this lumpectomy scheduled right away. Unfortunately, Christmas Eve is only a couple of days away, and I don't think I have to tell you that scheduling procedures around the holidays is a nightmare. I spoke to my team already, in the hopes you wanted to go ahead and schedule. The soonest we can see you is January third."

"That works," she answered. Aubrey was set to be in Denver until January sixth. Jenna would let her know then, after the procedure was over. She saw no reason to worry everyone for no reason.

"You'll need to have a couple weeks of recovery and be prepared for the radiation course. After I have a chance to look more closely at these tumors and at your body's response to their removal and treatment, we will know if…"

"There is cancer?"

"Right. It will also let us know if we've actually gotten rid of any and all concerning tissue. Now that we have a plan, I'll just need you to tell me who will be accompanying you, so I can pass that information on to my nurses."

"No one's coming. I'm not planning on having anyone there with me for the procedure. I'll make arrangements for a car service to bring me home."

"Oh, Jenna, I'm not comfortable with that."

"We have this under control, Raj. I don't want to worry anyone. I'll sign a release…"

Out of nowhere, Jenna felt someone from behind her grab the phone and remove it from her hand, causing her to jump out of her seat with a gasp, before spinning around in terror.

"What the hell…" she said in shock at seeing Trey standing behind her, a worried look on his face. "Trey, give me back the phone."

But he was already speaking to Dr. Kannan.

"This is her friend, Trey Adler. Hello. No, I will call you Dr. Kannan. That works for me. Don't worry. I'll be there with Jenna. Yes, I'll take her home. Of course, thank you. Let me give you back to her."

Trey held the phone out to her, simply waiting for her to take it back from him. She was still agape with shock, but she finally managed to grab it from him and struggle out a few words again.

"Thank you, Raj."

"You're welcome, Jenna. There's nothing to do now but wait. So, please try to relax and enjoy your holidays."

"I'll try. Happy Holidays to you, too, Raj."

Jenna hung up and slowly turned to look at Trey's face, guilt rushing through her at being caught with her secret.

Trey put down his coat on the kitchen table and Jenna jumped with nervous surprise.

"A little jittery, huh, Jenna?" he asked.

"Yeah, a little, I guess — especially when you barge into my apartment like this."

"I didn't barge in…Aubrey let me into the building when I passed her in the parking lot."

He looked at her intently enough to convince her he'd heard every word of her conversation and Jenna felt the features of her face fall in resignation. Somehow, keeping her fear a secret from everyone had made her feel more in control of the situation, but that had been a foolish crutch. She knew that now.

"Why don't you have a seat, Jenna," Trey asked, pulling out a chair for her.

"Huh?" she asked ineloquently, only to feel him push her down into the chair.

"What are we drinking?"

"You want a drink, Trey?"

"Sure. You want one, too. Where do you keep the hooch?"

"Cabinet next to the fridge. Glasses are to the right of that," she answered, almost dazed by his casual ease as he walked around her apartment, when her own emotions were tumbling over themselves with fear and dread that he would reveal her secret to everyone they knew.

"Great."

Trey moved quickly around her kitchen as though it were completely ordinary for him to be there.

He was in jeans and a plain white tee shirt that revealed multiple tattoos up and down both arms. Jenna chose to stare at those colorful markings instead of reflecting on the inevitable conversation she still wasn't ready to have.

Before she knew it though, he was sitting at the table and looking at her again with friendly concern that sent a spasm through her chest.

"I went with bourbon," he said simply, placing the bottle down on the table along with two half full glasses. Handing her one, he clinked it with his own, "Cheers."

"Cheers," she mumbled, taking a sip and counting each

silent second. He didn't speak for some time. Instead, he let her drink her bourbon while he leaned back in his chair sipping his own.

Oddly, his patience was almost maddening and Jenna couldn't bear the quiet anymore.

"What brings you here, Trey?"

"Well, I needed to get some stuff for Tea for Christmas. She said you have all the holiday stuff, not her."

"I do, I hadn't even thought about that. Ever since Jack died suddenly right before Christmas six years ago, she couldn't be near the stuff without having a panic attack. That's why it's all here."

"Wow, that's too bad. Well, I guess she's trying to rip the *Band-Aid* off," he answered simply, taking a last sip of his drink and refilling their glasses.

"Yeah, it looks like it. So you're spending the holidays with them?"

"Christmas Eve and New Year's Day, at least. They invited me to everything, but I figure they need some privacy. New family and all."

"You're pretty settled in here in Pittsburgh, then?"

"For a while. The feds still need help trying to figure out who bribed David. He claims not to know. Either he's more terrified of them than the US Government, or he really has no clue."

"God, I can't believe that all of that is still going on."

"It feels like that to you, but this case is still a baby, trust me."

"How do you know?"

"I just do," he said, with a hard edge to his voice.

"Tea and Griffen aren't worried about it, are they?"

"I don't think so. What are you doing for Christmas? You

know Tea said you were welcome to join us for Christmas Eve."

"I know."

"And Aubrey said you have a computer you need fixed when she let me in?" Trey continued.

"She was probably trying to get you to service something else. She thinks sex is the cure for any bad mood."

"I can't say I disagree — generally speaking. But I don't think it would help your situation right now. I mean..."

"You heard everything, huh?" Jenna leaned back in her seat and watched him. He had a calming influence on her, like a brother she never had.

Trey had loads of money, classic good looks, and a lean muscular body, offset by piercings and numerous tattoos. Not surprisingly, most people thought she was insane for only wanting to be his friend. Yet, they'd hit it off in a purely platonic way ever since he came to Pittsburgh to continue assisting in the investigation into Jack Taylor's death. Which meant she must be the only woman in America — hell, the entire world — that didn't want to sleep with him.

"I did. I'm sorry. But in my defense, I am constantly listening in on things."

"That's your defense?" she asked, with a snort.

"I didn't say it was a good one. It's a tool of my trade."

"You mean your computer hacker, residing in the gray area of the law, trade?"

"Something like that," he answered with a small smile. "Listening in or not, I had a feeling something was bothering you when we talked at the Christmas party. It also now makes a lot more sense why you're hooking up with that McCoy guy. He didn't seem like someone I pictured you dating."

"What are you talking about, Trey?"

"I saw you with him, leaving the coatroom at Carol's party, right before all hell broke loose."

"Oh, God." Jenna threw her face in her hands, completely mortified.

"I'm guessing no one else knows about you two?"

"There's nothing to know."

"There's not? You two didn't seem like 'nothing' to me. But what do I know? Look, do what feels right for you right now. You've got a lot going on."

"Are you always so nosy?"

"Yeah, pretty much."

"Does that mean you expect me to tell you all about what you heard?"

"Not if you don't want to."

"I appreciate that. Please don't tell anyone about any of this. I'm just not ready for them to know."

"It's your decision to make, so I'll keep it to myself. How about you get me some Christmas decorations so you can have some time to yourself?" he asked gently, and she smiled.

After gathering years of holiday decorations, they walked out to his car and loaded it up with lights, figurines, and any other tacky festive goodies they could find.

Jenna looked at him and said, "Thank you, Trey."

"For what?"

"For talking to me, for taking me to my procedure when it comes…"

"Of course, I'm your friend, Jenna. I'm not going anywhere."

"You seem like such a tough guy, it's all a bit surprising."

He leaned forward and whispered in her ear, "I like nice girls, but shh, don't tell anyone. Come here, you," he added, pulling her into a hug that smelled like leather and comfort.

Jenna allowed one tear to slide down her cold cheek, before rubbing it off on his jacket and backing away.

"You'll be all right, Jenna?"

"I hope so. Thanks," she answered with a soft smile that he returned.

"Call or text me if you need anything."

She nodded and walked away. After she'd made it almost halfway through the parking lot Trey yelled after her, "And let me know when you want me to pick you up after the New Year, okay?"

"Okay, bye," she said, with a smile and a wave.

Her emotions still felt incredibly raw as she turned back toward her building. Jenna had only made it about ten more yards before she saw Wyatt waiting for her, barely hidden behind the back end of his SUV.

She gasped a bit in surprise as she took him in — his arms were crossed and the expression on his face was one of pure fury.

"Jesus, Wyatt, you scared the hell out of me," Jenna said to him, her eyebrows raised and a hand to her heart in a cartoonish image of shock. Her cheeks were pink from the cold and her eyes a little red.

She looked beautiful to him, but he didn't let himself care. He was too busy feeling like punching a wall, or strangling her tattooed clandestine visitor.

"Get inside and get your stuff, Jenna."

"Oh, it's Jenna now, is it? Not Doc? What are you doing here? I thought we were meeting at your place?"

"I said get inside — now. Unless you want me to lose my

shit in your parking lot."

"Don't tell me what to do, Wyatt."

"It looks like maybe I have to, seeing as how I'm gone for one game and you're all over that asshole."

"You're kidding, right?"

"Fuck no, I'm not kidding. Is that why you said you didn't want anything to do with me after New Year's? Because that guy is coming by to pick you up?"

"That's what you think that was?"

"It sure as hell is what it looked like. If it's not, then just tell me what you're really up to with him."

"Right, because that's the only possible reason why he'd be here. I'm not really enjoying being around you right now, you know. I guess you're perfect and don't have anything you keep to yourself."

Wyatt couldn't speak. Everything was getting out of his control so quickly. He'd practically raced to Jenna's apartment from the airport. She was all he could think about while he was gone, though he didn't risk asking himself why he felt that way.

Her opinion about his shoulder had been the last thing on his mind. His mind had played over multiple scenarios of how she'd act when he saw her again, but none of them involved her hugging a guy who was far too close a friend for Wyatt's taste. They also didn't include her freezing him out like this.

It felt to him like she was making all the calls on the field, and he'd never gotten a chance to see the playbook.

How can one person turn everything upside down for me so quickly? He wondered.

All he'd understood was he needed to see her, especially after she sent him that picture of her chest. He felt like he was fourteen again, drooling over a perfect pair of tits.

It had shocked him how much he'd actually missed her.

He didn't even go home first. Instead, he'd headed straight to her apartment to start their planned holiday together. He was even excited to talk to her about the game.

Had she watched it? Did she notice how much better I'm playing right now?

"Oh, so now you're silent. Fine, Wyatt. You're unreal. I'm going inside now, by the way. Not because you told me to, but because I'm cold, I've had a shitty morning, and I *want* to go inside. You can stay here by your car and brood by yourself until the cows come home, for all I care."

Jenna walked briskly into her apartment and Wyatt stalked after her.

She opened her door and he could see her hand shaking slightly on the knob.

It was clear she was upset and part of him wanted to comfort her, but the rest of him was too overcome with frustration and anger to do anything but seethe. He needed her to be out of control, too — for her to remember he affected her, as well. Maybe she was mad, but he had to *make* her be glad to see him.

She threw off her coat, her back to him. Wyatt tossed his jacket on top of hers. This conversation wasn't over.

"I came here because I was looking forward to seeing you and getting our holidays started. But it looks like *you* didn't even notice I was gone," he growled out to her.

She spun around so quickly, that her blonde hair whipped aside with her, slapping her cheek. Gone was her cool exterior. Everything about her was raging and hot.

She pushed his chest forcefully and said, "Maybe I was thinking about *you* while you were away. Maybe I couldn't wait to go and see you. Maybe I was sure that seeing you would turn this day around. Maybe you'd know I felt that way if you let me speak before you started acting like a Neanderthal."

"But you touched him. You were so nice to him," Wyatt answered, but it came out quiet and almost confused.

"I can hug a friend. That's not what this is about."

"What *is* this about then, Jenna?"

"It's about you not knowing how to be with me — you're trying to direct what I do like I'm some rookie tight end. That's not how this will go between us."

"So you have me all pegged then? You think I've always had everything my way? Had the world handed to me?"

"The way you're acting right now? I'm thinking you haven't had the world handed to you. No it seems more like the world has waited on its knees at your front door begging for you to take everything wonderful it can give you. Well. My life's not like that and *I'm* not going to be like that with you."

"That's not how my life has been and that's not how I see you."

"It sure feels that way. What with you showing up here, furious over a conversation, that is *none* of your business."

"A conversation? You were all over each other."

"It was a hug, and it's still none of your business. You have no claim on me. You can't tell me what to do."

"You're mine for two weeks, so yes, I do have a claim on you."

"If you're trying to make me like you, Wyatt, you have a really fucked up way of doing it."

"You do like me. I know you do. More than that, I know you want me."

Jenna gripped Wyatt's tee shirt in her fists and pushed his back firmly against the wall by the front door.

"I don't want you, Wyatt."

Wyatt let her have her mini takeover for a moment. She

searched his face with hers, almost hesitant.

"You're a terrible fucking liar, Doc. Tell me, now that you've got me here, what are you gonna do with me?" he taunted. She kept staring at his lips until he took over again. He grabbed her ass with both hands and turned quickly, pressing her up against the same wall.

"Well, then, McCoy. What are you gonna do with *me*?" Jenna challenged back.

Wyatt slid his right hand around her body, then slowly running his fingers down the front of her jeans. She was hot through the thick cotton and responded almost immediately to his touch.

"Tell me…"

"Tell you what?"

"Tell me you want me."

"No," she sputtered at him, squirming against his hand. Wyatt popped open the top of her jeans and unzipped them so he could slip his hand into her panties. Her clit was already hard and swollen against his fingers. He rubbed it with his thumb as he curved two fingers inside of her. Jenna arched her body towards him, moaning despite herself. No matter what she said to him, her hot and wet body betrayed her. Wyatt could feel her already tightening around his pumping fingers and the circular movements of his thumb.

With his left hand he gripped her jaw, forcing her to look in his eyes, "Tell me you like the way I make you feel."

"No." She squirmed against his hand, clearly seeking sexual release, but he had her pinned firmly with the length of his body against hers and his hands, preventing her from controlling the motion.

"Tell…me…you…want…me."

"Why?" she demanded back. Her blue eyes sparkling with

anger, but it was clear she was desperate.

"Because I said so and...because I want to hear it...Jenna." He stroked her harder with his thumb, suddenly twisting his two fingers inside her until she was quivering against him.

"Y-yes. Yes! I want you so bad it makes me crazy, Wyatt. Are you happy now, you son of a bitch?"

"Very," and with a smile on his face, he thrust a third finger deeply inside her, caressing her to climax with his thumb.

He did need to hear it — loved watching her writhe against the hard wall, her perfect wavy blonde hair suddenly in complete disarray. Wyatt knew he was falling apart, too, but he wasn't sure he wanted to put himself back together again.

He released his hand from her jeans and she looked at him intently.

"Why do you care if I want you, Wyatt?"

"I don't know why, but I do care...very much," he answered, stepping away from her. He could smell her on his hand as he ran it through his hair, and it made him feel even more insane.

Everything was getting away from him so quickly. Yet, he couldn't make himself worry about it very much.

"I'm still mad at you, you know," she said quietly, looking up and trying to glare at him. She zipped her jeans closed and somehow managed to make it look indignant. Wyatt liked that a lot about her.

"You can't be that mad at me. I think you got over it."

"Charming," she snipped out, but a smile tickled her mouth.

"Are you still coming back with me?"

"I don't know, yet," she said, staring at her bedroom door.

He leaned toward her, placing his hands on her cheeks and forcing her to gaze at him again. His touch was gentler now, stroking the soft flesh of her lovely face until her eyes softened slightly. Her jaw was still set in a firm, stubborn line and she was breathing heavily, apparently with both desire and barely leashed anger.

"You're still angry, Doc. I get it. I'm kind of pissed, too, you know."

Her eyes narrowed and she huffed out a hard breath, wiggling her head in an attempt to free her face from his grip, but he tightened his hold and wouldn't let her go.

"Oh no, you don't," Wyatt whispered. Then he ran his thumb across her bottom lip slowly, feeling the gentle swell of the rosy, delicate skin, before leaning down. His lips were almost touching hers when he whispered, "I don't want you to be mad at me, Doc."

She began to open her mouth to speak, but he pressed his mouth on hers before she could make a sound. His tongue charted the path where his thumb had been, separating the tight line of her mouth, until she finally gave way to him.

Caressing her lips with his, tasting her tongue with his own, he gradually brought her back to the moment with him. She sighed slightly, and Wyatt let himself ease away from her.

Her hostility was gone. In its place were her soft blue eyes and gently parted lips.

"That's more like it, belleza. Let's get going. I hope you packed everything you need, because I'm not letting you out of my sight for a minute. Do you understand me?"

"I suppose I do," she said crisply.

"I'll carry your bag."

"No way, Wyatt. Not with the way you're still favoring that shoulder. You need to rest it if you want to keep improving your throw."

"You watched the game?" he asked, a smile cracking at his cheeks. "And you think I'm improving, huh?"

"Of course I watched you play. I've always watched you."

"You have?" his heart squeezed at the thought she'd been training her pretty eyes, and sharp mind, on him for years.

"Yes, ever since you started playing in televised games. And your performance really has been great lately."

Jenna disappeared into her room and emerged with a full duffle bag. With her head held high, she started to walk toward the front door.

"Not so fast," Wyatt said quickly, taking the bag and throwing it over his left shoulder while grabbing her hand in his right one. With a tug, he brought her flush against his side and rubbed his nose against her cheek until she giggled.

"Much better. Now get comfortable, because I'm not letting you out of my grasp, either," he added, before leading her out of her apartment.

CHAPTER THIRTEEN

Wyatt opened the door to his house for Jenna and she tried to force herself to relax. Even though she'd spent most of the short ride from her apartment collecting her thoughts, her nerves were still jangling inside of her. The bad news from her doctor and her fight with Wyatt had left her more unsettled than she'd been in years.

"Well, Doc, I guess you remember your way around, but here's the living room through here..."

Jenna's mouth dropped open at the sight of a massive tree, covered in lights and sparkling decorations. She walked toward it with slow, hesitant steps, as though the mirage would disappear if she walked too closely to it. Her toe knocked a box, drawing her eyes downward. At her feet one box held some goofy and well-worn ornaments, while a second box held others still in their packaging.

Her eyes shifted to the large bay window at the back of the room. The sparkling reflection of the tree in the glass gave way to an almost rural view of woods and snow covered trees, arching over the ice-specked Allegheny River. Jenna knew they were mere minutes from downtown Pittsburgh, but she felt like they were in their own isolated woodland cabin, where no one — and nothing — could ever burst their delicate little bubble. The whole sight sent a rush of emotions washing through her body.

"Um, Wyatt, does the White House know you stole their Christmas tree?" she asked, with a voice she didn't quite recognize.

"Too big?"

"Not if you're trying to build a habitat for the entire bird population of Pittsburgh through the winter."

Wyatt laughed and rubbed the back of his neck awkwardly before looking at her again.

"I had it delivered while I was gone. My assistant worked with a local nursery that brought it here and decorated the tree for us. I asked for the biggest tree they could fit in the room. I don't know, I thought if you were willing to spend Christmas with me, the least I could do was make it nice for you... If you don't like it, I can get something else."

Jenna felt a powerful twisting sensation in her chest and crossed the room to Wyatt quickly, not wanting him to misinterpret her response.

"No, please don't change a thing. I like it all very much. It's thawing out all my earlier grumpiness," she assured him, tentatively putting her fingers on his waist. Her feelings were such a jumble, but she knew she had to touch him.

"Then it was well worth it," he said, before wrapping his arms around her and nibbling at her neck. "I can get a bigger one if you want. Will that make you even happier? Would it make you want to walk around naked for the rest of the day?"

"Oh, no need for that. This tree is plenty big enough. Besides, if you want me naked, I think you and I both know no matter how mad I may get at you, you probably just need to ask," she said, with a teasing tickle of his waist.

"You've got it."

"I'm curious, though, if the nursery decorated the tree for us, what's with all these ornaments still in their boxes?"

"Some are from when I was a kid, the others are new ones I had them leave off the tree. I thought we'd want to hang some ourselves. Does that work?" He paused, staring at her with concern and asked, "Why do you look sad?"

"No, I'm happy. It's just been a long time since I can remember making good *new* Christmas memories."

"Why?"

"My mom died around Christmas, so I always had to be careful about it with my dad. Then Tea's husband died before Christmas, too, so I just treated the holiday the same way with her after that. You know, trying to be sensitive to her feelings."

"What about your feelings?"

"Oh… Those don't matter. I can take it. Someone has to be the strong one. It's just, looking at this…I forgot how beautiful it all could be."

"What would you have done if you weren't here with me?"

"I wasn't going to be rolling around with Trey, if that's what you're trying to stir up, Wyatt."

His jaw clenched and his eyes narrowed so quickly that Jenna felt instantly guilty. She reached her arms around his back and pulled him more closely to her.

"Calm down, Wyatt, I was just kidding. It was a bad joke. I'm sorry. I would've stayed by myself in the apartment."

"But you'd be all alone."

"I figured I can handle a Christmas by myself."

"Just because you *can* handle the world a certain way, doesn't mean you have to."

"You make a good point, Mr. McCoy. But that's enough of

all this sappiness. How about we go for a swim together again?"

"A swim?"

"I know you don't have some elaborate indoor pool here, but I would love to take a dip in your Olympic-sized tub."

"Would you now?"

"I may have been fantasizing about it since I brushed my teeth in there."

"Okay, but there's no lifeguard on duty, you'll have to rely on me to keep you safe."

"You'd *better* be in there. That's a major part of the fantasy."

Wyatt smiled and led her into his massive bathroom and began to run the water for them.

"My sister loves to throw all kinds of crazy girly shit in here when she visits. Check out that closet over there."

"'Crazy girly shit' sounds nice," Jenna teased.

After ransacking the closet, she placed the fancy shampoo and conditioner she'd found on the side of the tub and began filling the running water with bath salts and bubble bath. She stood up after lighting a few candles from the closet, when she felt Wyatt's hands at the edges of her sweater, lifting it over her head.

"Can this be a part of your fantasy?" he whispered against her bare neck, before kissing and licking her skin.

"Definitely."

Jenna turned around and unbuttoned his shirt, sliding it down his arms slowly. Wyatt began unfastening her jeans, but he hesitated at the zipper.

"So...we're cool?" he asked.

"Wyatt, I didn't like the way you acted earlier, but I could've been more understanding. I can only imagine how I would've felt if I walked up and saw you hugging that Olivia woman." Jenna removed her bra, then kicked off her shoes and reached for the button of his jeans.

"There's nothing going on with me and her," he answered with a bit of defensiveness in his tone, before pulling down her zipper and sliding her jeans down her legs. Jenna leaned on him slightly as she stepped out of one leg and then the other. Wyatt took advantage of his slightly crouched position to lick and nibble at one of her nipples, then the other.

"And nothing's going on with me and Trey," Jenna groaned out. "You still didn't want to see that. I get it. You aren't totally off the hook, but I understand. So I'm sorry I lost my temper."

"Don't be. I kind of liked it," he said, looking up at her with his face nestled between her breasts.

"What? You're crazy." Jenna laughed. Wyatt stood, still gazing at her left breast and stroking it with his hand, his thumb rubbing roughly over her nipple.

"I don't know, maybe I am." He looked into her eyes again. "Thing is, you always try to be so cool and calm. Collected. I can tell you want to keep yourself distant from me. Hell, you basically spent weeks telling me you wanted nothing to do with me. But I know I have an effect on you. I like that I drive you nuts. It's hot to see you get all worked up because of me — out of control. I know other people don't affect you like that... What can I say? I'm messed up."

Jenna swallowed around the lump that seemed lodged in her throat, before responding.

"Come on, you messed up thing. Let's get wet. That is if you can leave my chest alone long enough to get in the tub."

"I'll try," he answered with a chuckle, standing in front of her and placing a hand over each breast. "You're the one who texted me that these were my Christmas presents. They're the best gifts I've ever gotten. I intend to play with them as much as possible." Wyatt moved his face so it was planted fully between her breasts, pressing them against his cheeks. He hummed happily, suddenly moving his head quickly back and forth against the mounds of flesh, until all she could see was his hair and her own shaking breasts, as he reveled cheerfully in her body.

The silly attention made Jenna laugh out loud. She finally awkwardly bent forward to unbutton his jeans, effectively separating him from her bosom. He pouted at her, standing up with a sigh.

Wyatt looked despondently at her chest, adding, "Goodbye...for now." He quickly shucked off his jeans, followed by his underwear. Jenna stripped down the rest of the way herself, before he helped her into the steaming water.

There were about fifty scents swirling around their bodies, and Jenna loved every one of them. Wyatt sat down first and pulled her onto his lap, but his stiff erection was already bumping distractingly on her rear end. Jenna giggled at the sensation of his hard, slippery cock slapping and rubbing against her skin in the warm water.

"Don't laugh, woman. It's your fault, being all sexy and naked. You're not the only one here that fantasized about this."

Jenna turned around and faced him, moving her legs to straddle his hips. His responding groan filled her with joy and encouraged her to press her body more fully against him.

"Dammit!"

"What's wrong, Wyatt?"

"I didn't grab a condom. Hold on."

He began to move but Jenna gently pressed his chest, pushing him back down.

"Do you not want to?" he asked, clearly confused, and a bit distressed.

"No. I do. I thought about this while you were gone. I'm clean, and you have regular physicals. Are you…"

"Totally clean. I submit to all the tests, including STD tests. Are you saying what I hope you're saying?"

"I am. I'm on birth control, an IUD…" Jenna suddenly felt so shy, but continued, "I want to feel you bare inside of me, Wyatt. So…"

Before Jenna could say another word, Wyatt's mouth was on hers and his hands were tightly wound in her hair. As he pressed his body completely against hers, the water began sloshing against the sides of the tub. Wyatt moved his mouth down her jawline and sucked on her neck with a gentle pressure that made her pussy spasm in response.

"I guess that means you like my idea," Jenna managed to say, even though it was hard to formulate a thought. Wyatt simply grunted in return.

He leaned back to look at her, his eyes glowing like molten bronze, practically singeing her flesh. His hands moved to her hips, fingers wrapping around her hip bones and lifting her so that he was perched just at the cusp of her entrance. She pressed her hands on the edge of the tub on either side of his shoulders, balancing above him.

"Tell me you want me, Wyatt," she requested. Hovering above him, she looked in his eyes, wanting to give him a taste of his own medicine.

"You don't have to ask me for that. I want you so much, it's a little scary, Doc. And I like you, too, probably more than I should."

"Good," Jenna whispered. She nodded slightly and he began to slide into her. She could feel every part of his length inside of her, and with each inch, he was erasing the pain and fear of the day. Her hands moved to his hair, clutching it in her fists as she pushed herself down onto him.

His eyes never left hers as he gently eased in and out of her body. It was beautiful and sweet, but the excruciating cocktail of the day made Jenna need more...so much more. She wanted this water and his body to wash away everything ugly and leave nothing but the two of them behind.

She bounced up and down on him clumsily, but with determination. Wyatt noticed and quickly took over again. He pulled her off him, causing a disappointed grumble to escape from her lips. A wicked smile played on his mouth, before he moved his hands to her waist. Wyatt rose to his knees and turned her body to face away from him. She could feel his wet hands skim along her sides and then arms, until they covered hers.

Jenna was impatient, eager to have him inside of her again. She could feel his erection against her ass and squirmed backward to try and get closer, but his arms and torso were pinning her in place.

She felt his hot whisper in her ear, as he leaned over her, securing her hands to the edge of the tub. "You're right, I *am* obsessed with your breasts."

He paused, letting his hands caress the sides of her chest. But he didn't tease or touch them. She released a frustrated moan and pressed back against him again. A quick swat on her bottom made her jump. Jenna almost lost her balance, but Wyatt grabbed her quickly at her bent hips until she was steady on her knees.

"But, I also like this view. I'd hate to miss the chance to touch this perfect ass," he growled out, grasping the globes of her bottom firmly. Suddenly, he was inside her again. Jenna immediately groaned in pleasure. From this new angle, she could feel him even more completely than before. Each perfect inch of him, entering her so deeply she never wanted the feeling to end.

She gripped the edge of the tub, resting her hot cheek on its cool marble for a moment before lifting up on her hands to arch her body back and meet his powerful thrusts. Wyatt's strong fingers continued to grip the flesh of her ass, as he used his hold to gain leverage and increase his pace.

Soapy water swirled around them, creating a whirlpool, sucking and pushing at their bodies. Jenna felt him move his hands, one to her shoulder, while the other took a firm grasp of her hair and tugged on it hard. This allowed him to hit a point even more deeply inside her, causing her to scream out loud.

Electricity shot straight through to her core, as Wyatt leaned his large body across her back, moving his arms to hold her around her waist. He growled against the skin of her shoulder, biting it and pushing in short, hard thrusts until her own shouts were reverberating against the tile walls. They joined with his groans — creating an overwhelming crescendo of harmonious sound.

Wyatt released a deep grunt and she felt him spasm inside of her. She tensed and clenched around him, until her whole body went limp beneath him.

He breathed deeply, before sitting back against the tub, taking her with him. Returning her to his lap, he wrapped his arms around her from behind. Jenna grasped his hands, winding her fingers into his.

"You have such great ideas, Doc," Wyatt whispered, with a chuckle against her neck. Jenna giggled in return, resting the back of her head on his chest. He released her and began rubbing her shoulders. His hands began stroking down her arms and along her back, until she almost purred with pleasure. Sliding down the front of his body, she wet her hair with the water between his legs. When she sat back up, Wyatt began to rub shampoo into her hair.

"I hope washing my hair was a part of your tub fantasy, because it was definitely in mine."

"Making you feel good and having you at my mercy was my vision. This works for that," he said lightly.

Wyatt massaged her scalp with his strong fingers, and the relaxation she felt after her orgasm and from the pleasurable kneading of his fingertips was exquisite. The pain and fear of the day was ebbing away with each touch of Wyatt's hands on her scalp. The added tickling of his hairs against her smooth legs made her feel wrapped in protection from the rest of the world. The practical voice in her head was telling her she should hold back, but she couldn't make herself do it. It was *this* man that was making her feel so good.

Another voice in her head kept reminding her she may never feel this way again. It was getting louder and more overpowering with every one of Wyatt's insistent touches. Maybe he was her personal pied piper. In that case, for the next several days, Jenna was going to follow him anywhere he led her — even if it was right off a cliff.

After she rinsed the shampoo out and started to apply conditioner to her hair, Wyatt's hands began roaming over the rest of her body. He explored every inch of her, from her toes to her head, and then up again.

"Are you giving me an exam, Wyatt?" Jenna teased, working a small tangle out of her hair as she indulged in the sensuous slide of his hands on her body. After so many terrifying hours of *actual* examinations, she was grateful to have her body be her own again — even if only for these brief few days with Wyatt.

She had to wonder, *How many scared patients have I scrutinized objectively like my doctors have done with me? How many people were trying to hide their worry, while I poked and prodded them without taking the time to understand what my seemingly nebulous words could do to them, and their way of life? Was Wyatt one of them? Did I fail him in some way?*

His words broke through her spiral of anxiety.

"We've never had any time to just enjoy each other. I'm trying to make the most of this." His left hand settled on her knee, toying lightly with the raised flesh that was the remaining evidence of her arthroscopic surgery.

"That's a hell of a scar, Doc."

"It's from my knee surgery, but I guess you already knew that?"

"I did. Though I didn't get many details."

"I blew out both my ACL and MCL in this knee in the second half of a basketball game in college. We'd made it to the Elite Eight round of the championships my junior year. We were down five points with three minutes to go. I was a shooting guard and went up for a simple jump shot, just like I'd done a thousand times before. I came down funny and that was all she wrote. I couldn't walk and it took all my strength to keep from crying in front of all those people. They carted me off on a stretcher, it was all pretty humiliating."

"And you had to have surgery?"

"Yes, and a year of rehab. We lost the game, too. So it sucked all around."

"Were you able to play again?"

"Not competitively, no. My body was never the same after it happened."

"Did you miss it?"

"The game?" Jenna felt him nod slightly behind her. "Certain things, yes. My whole life had been in the world of competitive sports. It was how I related to my dad...and pretty much everyone else in the world, too. Everything was regimented and predictable. I always knew what the next day would hold, and that my body could provide me the security I needed to make a future for myself. All of that vanished with one misstep."

He went silent behind her, taking several deep breaths behind her, before asking, "Then you get why I don't want to have surgery?" he asked, gently rubbing the thin, raised skin on her knee with his thumb in a way that was at once soothing, yet also unsettling.

"I guess I do."

"All that security and predictability? I need that, too, but I don't have a brain like yours to fall back on. This game is all I can do. I'm not just a bum shoulder."

Her stomach flipped a bit at the reminder of Richard's advice. Maybe she hadn't taken into account the whole person when she examined Wyatt.

"No you aren't, Wyatt. I know that. I would've loved not to have that surgery. Thing is, it was the injury, not the surgery, that broke me."

He pulled her back flush against his front, and she could feel his chest move as he cleared his throat.

"I don't think you're broken, Doc." Wyatt leaned his head forward, nuzzling his face into her neck. "I think you're pretty amazing."

Bacon was sizzling and popping vigorously in a pan as Wyatt sang quietly to himself in his kitchen. He was also dancing a bit, mainly because he was only wearing a pair of boxer briefs, which required some careful cooking on his part to avoid burning himself.

It was early Christmas morning and he was making breakfast for himself and Jenna while she still slept. He'd kept her up pretty late, alternately watching Christmas movies on TV and delighting in her body as much as he could. The last two days had been great, probably too enjoyable, based on how quickly he was growing accustomed to having her around.

There was something very different about her. She made him forget about his shoulder, his career, everything. That was dangerous, he knew. But for now, he was going to let himself enjoy the holiday with her and sort everything out later.

While flipping the bacon, his phone buzzed against his granite countertop, declaring Jason Myers had finally called him back. Jason had been Wyatt's go-to wide receiver and one of his best friends while he was at UT. He also had the unique qualification of having played for Jenna's father in high school. Wyatt had left a message with Jason the day after he'd kissed Jenna the first time. Her indication at the ice-skating rink that a football player in high school had hurt her somehow grabbed his attention and wouldn't let go. Wyatt turned down the burner and grabbed his phone quickly.

"Jason, what's up? Thanks for calling me back."

"You're welcome, man. Sorry it took me so long. Ever since I joined the Canadian Football League, I feel like I never have much free time anymore. But I have today off. I hope it's okay I called you so early on Christmas."

"No problem, this is perfect."

"Your message said you want to know about Coach Sutherland?"

"Sort of. It's more that I want to know about his daughter. Jenna."

"Oh right. I heard she moved to Pittsburgh a while back. Do you know her?"

"She's my...friend."

"Wow, small world. That's great. How's she doing?"

"Pretty well, but I do really want to know about when she was in high school. It's important."

"Um, okay. Well, she was a junior when I was a sophomore, and she graduated a year early, so I didn't really know her too well. I liked her a lot, though. She really knew her shit — was practically our assistant coach. I remember her being on the sidelines at every practice and games, too. But she was less involved the season before she graduated."

"Why do you think that was?"

"Well, there were rumors..."

"What rumors?" Wyatt asked quickly, squeezing the spatula in his hand so hard that he had to put it down and flex his fingers until the joints stopped hurting.

"I don't know. It was a long time ago. She was always nice to me. I don't want to talk shit when I don't know anything for sure..."

"Jason, just tell me. I won't use what you say to hurt her."

"People saw her with this dude, Chase. He kept it on the down-low, but it was a small town. She was a nice girl, but really shy and totally separated from the rest of the school..."

"Dude, just say it."

"Chill out, man. Why the fuck do you even want to know this?"

"I have my reasons. Just tell me."

"Fine. People said he banged her to get her to fall for him so she would beg her dad to make him starting QB."

Wyatt felt so much anger coursing through his body he almost dropped the phone before continuing to speak. "Do you think he would've done that? Used her like that, I mean?"

"He's definitely a ruthless piece of shit, and he did end up starting that season, so it may be true. I didn't want to believe it. I liked her, and Chase was a total asshole. His family had loads of money and he pretty much figured the world owed him everything. Back in high school, he liked to brag he would always get what he wanted, no matter what. Chase was born on third base and thought he hit a triple."

Wyatt felt a twisting sensation in his gut. He was pretty sure it was shame. "I know the type." Wyatt growled out, thinking of his father with irritation. "What happened to him?"

"Coach Sutherland made him the starting QB. If Chase hooked up with Jenna, there was no way Coach knew it. He was crazy protective of her. Jenna graduated a year early, leaving the team when we were poised to have our best season ever. That should've been a huge success for her to enjoy. She was a big part of the team. It didn't make any sense."

"And Chase?"

"He got a scholarship to the University of Georgia. He's been a backup for Atlanta for a few years now, though he started for several weeks this season when Travis Cunningham had that concussion."

"Oh, right, Chase Matthews, yeah, I've heard of him."

"He always talked a good game, you know, bullshitting people to get his way. He was pretty good at tricking coaches into thinking he was an okay guy. I'm sure he's done that in Atlanta, too."

"So he's just a smooth talker?"

"No. Chase is worse than just being a dick."

"How?"

"He beat up a girl in college. It was so bad, I even heard about it at UT. His parents used their money and connections to buy her off so she didn't press charges. They got him out of that one. Who knows what other bad shit he's pulled over the years."

"Do you think he threatened Jenna somehow to become QB?" Wyatt asked so quietly that he could barely hear the words himself. There was a long pause before Jason answered.

"That's what the rest of the team figured happened. I would love to kick his ass just for thinking he did it, though."

Wyatt felt a pair of soft hands touching his bare waist, shocking him back to reality. He turned to see Jenna gifting him with a warm, sleepy smile. Her hair was a mess — blonde and tousled around her pretty face — and he felt actual pain in his chest at the thought of someone hurting her.

It tore him apart to think he could be another in a line of quarterback jerks to take advantage of her. He'd never intended to do that. His plan had seemed so innocuous to him at the time. Yet, it was all so different to him now.

"Wy, dude, are you still there?" Jason asked on the other end of the line.

"Oh, yeah, sorry, I have to go. Thanks for everything, I mean it," Wyatt answered, staring at Jenna's face so intently he could tell it made her nervous. She started fiddling with her hair, pushing it behind her ear. He reached up and stroked her face tenderly, then smoothed her hair back for her. He kissed her cheek and forced a smile around the bilious guilt filling his mouth.

"All right. Well, if you do see Jenna, tell her I say hi."

"Will do. Bye." Wyatt lied. After ending the call he held Jenna in his arms, probably more tightly than was necessary. He lifted his head and placed his chin squarely on the top of her head for a moment.

"Are you okay, Wyatt? Who was that?"

"I'm great. It was my agent," he said on a swallow, shocked at how awful yet another lie felt in his mouth.

"Agent? Calling you on Christmas? That's some service," she said with a smile, as she circled her arms around his waist. "Yum, is that bacon I smell?"

"Shit, I don't want it to burn. Let me get it off the heat."

Wyatt crossed the room to the stove. After putting the phone down on the counter, he looked down at the sizzling bacon, hiding his guilty face from her. He used the time it took him to remove the bacon from the pan to get his emotions under control.

When he was ready, he took a fortifying breath and turned to her with a smile.

"Merry Christmas, Jenna," he said. And he meant it. He was happy she was there with him, surrounded by the Christmas lights and silly decorations they had put up together over the last couple of days.

She sparkled in front of him, glowing in his kitchen like a delicate snow angel. Her time with him was also ephemeral. His original plan to sway her opinion such that she adjusted her diagnosis of his shoulder made that almost inevitable. Yet, that made the moment no less confusing.

Maybe the feeling would pass, once he got over the shock of imagining this strong, but vulnerable, beautiful woman being the victim of a villain like Chase. And now, Wyatt felt like he was just the latest predator — the carnivore that had dragged her back to his cave. He wasn't sure whom he hated more, Chase…or himself.

"Feliz Navidad, Wyatt Alejandro," she answered with a teasing grin. Wyatt leaned back against the kitchen counter and Jenna nestled her thighs between his legs. She looked into his eyes and lazily trailed her fingers across his chest, shoulders, and stomach.

"I like that you speak Spanish," Wyatt said, trying to shake off his dark mood. Jenna deserved a happy Christmas, and he would give it to her.

"Why, thank you. I like that I get to use it with you. But I think everyone knows *those* two Spanish words."

"It's still very sexy to hear them come out of that pretty mouth of yours. It reminds me of growing up."

"It's not too shabby coming out of yours, either. I think you have the sexiest mouth ever found in the real world. It's good you like me speaking Spanish, because my Irish accent is awful," Jenna teased.

"Why'd you study it?"

"An Irish accent? I never really studied how to do one. It's just more of a goofy thing I do when I drink…"

"Very funny, it's a real question. I thought you were supposed to be a serious woman."

"Oh, fine. I'll be serious. Well, I took it in school, but I worked really hard to become fluent because I wanted to do Doctors Without Borders in South America."

"Did you?"

"I was going to. About five years ago, I had to leave Atlanta." She paused and her eyes darkened, triggering that growling worry in Wyatt again. He clutched her hips and she leaned in more closely to him, before she continued on. "I thought that would be the perfect time to do it, but Tea's husband had died and after a year or so, she was still a mess. It was clear she needed me. That's what friends do for each other. If my mom's best friend Cheryl hadn't stepped in to help my dad raise me after she died…well, I don't even want to think about how much harder everything would've been. So, I decided to take an opportunity I found here in Pittsburgh instead."

"You guys must be really close."

"The closest. I'm the brown bird."

"The what?" he said, over a chuckle.

"The tattoo on my hip…" Jenna lifted up the tiny tank top she was wearing with one hand and drew down the side of her panties to reveal the colorful tattoo of three intertwined birds of varying colors flying in a circle. He remembered licking that design with abandon only the night before. "All three of us have this tattoo. That's each of us. Tea is the soft lilac one, Aubrey is the one with all the crazy colors, and me — I'm the sensible, boring, brown bird here."

"There's nothing boring about you, Doc, especially when you get me thinking about that tattoo on your hip. But I'm really trying to be good here and keep my hands off you long enough to make you breakfast. So you didn't get to do Doctors Without Borders? Is that why you do the free clinic and your charity work here?"

"How'd you know about that?"

"I've been trying to know everything about you, Doc, haven't you realized that yet? Eloni told me about it. I think it's great."

Jenna giggled and tickled his waist lightly in response.

"I think you cooking for me is great. I'm still recovering from the dulce de leche you made last night for Christmas Eve."

"I liked making it for you, I also liked licking it off you,"

Wyatt whispered in her ear, before sucking lightly on the lobe. "How about pancakes for your Christmas breakfast?"

"That sounds great!"

"Good, because I want to start opening presents."

"Yes, sir!" Jenna answered.

Wyatt took the plate of pancakes he'd made earlier out of the oven where they were warming. Jenna placed it on a tray, adding the bacon and other fixings. Wyatt went to grab the tray from the counter, but she slapped his hand.

"Oh no, you don't, Wyatt. You don't need to be straining that shoulder. I'll carry the tray," she ordered, grabbing it from him and bumping him with her hip. He followed her quietly, watching her rounded ass walk away from him in nothing but small, white panties, making him wonder if the presents could wait.

Jenna put down the tray next to the tree and turned in time for him to hand her a present.

"Wow, you don't mess around, Wyatt."

"Nope, open it. The food can wait."

Jenna giggled girlishly, and her big smile made his heart flip over in his chest again. She was allowing herself to enjoy the holiday, and he was relishing this new side of her. The paper flew everywhere, eventually revealing a box of ice skates.

"Ice skates?"

"Like our sort of first date. I know you weren't able to skate that day because it was a team thing, but next time, it will be just you and me. You need to be ready. I'm pretty experienced after my last skating session, so you can hold onto me. Don't worry."

"That sounds like so much fun, Wyatt. And I love them. Thank you." She leaned forward and kissed his cheek before resting back on the floor. "How'd you know my size for ice skates?"

"I peeked at the shoes you brought and snuck away to call about them. It was pretty hard to have them delivered here yesterday without you noticing, you know."

"I'm very impressed."

"Okay, now open this one." Wyatt handed her the smallest present in size, and the one he'd been most nervous about.

"But, it's your turn."

"I'll go next. Open it."

Jenna ripped the paper off and flipped the lid on the small jewelry box and gasped when she saw the delicate earrings inside. Her eyes misted a bit, but she tried to regain her composure before looking at him again.

"Wyatt, they look just like…"

"Your locket? I know. I saw them at an antique shop when we had an hour to ourselves during our Oakland trip. I remembered your locket had a woman's face on it, too. The sales lady called it a cameo."

"They're so perfect, Wyatt. They are one of the greatest gifts anyone's ever given me."

"I'm glad you like them. I told you I think you should have special things."

"Thank you." Jenna put on the earrings and leaned forward to kiss him slowly. Bing Crosby was singing over the sound system about being home for Christmas, only in his dreams. Yet, Wyatt felt like he'd never been more at home before in his life.

Jenna pulled back and the sense of loss was poignant. She thrust a present in his hands, adding, "Now you have to take your turn."

Wyatt tore into the perfectly wrapped, rectangular present. Inside laid song sheets of Christmas songs, with lyrics in

Spanish.

"Wow, these are awesome, Doc. I can't wait to play them for you."

"That's great. I'm so glad you like them, Wyatt. I was a little nervous. I mean, what do you give the man who has everything?"

"I don't have everything, and what I do have isn't guaranteed to stay with me."

"Don't say that, Wyatt. I know you're worried about the team keeping you. I don't need to be a mind reader to know that. But you've been playing better."

"That's not all I'm afraid of losing," Wyatt muttered, "but, yes, I'm definitely worried about that, too."

"Can I make an observation, Wyatt?"

"Oh, so now you're asking permission, Doc?" he teased, pulling her into his lap so she was straddling him, as they sat on the floor.

"I've watched you play for so many years. You know I think you're an amazing quarterback, right?" she waited for Wyatt to nod before she continued, "thing is, it's clear you don't play like you love the game. You play like it's an obligation."

"That's because it is."

Her mouth set into a stern and stubborn line.

"Tell me. When you stop reminding yourself you want to hate the game and how your dad fell for all of its traps…when you release a great throw and it connects with a receiver for a touchdown, how does it feel?"

"Amazing," he said softly, running a hand down the smooth length of her hair. She leaned almost imperceptibly against his hand and the motion made his throat tighten so hard he almost couldn't breathe.

"Exactly! It's okay to love the game. It's okay to want to be part of the team, a leader of it."

"It's not that simple, all of that can get out of control…"

"You're the most controlled person I know."

"Not compared to you, Doc."

Jenna laughed lightly. "Well, that's true. My point is you won't somehow become your dad if you let go a little. It will be okay."

"That's a big risk, Doc. I'm not smart. I didn't finish school. This is all I have going for me."

"You've got a lot more than that going for you, Wyatt. You *are* smart. And you've been playing so well the last few weeks, like a totally different man. I know the team has to have noticed."

"Thanks. Maybe I was just waiting for the right inspiration, Doc. I think you've helped me love it."

"Oh, stop buttering me up. You don't need me to do well."

But Wyatt was starting to think that he *did* need her, and not just for the game, or for what a change in her diagnosis about his shoulder could do for him.

He wrapped his arms tightly around her waist and started to make a comment about how surgery could ruin everything he was trying to build, but he bit back the words. He wanted to enjoy this simple moment with her while he could. Moving her hair off her neck, he trailed his tongue across her warm skin.

"How did you learn so much about football?" he whispered as he nibbled at the delicate skin by her collarbone.

"You mean because I'm a girl?" she teased, looking back at him and batting her eyelashes dramatically.

"No, because you know more about it than most of my coaches."

"It was my life growing up. After my mom died, my dad was really depressed. I was just a kid, but I knew. The only thing that cheered him up was coaching — and also, um, never mind. So I started helping him coach when I was about thirteen, until I basically became another coach on the sidelines — even when I was in high school and they were my classmates."

"Did that cause problems?"

"Yes. One problem in particular."

"Tell me about that problem." He was well aware she wouldn't tell him. But Wyatt knew its name now — it was that fucker Chase Matthews. Just the thought of him made Wyatt want to lock her up and shield her from anything in the world that could hurt her, even if that meant hiding her from himself.

"That was a long time ago. Let's keep talking about coaching. Um, anyway, I helped my dad out no matter what. Being a coach was like air for my dad. It's what kept him alive and was his reason for living."

"And you, too. You're pretty special."

"Oh, now you're just sucking up, Mr. McCoy."

"I thought I was being sensitive and supportive, but if sucking is what you want, I can certainly oblige."

Wyatt tilted forward, landing Jenna softly on her back on the floor, eliciting a surprised yelp from her smiling mouth. Kneeling in front of her, he took a moment to enjoy the view of her waiting for him in his home, beside the huge tree and the piles of wrapped presents he'd bought for her. Leaning over her, he slid her tank top off her body, stopping to whisper against her belly, "Enough presents for now. I need to unwrap you."

He licked down the warm contours of her breasts and sucked at the tightened buds of her nipples, before sliding those maddening white panties down her legs. She reached for his boxer briefs with her feet, grunting in urgent frustration, until he backed off to remove them quickly.

"Always so impatient, Doc," he teased, before parting her legs with his hands. Wyatt ran his face across her stomach, scraping his stubble over her smooth skin. She let her knees fall apart and began stroking his hair gently with her hands as she writhed beneath him with anticipation.

Wyatt moved so his face was completely between her thighs. Her smell engulfed him and he could feel himself getting hard and eager to be inside her again. That would have to wait, because he needed to taste her first.

For all the weeks that Jenna fought her attraction to him, she was completely open to him now — at least physically. Since they'd come back to his house, every time he reached for her, she'd been hot and ready for him, and this time was no different.

Separating her pink folds with two fingers of his left hand, Wyatt darted his tongue against her tightening clit. He licked at her in long strokes, sucking at the taut bundle of nerves that made her moan and wriggle beneath him. She pulled at his hair so hard it almost hurt, but it was worth it to see her lose herself with him.

Her legs began to tense and twitch against the floor. Wyatt moved his tongue repeatedly in and out of her warm opening. On a deep flick, he took two fingers from his right hand and plunged them into her deeply, making her shout out loud and bow her back far off the floor. He smiled and moved his tongue back to her clit, loving how loud and wild he made her. She was so wet and throbbing around his fingers he knew he couldn't wait any longer.

After her muscles spasmed deliciously around his fingers,

he removed them and raised his body over hers. Careful to put his weight on his left arm, Wyatt paused to gaze down at her face.

Her blue eyes were hooded and unfocused and her lips red from biting them with abandon. Wyatt slid the fingers of his right hand, still wet with her juices, into her mouth. Jenna met his gaze and sucked at his fingers. She scraped her teeth across the skin until he groaned out loud.

Removing his fingers from her mouth, he moved his hand to clasp the nape of her neck firmly before entering her in one smooth thrust. He was still amazed by the sensation of being inside her with no barrier. Every millimeter he felt of her was hot and tight around him — absolutely perfect.

Jenna wrapped her legs around his waist, looking up into his eyes. Wyatt could still feel her juices on his face. She smelled like she was a part of him. Her tight, athletic body met him thrust for thrust, until they were both grunting and moaning as one. With one more hard movement inside of her, Jenna squeezed around him, moaning his name in his ear.

The sound of his name on her lips sent him over the edge and he filled her, his throat releasing a long growl. He fell next to her, pulling her body to lie alongside his. She rested her head on his chest as they looked up at the sparkling lights of the Christmas tree beside them.

Wyatt kissed her forehead and whispered, "Feliz Navidad, belleza."

CHAPTER FOURTEEN

Jenna emerged from Wyatt's bedroom in nothing but the soft, Italian button-down shirt she'd found in his closet. Walking into his kitchen, she caught sight of his bare back and her stomach tightened.

"Are you planning to cook for me again, Wyatt? I swear you're spoiling me."

He turned and handed her a glass of white wine. The movement gave her the pleasure of looking at the chiseled edges of his muscular chest again.

Over the last few days they'd spent more time naked than clothed, intensifying the delirious way he made her feel. He turned her into a puddle of emotions and hormones every time she saw him. Increased exposure was only increasing her dependency on that feeling — rather than alleviating it.

"I like to cook," he answered.

"That's good, because if you had planned on having me feed you, we might've starved. I pretty much only know how to make steak," she said, before taking a tasty sip of the crisp and delicious wine.

"That works for me. I'm from Texas. That's one of our

major food groups, you know," he announced with a smile. He stared at her body, eyeing her up and down slowly, making her blood hum with desire. "Now, *that* is an outfit I like you in," he said, taking a step back and sitting on one of the bar stools in the kitchen as he bit his bottom lip.

"I'm glad to hear it. I saw this shirt of yours, and it looked very familiar to me…"

"It's the one I wore the night I met you."

"I know."

"How sweet of you to remember."

"I *am* very sweet, that's true. After how arrogant and cocky you were with me that night, I think I should get to keep it."

"Fine by me. It does look better on you anyway. I like this part the best," he added, grabbing her hand and leading her between his legs. He took her glass and placed it down on the counter next to his. Reaching his hands around to her bare bottom, he added, "oh yes, much better on you."

"You know what else of yours looks better on me?"

"What?" he asked.

"Those lips of yours, of course," she purred, right before she covered his mouth with hers. Her fingers splayed out across his hard back, playfully stroking the smooth skin, pressing herself more firmly against the cotton of his boxer briefs, and his hardening length between them.

They'd spent most of the day apart. He'd gone to a practice in preparation for the last game of the regular season in two days, and she had an eight-hour shift at the hospital. It worried Jenna a little how she'd actually missed him during that brief time apart. Yet, Wyatt had quickly dragged her to bed as soon as they reunited at his house, so it appeared she wasn't alone in her need to share as much time with him as possible.

Jenna began burying her face in the warm skin of his neck.

He'd showered after practice before coming home, but she could still catch a hint of the remnants of clean sweat on his flesh. No one smelled like Wyatt to her, and if she only had a handful of days left to enjoy the scent, she was intent on burning it into her memory.

She began to flick her tongue out to taste him and his groan made her smile. The sound of his pleasure became overpowered by the distant click of his front door opening and a woman's voice calling out to him.

"Alejandro...Hola. Surprise! Oh no, where is he? Is he home? Claudia, go look for him."

Jenna jumped away from him, letting out a tiny yelp.

"What's going on? Who is that?" she asked him in a loud whisper.

"Mierda. That's my mother."

"What? I thought you said you weren't spending the holidays with them?" Jenna squeaked out in terror. She darted her eyes around the kitchen as she desperately yanked Wyatt's shirt down a few scant extra inches on her legs, searching for an escape route. It was of no use, because a set of light steps was rapidly approaching them.

"It sounds like it's not just your mother," Jenna groaned.

"Wy, are you in the kitchen? We're here, and Abuela came, too, so you'd better be home," a younger voice demanded.

"That's my sister." He stood quickly, blocking Jenna's body with his own. "I hope you're ready to meet my abuela, too."

"Like this? Of course I can't. Maybe I can sneak out..."

"There you are, Wy, jeez, I know we surprised you, but you don't have to ignore us... Oh, crap. You're not alone."

Jenna hid her face behind Wyatt's back, her fingertips peeking out over the top of his shoulders.

"Claudia, this is Dr. Jenna Sutherland. Jenna, this is my

baby sister, Claudia."

"Doctor, eh? Just Claudia will suffice. I am an adult now."

"Just barely," Wyatt grumbled.

Jenna popped her head out around Wyatt's arm, extending her right hand toward Wyatt's sister.

Claudia rolled her eyes at her brother. Following it up with a saucy wink toward Jenna, she shook her hand.

"Hi," Jenna said shyly.

"It's so nice to meet you, Jenna. I'm Wyatt's *grown* sister. Um, maybe you'd like to chat with me on my way to the bathroom before you get a chance to meet the rest of us?" Claudia suggested, glancing meaningfully at Jenna's bare legs underneath Wyatt's button-down shirt.

"Oh my Lord," Jenna answered with a light laugh, her southern accent taking over in her discomfort. "Yes, please. That would be great." She stepped out from behind him, using one hand to prevent Wyatt's shirt from moving and revealing her bare ass.

Once safely deposited in Wyatt's bedroom, Jenna scurried around quickly, yanking on jeans and a sweater. Whatever she could grab to look presentable.

Claudia knocked on the door gently.

"Come in," Jenna answered. When Claudia entered Jenna could immediately tell she was much younger than Wyatt. She looked to Jenna to be around twenty-one, maybe twenty-two, but she was already quite striking. Jenna could only imagine how much Claudia's unique beauty must have worried Wyatt over the years.

Her figure was shapely, but surprisingly petite for being related to a giant like Wyatt, and she didn't share any of his lighter features. Dark eyes, rimmed in thick long lashes, set a sharp contrast to her smooth, olive skin. Her hair was much darker, too — pulled back into a sleek, shiny ponytail that made Jenna wish she could find a moment to brush her tousled waves before reemerging from Wyatt's room.

Claudia leaned back on Wyatt's dresser, crossed her arms and twisted her full lips into a beguiling half-smile.

That sneaky little grin is definitely hereditary, Jenna thought to herself.

"You're very pretty," Claudia said to her. She surveyed Jenna up and down with a sharp and clever look that belied her young age.

"Thank you. So are you," Jenna answered, with a smile of her own.

"Oh, um, thank you," Claudia said quickly, standing up straight and putting her hands in her pockets.

The compliment didn't seem to sit well with Claudia, which was odd, seeing as she was as patently beautiful as her once-famous mother.

"What are you a doctor of?" Claudia asked, diverting the conversation away from herself quickly.

"I'm an orthopedic surgical resident."

"Too bad you're not a neurosurgeon. I should warn you that Wyatt has a chronic case of hard headedness."

"I don't need to specialize in brains to know that," Jenna laughed, her tension easing immediately around the lively young woman. "So, you call him Wyatt? I heard your mother use his middle name."

"Yeah. From what I understand, my dad picked the name Wyatt. My mom and abuela picked Alejandro for his middle name. They'd love nothing more than to rid our lives of all things McCoy, I think. Seeing as we're stuck with his last name, they made that compromise."

"That makes sense, I guess. That must have been so hard

for you, dealing with your father's issues and the way he..."

"Disappeared? So, Wyatt told you about that? Interesting. I must say, Dr. Sutherland, you're a welcome change to the usual trash chasing after my brother."

"Oh, um, thanks. I don't think I'm really chasing after him, I mean..."

"Don't worry, I didn't mean it like that. I was just surprised to find you here. He's never actually introduced us to any girls or brought them here or anything. But it's hard not to miss the girls that tried to hook him over the years, some more successfully than others."

Claudia made a face at the memory, but Jenna couldn't focus on it. She was too distracted by the instant and shocking level of acidic jealousy that rushed through her at the mention of other women in Wyatt's life.

"I guess we can't hide in here anymore," Claudia said, interrupting Jenna's unwelcome bout of possessive thoughts. "Are you ready to face the Mexican Inquisition?"

"Excuse me?" Jenna asked with a laugh. Though she quickly stopped when she saw the serious look on Claudia's stunning face.

"I'm not kidding. Brace yourself. Those two are gonna get one look at a classy lady like you and sink their grandchild and great-grandchild wanting claws right into you."

"I didn't feel all that classy when you first saw me," Jenna said quickly. "And besides, they can't be that bad..." Jenna added slowly.

"We'll see. Wyatt's driven them crazy over the years with his..."

"Claudia," Wyatt said gruffly. He was standing at the door, glaring at his sister with an intimidating look on his face.

"Oops, busted," Claudia said, with a little smile thrown

Jenna's way. As Jenna left the room, Claudia whispered in her ear, "He must like you a lot. I've never seen him that mad about my big mouth."

Jenna tried to respond, but no words came out. She was too stunned by Claudia's words.

Wyatt walked over to Jenna, placing a hand at the small of her back, "Don't believe a word she said about me," he whispered into her ear.

His touch calmed her a bit and she turned to him before they left the room.

"Well, you came in too soon. If you hadn't interrupted, I might've gotten a chance to hear something I shouldn't believe."

"Then my timing was just right, after all. Look, are you ready to do this?"

"I'm not going to just ignore them."

"You didn't answer me," he whispered.

"It's okay. I should be asking you if you're ready. I got the impression from Claudia that…"

"Enough about what she said. Stop stalling and let's get in there," Wyatt commanded.

Jenna suppressed a smile, but she quickly followed his instructions.

"We begged Alejandro to come home for Christmas, but he said he couldn't. I think I know why now," Wyatt's mother said to Jenna, with a teasing tone. Wyatt glanced at Jenna, worried about her reaction to his mother's revelation.

"What? I don't understand…" Jenna whipped her head in Wyatt's direction.

Dammit, he thought.

She was clearly confused. Wyatt could almost hear the gears in her brain churning, trying to process why he'd lied and told her his family didn't want to see him for the holidays. He searched for words to end the tense moment, but his sister was already on it.

"Mom, don't embarrass her," Claudia said to their mother.

Wyatt was instantly grateful to his sister for trying to ease his mother's interrogation of Jenna. He was surprised by how much he liked having Jenna meet the women that meant so much to him. But the last thing he wanted was for her to hear something from them that made her suspicious of him in any way.

"Mama, I'm sorry I couldn't make it," Wyatt interrupted, "but I hope you had a great Christmas. I did call, you know."

"You did. You're such a good boy. And we were going to stay in Texas and not bother you. But, your brother cancelled his visit at the last minute. He is off to who knows where. So we decided to come up and see you."

Wyatt's teeth gritted at the mention of his little brother. He was always "off somewhere," satisfying whatever latest whim — or woman — that appealed to him. Worrying about whether his family was all right without him over the holiday season had never interested him. Yes, Wyatt had deserted them this time of year, but it was for a very good reason.

"Do you like children?" he heard his abuela ask Jenna, quickly pulling him back to the conversation.

In the twenty minutes since he'd taken Jenna into the living room to meet the rest of his visitors, they hadn't been overly pushy with her. They must've been just getting warmed up before diving into the weighty topics.

Before Jenna could even answer the question, he could see

they were already examining her hips. He assumed they were trying to gauge if they were wide enough to accommodate the many grandbabies his mother wanted.

"I love kids," Jenna said, with a smile, and Wyatt felt a bit of relief that she hadn't been offended. "I've helped to raise my best friend's son over the last several years. Her husband died when she was only a few weeks pregnant."

"And she volunteers with local underprivileged kids in the area. She helps them with their health, athletics, tutoring...you name it," Wyatt interjected.

"Thanks, Wyatt," Jenna said softly, her cheeks flushing a bit.

"It looks like our Alejandro knows quite a bit about you, my dear," his mother said sweetly. She glanced at his abuela, quickly turning back to Jenna, "But do you want kids of your own?"

"Mama, lay off her a minute, will you?" Claudia said. "I'm sorry, you don't have to answer all their nosy questions. It's just rare that we get to see my brother care enough to know a girl's last name, much less all these sweet little details."

"Claudia!" Wyatt said, with a chastening voice. He'd been lucky to catch Claudia in his room before she said anything too awful to Jenna about him, but he knew she wasn't done trying to torment him.

"Um, no, it's okay," Jenna answered quietly. "I would love to have kids of my own. It's something I've always wanted."

"That's wonderful," Wyatt's mother exclaimed. "Maybe you will want to have kids soon?"

Wyatt felt Jenna's whole body tense up next to him. He looked over to her and was shocked to see she'd turned completely white. Any smile on her face was gone, replaced with a look of pure anguish and panic.

"Are you okay?" he asked, leaning forward to whisper in her ear.

She shook her head and jumped up out of her seat.

"Um, I'm so sorry, but I just realized I have to go. It was really nice meeting you all. Please forgive me." Jenna quickly darted out of the room toward the door, leaving all of them with shocked faces.

He tried to catch her, but she'd already gotten on her shoes and left before he could talk some sense into her.

"I'm sorry, I have to go get her. I'll be right back."

Wyatt quickly put on shoes and a jacket and ran after her.

Jenna rushed to her car in Wyatt's driveway as fast as she could. Her hands were trembling as she tried to unlock the door. She'd rushed out so quickly that she hadn't even grabbed her coat, but there had been no time for that.

Shame filled her at making such a scene in front of his nice family, but Jenna knew she couldn't be in that room with them anymore. Her emotions were out of control, and she couldn't let anyone see her that way. She needed to be alone until she could collect herself again.

She'd let the magic of these few days so completely consume her that she'd barely thought about the painful procedure and lengthy treatment awaiting her. With that much desired escape, came the fact that she hadn't even let herself think about what this could mean for her future — and the life she'd dreamt to have for herself one day.

What if this course of treatment doesn't work? What if I need invasive chemo and end up not being able to have kids? she thought in a panic. *Will cancer just keep taking from me? It took my mother at the beginning of my life. Is it going to take my chance to create it? Will I forever be alone in this body?*

That bleak possible future flashed before her eyes — it would be a life of smiling at happy women with *their* swollen bellies, as they celebrated their own granted wishes. She would probably deflect questions when people asked if she would ever want a family. Maybe provide some bland excuse, or change the subject, all the while hiding the pain of knowing she'd never experience the joy of creating life.

Or worse, what if I really am sick? What if it simply kills me? The only remnants of my mother will die with me. How will my father ever get through that?

Jenna's throat closed and it felt like she was suffocating — as though her knees were rubber and would never hold her weight. This place wasn't for her — a place full of big families and hopes and dreams. She was days from embarking on a painful medical process that might not be successful. Jenna had walked that path before and she knew there was a good chance it would only devastate every person around her. She didn't want to drag Wyatt, or his lovely family, down with her. All she could do was run.

She grabbed for the door handle, but before she could open it, she felt Wyatt's firm grip pull her back.

"What the hell was that about, Jenna? Don't you like my family?" he asked angrily from behind her. It made her feel sick that he thought her response was to his family, who'd been nothing but kind to her.

"No, of course not. It's not that," Jenna answered, turning her body to him but staring at her feet. She felt his calloused fingers stroke her chin and lift her face, so she was staring into his eyes, her teeth chattering lightly. "I just realized I need to go home. You should have some time with your family, and…"

Before Jenna could control herself, a lone tear slid down her cheek. Wyatt reached up his other hand, wiping the tear away with his thumb. His touch was so caring that Jenna wasn't sure if she could breathe without releasing the sob she was fighting hard to hold back.

"Hey. What's all this about, tough girl?" Wyatt removed one hand from her face so he could take her keys and slip them into his pocket. "Talk to me, belleza."

Wyatt took off his jacket and put it around her shoulders, then brought her into his arms.

"You know you never call me by name unless you're upset," she laughed out harshly against his chest.

"I *am* upset, and don't change the subject, *Jenna*," he said sternly, leaning back to look down at her face.

"I think I liked belleza better."

"Me, too," he said, with a soft smile. "Now, please, tell me." He leaned forward as he whispered against her cheek, dropping the lightest of kisses on her skin.

"I can't."

"Why not?"

"It's not because I don't want to tell you. It's just that I'm…I'm not ready."

"It *is* something though, isn't it? Something that made you want to run from me?"

"Yes. I didn't want to leave you all. I think I panicked. I'm sorry. I'm sorry for so many things, Wyatt," she added, looking down again.

And she *was* sorry. Sorry Chase made her reluctant to trust Wyatt. Sorry her body may be a ticking time bomb of genetic brutality. Sorry she ever consulted on Wyatt's shoulder and delivered a diagnosis that could threaten his whole career.

"Then make it up to me and come inside. Remember Mama said she's going to make tamales. You don't want to miss that."

Jenna's stomach growled and he laughed, pulling her in to a tighter embrace. He turned them around so he was leaning his back against the side of her car and rested his chin on the top of her head.

Jenna kissed his neck and breathed him in before shivering slightly.

"You're still freezing, that settles it. I'm dragging you inside, but this conversation isn't over," he said, standing upright. Jenna looked up at him with embarrassment in her eyes.

"Wait, are you sure I'm invited? After the way I acted..." she asked softly, amazed by her own desire to just curl into his warmth and never leave.

"You're a smart and beautiful doctor that doesn't take my shit and loves kids...I think *I* wouldn't be welcomed back in if I *didn't* bring you with me," he teased, gently lifting her chin again and lowering his lips to hers for a brief moment before continuing. "They weren't offended or anything when you left. Just confused. I'll come up with an excuse."

"Okay, thank you. But before we go in...will you please kiss me again, for real?"

He smiled down at her with a broad, open grin that filled her cold body with warmth.

Wyatt took her face in both of his hands and leaned down to kiss her lips with a light, cautious touch. She could tell he wanted to be gentle with her, but she needed more. Jenna licked the seam of his lips, pushing through to touch the smooth terrain of his teeth.

Wyatt growled against her mouth and drew her more

closely to him. He allowed her tongue entrance, quickly reaching into her mouth with his own, tasting her right back.

Jenna breathed him in and just gave into the feeling. She let her arms wrap around his waist, her body mold to his, and suddenly realized that all the unhappy thoughts in her head had simply...disappeared.

She knew it was impractical and all kinds of foolish to let herself be so open with this man. Yet, relaxing into him — being connected to him so fully — felt just too right, too complete. She refused to deny herself this moment.

What if the news is terrible next week? I don't want to regret missing this time with him...this chance to make more of my life, if only for a few more nights, Jenna thought, as she let his tongue lazily explore her mouth and he swallowed every sigh she uttered.

Life was right here at her feet willing to give her something great. She so desperately wanted this chance with Wyatt, and needed to take it — because life was one cruel breath away from possibly taking so much from her.

He pulled away from her mouth and Jenna breathed out heavily, resting her head on his chest.

That sense of release, that openness she felt with Wyatt was inexplicable to her. There was no logical explanation for it. It was terrifying that this feeling could come to her from just one person.

If she were smart, she'd walk away now before they both got hurt. But Jenna was tired of being wise. She was sick of doing the right thing. All she wanted was to rest in this man's arms and just let everything go away.

It suddenly made sense to Jenna the way Tea looked at Griffen years after she'd been so devastated from losing Jack. Jenna had never seen happy devotion as an adult — she had only seen the loss after it was gone. The loss that lived in her father's eyes every day after her mother died. If there was any chance Wyatt felt that way about her, would her own illness, and all the risks it entailed, break him, too?

"You still with me, Doc?" Wyatt asked softly against her hair.

"Yeah," she choked out.

Whatever happened next, she would let herself have this rush in her veins, an intoxicating sensation of being tethered to him, yet still feeling free, all at once.

"Does that mean you're ready to go inside with me?"

"Yeah, maybe another kiss, first?" she whispered.

"Good idea." And then he stole her senses again, caressing her lips with his own. With each stroke of his tongue in her mouth and his fingers through her hair, he wiped those bad thoughts away, yet again.

When he finally leaned back from her, she felt bereft. Her desire for more must have shown on her face because Wyatt chuckled deeply in response.

"I should get you inside and to my family before they think I ran away to Vegas with you."

She looked up quickly, his words shocking her back to reality.

"What?"

"Relax, Doc. Come on," he said, with a chuckle, stepping aside and holding out his hand to her.

She looked at his tanned skin, fingers curled in toward the most welcoming of invitations, and Jenna had no desire to resist it. Instead, she simply slid her hand into his and let him take over the moment, pulling her close to his side and leading her back into the warm security of his home — and his life.

CHAPTER FIFTEEN

Wyatt pushed through the door to his home. He swallowed his concern at not seeing Jenna right away, and called out into the emptiness, "Doc, I'm back."

He'd rushed straight home to her from the stadium after his post-game shower. It had been the last game of the season. As with every one since Jenna had consulted on his shoulder, he'd played better than any other time he could remember. Her observations about his playing were beneficial to him, but it was also the hope that she'd watch and be impressed that pushed him even harder.

Wyatt threw down his bag before venturing further into the house. It might raise some eyebrows that he hadn't stuck around to talk to the press after the game, but Wyatt had been worried about Jenna ever since she'd run off the night his family made their surprise visit. A small part of him wasn't even sure if he could trust that she'd really waited for him.

He braced himself for disappointment as he wandered towards the kitchen. But there she was, in cotton shorts and a thin top. She had earbuds in and was cleaning his counters, singing something to herself, so off-key he couldn't recognize it. The sight was surreal and cute, making him laugh out loud.

"Shit!" Jenna jumped up in shock and dropped her rag. She turned to him, removing her earbuds. "Dammit, McCoy. You scared the hell out of me."

"Sorry, Doc."

"It's okay, I just didn't expect you home so soon."

She crossed the room to him and wrapped her arms around his neck to give him a quick kiss. When she squeezed him to her a bit too eagerly, Wyatt couldn't hide his wince from the pain emanating off his right shoulder.

"Oh, shoot, I'm sorry. Let me ice your shoulder down. How are you feeling? You took another brutal hit in the third quarter."

"I'm fine, but I'll let you worry about me if it makes you feel better."

She rolled her eyes at him before gathering an ice pack and compression wrap. He could tell she was making herself at home and he liked it. It felt nice having her waiting for him after he returned from another tough game.

"Sit down on this chair," she instructed.

"Doctor's orders?"

"Yes, not that it ever mattered to you before," she teased, nudging him down into the chair playfully. "Here, what if I do my exam sitting on your lap. Will that make you behave?"

"Now why didn't you take that approach to begin with? I might've been much more cooperative."

"I doubt anything would've had that effect on you." She perched on his lap carefully and covered his right shoulder with the ice pack and began securing it to him with the wrap. "I swear, if they don't pick up a quality offensive tackle in free agency, your shoulder will be the last thing I worry about," she said sternly, before pinning the wrap down.

Her touch was amazing. It could make him hot and crazy, but in moments like this she filled him with a sense of calm, almost as though he were being cherished.

"Did you see the trainer after the game?" she asked, leaning back on his lap to look at him.

"No."

"Wyatt, you have to be committed to the process in every way if you want them to believe you're serious. You know that includes your own health, too."

"I *was* serious — seriously ready to get home to you."

She paused and gaped at him, before a blush streaked across her cheeks.

"Come here," he said, more gruffly than he intended, quickly smiling and wrapping his left arm around her, pulling her to him. He kissed her slowly. When he felt her sigh in his mouth he released her, thrilled to see how hazy her eyes had become.

"I missed you, too, Wyatt. If that's what you were wondering," she said lightly.

Wyatt laughed and brushed some of her soft hair behind her ear awkwardly with his left hand.

"You played great."

"Thanks. I wish you had let me get you that ticket, though. You could've been there cheering me on."

"I'm sorry I wasn't there. But you know that wouldn't have looked right, you pulling strings for me. Even though my consultation is long over, I can't take any risks with my possible fellowship. I'm so sorry."

Wyatt's stomach flipped over at her words. He was slowly coming to terms with the fact that he cared for her, a lot. The idea of jeopardizing her career for his own was becoming more unpalatable to him by the day. Even if it was for the benefit of his family's security, Wyatt was beginning to feel like he needed to let the whole plan go and face his chances with the team as they stood now.

"Have the coach or GM talked to you about your contract? This winning streak is great for your chances of sticking around."

"Maybe, but the season's over. We needed Baltimore to lose to make the play-offs."

"I know. They won just minutes after you guys. Assholes," she laughed.

"I don't want to talk about Baltimore, or the trainers, or even about football. I want to talk about you."

"What about me?" she whispered. Her voice sounded nervous and she looked down so her shiny blonde hair created a shimmery veil between them.

"Hey," he said softly, moving his left arm from her waist, so he could tilt her chin up with his fingertips. "I want to talk about how you are what I couldn't stop thinking about during the game. And you're the only person I want to be around right now."

"Yeah?"

"Yeah."

"Well. That's not too shabby," she said, with a teasing smile.

"Not shabby at all, and I've got to say, you're very good at this doctor stuff. My shoulder feels better already."

"Thank you very much," she answered, with a playful smirk.

"But I was hoping you could take some time away from the whole doctor thing. After New Year's, how about we go to Mexico together? I know this great place in Cabo San Lucas. It's really private, so you'll just need that tiny bikini I got you for Christmas. We'll swim together again. I'll let you practice that great stroke of yours some more. You can rub ice all over me there, too."

"Oh, that sounds so wonderful," she muttered quietly, all that nervousness taking over her face again. She looked away and said, "But, I don't think I can get away."

"Come on. Okay, what about a weekend away?"

He turned her face to his and her eyes looked wet with unshed tears.

"All right, that's it. I was patient a couple days ago, but not anymore. Tell me what the hell is going on with you."

Jenna stared at him, the fear and sadness on her face sending a chill of anxiety through his body. His heart started to pound violently in his chest.

"A couple days after you first kissed me, I had my annual exam. They found lumps."

Wyatt felt like a three-hundred-pound lineman had just barreled helmet first into his gut. All the breath left his body and he was having a hell of a time making sense of the words Jenna was saying to him.

"What do you mean? Are you saying you could have…"

"Cancer? They don't know. The tumors are borderline benign and malignant."

"What does that mean? What happens next?"

"They need to take them out. It's a surgery called a lumpectomy. That's happening on January third."

"Will they put you under anesthesia? Is it dangerous?"

"Yes it will be general anesthesia. I guess it's no more dangerous than any other surgery."

"You *guess*?" Wyatt's head was spinning, his chest twisting with worry. The thought of Jenna being put under and possibly never waking up was terrifying, but not as much as the chance she could have a devastating condition he was powerless to fight. Jenna tried to give him a comforting smile, clearly distressed by his response.

"The surgical team is excellent, so that part of the treatment should go smoothly. It will be painful afterward..." Jenna paused and looked away from him for a moment, then met his eyes again. "I may not look the same."

"But the surgery will take care of everything? You'll be okay, right?"

"If they are cancerous and have already spread... Well, that would be really bad. Even if they find the tumors aren't cancerous, I need to go through radiation, no matter what. These tumors can come back if I'm not aggressive. So you see, I can't go anywhere..."

Wyatt pulled her tightly against him.

"I want to be there," Wyatt said roughly.

"Where?"

"The surgery, the radiation, all of it. I want to help you."

"You don't have to do that, Wyatt. It's an ugly process. Believe me, I know."

"I can take it. Are you telling me you don't want me to be there for you?"

"It's not that, Wyatt. Tumors like this are what killed my mother. Hers were malignant. After months of chemo, she was so weak she contracted pneumonia that severely affected her respiration. She went into sudden cardiac arrest... I was there when it happened. I won't ever put someone through that, not *any* of it."

"I hate that you had to go through that, but this isn't your choice, Jenna. I want to be there with you. I'm *going* to be there for you. My sister got really sick when she was seven. Juvenile diabetes. But before we got it under control, we almost lost her. I'll go nuts if I'm not there with you. What about your friends? Your dad? Will they be there?"

"No. I didn't tell them. Trey is taking me to the surgery."

Red flashed before Wyatt's eyes. "What? You're going to let him be there, but not me?"

"It's not like that. He's the only other person that knows. I didn't even mean to tell him. He overheard me talking to the doctor. I can't put my dad, or Tea and Aubrey through that."

"You're just going to hide it from them?"

"Have you ever kept a secret or done something you aren't proud of to help take care of people you love, Wyatt?"

He swallowed so hard it hurt. Wyatt knew all too well about that.

"Yes…I have."

"Then you understand why I can't tell them."

"I guess I do."

"Thank you, Wyatt."

He held her closely to him with his left arm for several minutes, as the news she gave him steadily sunk into his brain.

"And this was why you were so upset when my family visited?"

"Yes. Wyatt, if this turns out badly, there's a chance I can't have kids. Hell, it's possible *I* don't make it through. You didn't sign on for all this. It's okay if you just let me go."

"I'm not going to do that, Doc. So you can just knock that shit off right now."

Jenna leaned back and looked at him, stroking the hair away from his face. She placed a soft and soothing kiss on his forehead, before gazing into his eyes.

"Okay, you can come with me to the hospital on the third. I'll tell Trey I don't need a ride to the surgery anymore." She stood up off his lap and he immediately reached for her again.

She smiled softly at him. "I'm going to take a shower. I know you took one after the game, but do you want to join me?"

Wyatt nodded and she removed the wrap and ice pack from his shoulder. "Let's go," Wyatt said, but as he moved to get up his phone rang in his bag before he could touch her.

"Dammit, that's the ringtone for my agent. I have to take it. I'll meet you in there."

"Hey Gabe, what's up?" Wyatt grunted out in greeting, watching Jenna disappear into his bedroom.

"Hey, man. You sound like shit, are you okay?"

"Sure, I'm fine. Just tired."

"You played great out there today. Did they give you another cortisone shot to your shoulder before the game?"

"Yeah, those work wonders."

"So, you wanted me to find out who was jockeying to be your backup? Well, I talked to all my contacts at the Roughnecks and it looks like that Chase Matthews guy who's been playing in Atlanta the last few years is in talks to go to Pittsburgh for next season."

"What? That can't happen, he can't come to Pittsburgh."

"He started for several weeks in Atlanta and he'll definitely try for the starting spot in Pittsburgh."

"We need to block him, he can't come here."

"Christ, Wyatt, after what you did in Dallas, you have no credibility here."

"I know it looked bad that I wouldn't train my replacement, but that was business. This is different."

"How?"

"I can't tell you. Chase Matthews is a problem. He can't come here."

"Wyatt, I can't help you if you won't be honest with me. Look, if you get cut or traded, you won't even see this Chase guy. And the way things are looking, with your shoulder and their locker room worries, that's probably what's going to happen. If your shoulder's really not better, they're going to trade you."

"Fuck."

"You've played great the last few weeks and they've noticed your attitude has improved. They are skeptical whether it will last, though, especially if the surgery diagnosis sticks. Plus, they still worry about your long-term leadership qualities. Other teams have seen how great you've played. I may be able to get you a starting gig in San Diego."

"That's the other side of the goddamn country!"

"Wyatt, you're not making any sense. I thought you wanted to start no matter what?"

After all these years of playing, he could lose everything he'd fought so hard for — a safe and secure way of life for him and his family that would last as long as they were alive. Yet, for the first time, that didn't matter to him.

All he could think about was that if he left Pittsburgh, he could lose Jenna. She needed him to be there for her during the terrifying struggle she was facing.

As if that weren't bad enough, the idea of that bastard Chase being in the same city as her without Wyatt there to protect her made him want to punch his fist through the wall.

Suddenly, Wyatt felt more desperate than ever for her to change her opinion about his shoulder.

I'm damned if I do and damned if I don't, he thought to himself bitterly. *If I don't get her on my side, I'm traded and far away from her most of the year. If she finds out I tried to use her to sway her opinion about me, then she hates me for it. Well, isn't this some fucking shit?*

Wyatt could hear Jenna in his shower. Every muscle in his body was tense with the desire to join her and have all that pretty blonde hair and smooth flesh covered in water and open to him.

Wyatt curled his hand into a fist.

I won't give up this easily.

"Gabe, schedule a meeting for us with the team for the week after New Year's. Tell them that we are going to change their minds."

Water sprayed across Jenna's face, sliding down her throat and between her breasts, before splashing onto the smooth marble tiles beneath her feet. She turned her body to allow the stream to wet her hair and traverse her back. Each drop tickled and teased her body, like thousands of tiny wet kisses.

Since her time with Wyatt had begun, it felt like every part of her was more alive and awake than ever before. Amidst that euphoria, she was also incredibly confused. The whole purpose of this arrangement had been to break free from her serious life. Yet, instead of escaping from the terrifying realities of her life, Jenna was becoming more intensely connected to Wyatt with each passing moment. Even more troubling, she'd confessed her diagnosis to him.

Now he wanted to be there for her and the offer had left her feeling relieved and cared for in a way she couldn't recall ever experiencing. Rather than try to make sense of it, she chose simply to let the water rush across her skin.

Jenna tried to ignore the sense of disappointment she felt when Wyatt hadn't joined her in the shower, and turned off the water. She stepped out and wrapped a soft towel around her wet body, securing the ends between her breasts as best she could. She could just as easily have walked around naked, seeing as her body was truly no longer secret from Wyatt in any way.

It surprised her not to find him in the bedroom, but she quietly wandered down the stairs. She didn't see him in the living room, or any of the other rooms in his elegant house with which she had become familiar.

Jenna suddenly began to feel a little silly padding around his house on her wet feet, and was about to call out for him, when he suddenly came into view. He was seated in the shadows of the very formal sitting area she'd only barely noticed before. Her feet stopped so quickly at the sight of him she almost tripped.

The light in the first floor had darkened to a soft, hazy purple as dusk finally conquered the sun outside the windows overlooking the icy Allegheny River. Wyatt was sitting in the back of the dark den. He was still in his fine slacks and shirtless, just as when she'd placed the ice pack on his shoulder.

His whole form was encased in shadows, disturbed only by the flickering glow cast from the blazing fire next to him.

When had he started that? Christ, how long was I in the shower? she wondered.

Not only had his location changed, so had his temper. He'd been concerned and caring before, but now, he looked as if he was downright brooding. Her stomach turned over with guilt at the thought she had made him sad with her news, a sign that the painful side of this process had already begun.

Jenna tried to discern the most logical approach to addressing the situation. Yet there were no charts to examine, no tests or X-rays, or blood work. There was only the tingling in her fingers and the heat of his stare, to guide her brain, and they were certainly no help. His gaze felt like it was boiling every wet droplet still on her skin or dripping incessantly from the ends of her hair.

"Come here," he commanded.

"Why?" she asked, attempting a teasing tone, though she felt her legs move independently from her body as she made her way over toward him.

The effect he had on her was unreal, like some kind of gravitational pull, and she knew he felt it, too. They were like two lonely and confused planets that had found each other and created their own solar system. Neither had any clear sense of which one of them had the more powerful force of attraction over the other. They just understood their paths were forever linked to the other.

Wyatt was sitting in an oversized, leather chair that looked like something Ernest Hemingway would've gotten drunk in after finishing *A Farewell to Arms*. Like the great writer, he looked equally tormented.

The room, the furniture, combined with Wyatt's confusing mood, and the half empty tumbler of something potent in his right hand made Jenna uneasy. Yet, before she knew it, there she was — in front of him.

Wyatt reached out his free hand and grabbed her wrist, pulling her into his lap. The smooth material of his pants combined with the warmth of his bare chest caused her to curl into him in a way she never had with another man. This feeling of being so small and reduced to another's care had always terrified her, but not now. Not with him.

Why am I so calm? Why does the feel of his arm around me and the sound of him smelling my freshly washed hair seem so...perfect?

He breathed again and squeezed slightly and the moment turned from calm to chaotic so quickly Jenna felt completely off-balance.

She leaned away — as far as he let her — and looked in his eyes.

"What's wrong, Wyatt?"

He stared back into her eyes, searching for something, but she didn't know what. He placed his glass on the floor with a thud and reached up both his hands to her, his arms tense, and ran his fingers through her damp hair until time disappeared and Jenna's heart went from a gentle insistent patter to a frenzied pace.

The turmoil in her chest reminded her of the sleeping patient's EKG she had watched one night during her last experience in the emergency room as a young med student. At that time she'd still been fooling herself she could fulfill her long-held dream of being a trauma surgeon and helping patients in the most dire of straits.

The patient was an older man who had been in a terrible accident. It was a quiet interlude she'd shared with his resting form, watching as his chest rose and lowered regularly. The gentle, steady *beep-beep-beep* transfixed her with the torturous memories it evoked.

When suddenly his body became possessed in an erratic frenzy just seconds before he went into cardiac arrest and blurs of humanity rushed into his room with the crash cart.

She'd completely panicked, and stood frozen in place the entire time. Like a true coward, she hid in the corner, watching these doctors act on adrenaline and instinct. Yet for Jenna, there was only buzzing in her ears, lead in her limbs, and shame in her heart.

Jenna was still haunted by that night in the E.R. when she yet again faced down the specter of violent death and failed to beat it. Her lack of control over what was coming next and her own horrific memory of being a weak child consumed her. She knew she was no match for the feeling of complete helplessness as the world spun around her — each life and soul so precariously close to disappearing. That old man died that night, just like her mother, and she'd failed to save either of them.

Resigned to her inadequacies, Jenna embraced orthopedic surgery. Each second was scheduled and choreographed in advance. The room was sterilized and prepared for anything, making an environment so completely predictable that Jenna felt in absolute control. There she was a champion, even if it was only in her own world.

Nothing about this moment with Wyatt and her racing heart were controlled. It should have made her feel like that twitching and ailing man in his antiseptic hospital bed, so completely at the mercy of fate and spontaneous decisions. Instead, all she could do was look into his brown and golden eyes and let the mass of sensations take over her nagging sensibilities. Finally, she willed herself to breathe slowly — in and out, in and out — to calm down and bring this overwhelming experience somehow into focus.

"Wyatt?" she whispered, leaning her head forward to him as he cupped the sides of her face. Jenna reached up a hand to stroke his face and he leaned into it heavily — his flesh almost feverish against her cool palm.

Ever since she was a child, people had told her she had "healing hands." She thanked whatever force gave them to her if they managed to help her maneuver through this moment — the intensity of which was starting to pull her under with unseen hands of its own.

"Shh. I'm okay. I promise," he said softly, his breaths feathering across her lips. "I just want to look at you. Make sure you're here."

"I'm here, Wyatt. I promise. I'm here. *We're* here."

"You are...for now. It's not enough. I need you to stay." He moved her thighs around his waist and her towel fell around her, blanketing the two of them lightly.

"Tonight? Or..." But before she could speak any further, his strong hands left her face and gripped the back of her head, tangling his fingers into her hair and crushing her lips to his.

It was almost painful, but she needed it that way, too.

Jenna wiggled her hips, fully seating herself atop him until he groaned. Wyatt snaked his other hand around her waist, pulling her tightly against his chest until her damp breasts pressed against his hot skin.

"Wyatt, I mean it, is something wrong? Is this about what I...told you? I didn't mean to upset you, I'm sorry."

"No, don't ever apologize for trusting me with the truth. Nothing's wrong. I just want to relax with you."

He held her and she was relieved to feel him start to calm down next to her.

She leaned back and glanced around the darkened room, which was lit only by the flickering fire. Even so, she could see numerous sculptures and works of art throughout the space. Sensing Wyatt wanted to change the subject to anything but his own distress, she searched her mind for something pleasant to say.

"This is some room. I like all these sculptures in here."

"You do?"

"Of course, they're beautiful. Where'd you get them?"

"Some are from little art galleries I came across over the years and others..."

Wyatt hesitated and Jenna studied his face closely.

"Wyatt McCoy, are you blushing? Where are the sculptures from?"

"That depends, which are your favorites?"

She looked around thoughtfully. "I really like the ones of people, but that one of the water crashing on the shore is really beautiful, too."

He smiled broadly and hugged her tightly around the waist. "That's great."

"Now tell me where you got them, stop being so mysterious."

"I, um, I made them."

"Are you kidding? Why would you be shy about that? They're so great."

"Having your sculptures in your house is kind of arrogant, don't you think? It's like a band wearing their own tee shirts at a concert."

"No way, my apartment walls are covered with Aubrey's photographs, and I think they look great. But I do find it adorable — and surprising — that someone who comes off as larger than life, like you, has all this humility."

"I'm adorable, huh?"

"Very, and full of surprises. You're quite the artistic man, I'd say." She leaned back to look at him better, feeling ever more relieved to see the hint of a smile on his still somewhat troubled face.

"Is that a good thing?"

"I'm quite partial to adorable and artistic, so…"

"Then it's a great thing," he said, burrowing his face into her neck and breathing quietly, and she indulged him until that creeping sense of worry started to overtake her again. She knew there was something bothering him, but it was clear he didn't want to talk about it. If anyone understood the need to ignore unpleasant things, it was Jenna. So she decided to keep humoring him with the distraction he so clearly needed.

"How'd you get into it?"

"Sculpting? Well, I loved art history in college. It was a nice escape from a lifetime of being the next 'McCoy.' I also have a little sculpting studio here in the city."

"Ooh, now that I'd like to see. Maybe you can help me make a coffee mug."

"I'd like that, especially the idea of spending more time with you."

"Really?"

"Yes, really. Now who's adorable?" he teased, kissing her softly.

Jenna ran the fingers of both her hands through his thick, wavy hair, letting the softness of the strands slide across her skin as she pressed her body closer to his chest and wrapped her legs around him again. She could sense the darkness in his heart descending again. Before she would let it take him over, she tugged slightly on the fistfuls of hair in her hands and tilted his head back until he looked directly into her eyes.

He smiled slightly and her heart eased up a bit, sensing he was back with her again.

"Maybe sculpting is your thing. You know, your outlet to improve your game?"

"No, I've done it for years, I think you're what makes me better. Maybe I should sculpt you?" he proposed, steadily running his hands up and down the sides of her upper body. "I'm starting to really like that idea. Get my two favorite things together."

"What do I have to do?"

"Stand still and do what I tell you. That may be hard for you."

Jenna leaned down and kissed him deeply. Pulling up, she whispered, "I could probably manage, especially considering I think you've done quite a bit of bossing me around so far, Mr. McCoy. You just need to keep up your form of positive reinforcement."

"I can definitely do that. I bet having a sculpture of you around would make me invincible. Since we got together, I can't lose. If you'd resisted less in the beginning, I might've made the play-offs," he teased, tickling her waist lightly.

"A couple weeks earlier would've made you even better? Come on, please," she said, laughing and writhing away from his tormenting fingers.

He suddenly stopped moving and held her to him.

"You make everything better, Doc."

"Wow, how about that? Wyatt sometimes I feel like you get out of bed each day just to find another way to shock me."

"That's good, because the person you thought I was...that's not someone I want to be."

"I'm sorry I made you feel that way."

"Don't be."

"But I *want* to be sorry, Wyatt. I know I was too hard on you. I prejudged you and that wasn't fair. You make everything better for me, too, you know? So, I want to believe in you."

"But what if I let you down?"

"I hope you don't. I *trust* that you won't. That's what believing in someone is all about. But if you do let me down, well, then I'll stop and consider the situation and where we stand, and then decide what to do."

"Always so logical, huh, Doc?"

"Unfortunately so. I've always been that way."

"I like it."

"Oh yeah, logical is *so* sexy."

"Everything about you is sexy to me, can't you tell?" he said, with that cocky smirk back on his face. But it didn't irritate her anymore. Instead it thrilled her to see that crease in one cheek and sparkle back inside his eyes — each time only for her.

He slid his hands down from her waist and grasped the globes of her bottom with firm hands and pulled her flush against the pressure of his hardening cock.

She giggled slightly and squirmed against him until he groaned.

"I told you — you're so sexy, Doc," he whispered.

The oddest wave of fear suddenly washed across her out of nowhere, as if with each contented breath she took it brought with it an insecurity and nervousness she couldn't quite place.

Before she knew it, she asked him, "What if *I* let *you* down, Wyatt?"

"You couldn't do that."

"Wyatt, I mean it, what if..."

But he kissed her firmly before she could finish her thought and she quickly lost track of all her worries, releasing them from her mind so she could take pleasure in him yet again. As his teeth nibbled her lips, she felt his warm, smooth fingers venture across the skin of her cool chest — a contrast that sent a thrilled shiver down her spine. A rush of air struck her when she watched her damp towel flutter to the floor beneath them.

He reached a hand down, undoing his pants and Jenna lifted her bottom and helped him slide them and his boxer briefs down his legs and onto the floor.

Wyatt teased her opening with two calloused fingers and she squirmed against his touch, already wet and clenching around his fingers. His thumb worked her clit in a tight circle until her arousal was almost painful. Her back arched, thrusting her breasts into his face.

When Jenna didn't feel his mouth on her she opened her eyes and looked at him. His face was twisted with emotion.

"Please don't change the way you are with me, Wyatt. I can't bear it if you look at me differently now that you know," she pleaded, never feeling more aware of her traitorous body than in that moment.

"You're even more beautiful to me now, Jenna. I promise."

He leaned down to lick her breasts gently, nibbling on one nipple, then the next. One hand reached up to her head, pulling her mouth to his now upturned face. When their lips met, he used both hands to lift her body and thrust himself into her with potent force.

Jenna cried out at the potent sensation of him fully seated in her body. His hands were everywhere — in her hair, on her breasts, at her waist, teasing the flesh of her nape — but it wasn't enough. Jenna touched every part of him that she could reach, from the hot corners of his shoulders, to the ridges of his biceps, and the tensing edges of his abdominals.

Their kisses mirrored the movements of their bodies. As their tongues moved in and out of each other's mouths, Jenna rocked up and down on his rigid length while he arched upward to meet her. His movements became more frantic and out of rhythm as they both gasped heatedly from the passion of the moment.

"Wyatt," Jenna breathed out desperately.

"Yes, Jenna. Now," he whispered. He pulled her down against him until they were completely connected, and she could feel a pulsing rhythm inside her as his release entered her. Her body convulsed above him. The sensation was beyond an orgasm, and all she could do was collapse against his chest as her body relaxed into gentle twitches.

Wyatt stroked her hair and rested her face in the crook of his neck.

"Don't move, belleza. Please."

"Okay," she whispered, against the pulse beating at his throat.

Jenna closed her eyes and breathed him in as deeply as she could, allowing every inch of her body to melt into his.

CHAPTER SIXTEEN

"How's the hot cocoa? It's my abuela's recipe. I hope it's not too spicy?" Wyatt asked Jenna, making sure she was wrapped up snugly in her coat and enough blankets to keep her warm on the love seat on the veranda outside his bedroom.

He'd spent the last two days trying to focus only on the joy being with Jenna brought him. Yet, he knew that with each second they came closer to the New Year, the pressing reality of all the obstacles they faced waited impatiently in the wings. Her surgery, the machinations he'd made to further his career, and the precarious nature of their relationship, were the evil supporting cast in the play of their lives together. He wished he could close the curtain on all of them.

"Mmm, it's delicious, Wyatt. I love Mexican chocolate. Thanks. But, do you really think we'll be able to see the downtown New Year's fireworks?"

"It's worth a shot. We may have to lean over the edge, though."

"Um, then never mind. I'd rather stay over here."

"Wait a second," he said, pulling her between his legs and stroking her under the blankets lightly. "You're not afraid of heights, are you? Tough girl like you?"

"No, I'm not afraid of heights. I am afraid of *falling*. That is completely rational and the result of thousands of years of productive evolution."

"I don't buy it. You're scared of heights. Back ba-ba-back," he teased, flapping his arms lightly like a chicken.

"Very mature."

"Hey, you did it first."

"Don't remind me. That was *not* my finest hour."

"I actually thought you were pretty funny."

"You keep teasing me like this, you might lose your nooky privileges."

"'Nooky?' Now who sounds like an eighty-year-old?"

"I'm warning you, McCoy, one more joke, and no more nooky. It's up to you."

"All right, I give. You're right, Doc. All the time. In every way."

"Much better. Now get those arms back around me and warm me up. I'm out of cocoa."

"I could get you more."

Jenna turned and glanced at the New Year's countdown on the TV through the glass French doors leading to his bedroom.

"No. It's almost midnight. I don't want to miss the countdown."

"Oh, you're right. Come on. Stand with me so we can try to see the fireworks. I'll warm you up."

Wyatt took the mug from her hand and put it on the small side table before lifting her up and pulling her body tightly to his. From inside he could vaguely hear the voices on the TV indicating time was quickly running out.

He pressed her body close to his as she joined him in counting down from ten.

"Happy New Year, Jenna," he whispered.

"Happy New Year, Wyatt."

The sound of fireworks they could just barely see rumbled in the distance, syncing with their linked heartbeats.

Wyatt began singing *Auld Lang Syne* in her ear. With the last lilt of his temporary brogue across the words "auld lang syne," he kissed her temple. On a quiet breath, he silently prayed they could have the courage to move past the misfortune of old times past, and find the strength to face an uncertain future together.

"That was beautiful. I would have sung along with you, but I think I'd make your ears bleed."

"I won't comment on your singing. Let's just say, you don't have to be great at everything, Doc. You can leave the singing to me," he teased.

"How diplomatic of you," she said softly against his neck, with a light chuckle. "I wouldn't have been able to anyway. I don't know those words."

"It's the Gaelic version. Grandma McCoy taught it to me when I was very little. I only met her a couple of times before my dad was out of our lives. This is the first time I've sung it since then."

"I loved it. Thank you for sharing it with me."

He leaned away from her and searched her eyes for some relief from the anguish that had plagued him ever since she'd told him about her diagnosis.

"Wyatt, you can't will it out of my body," she declared.

"What are you talking about? I just like looking at you is all."

"Don't play dumb," she remarked, lifting a hand to his cheek. "I know that look. I saw it on my dad's face in the months my mom got worse and worse. You can't ever make the bad go away. If it turns out I can't kick this... Then all we can do is hope — hope that I'll get better."

"But it's not fair," he insisted, clutching her shoulders with more force than he intended. Willing himself to loosen his grip before bruising her, he added, "We only just found each other..."

"Before she passed away, my mom told me it isn't about whether life is fair. It's just *not*. You'll drive yourself nuts if you try to make it to be. Life can actually be a real son of a bitch." Jenna kissed the skin of his throat tenderly before continuing, "All you can do is grab at something great when life is willing to give it to you and cherish it. She was right. We need to treasure these moments we have together. We can't worry about what will happen next, or wonder which kiss or breath could be the last. Look at my dad. He didn't get to say goodbye to my mother. She'd promised him she'd be there when he got back, but instead, it all ended while she was talking to me. I took that moment from him, and I didn't even make the most of it."

Wyatt stroked her hair and looked over her head, swallowing hard.

"You can't think like that. Your father loves you."

"I know, but nothing about that day was fair. We let the moments get away from us. I won't let these moments get away from you and me, Wyatt. I refuse to."

She shivered against him and he reluctantly pulled away from her, taking her inside. They tossed the blankets and their coats on the floor. Wyatt undressed her carefully and let her undress him, before they climbed into bed.

He lay alongside her beautiful body and stroked the full length of her curves. She was naked and bare before him, wearing nothing but her mother's locket and the matching earrings he'd given her. Wyatt swore she'd never looked prettier.

After a silent moment, Wyatt felt the need to share more with her. "No one knows the life I've really lived, except my family…and you. They all thought I was a spoiled, entitled jerk with this famous dad. I let them believe it. But sometimes I wonder what life would be like if I were just me. Not Wyatt McCoy — son of the greatest quarterback ever, always living under a microscope. But just *me*. Just *Wyatt*."

"But you're just Wyatt with me, isn't that something?"

"Fuck, Jenna. That's everything," he answered. Wyatt rolled on top of her so that he could kiss her cheeks and eyelids. "I like who I am with you, belleza. The influence you have on me."

"Oh yeah. I like a lot about you, too, Wyatt. I like when you sing to me. In Spanish or in Gaelic."

"Half-Mexican and half-Irish makes for a lot of singing…and a foul temper," he said, between nibbles at her neck.

"I'm okay with that. I also like this little scar on your chin," she said, touching the remnants of a long-since healed gash lightly.

"I got it during a backyard football game when I was thirteen."

"I think it's sexy," she said huskily, before licking the raised flesh. Wyatt felt like he was turning inside out and groaned a little. "You like *that*?" she asked against his cheek.

"You know I do. I like pretty much everything about you. You get that, right, Doc?"

"I think so."

He leaned down against her body more heavily and kissed her lips.

"Don't you mean that you *know* so?"

"Yes, I'm pretty sure that I do know so. I like the hell out of you. I don't know how to deal with that, but…"

"I think I more than like you, Doc."

Jenna swallowed hard beneath him, running a silky hand across his face.

"I think I more than like you, too, Wyatt."

"Is it okay if I think I love you?"

"Yes, it's okay. Because I think I love you, too."

If life really were so unfair as to take her from him, then he would relish every little moment of good it was willing to give them together.

He finally accepted that even if it meant being on the practice squad in Pittsburgh until he was forty years old, he'd do it to be near her. She needed him, and he would do whatever it took to be there for her. Wyatt ran his face across the warm skin of her chest before kissing every inch of her breasts and throat. He let happiness wash over him — losing himself in it, worshipping it.

"Wyatt…"

He looked up to her face. Her voice was so tentative he could barely recognize it.

"Yes, belleza?"

"I have a confession to make."

"Yes?"

"I-I'm kind of scared."

"Of course you are. I'm pretty scared, too."

"Wyatt, please know…I also wish life were fair. I don't want to leave you." A sob broke from her chest, the sound was like shattering glass, and he lifted up quickly, rolling on his side to bring her into his arms and held her close. He stroked her hair too hard, as he felt the emotions tearing him apart.

With a rough motion, he squeezed his arms even more tightly around her, trying to use all his strength to keep her safe.

"I know, Jenna. I know. I wish you'd told me sooner, but I'm glad you finally did," he whispered, kissing her hair, her cheeks, eyelids, and every inch of her tear-streaked face.

She leaned back from him, wiping her face and forcing a chuckle.

"Wow, I'm a real mood killer. How about a more fun confession? I wanted to say yes to you from the first day I met you."

"I knew it," he whispered, kissing her cheek with grinning lips.

"Down, boy. That kiss by the car probably confirmed that to you," she said, with a soft laugh. "I was nervous, though — about what it would look like from the outside, since I'd consulted on your shoulder. I also worried you were like another athlete I've known — selfish, dishonest."

"Oh," he muttered out roughly. Wyatt's heart seized with pain at the reminder of those gruesome characters that haunted them. They were trying to take center stage in their lives again and he hated it. The mere thought of Chase Matthews anywhere near her unleashed a whole new slew of protective fury in him.

"But now I see you aren't like that," she said reassuringly, turning her body to face him. She kissed him repeatedly until his body started to relax. "I think I got reminded life is shorter than we realize. I knew that, but I guess I let myself forget for a moment. Maybe these tumors were a blessing? Forcing me to take a risk with you." She paused, before asking, "So, why did *you* agree to this time together, Wyatt? I mean, I know I wasn't exactly sweet as pie to you," she teased, hugging him more closely to her.

"You may have been trying like hell to be a tough cookie on the outside, but I had a feeling I could be your big glass of milk — soften you up."

She groaned at his lame joke, but the sound turned to a moan as he stretched over her body and slipped his legs between hers.

"I think we're a good match, Jenna."

"You do?"

"Yeah. You're aggressive and want to be in control…"

"Hey, that makes me sound…"

He pressed into her harder, his stiffening penis nestling between her folds and rubbing against her most sensitive parts.

"Shh, I like you being strong. But I need to be in control sometimes, too. That's why I'll let you have enough rope to make you happy, but then I'll turn around and tie you up with it."

"Ooh, now that sounds promising," she giggled, then added, "I'm glad I told you about the surgery, and what's coming next. That way we don't have any more secrets."

Wyatt opened and closed his mouth like a dying fish, gasping for air. He wanted so much to tell her the truth, to explain why he was so desperate to make her change her opinion on his shoulder. That even though his motives for spending time with her hadn't been pure at the beginning, his feelings now *were*. Yet, no words came.

"Wyatt, are you okay? Is something wrong?"

"No. I'm just really glad you told me, too. No secrets."

The shame in his gut ate at him, but it was too important he be there for her. Their feelings were a tender new plant that could grow into a strong tree someday. He simply needed to protect it from harm — even if one of those threats was of his own making.

"That's great. You know, they say what you do at midnight is what you'll do all year," she said, with a mischievous smile.

"Is that right?"

"Yep. So, I was thinking... What I'd like to do this midnight is *you*."

"That sounds like one hell of a year, Doc," he replied, with a deep laugh.

"Now get those lips of yours over here, Mr. McCoy, and make my New Year's wish come true."

"I told you...to call me, Wyatt," he teased, before closing his lips over hers. He relaxed his body against hers, reveling in the way she fit perfectly against him. As he slipped inside of her, he let all his fears disappear.

She was falling for him, too.

Everything was going to be okay.

A slight tickle at the skin of her cheek interrupted Jenna's slumber. She rolled over and a whiff of coffee pleasantly wafted into her nose. As her eyes fluttered open, she smiled at the sight of Wyatt seated next to her on the edge of the bed. He was stroking her face lightly with his left hand and wearing nothing but light cotton pajama bottoms. Two coffee mugs steamed next to him on the bedside table.

After the intensity of the night before, Jenna was filled with joy at their easy domesticity. Maybe they were just playing house, for now, but she felt confident she didn't want this wonderful game ever to end. She clumsily reached up a hand to stroke at the smooth muscles of his chest, letting her fingers slide down the rippling edges of his stomach.

"Morning, Doc. Are you having fun pawing at me?"

"Yes. I can't help it. I think I may be obsessed with your body," she mumbled, still groggy.

"That works, since I *know* I'm obsessed with yours. Though, it really interferes with finding the motivation to leave this bed."

With a sigh, she reluctantly stopped groping him and sat up.

"Oh, that reminds me. I need to get my butt in gear. I have to be at Tea's house in a couple hours."

"Is everything okay?" he asked, and the wrinkles in his brow looked so cute, that Jenna had to nuzzle his neck for a moment.

"It's all good, I promise. Every year we make a traditional Southern New Year's dinner. Well, she cooks. I mostly try to keep her from dropping things while I watch the Rose Bowl. I'd probably poison everyone if I tried making actual food."

Wyatt moved so he was sitting next to her and gently stroked the part of her leg that had escaped from under the sheet.

"You know, Doc, after you help me do my shoulder rehab exercises, I don't have any other plans today. One of the few benefits of not making it to the play-offs is getting some more free time. How about I come with you today? You can finally tell your friends about us."

Jenna's heart squeezed at his question. The idea of opening their relationship to the world was thrilling, but also terrifying. His eyes hardened with her hesitance and she could tell he felt hurt. The realization made her feel terrible.

"I'm your dirty little secret. I get it."

Jenna wrapped her arms around his neck and kissed him quickly.

"It's not like that at all, Wyatt. I promise."

"They're important to you...part of your family. You met my family. They know we're together."

"And I love that they know about us. I can't wait to tell my friends about us, I swear. I just want to handle it perfectly. Tea has a lot going on right now. Plus, she's got a full house for the holidays, so it's extra crazy over there. I also feel bad now that I didn't say anything about us sooner. That means I have to handle the news carefully."

"Why do these sound a lot like excuses, Doc?"

"They aren't! I mean it. I'm going to tell them today. I have a whole plan I've been working on. I was thinking I could call you after I tell her and you can come over then?"

"Yeah?"

She nodded and he kissed her. "That's a promise and I'm going to hold you to it, Doc," he murmured against her lips. Wyatt's strong hands snaked around her bare waist and she immediately considered canceling every appointment she ever had for the rest of her life. Wyatt broke the kiss and she leaned against his chest in comfortable silence. His voice finally broke through the calm.

"Are you going to tell them about your...you know..."

"My lumpectomy? Maybe. And you know you're allowed to say the word." He hugged her so forcefully to him she was worried he'd crack a rib. "Wyatt, you're gonna squeeze the stuffing out of me."

"Jenna, it's okay to be emotional. You didn't tell anyone because you know it's a big deal. Let me worry about you. I'm good at worrying. Just ask Claudia. She'll tell you it's kind of my thing."

Jenna reached her arms around his waist and kissed his neck.

"Fine. I'll let you worry about me. I'll warn you, though, I might get used to it."

"Good. That's my intention, Doc," he answered, with a kiss to the top of her head that made her sigh with contentment.

Wyatt was dressed and trying to distract himself as he waited for Jenna to call him. His phone rang and he jumped for it. A stab of disappointment shot through him when he saw it was his agent. He'd just have to wait a little longer before Jenna was ready for him.

"Hey Gabe. Happy New Year."

"Cut the bullshit, Wyatt."

"What bullshit?" Gabe was clearly furious about something, but Wyatt didn't have a clue as to what could have him so riled.

"I've put up with a lot of shit from you over the years, but this is beyond fucked up. I should fire you as a client right now."

"Christ, Gabe, calm down. What the hell are you talking about?"

"It's my fault for not having the balls to nix your stupid Dr. Sutherland scheme in the first place."

"Wait, what about Jenna...I mean Dr. Sutherland?"

"I know you're driven, but I never thought you'd pull something like this. This is so fucking low."

Wyatt suddenly felt cold fear oozing down his spine. He fought to breathe and bit out as many words as he could through the invisible fist squeezing at his throat.

"Dammit, Gabe! I need you to tell me what happened.

Right now!"

"Let *ESPN* do it. Or *Fox Sports,* or any goddamn sports news channel you can find."

"What do you mean?" Wyatt asked, but he was already pulling up *Fox Sports* on his laptop. And immediately wished he hadn't.

The title of *Fox Sports'* latest exposé was: *Gunslinger McCoy Romances His Own Doctor in Desperate Ploy to Stay on Team.*

There he and Jenna were — every aspect and stage of their relationship seemed to be plastered all over the Internet. There were pictures of them at the ice-skating rink, afterward in the parking garage, and of him walking into Carol's restaurant. There were even images of him waiting for her in her parking lot after he returned from the Oakland game, and was so furious at the sight of her with Trey.

No matter what page he went to, there they were. The main focus was the salacious story about his illicit affair with the voluptuous blonde surgeon that consulted on his shoulder. The worst part though, was how the story asserted he was only involved with Jenna so he could use her position to save his career.

"Gabe, what the hell is this? Where the fuck did this article come from? I didn't want this to happen."

"Then how did Olivia get all this?"

"Olivia?"

"Yeah, it's her story. Her pictures. She quotes you as saying: Dr. Sutherland was going to see things your way one way or another. Did she make that up? If she did, we can sue her."

"She didn't make it up," he whispered. "I said it after the New Orleans game. I was all amped up and trying to get her to back off."

"That explains when the pictures started. The first ones came within days of that game."

"Fuck, Gabe, you're right. She must've been following me, stalking the two of us. She's here in Pittsburgh all the time." Wyatt scanned through one shot after another of him pursuing Jenna all the way through to them on his veranda the night before. The image looked like it was taken with a night vision camera. "Me at yoga with her...meeting her for ice-skating. Christ, even us kissing for the first time. It makes it look like we were together while she was still consulting on me."

"At least her opinion on your shoulder was unfavorable. That may help her, ethically speaking."

"Christ. You're right. This could ruin her career. We have to fix this."

"Why do you want to fix it? And you better be honest with me, Wy."

Wyatt sank heavily in the chair in front of his laptop, his eyes fixated on a picture taken in his driveway. He was holding Jenna in his arms after she'd been so upset that she ran from his family. They were kissing and the intimacy of the moment was almost too perfect. Olivia violated that beautiful experience, and now Jenna was bound to hate him. After everything she'd been through with Chase, she would think the absolute worst of him.

And why wouldn't she? He *was* the worst. His own words made him look like a brutal manipulator. She'd probably hate him, and he might actually deserve it.

"Are you still there?" Gabe asked with a frustrated tone.

Wyatt cleared his throat hard and answered, "I'm here, Gabe. We have to fix this...because I love her."

That answer seemed to appease Gabe, because he sighed and said gently, "Good, but you've really fucked up big time,

Wyatt. I'm sorry to say that this may not be fixable."

"I know, man. I know."

Jenna opened the door to Tea's house. She was a little early, but she knew Tea wouldn't mind. It made it that much sooner that Jenna could tell them about Wyatt and get him over there. Then she could stop feeling like a fool for missing him already.

The kitchen was empty, but she heard the soft hint of voices from down the hall and followed them. The door to the small back room Tea had turned into Griffen's writing area was slightly ajar. She almost walked in, but quickly realized this was no conversation to interrupt.

Tea was seated on Griffen's lap in a cute little two-piece shorty pajama set. Griffen's left hand was resting on her leg, while his other hand was holding her chin firmly in his grip. Jenna felt horrible for eavesdropping, but she could tell they were just talking and she was too curious to know what was going on with these two.

"Why didn't you tell me how you were feeling, Althea?"

"I did tell you. This morning."

"But you should've told me sooner. You have to talk to me, gorgeous. I want to fast-forward through all this preliminary stuff and go straight to our life together. *Our* family. You need to be ready to put on the brakes if I go too far or too fast. I need you to tell me if it's too much. If you don't like something I'm doing..."

"That's the thing, I love everything you're doing. Our life together — you, me, and Johnny — us as a family...it means the world to me. I don't want to do anything to risk harming it.

I don't want to mess this up. I want us to be forever. I don't want to hurt you, or risk you leaving us, just because I feel overwhelmed."

"You could never do anything to make me leave," he whispered, moving his hand to hold her jaw, kissing her deeply. When he pulled away, Tea's eyes were heavy and almost drugged-looking. "I know I've been pushing, but that's because I want us to have everything this life together entails, right now. If you aren't honest with me about how you feel, then I'll just unknowingly push more."

Tea grinned and nibbled at his chin.

"That's because you're incorrigible, Griffen Tate. I don't want you to change, but I will try to be more open with you about how I'm feeling. Losing the last parts of Jack that are in my life is terrifying to me. I won't lie."

"You can't lose him from your life. I would never let that happen. He'll always be with us."

"I know that, Griffen. So, I've been thinking. How do you think the name Althea Taylor Tate sounds? I would change my middle name to Jack's last name when you and I get married. I'll still take your last name, though. Would you be okay with that?"

Jenna's heart swelled with relief to hear Tea had apparently been handling her issues just fine without her and Aubrey constant meddling into her life.

"Gorgeous, I think that is the most beautiful name I've ever heard."

"And please know I love everything you're doing with Johnny. I appreciate it so much. I'm sorry I wasn't more receptive to your idea to adopt him. Of course you're worried about what could happen if you don't have a legal claim to him. What if I died…"

Griffen clutched her arms and moved closer to her body.

"Don't even say that, Althea."

She giggled lightly and stroked his hair.

"Sorry. See, you share your feelings with me right away. That's so wonderful. My point is, I get it, and I think it is a beautiful thought. I know it would make Johnny happy, too. And your idea about moving…"

"I've had a lot of ideas lately, haven't I?" he laughed.

"You have. To show you how much I love them, I found a house on Shady Avenue in the Squirrel Hill area of the city. It's kind of big, but it's old and historic and completely beautiful. It has an amazing yard and a wrought iron gate, just like in some nineteenth century novel. I won't have a view of the rivers anymore, but maybe that's a good thing. Plus, it's really close to Jenna and Aubrey. I think it would be good for them, so we can make sure they see Johnny as much as possible."

"Althea, it sounds perfect. I'll buy it for you today."

"You haven't even seen it!"

"Don't have to. If you love it, I love it. I love you."

"I love you so much, too. Not sure if the realtor will pick up the phone on New Year's Day, but I'm getting excited!"

"Speaking of excited…" Griffen growled at her, creeping his hand underneath the hem of her shorts.

Jenna started to realize just how inappropriate her snooping was becoming. As Griffen moved his hands to start undoing the buttons of her pajama top, Jenna turned and quickly ran toward the kitchen. In her haste, she knocked a book off a small table in the hallway.

She cringed and heard footsteps behind her. With a blush, she turned and saw Tea walking toward her, cheeks completely flushed, as her fingers fumbled with the buttons of her pajama top.

"Jenna...um, you're early."

"I know, I'm sorry."

"It's okay, let me just get dressed. Johnny is playing with my mom at that little park nearby. There's only an inch of snow from last night but he was insistent he wanted to make a snow man."

"No rush. I'll just go watch the parade. Go spend some more time with your man," Jenna instructed her with a wink.

"Thanks, Jenna," Tea said, giving her a hug.

Jenna relaxed in the kitchen for half an hour, watching the parade on the little TV Tea had on her kitchen counter before Vivian and Johnny barreled into the room.

"Dang, Miss Jenna. You are positively glowing. What have you been up to?" Vivian asked after pulling her into a warm hug.

"Auntie Jenna! Hi," Johnny exclaimed, waiting for her to sit back down so he could climb into her lap. Tea and Griffen joined them, both looking flushed and relaxed in a way that had Jenna very eager to see Wyatt again.

"Hi, Jenna, good to see you again," Griffen said, with a happy grin, as he put an arm around Tea's shoulders.

"Hi, y'all. I'm so glad to see all of you. I'm hungry, too. Tea, I swear you and Viv make the best expatriated Southerner's New Year's Day dinner on earth."

"It helps a lot to have my mom here to help."

"I'm sure."

"I love those earrings, Jenna. Where did you get them?" Tea asked.

"They were a gift."

"Oh, really? Who is this generous person?" Vivian asked meaningfully, as she handed the grown-ups mimosas, with a plain OJ for Johnny. "Could they be the reason you're fixing to make me need to dim the lights with how bright that smile on your face is, girl? Who is he?"

"What?"

"Come on, you can't kid a kidder. I know that look, and it's pretty obvious since you're usually the serious one amongst all these maniacs," Vivian added with a conspiratorial wink.

"Wait, Jenna, are you actually seeing someone?" Tea asked. Jenna caught Trey's knowing gaze out of the corner of her eye as he entered the kitchen. He was holding a very expensive-looking bottle of French wine.

"What's everyone so worked up about?" Trey asked.

"Jenna has a new man in her life," Tea said effusively.

Trey looked at Jenna with the hint of a conspiratorial smile, but didn't comment.

"Well, um, it's Wyatt McCoy. Oh, speak of the devil," she added when her phone began buzzing. Wyatt was calling her, but she would need to call him back. Sharing this with them was too big a moment.

"What? Oh my God, that's amazing," Tea said, clearly shocked. "Are you two a thing?"

"Yeah. A very real thing. I was wondering if you'd mind if I had him come over today to have dinner with us?"

"Of course, we don't mind," Tea exclaimed. "This is so neat."

"Wait, why does that name sound so familiar?" Vivian asked.

"He's the quarterback for the Pittsburgh Roughnecks, Mom. And he's insanely good-looking. Not as handsome as Griffen, of course," Tea added, kissing Griffen's cheek. She grabbed her laptop and started messing with it before adding, "Let me *Google* him for you."

After tapping on the keys quickly, Tea gasped loudly and

threw her hand to her mouth.

"What is it, Althea?" Griffen asked, looking over her shoulder, before gripping the edge of Tea's chair so hard it looked like it would break in his hands.

"What's wrong, you guys?" Jenna stood and walked around to try and catch sight of what had them so upset.

"Jenna, I don't know if you should look. Oh, honey…"

Violent waves of nausea racked her body with each photograph that flashed across the screen. It was so surreal Jenna could almost convince herself she was dreaming…*almost*.

Almost every moment she and Wyatt had shared were somehow now broadcasted for the world to see, and mock, in vibrant high-definition.

Oh God, these pictures are everywhere. Was every day together a setup? An attempt to discredit me? How could Wyatt not have known — not been involved with it?

These had been special and exciting experiences for her, but now, they were all frozen in time with a patina of betrayal and hurt. Every memory of falling in love with him had morphed into something evil and ugly, as though the last few weeks were being twisted in the reflection of a fun house mirror. Where beauty and hope had previously been, now only remained disgrace.

She felt hands on her shoulders and the nudge of a chair behind her knees. Jenna was so light-headed, she thought she might actually faint. In the distance she saw Trey smack his hand hard against the wall of the kitchen.

"I'm gonna fucking kill him," he growled.

"Not if I kill him first," Griffen added.

Jenna kept staring at Tea's laptop screen, pulling up one Web site after another. It seemed like the whole world was looking at her — laughing at her. Distant voices were trying to speak to her, but she could focus on nothing but her own internal words of shame.

"Jenna, say something," Tea pleaded.

"You need to stop looking at that shit. I'll throw that laptop out the window if I have to," Trey threatened. Practically mute, she shook her head and clicked over to another Web site.

Tea grabbed her hands and yanked them away from the keyboard, forcing Jenna to look at her.

"Let me go! I have to see it. I have to see what he did to me!" Jenna suddenly shouted, trying to pry her hands out of Tea's grasp.

"Auntie Jenna, what's wrong?" Johnny asked her.

"She's okay, Johnny," Tea answered. "Mom, can you take Johnny to his room to watch cartoons?" Tea quickly looked back over at her, ready to deliver a command. "Jenna, you need to snap out of it. Now. Maybe it's not as bad as it looks."

Jenna breathed deeply and finally responded, "They quoted him, Tea. They don't do that unless they aren't worried about being sued, right?"

"Well…"

"That's what I thought."

"But maybe there's something we don't know. Remember when you told me to talk to Griffen after he admitted to investigating Jack's death?"

"You were mad because you didn't like *what* he told you. I don't even have that luxury. Griffen didn't make you learn about what he'd been doing from the *New York Times*."

"I just don't want you to jump to a bunch of conclusions you'll regret. It's hard to know exactly what to think about his motives. I only just learned you were dating him."

"Tea, don't add guilt to the mix. We can't really talk about keeping a relationship secret," Griffen interjected.

"I didn't mean that at all," Tea insisted, as she began stroking Jenna's hair. "It's just I can't really know if all these things this reporter, Olivia 'whoever,' says about him using you are true without knowing more. Maybe he has an explanation. The existence of these pictures may look bad, but you can't deny how happy you look in them."

"I look happy in them because I am...I mean, I *was*. I love him, Tea..."

"Oh, honey." Tea wrapped her arms around Jenna trying to soothe her, but she wasn't even sure if she remembered how to breathe.

Leaning back, she stared into her dear friend's shimmering hazel eyes, watery with emotion, and whispered, "It looks so bad, though. Like he set me up. How could she have all these pictures of us — know where we were all the time?"

Tea furrowed her brow, clearly trying to come up with a good counterargument. Before she could speak, Jenna jumped in her seat at the sound of a loud knocking at the door.

"I'll get it," Trey said as he strode over, motioning for everyone to stay seated. "We don't know who it could be."

Jenna heard Wyatt's voice in the distance and her heart was overcome with pain. She wanted so much to run to him and let him say it was okay, but the weight of her fears had immobilized her.

Tea stared at her intently before asking, "Jenna, do you want to talk to him? Give him a chance to explain?"

Jenna looked at her worried eyes and shook her head, "I can't see him right now. I don't trust myself to even know what is the truth or a lie. Tea...I don't think I know how to love the right person."

"Don't say that, honey. Maybe it *is* better you have a little time. Come here."

Tea drew Jenna back into her arms and she could feel her friend shake her head in the direction of Trey. He must've been watching for her answer because she saw him turn back to the door.

"She doesn't want to see you, man."

"Move it, Trey. I need to talk to her."

"Leave before I make you leave," Trey growled at him and slammed the door.

"Jenna!" Wyatt was screaming on the other side of the door, banging on the wood for several minutes.

"Dammit, that boy needs to quit while he's behind," Vivian said, from the other end of the room. "I put Johnny in his room. He doesn't need to hear all this. Let me mix up something stronger than mimosas. I have a feeling we're going to need them. Let's each have an old-fashioned. Tea, honey, where do you keep your sugar cubes?"

When the pounding and shouting finally ceased, Jenna thought her heart stopped beating with it.

CHAPTER SEVENTEEN

Tea handed Jenna a cup of coffee before spooning out a bowl of buttery grits for Johnny's breakfast. He began shoveling the hot cereal into his mouth without a care in the world. Jenna, on the other hand, still felt like hers was ending. She'd taken Griffen and Tea up on their offer of staying with them for the night. The mere thought the press might be waiting outside her apartment was enough reason to hide out in Tea's crowded duplex for a little while longer.

Before she could take a sip of her coffee, the front door opened and Aubrey barreled inside, throwing her purse and duffel bag on the floor.

"What are you doing here, Aubrey? You're supposed to be in Denver!" Jenna said, completely shocked.

"I told her you were here. She saw the Olivia Hayes article," Tea answered.

"Auntie Brey!" Johnny jumped out of his seat and rushed into her arms.

"Hey little man. Wow, you're really sounding like a big boy. Your 'R's' are coming along great. Can you head to your room and grab some face paint so we can make a mess with each other?"

"Man, you guys keep making me leave. This sucks."

"Johnny! Don't say that word," Tea chastised. "I know it stinks, but we'll have fun in a couple minutes, okay?"

"Sorry, Mom," he pouted. Tea leaned down and gave him a kiss on the cheek and he kissed Brey's cheek before running off to his room.

"Jenna, of course I'm back. The second I saw those headlines, I got the first flight home. It was a total bitch to fly home on New Year's Day, but I knew you'd be having a meltdown."

"Thanks, Brey," Jenna said to her, as Brey hugged her seated form.

"You're welcome, babe. Though I am disappointed you kept your sexy times from me."

"I'm sorry."

"Hey, Brey," Griffen said, walking into the kitchen. He wrapped an arm around Tea and kissed the top of her head. "I was just on the phone with my lawyer in New York. They're going to try and get an injunction to stop further distribution of the article and pictures, but he said it's a long shot. I'm sorry, Jenna."

"Not to add onto the bad news," Aubrey said. "But it's good you stayed here last night. My flight didn't land until almost midnight last night, but the paparazzi were camped outside our apartment even then."

"Oh, no. You're kidding?" Jenna said, feeling completely desperate.

"I'm sorry, but it's true," Trey said, walking into the kitchen in his boxers. He was pulling an undershirt on over his bare chest, covering his many tattoos and nipple rings. He looked exhausted as he smoothed down the tee shirt and ran his hand through his tousled hair. He'd refused to leave after he saw how upset Jenna still was the night before. With Vivian set to emerge from her room upstairs soon, too, they were having the most depressing slumber party in history. "That's how these vultures work, Jenna," Trey continued, "they're probably at your work, Wyatt's house, everywhere either of you would go."

"Well, that blows," Aubrey said, as she scooped out some grits for herself.

"Griffen, what are we going to do?" Tea asked, "should you take Jenna to your place in New York?"

"You mean *our* place in New York," Griffen corrected Tea, planting a kiss on her cheek.

"Yeah, our place," Tea said with a smile.

"That's better, gorgeous. But no. I really think she's better off here. Pittsburgh is less celebrity-crazed than most places, especially compared to New York. Movie stars are here all the time for filming and pretty much no one bothers them. Besides, I don't want to leave you and Johnny. Trey and I can keep an eye on her, at least for now."

"Thanks for thinking of it, Tea, but I don't want to go anywhere," Jenna said.

"You're right. Besides, here we have a better chance of making sure the cops take the time to make sure none of this attention gets out of hand. Carol called me last night. She was really worried about Jenna's safety and already had calls in to her friends at the Pittsburgh Police Department, so hopefully that will help, too," Tea added.

"Good for Carol," Aubrey said. "I have to say, though, none of this makes sense to me. Is this reporter obsessed with Wyatt, or something?" Aubrey asked, sitting down to her grits and coffee.

"It seems like more than that to me," Trey said. "Not sure what, but my instinct says she's got something bigger in mind than a crush on a football player."

"Yeah, my bet is she wants a primetime feature on *Fox Sports*," Griffen said bitterly. "And she'll probably get it."

"Oh God," Jenna suddenly started to panic. "My face will be everywhere." Her heart went cold at the sudden thought of Chase reading about her, staring at the photos of her with Wyatt. She figured he knew where she was, but it made her sick to think of him looking at her.

Aubrey sat next to her and put her arm around Jenna's shoulder. "It already is, girl. We just need it to blow over."

"Blow over? You know how hard I worked to get to where I am today."

"But you really should lay low. What if you stay with us? Griffen will be here, Trey, too. That would make me feel better," Tea said, sitting down next to her with worry creasing her face. "You don't have to go anywhere, right? I think you should stick close. Aubrey, you can stay here, too."

"Duh, of course. We'll hide out in our pajamas and watch chick flicks with our phones off. It'll be fun."

"Um, I have an appointment I can't miss tomorrow," Jenna responded softly.

"Work?"

"No."

"What is it, Jenna? Why are you being so cagey?"

"I don't want to worry you."

"Well, you're worrying the hell out of all of us right now."

"If she doesn't want to tell you, she doesn't have to. People are entitled to their secrets," Trey said sternly, squeezing her shoulder in a brotherly way that made her heart hurt. It felt nice to have someone on her side.

"I know you feel that way, mystery man. Jesus, Jenna, what else is going on? I can only worry so much before my heart explodes," Aubrey demanded loudly.

"Don't yell at her," Trey said firmly, quickly standing between Jenna and everyone else — protecting her.

"Who the fuck do you think you are, barging into our lives and telling us what to do? Griffen, you need to control your friend."

Aubrey was standing up, her finger in Trey's face. It looked like she was releasing all her pent up frustrations on him, and it made Jenna feel terribly guilty.

"Enough!" Jenna shouted, finally finding her voice. "I have a lumpectomy scheduled for tomorrow to remove several tumors."

Everyone in the room, except for Trey, looked shocked. He put his hand back on her shoulder reassuringly.

"Oh God, Jenna. What? Do they think it's cancer?"

"They can't be sure until they remove them tomorrow. I have to go through radiation, too."

"But you are the same age your mother was when she found out she was sick," Aubrey said, her voice choking with emotion.

"I know. She died four months later. So, no, I can't miss this appointment." Jenna flopped against the back of her seat, trying to ignore the queasy anxiety in her stomach.

"Why didn't you tell us?" Griffen asked, his voice rough with frustration.

"I didn't want to worry you guys. I didn't tell my father for the same reason."

"Your dad needs to know, Jenna," Aubrey remarked.

"No, he doesn't. It would tear him apart. Besides, I have enough to worry about today. I got a voicemail from Richard. I have to go meet with whatever members of the ethics board they could pull together on such short notice this afternoon. I mean, the meeting was already leaked on *Deadspin*, so I should probably get going." Jenna felt so defeated, but it was time to face the music — the very loud and depressing music.

"Jenna, you shouldn't go alone. Let me take you," Trey whispered.

"Sure, that would be nice, Trey, thanks."

"Jenna, I'm not done worrying about you," Aubrey said, breaking into their conversation.

"Griffen?" Tea whispered. Jenna was able to catch her meaningful glance at him.

"Yeah, got it. Trey, come with me. Let's give these three some privacy."

"Jenna, I can stay if you need me," Trey offered.

"No, Trey, I'm good, I need to talk with my girls. I really appreciate you going with me today, though."

Trey and Griffen walked out and two sets of anxious eyes immediately focused on her.

"I don't know why you would keep the news about these tumors from us," Aubrey huffed out.

"Ease off a bit, Aubrey. I know we're hurt, but you have to understand where Jenna is coming from."

"Thank you, Tea," Jenna whispered.

"Don't thank me, yet. It doesn't change that we're really worried about you."

"Please don't be. This is my problem."

"That's not how this works, honey. We're family. That means we are each other's problems. Nothing you could ever do would ever change that," Tea said, crouching in front of her and clutching Jenna's knees. "I wished you'd told us about all of it. We want to be here for you. Plus, Aubrey and I are really nosy."

"Seriously, Jenna, after all we've been through together, how could you keep that secret from us?"

"I'm sure each of us has secrets," Tea said, and Jenna was shocked to see Brey finally shut up, for once.

"I know, you guys. I should've told you. I'm sorry."

"You were going to tell us when you were ready. We won't torture you anymore. Right, Brey?"

"Right. We're here for you. It's not about us."

"Wow, Brey, you're really growing," Jenna teased.

"I know. Go figure. I still want to beat up this Olivia chick, so I'm not fully matured."

"If maturity means not wanting to boob-punch that bitch, then I'm a little brat, too," Tea exclaimed.

They laughed and Jenna finally felt the fear in her chest ease slightly as they sat together in silence. Aubrey and Tea gently stroked her back and she forced herself to be okay with how nice it felt to let other people comfort her for a change.

"I love you both so much," Jenna whispered.

"We love you, too. And we promise, this is all going to be okay," Tea added, just as softly.

"When?"

"Now *that* we can't say. Sorry," Aubrey answered.

"But we promise we'll be here for you the whole time," Tea added quickly.

"Thanks, you guys," Jenna answered with a sigh.

Wyatt paced back and forth on the linoleum floor of the hospital hallway, well out of sight of the conference room he'd left half an hour before. His legs wouldn't stop moving. He felt like a caged lion, desperate for freedom. Inside that room was a collection of doctors designated to decide Jenna's fate, and he couldn't do anything else to help her.

He and Gabe had made every call, and pulled every string, they could think of to get him in front of that ethics panel before Jenna faced them. In the end, his head coach had come through. It filled him with a sense of gratitude and loyalty that had rarely invaded his heart related to the game of football.

When he'd walked into the room, three older men stared back at him. He'd never been very good with words, but he had no choice but to try.

"Mr. McCoy, I'm Dr. Richard West, head of Dr. Sutherland's department. I've been informed you wanted to meet with us first."

"I do, sir. Dr. Sutherland did nothing wrong. Her opinion was delivered to my team well before anything happened between us — romantically."

"Those pictures imply a relationship began much earlier."

"I pursued her from the first second I met her. That's no lie. But she was always professional. If you could punish me somehow instead, I would jump at that chance, because she did nothing wrong."

"Fine. Then why does the article say you were scheduled to have a meeting with your team this week that would 'change their minds'?" an elderly doctor asked.

"She had nothing to do with that. I had my agent schedule it. I have no clue how it made it into that article. Trust me, I'd love to know. I was going to tell the team I was willing to make sacrifices to stay in Pittsburgh. I'd given up on changing Dr. Sutherland's mind. She never would've compromised herself that way. I shouldn't have even considered she would."

"Yes, let's talk about your desire to change her opinion. Seeing as you were quoted in the article to that effect…"

"I never approved that article. I didn't even know it was being written."

"But you don't deny that you said it?"

His heart nose-dived into his stomach. It took a quick swim with the shame already swirling around in there, before he found his voice again.

"No, I don't. I did hope to persuade Dr. Sutherland to change her mind, but she would never do something like that. If anyone is the problem here, it's me."

"The issue is, you're clearly biased in this situation, and that article doesn't establish you as very trustworthy. Though, it does seem quite unlike Dr. Sutherland to do anything of this nature with a patient. Consult or otherwise," Dr. West mused.

"Correct," Wyatt answered.

"But even the appearance of impropriety is a risk. We can't have this kind of negative attention."

"I'm willing to do whatever it takes to make this right. I'll do free advertising for the department. I'll volunteer my time. Whatever you need."

"That certainly is an intriguing offer," Dr. West added. "Our relationship with the Roughnecks is a source of great pride to the department."

"Thank you, Mr. McCoy," the oldest one added. "We will take your comments under consideration."

He'd then waited in the hall for Jenna to have her meeting with them, only briefly catching sight of her as she walked into the room. She hadn't spotted him, but he could tell from the straight line of her shoulders and stern set of her jaw, she was trying to hide deep sadness — hurt *he* had put there.

Jenna finally emerged from the room. Her perfectly sculpted face was twisted in grief and pain. He'd let her down, made her feel wounded and betrayed. That knowledge twisted in his gut, making every breath more painful than the last. He stalked toward her, feeling a moment of relief when she didn't immediately sprint in the other direction.

"Hi, Wyatt," she said faintly. Her blue eyes lacked some of

their usual brightness, but she held his gaze.

He slowed his steps, walking to her carefully, fighting the urge to grab her and hold her close to him. Wyatt didn't want to risk pushing what little luck he might have left with her.

"You look so beautiful, Jenna. I've missed you." She was wearing the earrings he gave her and his heart felt like pure oxygen had just been released on a dying fire. He could hear her breath catch in her throat. She looked away from him as she shrugged on her coat and smoothed back some hair that had escaped from her sensible bun.

Finally, she asked, "So, I guess you helped me in there?"

"Yes. Are you able to go back to work right away?"

"No, but I think my medical license may be safe. I've been asked to take a brief leave of absence. Richard — Dr. West — knows about my surgery tomorrow. He'll have my leave overlap with my recovery. Not sure what that will do to my fellowship hopes, but that's the least of my concerns right now," she replied, looking away from him again, and his whole chest tightened at how lost she appeared.

"Jenna, talk to me," Wyatt said softly, reaching for her, but hesitating before actually touching her.

"It appears I'm not cut out for risk-taking after all," she mused over a mirthless laugh.

"It'll be okay...I promise. Whatever I can do to get you back on track for that fellowship..." he declared, finally allowing himself to touch her shoulders and wrap her in his embrace.

At first, she let him hold her. He could feel her relax against him. She breathed him in, while he inhaled the familiar scent of her hair. Yet, just as quickly, she shook him off and stepped backwards from him.

"Wyatt, I need you to be honest with me. Is it true? The

article? Was that why you went after me so hard? To sway my opinion about your shoulder?"

His mouth started working its way around a lie, but he fought it back.

"I had nothing to do with that article, or those pictures. You have to believe me about that."

"You didn't answer my questions. Is the article accurate?"

"What the article said was true, about my plans. What I hoped I could get you to do. But I never intended to hurt you. It wasn't about that."

"What was it about, then? Was your plan to fuck me then discredit me? Make me look like some kind of spurned psycho, so you could keep your precious position?"

"No. It wasn't like that at all. You really think that of me?" he said, so low that it was unclear even to him if he was growling or talking.

"I don't know what to think, Wyatt! Don't you get it?" she shouted, and he immediately saw her try to calm herself down.

He turned and roughly ran his hands through his hair. When he looked back, her expression had relaxed slightly and it made his heart soar with hope, only to crash down when he had to speak again.

"I just thought that with more time, Jenna, you'd decide on your own to help me out."

"How could you even imagine I would do that? Compromise my medical opinion?"

"I'm stubborn and stupid. I figured you just needed to know me better. Spend some time with me. See me in action."

"And that I'd care about you?"

"If that helped you see clearly, I guess I would've been okay with that. I know that sounds awful, but I was desperate. I feel so terrible to see you hurt now. It's killing me. Initially, I wanted everything — to stay on the team so I could get the best contract possible to look after my family for as long as I could. But then I wanted you, too, so I did whatever I could to have you."

"Oh, so you wanted it all? Well that makes it all okay."

"It's not okay, I know that. Come on, stop being sarcastic."

"All those times you wanted to talk about surgery, and my knee injury…it was all part of the plan?"

"Yes." She cringed at his brutal honesty, but he went on, "But I know we can get through this. We can take that leave of absence and I'll help you recover. After your surgery, we can start over."

"I don't think there is a *we* anymore," she muttered, looking down.

"Jenna…"

"I don't think I can start over, Wyatt. How can I trust you after all of this? I wish I didn't love you. That I could say I don't want to see you again. That I don't want to know you, but…"

"You can't say it because it's not true. You're the most honest person I know."

"And I honestly feel like I'm dying inside. You thought you could will your shoulder into feeling better. Now you think you can will me into forgiving you. You want to call an audible — adjust the play on the field and everything will be better. That's not going to work this time. Those pictures? They were every moment we were together."

"Olivia did that all on her own. We can't let one person's actions take what we have from us."

"Even if I believe that to be true, it wasn't her actions that broke my heart. It was yours. Your words gave her the lead she needed."

"Jenna, I hate that you're in pain, but you have to listen..."

"No, Wyatt. I've *been* listening, but I haven't heard you once say you regret what you did. You just hate that you got caught. You can't even imagine how much it hurts to have the whole world laugh at me like this. Do you have any idea how long it took me to get here? How much more I have to do? This isn't a game!" Jenna finally shouted, only to breathe out slowly and let her shoulders slump down.

"Believe me, people will lose interest. A new story will come along."

"It'll never be the same for me. I'm always going to be that lady doctor you used. That's how the world will see me *forever*. You've lived your whole life in the spotlight, but I haven't. I'm not cut out for this."

"I don't want to give up whatever chance we may have to be happy together."

"Why didn't you think about that when you kept this from me? New Year's Eve...I thought we agreed to have no more secrets."

"I wanted to tell you, but I couldn't risk you pushing me away with your surgery coming up. You need me."

"Maybe I do, but I'm going to have to learn how to live without you."

"Jenna..." He reached for her and she slapped his hand down.

"No! I give up, Wyatt. I give up." Her voice caught again and Wyatt couldn't decide what he felt more — panic or heartache. Nausea was pretty prevalent, too.

"Don't say that, please. I told you, I didn't have anything to do with Olivia's story."

"Even if you didn't help her with it, at the least you set this horrible machine in motion. And that tank just rolled right over me."

"I can make it okay. Let's just go back to New Year's morning."

"That's simply not possible."

"How can you be so matter-of-fact about all this?"

"Because these *are* the facts, Wyatt!" Her voice raised an octave and there was something about the hint of hysteria in it that made him think he had a chance. It was when he broke her cool demeanor that he was most able to get through to her.

"The *fact* is that I'm crazy about you and I want to make this better. Don't you want to see what we can be? We can fight this. I can fight this. I *will* make it right."

Jenna swallowed hard and said roughly, "We don't always get what we want in life. Fighting just makes it hurt more."

"You don't want me?"

"I wish that were true, but you know it's not. It would be easier if I could go back to the day before I met you. But I don't want that. So, I'm screwed, because how can you think I would just move on from this? What you did was so wrong. So humiliating! I was so scared you would break my heart, Wyatt. I suppose I had this coming. I knew better."

"Stop it. Don't be like that. Please. I'm not giving up on us. I'll do whatever it takes to stay here and be near you. I promise."

"I want to believe you, but it feels like us…this, it was all fool's gold, shiny on the outside, but inside just a sham. And I'm the sucker who believed it was real — believed you loved me."

"You're not a fool and it wasn't a sham. I do love you," he growled.

Tears welled in her eyes. This time, she did run. He hurried after her to the parking lot.

"Jenna, stop." He grabbed her arm, and when she looked down at his hand, her bottom lip quivered, either from cold or emotion, he couldn't tell. Though he was sure his own insides were on fire. "You know I'm in love with you. I'm crazy about you."

"Wyatt, you've lied to me so much. How can I trust you again? Any time I've loved someone, I got so hurt. My mom, Cha—"

Wyatt swallowed hard at the realization she could equate him with a monster like Chase, that he thought he'd digested his own Adam's apple.

"Jenna, I promise…"

"No more promises, Wyatt. This is my career. My heart. My *life*. And you ruined it. You ruined us…you ruined everything," she added with a desolate whisper.

"I'll figure something out. I'm a part of your life."

"You'll always be a part of me, but I don't think I can let you be in my life."

"Jenna. Please. You need me. Let me be there for you. Just a couple more days — at least until the surgery is all done. You kept secrets from me, too. You waited forever to tell me you're sick."

The sadness left her eyes, with rage quickly replacing it.

"You son of a bitch. How *dare* you compare the fact I could have the same disease that killed my mother, to your selfish obsession with playing this fucking game on your own goddamn terms?"

She brought her hand back and swung at his face to slap him, but he grabbed her wrist and yanked her to him quickly. He whispered roughly in her ear.

"It's not like that, belleza. It's not. I just mean we do things to protect the ones we love. Maybe my actions were wrong, and my motives, too, at the beginning. But I'll do anything to keep you. That's why I kept lying. You didn't want to hurt me, that's why you kept yours."

She was letting go like she'd done every time he held her. He breathed in her incredible fresh scent and began to press her completely against him. "I need you, Jenna."

"No! Let me go. I can't..." she cried out, pushing him away, almost knocking the wind out of him.

"Belleza." She shook him off, but before he could grab for her again, he felt a strong hand pull him back.

"What the hell?" Wyatt yelled.

"Let her go, man. Haven't you hurt her enough?"

"You brought *Trey* with you? Are you with him? Are you trying to punish me?"

"I told you there's nothing between us. Christ, you're seriously going to pull that jealous shit now?" she asked in an exasperated tone, throwing her hands up.

"No, I just... Fuck. You know what I mean."

"Fine. Trey was worried about the press. He thought I might need protection."

"She's right, and I'm still worried about them, so how about you let us go and just accept that you lost this time, all right, man?"

I really hate this fucking guy, Wyatt thought as his hands curled into fists.

"I just want to talk to her for a minute."

The words were getting harder for him to squeeze out. Trey was right. He was losing — big time. He wished he could call a play and dictate the movements of everyone in front of him. But this wasn't a game, and he'd never be able to control her.

"Just let me go, Wyatt. It's too late."

He couldn't — *wouldn't* — do that. He reached for her and wrapped his fingers around her firm arm. She just shook her head.

"You know I feel awful, Jenna. Nothing was supposed to happen like this. That wasn't my intention."

"Yeah, I feel pretty bad, too." Jenna moved away, but Wyatt was desperate and couldn't bring himself to release her.

"Let her go, man," Trey growled at him.

Wyatt looked over at him, sizing him up as an opponent. He was so crazed, it suddenly seemed like he was capable of anything. Wyatt stared Trey down. The guy was a little shorter than him, if just by a couple of inches, but he looked pretty jacked for a regular guy. To his credit, Trey looked unfazed.

"I said I just want another minute to talk to her, asshole."

"The only asshole I see is the one in front of me. You fucked this up, now you're going to let her go. That's how this works. But I'd love it if you gave me some trouble, because I've wanted to beat the shit out of you since I heard what you did, so it's all good for me."

"Fuck off," Wyatt simply responded. Trey was keeping Wyatt from Jenna, and talking sense into her, and that was all that mattered. He released Jenna's arm and pushed Trey out of the way.

Wyatt was met with a hard right hook to his jaw that made lights burst behind his eyelids and his teeth shake inside his mouth.

It took a moment, but Wyatt regained his bearings and pulled his right fist back, reaching around with a powerful swing, landing a blow directly onto Trey's left eye. His shoulder screamed in response but Wyatt wouldn't let it slow him down.

"Stop it, you idiots!" He vaguely heard Jenna shout at them, but all he could think of was getting through with this guy and back to Jenna. Then he heard shouts in the distance.

"Wyatt, over here! Shit, I can't get a good shot, can you?"

Fucking paparazzi. Here? In a Pittsburgh hospital parking lot?

"That's it! I've had it. You two can kill each other for all I care. I just need to get home."

The two men backed away from each other, panting, just in time to elude the interloping photographers of their dream shot. Wyatt moved his body so his back was to the cameras and he was blocking Jenna.

He could see the *TMZ* headline now: *Struggling QB and His Personal Love Doctor in Violent Love Triangle with Tattooed Mystery Man.* He couldn't let that happen. Jenna hated him enough as it was, the last thing he needed was to contribute to new stories about her. Wyatt looked at her intently.

"Jenna, I know you don't have any faith in me, but I'll fix this. I'll make it right again. Because, belleza, you're what I want. *You're* my everything, now."

"You don't get to have everything, Wyatt. You don't get to have me." She turned her face to hide the tears in her eyes. "Wyatt, please let me go. This is just too hard."

"No. Belleza...Jenna. No. Please."

She shook her head and finally met his eyes. Her voice was terrifyingly steady when she said, "We had a perfect Christmas together. But I can't let you be in my new year...and damn if that doesn't hurt like hell. I'm sorry, but it's time to say goodbye."

All Wyatt could do was watch as that son of a bitch Trey led her away. With each step, she took with her all his hopes of a happy life of his own and a future he could call theirs.

Like fuck it's over, he swore to himself.

CHAPTER EIGHTEEN

"Jenna, are you comfortable?" Tea asked her as she smoothed out the thin hospital blanket covering Jenna's bare legs.

"As comfortable as anyone can be in this hideous surgery gown," she answered, trying to force a smile.

The room that she would soon return to after her surgery was packed with well-meaning, but worried, faces. Tea and Aubrey were beside her bed and Johnny was seated on Vivian's lap in the corner.

Trey and Griffen were in the other corner talking heatedly about something, most likely how they could make sure no images of her as a drugged-out postoperative patient appeared on the Internet somehow.

Griffen's attorney from New York had threatened to file suit against the hospital, its administrators, and staff, if there was even a hint that a HIPAA privacy violation occurred related to Jenna's surgery or treatment. It had apparently worked, because the whole floor felt like it was on lockdown.

Brey had even heard people had to surrender their phones in order to ensure no one took a picture. The precaution was a relief, but all the attention made her feel a bit embarrassed. Though the alternative — further exposure of her life when she was in the most vulnerable of times — was too terrible to consider.

Even Carol was in the waiting room. Everyone else would soon be shuttled off to join her, but Richard had pulled some strings to let her have more visitors than usual.

Jenna swallowed hard and continued speaking, this time to everyone in the room.

"Thank you for coming to support me with this. I hate that I worried all of you this way, but it really does make it easier with all of you here."

Tea and Aubrey looked at each other with guilt in their eyes.

"What's going on, you two?" Jenna asked.

"Don't be mad, Jenna," Aubrey said quickly, getting up to go to the door. "I know you didn't want him here, but we thought it was too important he be here for you right now."

A powerful surge of treacherous hope wrenched at her heart as she wondered if they had invited Wyatt to come see her. He'd called and texted her multiple times before she'd gone to the hospital, leaving messages that he loved her and was worried about her.

Jenna had almost caved. Each time the image she'd assigned to his phone contact popped up, she was that much closer to giving up all she believed in if only to let him comfort her. She'd assigned him a graphic of *Yosemite Sam*, because Wyatt was her own crazy little gunslinger. But he wasn't really hers, not anymore. Maybe he never really was.

The world knew he'd taken advantage of her, broken her heart, and lied to her. That didn't stop her from wanting to see him just once more, and Jenna despised herself for her own weakness.

"He's here?" Jenna asked with a crack in her voice, overwhelmed with anticipation.

"He is," Tea said, opening the door to reveal Jenna's father on the other side. Shock and deep love overtook her all at once instead.

"Daddy?"

Tears filled her eyes and she felt like she was suffocating under the weight of her own emotions. Jenna quickly pushed down her own treacherous disappointment at not seeing Wyatt in front of her.

Man, I truly am pathetic. I need to get used to missing him. Might as well start today, she told herself

"Baby girl, it's okay. I'm here. Cheryl's here, too."

Everyone else cleared out of the room as her father and Cheryl rushed across the room. Her father kissed her forehead, while Cheryl hugged her hard, making Jenna yelp when Cheryl's purse snagged the IV connected to her hand.

"Oh shoot, honey. I'm so sorry. Are you okay?"

"It's okay, Cheryl. I feel so bad they told you, though. I know this must be so hard for you guys to face this again."

"The only thing you should be sorry about is keeping this secret from me, baby girl," her father said sternly. It was hard for her not to smile as he used a tone with her she couldn't recall hearing since she was in high school.

"Am I grounded, Dad?" she teased.

"If I could ground you, I would. But I understand why you didn't want to tell us. You've always worried more about other people than yourself. That's admirable, baby girl, but sometimes you have to accept that it comforts us to be able to take care of you for a change."

"I know and I'm sorry. How'd you two get here so soon? I

didn't even tell the girls until yesterday."

Cheryl sat beside her on the bed and smoothed her hair down, her face twisted into a sad grimace.

"We started driving up here from Georgia on New Year's Day, honey."

"Oh, no," Jenna hid her face in her hands. The shame was so acute she couldn't even open her eyes. With muffled words she asked, "Y'all saw the article and pictures, didn't you?"

"We did," her father whispered. "We knew you'd need support, so we came right up. Cheryl had a hunch you'd tell us to turn right around if we told you we were coming up to support you."

"She was probably right," Jenna mumbled.

"And we didn't want to give you the chance to be a stubborn mule, so I called Tea on the way," Cheryl said, adding, "she later told us about your surgery, so we made sure to get our butts here today to help you."

"I can't believe I didn't realize you'd see it. You watch *ESPN* every day. The article is pretty much mentioned on every sports news channel. You must be so humiliated because of me. Dad, please tell me this isn't going to hurt you with the school or your camps?" Jenna pleaded, dropping her hands to her lap heavily.

"Don't worry about me. You've been through enough. Cheryl and I only care about making sure *you're* okay." Jenna's father perched carefully on the other side of her bed before continuing. "There is one thing, though. I know Mr. McCoy's head coach, Coach McGill, from back when his son still played. He went to one of my camps and McGill was very grateful for the improvement his son made. He said he owes me a favor for getting his son a starting position in college. If you want, I can make a call and encourage him to get this

Gunslinger McCoy on another team — far away from you. Anything you want, baby girl, I'll do it."

"Oh God, *no*. Please don't do that, Dad. Wyatt's livelihood is so important to him and his family. I know I can't be with him after what he did...but, I don't want to see him get hurt."

She watched as Cheryl and her father exchanged a worried, parental glance.

"Honey," Cheryl said, as she stroked the top of Jenna's head, "do you love this boy?"

Without looking up from her hands, Jenna whispered, "I do, Aunt Cheryl. But, I'm just going to have to learn how to get over that, I guess."

Her father cleared his throat, and said, "Let's get through what's in front of us — this surgery — and we'll take our next step after that."

Jenna took one of each of their hands in hers and smiled wanly, unable to offer any other solace or encouragement.

The door to her room opened slowly as the nurse assigned to her and her assistant entered.

"Dr. Sutherland, I'm sorry to interrupt, but it's time."

Jenna nodded, letting go of their hands. She leaned back against the pillows and allowed herself to be wheeled away to her fate.

Wyatt pulled his baseball cap down low across his face and leaned against the wall outside of the hospital where Jenna was having her surgery. His friend, J.J., had generously let him borrow his car so he could get around without tipping off the media to his presence. It was brutally cold out, but Wyatt was completely stir-crazy. He quickly found he could only bear so much time cooped up in any one space that day, much less a little sports car.

He'd seen Jenna go in with all her friends a couple hours before and could only presume she was in the thick of it now. The thought of her going under the anesthesia scared him so much he had to force himself to think about anything else.

For the last two hours, he'd been mentally going through every aspect of the Roughnecks' offensive playbook in his head. With each lap he paced, Wyatt recited a different play to himself. He distracted himself by thinking of ways he could improve his game at each formation. If he was really going to show the team he could change his approach and become the quarterback they needed, then that process had to start immediately.

Wyatt switched his brain to planning how to advise his teammates on ways they could work together more effectively. He was toying with proposing optional off-season practices or meetings with his receivers to learn from the mistakes of this season. The process was so engrossing he hadn't even noticed the man standing in front of him, until he heard his own name.

"You must be Wyatt McCoy."

Wyatt looked up quickly and was frozen in his spot. Although the man was in his fifties, he was clearly athletic. He was also brimming with authority, to a degree most would find him imposing. Yet, that wasn't what had Wyatt's heart stopping in his chest. It was the sight of the same light blue eyes that had haunted him ever since he'd lost Jenna.

"Do you have anything to say for yourself? I know you can speak, because you did enough of it to that reporter."

Wyatt stood up straight and held his hand out, only to put it down by his side when the other man just glared at it with disdain.

"Yes, I'm Wyatt McCoy. You must be Kevin Sutherland, Jenna's father. I saw your picture..." Wyatt cut himself off before admitting to seeing it at Jenna's place. The thought of how he'd made her come with his hand in that apartment, not even two weeks before, was probably not something he needed on his mind while speaking with her dad.

"I'm her father, you're right," he answered as he looked Wyatt up and down, his face full of both interest and disgust. "You look like shit, son."

"I *feel* like shit, sir."

"Well, I suppose that's something. From that bruise on your jaw, it appears someone already whooped your ass. I'm grateful they saved me the trouble, especially because my daughter told me she doesn't want you to get hurt."

The tiny flicker of hope those words put in Wyatt's chest was the best he'd felt in days.

"That's because she's an amazing person, sir. I'm so sorry for what I put her through. What I put all of you through."

Blue eyes squinted at Wyatt, and he gave him an appraising look that reminded Wyatt so much of Jenna's expressions and her quick mind, it was actually painful.

"What are you doing out here? Are you going to try to go into the hospital?"

"No, she doesn't want me in there. Even though it's killing me not to be with her right now, I know it will only upset her at the worst time if I try to barge in there."

"But you're out here anyway? After she rejected you?"

Wyatt looked away for a moment, clenching his fists to try and collect his thoughts.

"I have to be near her now, sir. If things turn out badly in there, or if the results aren't good..." Wyatt swallowed hard and continued, "I need to know she's safe in the world, even if I'm not able to share it with her."

Jenna's father gave him the tiniest hint of a smile and reached out his hand. Wyatt shook it firmly.

"I want my daughter to be happy, but she's not good at letting herself feel that way. Maybe you don't deserve her. It sure as hell looks like you don't right now. But if you make her happy, that has to be worth something."

"Sir, I know I made her happy once. I believe I can do it again."

"People make mistakes. That's a part of life. I've made more than my own share. You've made a very big one. If you learn from it, get back out there, and try to make it right...then maybe you can show us all that you're a real man."

"I'm going to do everything I can to turn this around, sir."

"I hope you do. Good-bye, Mr. McCoy."

"Good-bye, sir," Wyatt answered, before watching him walk away.

The relief that surged through Wyatt when he saw Jenna leave the hospital had been short-lived. She'd looked groggy and needed help with every single one of her movements, but at least she was in one piece. It felt like his heart was going through a meat grinder knowing he wasn't allowed to be the one to help her. Every time she winced or leaned on one of her friends, his muscles would jerk with an involuntarily spasm, as though *he* were the one supporting her body.

I'd do anything to be able to feel that pain for her, he thought.

It was even worse that once Tea had deposited her in the backseat of her SUV, Jenna was gone from his sight all over again. He swallowed his sadness at seeing her disappear and went back to trying to make her world right again.

He wasn't lying to her father when he said he wanted to fix things. That had been all he could think about ever since Olivia's story became plastered across every form of media he knew of, and in multiple languages. It was also how he'd ended up hours later staring at the door of Trey's rented townhome. Luckily, at least some people were still talking to him, and one of them was his sister. Claudia had used her impressive computer skills to help him figure out where the elusive Trey Adler was staying while in Pittsburgh. Though, it had come at the price of listening to her give him hell over the phone.

"Wy, I hope you realize you are a complete asshole," she'd informed him. "I really liked Jenna, you dummy. I'm officially taking her side. If she ever speaks to anyone related to you ever again, I will be her friend."

"Glad you made that clear, Claudia. Were you able to get that address I needed?"

"I was. Though I can't figure out why you want anything to do with this punk. It looks like he spends as much time on the wrong side of the law as the right one."

Wyatt was counting on exactly that.

"Don't worry about it," he'd said brusquely.

"Wow, you're in a rotten mood. Not that I feel bad for you. I'm still mad at you. I thought you liked Jenna? I don't get it."

"I more than like her. I love her. That's why I need this guy's help."

"Okay, but if you do somehow get Jenna back, from now on, please make your decisions based on what will make the two of you happy together. I better not ever hear again that you used your worries about me and mom and abuela to do something messed up like this. Do you know how hurt mom is right now? She thinks she's a total burden. Like she's been the reason you screwed up your life."

"Dammit. That's not what I wanted. None of this is what I wanted."

Claudia finally gave up Trey's information, and he headed straight to him. Trouble or not, there was no turning back. A lot of memories tormented Wyatt, but nothing came close to the torture he felt at his recollection of the look on Jenna's face when she'd left him the day before in that hospital parking lot. Her big blue eyes reflecting how much torment and disappointment he'd caused her.

It had been as though he could hear her heart breaking, could feel her blaming herself, and taste the bitterness in her mouth from his betrayal. Wyatt experienced every brutal sensation right along with her, but his had the added pain of knowing he'd caused it.

Wyatt had forced her to open herself up to him, and he'd gone ahead and broken her.

For the first time, he believed he might be worse than his father. At least his dad had broadcasted to those who loved him just how shitty he was. Wyatt, instead, had hidden his ability to harm behind the love for his family, whether they'd demanded that sacrifice or not.

He knocked on the door. Asking for help wasn't Wyatt's strong suit, but he had no choice. It opened and Wyatt fought the urge to curl his hands into fists.

"If it isn't Shithead McCoy," Trey sneered at him, leaning against the doorjamb. "How's the jaw?"

Wyatt resisted the urge to rub his still-aching face and instead straightened up to his full height. He didn't enjoy eating crow, and he really didn't like Trey, but he was getting frantic.

"Jaw feels awesome. How's the eye?" Wyatt felt a moment of glee when he saw the dark, bruised ring around Trey's left eye.

"Never better. I'm kind of busy, dude. If you need me to kick the shit out of you again, I'll find the time, but otherwise,

I'm really not in the mood to deal with your spoiled ass."

"I'm not here to fight. I need your help so we can make things better for Jenna."

"I'm listening."

"You were with her today. Is she okay? How's she feeling?"

"It's none of your business…but she's doing all right. Griffen is watching after her today. It's not easy, Jenna's being followed everywhere she goes, people are always trying to take her picture, yelling at her. That's not even counting the shit being said about her in the press and online."

Wyatt felt his fury surge and slammed the wall by Trey's door hard.

"Easy dude. Listen, there's a reason why guys like us aren't meant to be with nice girls like her. We will always destroy them, so word of advice from one asshole to another — I wouldn't try to see her if I were you. She's still upset and Griffen may kill you. He's pissed. Wants to fuck you up worse than I did. Hmm, on second thought, let's go over together. I'd like to see that."

"Shut up. I…look, I don't know what your feelings are for Jenna, but I know you like her."

"Jenna's my friend."

"Right, your friend. I thought guys like you don't have female friends?" Wyatt couldn't help but ask with a snort.

"Hey, fuck you, man. *You're* gonna tell *me* how to treat women? And yes, she's just my friend. She reminds me of…someone I used to know. And she deserves better than the shit you've done to her."

"We can agree on that. I think you know how little I want to ask for your help, but I hear you're good at using computers in a lot of ways."

"That's one way to put it. I'm going to guess that what you have in mind is not completely legal. Am I right?"

"You'd be correct. That's why Jenna can't know anything about it. I'd do it myself if I had any idea how. What's the problem? Are you afraid, punk ass?"

"Of course not, fucker. Just wanted to make sure we're on the same page. I'm already in hot water after using my *special* skills to help Griffen with his investigation. I might as well push my luck even more."

"Thanks, man."

"Don't thank me, asshole. I'll try to take care of all this bullshit. But I'm doing it for Jenna, not for you, got it?"

"Got it. Trust me, I'd be happy never to see you again after all this."

"I'm with you there. You might as well come in so we can get started. I've poked around some — trying to figure out why your little friend did this to her."

"Olivia Hayes is not my friend."

"Whatever. You know you started this whole mess. We each need to accept the harm we cause."

"That's why I want to fix it, even if she doesn't want me after all this."

"Good. So I need you to tell me what you know and what you're willing to do."

"I'm willing to do anything to protect her. *Anything*."

CHAPTER NINETEEN

Jenna gazed out the window in her living room, breathing slowly through the throbbing soreness in her breasts. It had been several days since her surgery and she had a lot to do to prepare for the next phase of her treatment. She could hear the instructions as though she were objectively providing them to a patient herself: *take medicine when you are in pain, rest as much as possible, and try to relax because you've been through an extreme physical event.*

Yet, the words were still hollow to her. She couldn't follow any of the advice, because the pain in her body was a welcome distraction from her much more agonizing heartache. Wyatt had stopped trying to reach her. It was what she'd told him she wanted. Yet, with the loss of his constant calls, she knew it was time to accept that the love bubble they'd lived in for the holidays had truly burst.

She heard the doorbell ring and Aubrey greeting Trey. Jenna gave him a weak smile, before returning her eyes to the window.

"Hi, Trey," Aubrey said, "you've got a lot of stuff there. What did you bring us?"

"I met with Wyatt and got the things she'd left at his place," Jenna was able to hear Trey say quietly to Brey. Her right hand moved unconsciously to the earrings Wyatt had given her. She still hadn't been able to stop wearing them and didn't want to try.

Jenna turned to see her suitcase and the box of the ice skates Wyatt had also given her. She turned so quickly away from the sight she had to breathe in sharply through a responding shot of pain in her chest.

"Dammit, Jenna. I heard that," Brey shouted at her.

"Griffen's worried about her, too. I guess she's not doing so great?" Trey asked.

"No. She's been over at that window seat all day. She's refusing to take her pain pills, she's not eating, plus she's testy as hell."

"*She* can hear you," Jenna said loudly, from across the room.

"I told you. She's *very* cranky," Aubrey grumbled out.

Everyone was worried about her, but they had to understand she just needed enough time and quiet to get over him. Her plan had to work, because if she spent the rest of her life feeling this way, what kind of existence would she have?

"How are you, Trey?" she asked him, turning carefully to face the middle of the room.

"Good. I brought you something else."

"Oh, yeah? What?"

"Tea's mac and cheese. She said it's what heals a broken Southern heart. She made me promise I would say that. I feel like I need to man up now, maybe I should spit or grill something?"

"Your manhood is threatened, huh?" Aubrey asked with a laugh.

"Never threatened — it just likes to be coddled is all."

"Well, we're short on coddling here, though we do have bourbon. I could use a shot if you're pouring," Jenna said, never budging from her perch at the window.

"I'll get the bourbon," Aubrey offered.

"Is she allowed to drink, you know, after…"

"Aubrey told you I didn't take any pain meds, so yes."

Jenna could see Aubrey look at Trey and roll her eyes.

"I saw that, you know," Jenna sniped.

"I know. That's because I wasn't hiding it. Good luck, Trey, she's the best doctor, so that means she's the worst patient ever. If I didn't love her so much, I'd strangle her."

"Humph," Jenna grunted out loudly. "I hope you heard *that*."

"I did, my darling. She's all yours Trey. And you can give me that cheesy noodle goodness. I'll put it in the kitchen and serve it up for our cranky patient over there. I was worried you'd say you brought a gossip magazine. I've been trying to keep this place clear of them. Though I might want to get a copy of the National Enquirer for my own amusement. That one says Jenna and I are lesbians and she was using Wyatt to advance her career," Aubrey informed them.

"I saw that one, too. That was my favorite article for sure," Trey said, with a smirk.

"Oh, brother. We're lesbians, huh?" Jenna asked.

"Hey, you could do worse," Aubrey huffed out defensively.

"Very true, Aubrey. Though you'd love me and leave me. I've seen how you are with men. I'll pass."

"What's that? Was that a *joke* from your room at the Depressed Days Inn over there? I am shocked."

"Go get me some mac and cheese woman and let me talk

to my friend, Trey," Jenna teased.

"Friend, huh? Trey, are you really just being a big brother type here? You aren't swooping in with your tattoos and piercings, hoping to guard more than just her body, are ya?"

"Jenna, why is it that no one understands us?" Trey asked her, acting deeply wounded.

"Easy, Aubrey. He's just helping me. We're buds now. Sorry, Trey, Aubrey likes to jump to conclusions."

"It's true, jumping to conclusions is my favorite form of cardio," Aubrey added.

"It's all right. I can take it. All this ink toughened my skin. Besides, I wouldn't take advantage of a woman under my care, and I don't think about Jenna that way."

"Hey!"

"What? I don't get it," Trey said, honestly confused.

"I don't think of you that way either, but my ego's been bruised enough lately. Lie and tell me I'm irresistible, at least until I get my head back on straight."

"So I guess that means Trey still needs to find the right woman. One that's not under his care, but just under him."

"Get in that kitchen, you busybody," Jenna said, finally letting herself feel a twinge of humor.

"But I can make you feel better, I promise. Do you know Joe Stevenson thinks you're beautiful?" Aubrey interjected playfully as she headed to the kitchen with the macaroni and cheese. "They had a whole segment about you on *By The Way* and he was all about what a catch you are. You love that show on *ESPN*."

"Oh yeah, a dream come true. Which picture did they use?"

"They said the pictures disappeared from the Internet. Every time they appear anywhere, they're gone again right away. So they had to use your *UPMC* official photo. Man, that one is so bad."

"Thanks, Brey, you really know how to keep things in perspective," Jenna grumbled at her.

"You're welcome," Aubrey responded, eliciting a withering glance back from Jenna.

"That is so weird about the pictures. Don't you think, Trey? Nice, but weird," Jenna wondered.

"Those things happen," Trey responded quickly. "Um, I think I want mac and cheese, too, Brey. If you don't mind."

"So polite. Sure."

"What do you expect to see through that window, Jenna?" Trey asked her gently, as he sat on the sofa.

"Nothing, I just like the view of the hills from here. Plus, I don't think the press can get a shot at this angle, and I don't really have anywhere else to be."

"Stop feeling sorry for yourself. Come here and sit with me."

"Okay." She hauled herself up and made her way over to the sofa. "I don't think I do misery very well. I tried it on these last few days but I'm not good at it."

Sitting down, she leaned back on the cushions and let loose a sigh.

"Everyone has the right to wallow once in a while, Jenna. But not right now for you. I'm here, so you have to pretend to be happy to see me."

"Fine," she said, smiling slightly, then looking questioningly at the computer Trey was starting up on his lap. "You brought your laptop with you to be my bodyguard?"

"Yep. I'm working on something."

"Always so secretive. Let me see."

"Now you're feeling frisky again? How about you go back

to pining away and give me some privacy?"

"Pining? Me? No way. I'm not pining."

"Sure looks like it to me. Have you been sleeping?"

"No."

"Why not?"

"I'm not tired."

"Are you thinking about him?"

"Who?"

Trey simply raised an eyebrow at her skeptically.

"Fine. Maybe I've thought about him — a little."

"Dreaming about him?"

"That's none of your business."

"So the answer is yes."

"For your information, since I haven't been sleeping, I can't dream about him."

"Great comeback," he teased.

"Why do you care? You hate him, right? Besides, how do you know so much about this?"

"I'm just smart, I guess. Fine, if you want me to leave you alone about him, then relax. I'll start doing something boring that I can let you eavesdrop on."

He tapped away quickly on his keyboard, when, just like that, his screen was full of kittens and puppies playing with each other on *YouTube*.

Jenna couldn't help but giggle as she watched them frolic and paw at each other. She curled her legs underneath her and leaned her head on Trey's shoulder to get a better view.

"*You* like kitten and puppy videos?" Jenna asked Trey incredulously.

"They're good medicine for almost any ailment. Now stop chattering, I like the music on this one."

Jenna made a gesture of zipping her lips shut and went

back to watching the fuzzy cuteness, until her eyelids started to feel incredibly heavy and she let everything go dark. Her dreams were scattered images of Wyatt's half-smile and his arms around her on a shimmering Mexican beach. They were healthy and together. It was perfect and Jenna dreaded the time when she would wake up again.

Okay, I hesitated too long before passing toward the wide receiver. Jenna was right. I do drop my shoulder before throwing. That hesitation and tic made me a sitting duck. I got the ball off, but the pass was rushed and inaccurate. Incomplete.

Wyatt paused the digital playback from week four's game against Carolina to jot down some notes on the mistakes he'd just noticed. He leaned back heavily in his desk chair and rubbed around his eyes, which were dry and painful after watching hours of his game films from that season.

The last two weeks had been a blur. He'd divided his time between meetings with his team, attempting to improve his future performance, and trying to find some way to eliminate the media's interest in Jenna. Trey chasing after the pictures and taking them down as fast as they went up had just been a *Band-Aid*. It was also impossible to catch all of them — like trying to bail out a sinking cruise ship with a *Dixie* cup.

The story about his attempt to take advantage of Jenna's position was sexy and scandalous, but he'd really believed interest in it would eventually wane — especially with the *NFL* playoffs there to distract the media. Yet, every time their story left the news, Olivia produced some other juicy tidbit about locker room strife, or another new feature of his relationship with Jenna. That would then stir up a whole new round of interest in them.

He and Trey needed something to discredit Olivia and make her leave the story alone, so it could die the quiet, eventual death of every other pop culture phenomenon. Thus far, they'd hit one dead end after another. Olivia was ruthless in the pursuit of bettering her career, and they'd found nothing that would silence her.

With each new buzz of attention, Wyatt lost more hope he'd ever show Jenna he could protect her and make things right. These follow-up stories also consistently derailed any progress he'd made with the Roughnecks to negotiate a compromise contract extension.

He ran his fingers through his hair, tugging a bit before letting go. Wyatt was worried he was possibly only making things worse. His mere existence was too enticing for the press. Now that Jenna was in his orbit, he worried the press would never let her out of their telescopic lenses.

His fingers itched to call her and see how she was — to tell her how much he missed her. He fought back the urge. Part of his plan was to show her he could actually listen to her wishes. If she wanted him to stay away, then that's what he would try to do. But it was starting to get almost impossible, especially after Trey begrudgingly admitted to him she was sad.

Having Trey take the ice skates to her apartment had been a bit of a low blow. His own sneaky attempt to get her to think about him. He was attempting to be mature enough to honor her wishes and give her space, but he couldn't bear the idea she might have evicted him from all her thoughts. Maybe he was still a stubborn, selfish son of a bitch after all.

Wyatt sighed deeply and sat back up, leaning his elbows on his desk. Sick of watching himself on video, he brought up one of Chase's games as a starter. The Roughnecks GM was still hot to acquire that piece of shit. This left him no choice but to watch film of Chase, too — see what he was up against.

He hadn't made it through five minutes of the video before he slammed a fist down on his desk. His heart was racing in his chest, but he tried to think clearly.

"What in the hell?" he said out loud, grabbing his phone to call Trey.

"Hello."

"Hi, it's Wyatt. Remember how I told you about that asshole Chase?"

"Yeah."

"I've got a video of Olivia at his game in Atlanta during Pittsburgh's bye week. She's on the sidelines talking to him. I can't tell for sure, but I think he handed her something. She doesn't cover Atlanta. She's spent the last three years kissing ass to be assigned to Pittsburgh's division. What the hell was she doing in Atlanta?"

"That might explain some of her emails. She has a lot of message exchanges with someone she only referred to as 'C.' I've tried to get his emails, but he's not as careless as she is."

"How do you have Olivia's emails?"

"When will people learn not to ask me questions they shouldn't know the answers to?"

"Message received."

"You should know that Olivia's in Pittsburgh now."

"Are you sure?"

"Yeah, I'm outside of her hotel now. She checked in yesterday and is staying in the East End of the city, really close to Aubrey and Jenna."

"Fuck. That devious little bitch."

"She emailed her boss that she's got a juicy story about Jenna being sick and you knowing about it — that you victimized her specifically because she was vulnerable right now."

"That story can't happen! The other stuff was bad enough, but this would destroy Jenna. What is Olivia's obsession with this story? The team is fed up with her, she's simply burning her bridges. It's like she has a vendetta against Jenna. This can't be about wanting to be with me. She never liked me that much to begin with, and I certainly hate the fuck out of her now after what she did."

"I don't know if Jenna was the real target here," Trey mused.

"What do you mean?"

"You're the one who looks the worst. That article was released before your planned big meeting with the team. If Jenna had changed her opinion like you wanted, no one would have taken her seriously after your relationship came out."

"You mean, maybe they wanted her opinion to stand?" Wyatt asked.

"Yes, and make the team view you as undesirable, and too much of a risk. That's kind of what happened, isn't it?"

"It is. And it's really helped Chase. We know he's a piece of shit, but he's made himself look squeaky clean for the rest of the world. What did they talk about in their emails?"

"Some are about meeting up. She went to Atlanta a few times, but she had more trips to Vegas. This all occurred over the last few years, only during the football season. They also have the names of Atlanta players and their injuries. For the few weeks he started, there's a series of numbers. They could be scores, but I'm not sure."

"Holy shit. Trey, send everything you can to me. Your friend, that Griffen guy. He's not just a writer, isn't he an investigative journalist, too?"

"Yeah. I help him with the investigations."

"Do you think he could complete an article and get it published by tomorrow?"

"If it'll help Jenna, then he'd have it done in an hour."

"Good. Let's meet with him ASAP. I want this feature to come out before Olivia's article about Jenna being sick. And if Olivia and Chase were doing what I suspect, no one will give a shit about me and Jenna anymore."

"Gabe, this is Griffen. Thanks for setting up this press conference for us," Wyatt said to his agent before buttoning, and then unbuttoning, his suit jacket. His whole body was humming with anticipation.

This was as antsy as he'd felt before the Orange Bowl. He'd gone on to win the national championship for the University of Texas. Hopefully this day would be similarly successful. Though, unlike that game, this milestone was guaranteed to be humiliating for him.

"It wasn't hard. After Griffen's article in the *New York Times* yesterday, I couldn't find a hotel conference room big enough to fit everybody that wanted to come."

"It looks like Super Bowl media day in here. But I can't take too much credit for that excitement. A story revealing that Olivia Hayes and Chase Matthews were involved in an interstate gambling ring was bound to cause an uproar," Griffen interjected.

Wyatt could tell the guy still hated him, but he'd managed to put that aside for Jenna's sake. His article was explosive. He and Trey took Wyatt's gambling theory and ran with it so well that his head was almost spinning. Wyatt even got a quote from an "anonymous" Roughneck's front office man stating all of her team privileges were revoked, and negotiations with Chase had officially ceased.

She'd been sleeping with men at every level, all over the league, getting inside information on injuries and game plans. Then turning over what she learned to her gambling contacts in Vegas. Wyatt figured his refusal to share anything at all with her during their now cringe-inducing random sexual escapades, was probably infuriating to her.

But the real jackpot came when she hooked up with Chase. What began as one of her information conquests, quickly turned into something bigger when he lucked into a starting quarterback position for Atlanta. With Chase running the game, he could shave points in a way that made everyone involved very rich — and also felons.

The only problem was that Chase wasn't going to start in Atlanta next season. If Chase could start as QB in Pittsburgh, that would've been perfect for Olivia. When Wyatt opened his big mouth about Jenna "seeing things his way," he'd gift wrapped the perfect way for Olivia and Chase to unseat him.

That was all over now. *Fox Sports* had suspended her indefinitely. Trey found her computer and other files in her hotel room. He erased all the contents relating to Jenna. How he'd managed that was another one of those questions Wyatt wasn't supposed to ask. She would never post another sentence about Jenna as a reporter and Wyatt could finally breathe a bit more easily.

"You all right there, Wy?" Gabe asked.

"I'm great. Let's do this."

Wyatt and Griffen sat at a table in front of dozens of microphones. He cleared his throat and began to speak.

"Thank you for coming. I know you all have a lot of

questions for Griffen Tate. After I make a brief statement, I'll hand full rein to him. You've seen a lot about me in the news lately. That I'm a selfish bastard. That I used Dr. Sutherland to further my own agenda — to try and manipulate her into giving me a favorable opinion on my shoulder. That I am willing to do anything to stay on as starting quarterback of the Pittsburgh Roughnecks... All of those things are true."

Some people in the room gasped, and the shame burning at Wyatt's throat made it difficult to speak. He swallowed, steeled his jaw and looked straight ahead at the undulating sea of reporters before him.

"What you haven't heard is the rest of the story. All of these reports left out that Dr. Sutherland is an incredible physician, with a better football brain than any man I've ever met. She's way too good for me. So, I guess, it's the only fair punishment for my actions, that I fell in love with her almost right away. She did nothing wrong in any of this — unless you count trusting me. I rationalized my behavior behind my good intentions. And that's how I also decided it was okay that I was trying to have her, while keeping the truth from her."

Wyatt cleared his throat, and continued, "Dr. Sutherland is not weak, or a victim. She's not an accomplice in my bad acts. She is the most beautiful person I know, inside and out. I still love her. I will always love her. I'm not with her now. That's because I wasn't brave enough to be the man she deserves. But, I refuse to let any of you hurt her or misjudge her. Come after *me*. Hate *me*. But leave her out of it. Thank you for your time. And for the record, that is the last statement you will ever get from me about Dr. Sutherland. Griffen, you're up."

Griffen gave him a nod and small smile that made him feel oddly proud. Maybe he could clean up this mess after all.

Wyatt waited patiently for the press conference to end. He

left quickly to avoid the onslaught of reporters trying to get one more quote and made his way to his SUV in the same downtown parking garage where he'd first kissed Jenna. It had been a bittersweet surprise when Gabe had told him the press conference would be held at the hotel on the other side of the garage from the ice-skating rink.

He hadn't been able to resist the urge to park there, perhaps in some pitiful effort to be closer to the memory of that moment. The thought of how shy, yet sexy, she'd been that day was enough to make him want to scream with self-loathing. After he glanced into the backseat to make sure his duffel bag was secure for his upcoming drive, a figure emerged from behind a pillar in front of him.

"If it isn't Gunslinger McCoy. In the flesh," the person slurred at him, and moved into the light. Wyatt's fists immediately clenched.

"Chase Matthews. Shouldn't the FBI be giving you a body cavity search, or something?" The stench of booze on Chase's breath was undeniable.

"I saw your press conference online while I waited here for you. It makes sense Jenna would fall for a pussy. Too bad your precious *doctor* is going to really hate you. Well, even more than she does already. Now that you busted me."

"What the hell are you talking about? She hates you, you piece of shit."

"You think you're so clever. Why do you think she never tried to mess with me? Why she helped me?" Fear started to pulsate in Wyatt's chest. He wanted to shut Chase up, but he couldn't form words before the shithead spoke again. "There it is. You're scared now, pretty boy. Nice. That's what I want to see. Thing is, I always loved gambling. That's how I found out her dad — the *great* Kevin Sutherland — shared my hobby. I saw him gambling on sports and took pictures. I made it look like he gambled on his own team. Jenna covered for me, but there's no need for me to protect her daddy's secret anymore."

Wyatt gritted his teeth. "If you fucking hurt her…"

"Funny you should bring up fucking. She's not too bad at it, is she? I bet she's gotten better since I broke her in, back in the day."

Wyatt grabbed Chase's jacket and yanked at him hard, pushing him back against the pillar, but he just laughed in his face.

"I'll fucking kill you if you say her name again."

"Are you going to risk that shoulder of yours?" he taunted. Wyatt hesitated. "I didn't think so."

"If you're smart, you'll shut up, Chase," Wyatt said, pushing him against the pillar again.

"Did you like Jenna's big tits? They were nice back then. Too bad they're all fucked up now, according to Olivia."

"That's it, motherfucker!" Wyatt saw nothing but brutal, hot red, as he pounded fists into Chase's stomach and then a left hook to his jaw. Chase managed a couple glancing blows to Wyatt's face, but Wyatt quickly knocked him down to the ground. His foot stomped onto Chase's stomach.

Wyatt's body was moving on its own. All his anger and frustration of the last two weeks was focused with pinpoint accuracy on destroying the man beneath him. "I'm going to fucking kill you!"

"Wy, stop!" Wyatt vaguely registered Gabe yelling into his ear as he pulled him away from Chase.

"Let me go, Gabe! I'm not done with this lowlife. He gets off on intimidating women. I'm going to show this sick fuck what it means to really suffer." Wyatt kicked at Chase again. "Get up, bitch!"

Chase groaned from the ground, clearly in agonizing pain. The sight filled Wyatt with a mixture of triumph and a desire to deliver even more hurt to the bastard.

"Stop it, Wy. If you stop now, I can make this go away. It's over…it's over."

CHAPTER TWENTY

Jenna sat in her rental car in the driveway of her childhood home. The windows were rolled up and the air conditioning was running. Yet, it wasn't the rainy April Georgia weather holding her firmly in place.

The sadness to which Jenna had grown accustomed hung as heavy in her limbs as lead. Her father had called her the week before to say he needed her right away. Her radiation treatments were finally done and the tumors hadn't returned. They hadn't been malignant, but they were certainly dangerous. Having them gone and this clean bill of health should've left her feeling relieved. She was even practicing in the orthopedic surgical group again, thanks to Wyatt's press conference and Richard's support. Even so, she still felt miserable and alone.

Jenna took out her cell phone and played Wyatt's press conference from January for about the thousandth time. At first, she'd wanted to be mad at him for it, worrying it was a ploy to make himself look good. But she couldn't deny the clear anguish on his face, because she'd seen it in her own mirror ever since the day she told him goodbye.

The conference was by all accounts embarrassing to him,

and on top of that, he'd simply disappeared after it. In fact, he'd been off the grid for months. There'd been rumors he'd beaten up Chase Matthews, but that story petered out after the FBI took Chase into custody and indicted him and Olivia for racketeering, and various other charges. Chase being so discredited also eliminated him as a threat to her father's career.

She and Wyatt had been apart much longer than they'd been together, but she could still feel the sensation of her face beneath his fingertips and his lips on hers. Jenna hated that she couldn't get over him, but at least the love she held for him deep inside was something the world could never take away from her. She paused the video and finally left the car, throwing her bags over her arms. Her father waited for her at the door and took them from her. Jenna couldn't make sense of his smiling face and all-around good mood. She gave him a hug and sized him up.

"Hi, Dad. You know, for someone so desperate to see me, you look pretty great. I thought you were sick."

"No. I'm not sick. I just wanted to see you. Come on, let's get these up to your room."

They walked up the stairs and nostalgia hit her hard at the sight of her unchanged bedroom. The walls still featured posters of her favorite *NFL* players, and her bookshelves were lined with her many trophies and numerous textbooks.

Her father put her bags on the floor and turned to her with the most serious look on his face.

"How's my baby girl?"

"I'm okay."

He looked at her skeptically, "Come on. I know I didn't raise a liar."

"It's been a rough couple of months. With the treatments,

and…"

"And not seeing Wyatt?"

"No, that wasn't easy. Not like it matters. You know what he did, and no one's heard from him since the press conference."

"I've heard that," he answered slowly. After pausing, he added, "Everyone makes mistakes, Jenna. I also learned you covered for mine for far too long. You were living your life for someone else for years. That's a mistake, too."

"I was protecting you, you shouldn't have had to lose everything for one error of judgment."

"That was my choice to make, Jenna. I'd rather never coach again, than let something I did hurt you. But that's not why I wanted you to come here."

"Then why, Dad?"

"Because I wanted to ask you why you'd risk your whole life to cover for my mistake, but you won't even let Wyatt have a chance to make up for his."

"That's not fair. That was…"

"What he did to you was wrong. But our lives aren't judged solely by our failings. They are also defined by what we do to atone for them. If you have a chance at happiness, you have to take it. It may turn out badly, but that's why it's a chance and not a guarantee. You've got a shot at something that could make you happy in your own life. That's why I want you to consider forgiving him."

"It's not that simple."

"Of course it is. Love is the simplest thing we do in life. It's the living together and the day-to-day that's the hardest part."

"You're still a great coach in every way, Dad."

"That means you have to listen to me. You know I love

you, but I don't want you worrying about me. You look after so many people. But you also need to give the rest of the world some credit. I know better than anyone about putting your life on hold — of being scared. I don't want you hiding behind me, or anything. And that's what you're doing — hiding. Your mother would never have wanted that."

Jenna sat heavily on the edge of her bed. Her father walked to her bookshelf, and ran his hand across the frame of an old photograph. It was her mother holding a three-year-old Jenna in her arms. Her long wavy blonde hair was blowing in the breeze, as they smiled at each other. He cleared his throat, before turning back to face Jenna.

"I never wanted you to be afraid of living. Getting hurt? Getting knocked down? That's all a part of living, baby girl. Your mother told me what she was going to say to you that day that she…died. You've followed all her instructions, except for one thing."

"What's that, Dad?" Jenna couldn't look at him. She could evade questions and solve other's problems, but it was brutal to face him challenging *her*.

"She told you never to give up and to accept when something good comes your way. But you seem pretty happy with throwing in the towel. In fact, it looks like that's all you want to do."

"I don't want to fight a losing battle, Dad."

"You're guaranteed to lose if you never bother to try."

"I can't fail again. I feel so lost, Dad. I just…I need more time."

"Time for what? The surgery and treatment were a success. You have your life back. The question, baby girl, is what are you gonna do with it?" He leaned down to kiss her cheek, and then added, "I'm going to head over to Cheryl's place while you get settled in."

"You're leaving?"

"I think you'll be fine," he said, tapping her gently on the chin with his fist and smiling down at her. He left the room and the sight of his back tore at her heart.

Jenna felt her throat close around a swollen ball of her own sadness. The desolation of the last few months was suddenly accentuated by the terrible sensation of disappointing her father, and the fact she knew he was right.

Heaving a deep sigh, she just let the loneliness take her body. She fell back on the bed as silent sobs shook her shoulders until it felt like her teeth would rattle out of her mouth. Her hair spread around her face as she tried to catch her breath, even as more tears filled her eyes.

Pressing her hands to her overheated face, she stopped holding back and let the tears fall. They spread against her palms until she couldn't remember a world in which she wasn't crying. The sound of her own pain was so loud, she almost didn't hear the hesitant question that came to her from the door.

"Hi, Doc. Are you okay?"

Jenna sat up quickly, wondering if she was hallucinating. Yet, it wasn't an illusion. Wyatt was standing inside her old bedroom, and he looked amazing. His right arm was in a support sling and he had a tentative look on his beautiful face. She frantically wiped at her cheeks and tried to compose herself. For so many months she'd convinced herself letting him go was the correct, albeit torturously painful, choice to make. That wisdom was now replaced with her intense desire to rush to him.

"Cat got your tongue?"

"Huh? Uh, um."

"You always did have a way with words, Doc."

"Wy-Wyatt, what are you doing here?"

He walked to her slowly. She could tell he was nervous. It was subtle, something only she could see. His eyes darted around the room, landing on a box of tissues on her desk. He handed it to her and she couldn't help but notice how large his tall, muscular frame looked in the small space.

"I've been working with your dad. I can't do too much since the surgery, but my rehab is coming along well and he's coaching me…"

"What did you say?"

"Um, which part?"

"Let's start with you being here. I can't believe Dad didn't tell me."

He cleared his throat and stepped closer to her. His scent was overpowering all her senses. It was as though every cell in her body had become a full cheering squad, shaking their pom-poms at the discovery he was close to her again.

"I drove down here after the press conference to have the surgery at Emory, so I could be near your dad. We didn't tell you because I needed to prove to him, and to myself, that I could somehow be deserving of you. Your dad has been coaching me and showing me how to have passion for the game."

He paused to let her respond, but Jenna could only stare at him. Wyatt swallowed and continued speaking.

"I *am* really enjoying the game now. It's amazing. We're also working on an after-school program with tutoring, co-ed teams, and medical help for underprivileged kids. We want to have it in Pittsburgh first, so your dad can transfer up there to be near you and keep working with me."

The shock of this statement helped Jenna find her voice again.

"Wyatt...setting up something like that has been one of my dreams for so long. How..."

"Your dad told me," Wyatt looked around nervously, pacing slightly in front of her. When Jenna couldn't find any words to say, he became even more uncomfortable. "Um, and I needed to make it up to my own family. They were really upset by what I did. I thought I was helping them, but all I did was hurt everyone."

Jenna swallowed hard, trying to make sense of all his rambling statements. She managed to formulate another question through her fog.

"How did I not hear about you doing all this, or anything else about you for months?"

"We all worked hard to keep it out of the press. Trey helped me keep it off the Internet, like he did with your pictures and articles."

"You guys did that? I thought you hated Trey."

"I'm still not a fan and I'll never believe he wasn't trying to take you from me, but I did enough on my own to lose you." Wyatt kneeled in front of her, bringing him to her eye level. He moved a hand toward her knee, but quickly snatched it away before touching her. Jenna's heart squeezed at the lost chance to feel him. "I decided to suck it up and do whatever I could to make it better. Did it? Make it better...at all?" he asked, searching her face with his desperate gaze.

"It did. I hated seeing those pictures. I mean, I hated being so exposed, but then I liked seeing you hold me. And it hurt all over again to think about what you hid from me. It was all such a fucking mess."

"I couldn't handle anyone seeing those pictures, Jenna. Those were our private moments. I messed up so bad. I know that. The fact I used anyone like that, especially you, is terrible..." Wyatt took a deep stabilizing breath before continuing, "You wanted me to say I regret what I did."

"Do you?"

"At first it was hard for me to regret it, because my actions were part of what brought us together. I will always be grateful for that. But what I did was wrong. If I could do it all over again, I wouldn't. Even if it meant I couldn't have you, I'd accept that if it spared you all this pain." Wyatt sighed as he rubbed the back of his neck nervously before continuing. "I never want you to be hurt, Jenna. And I did that to you. I should have told you when I had the chance. You opened up to me, but I was scared about you being sick. I went kind of nuts. And then I lost the right to support you when you needed me the most. I know I broke your heart. I hate so much that I did. If it helps, I've been really miserable."

"Yeah, it helps some," Jenna replied, with the slightest smile. "Wyatt, I've been miserable, too."

His face was full of worry and anguish. "Jenna, I'm so sorry. I've been trying to fill every moment of every day with anything I can do to fix what I did...fix myself. If I had a free second my mind would just go back to remembering your smile, your eyes, the way you make me believe I can take on the whole world and win. And then I think about how I lost you."

He looked down for a moment. When his eyes met hers again, they were red and slightly lost looking.

"I wish I'd paid better attention in school, because I don't know enough words to tell you how much I've missed you.

And I've missed you so much. You were the best thing that ever happened to me and I totally fucked it up. I want to be a better man for you, belleza. Will you please let me try?"

Jenna paused before answering. Wyatt looked frantic and began to open his mouth again to speak. She pressed two fingers against his lips, silencing him.

"I have to let you try. I've given life without you a shot and I can't do it. I'm terrible at it. I need you, Wyatt."

He grabbed her hand from his mouth, holding it in his before stammering out, "So you can forgive me?"

"You're the good thing that life is willing to give me, Wyatt. The least I can do is take a crack at forgiving you."

Wyatt kissed the palm of her hand, and she moved her fingers to cradle his cheek. The feel of his rough stubble against her palm was simultaneously thrilling and calming in varying degrees. She needed him closer, though.

"Come here," she whispered. He responded with a huge smile before sitting next to her on the bed. Jenna held his left hand in hers and looked up at his face. His smile faded, his face clouding again.

"What's wrong? Are you worried about committing to Pittsburgh like that... What if you don't get re-signed?"

"Well, Coach McGill really respects your dad, and he's liked what I've done to address the team's concerns. We'll figure it out. I'm not losing you again."

"Then why do you still look scared, Wyatt?"

"Because I hope you'll let me kiss you."

"Oh. Well, I'd like that," she whispered, and watched as he slowly leaned toward her. He stopped so close to her lips she could feel his hot breath against her eager skin.

His eyes locked with hers, as he said, "I love you, Jenna." Then he closed that final distance between them, pressing his lips on hers and sending a rush of pleasure through her body. All those painful months, weeks, days, and seconds apart disappeared, as Wyatt moved his hand to the back of her head, winding his fingers through her hair.

Jenna moved her hands to his face, desperate to feel more of him and convince herself he was really there with her again. Their kiss was tentative at first, until she couldn't resist the urge to press her mouth more passionately on his. Wyatt groaned in response and nibbled at her lips, and then slid his tongue between them. Laying back on her childhood bed, she pulled him down on top of her, only to stop quickly when she felt him wince against her mouth.

"Oh no, your shoulder! Are you okay?"

Wyatt chuckled and rolled onto his back. "I'm with you again, Doc. Everything is perfect. You can tap dance on my chest, if it makes you happy."

Warmth filled Jenna's whole body and a huge smile broke across her face. "I don't need to do that, but I would like to free you up a bit."

She gingerly removed his sling, before stretching her body along his and kissing him again. Sliding one leg between his, desire began to build inside of her at the pressure of his muscular thigh against her warm center. Jenna rubbed against him harder, as though she were a teenager again, complete with the accompanying creaking of her childhood bed.

Wyatt leaned away from her kiss. He stroked her hair from her face with his hand, taking the moment to stare at her silently. She saw desire in his eyes, but also deep concern.

"Wyatt, what's wrong? Why did you stop? Is it because of my surgery?"

"Are you okay? I mean, is it safe? I can't tell you how scared I've been while you went through all that. Your dad kept me updated, but not being able to be there for you…it killed me. I don't want to cause you any pain."

"I'm not made of glass. It's still me. Please, I *need* you to touch me." The agony of so much time apart weighed heavily inside of her. His warm caress was the only thing that seemed to provide her any relief.

She pulled off her shirt, and slid down her pants. Wyatt's warm gaze moved over her body slowly, fanning the heat inside of her until it was a full blaze. Jenna carefully removed his shirt, dragging her mouth across the hot, smooth skin of his chiseled chest. When she heard him pop the button of his jeans and slide the zipper down, her heart filled with happiness.

Wyatt's hand undid the back of her bra and gently caressed her newly freed breasts. He eased back and stared at her again, seemingly transfixed by the sight of his own hands on her body. A tickle of fear invaded Jenna's throat. She tried to swallow around it.

"I know I look a little different. Do my scars bother you?" she asked in a shaky voice.

His eyes turned upward to hers quickly and he whispered, "God no. You're more perfect than ever to me — because now you're safe. I love you, Jenna. It's just…I dreamed so much of being with you again…"

"I dreamed about you, too. This is *real*."

He smiled at her, as his hands moved to her panties and pushed them down her legs. She eagerly shoved down his jeans and boxer briefs, so their bodies and emotions were completely bared to the other.

"I can't wait anymore, Doc," he grunted, his left hand gripping at her bottom and squeezing it hard.

"Then don't."

Wyatt sat up and buried his face into her neck and growled

at the invitation. Leaning back to smile devilishly at her, he moved her leg so she was straddling him. She curled her legs around him, squeezing him tightly to her with her thighs. Kissing across the edge of her neck and jaw, he found her mouth with his, just as he pressed hard at her entrance.

Jenna opened herself to him, sighing heavily as he entered her steadily. His right hand moved up her back. He moved his left hand to the bed for support, his legs becoming powerful pistons, driving his length into her body over and over again. She leaned her head back, letting him lick across her throat.

With her arms wrapped tightly around his neck, she could feel his soft hair tickling her chin. It was a gentle contrast to the potent and welcome sensations occurring below. Wyatt had taken complete control of her body, and Jenna was so grateful.

She needed him in every way, and no amount of his body so close to hers seemed to be enough. His touch was finally erasing the memory of so much loss and time apart. She couldn't wait to let him keep trying to make it all better.

Jenna's body exploded with convulsing spasms of bliss. She screamed his name, as he whispered, "oh, belleza," hotly against her neck.

He growled against her skin, thrusting into her one more time, before resting inside of her. She relaxed her legs around his waist, but he kept holding her.

Jenna leaned away so she could see his face. Brushing the damp hair off his forehead, she whispered, "Thank you for fighting for us, Wyatt."

He kissed her forehead, and answered, "I'd go to the ends of the earth for you."

"Lucky for you, you just had to head down to Georgia."

EPILOGUE
Approximately Three Months Later

"Mr. McCoy, I must say, I am very impressed with your progress. This type of surgery usually takes six to eight months for recovery. It's July and you're looking stronger than ever. Let me just make a note in your file," Jenna said, her glasses perched on the end of her nose.

"That's great to hear, Doc. I've been working hard."

"I can tell. I think your performance on, *and off*, the field, is phenomenal. I was particularly impressed with your stamina just now. I can tell you've been taking your training and rehab very seriously."

She strutted away from him in red stiletto heels, avoiding a box labeled *Doc's Tee Shirts (Box 1 of 3)*, so she could bend over her old dressing table that they'd decided to put in Wyatt's bedroom. Wiggling her hips, she made sure her lab coat crept up, revealing her bare bottom, with its tan lines from their recent trip to Cabo San Lucas, Mexico. She'd added a red garter belt and thigh-high stockings to the look this time.

They'd already played a round of Wyatt's favorite game, *Dirty Doctor Sutherland*, but it was still fun for her to prance around for him as his own personal sex kitten. His answering groan gave her all the confirmation she needed, to know he enjoyed it, too.

Jenna pretended to write a note on the pad of paper, when she felt Wyatt's hands slide around her waist and he pressed himself against the crease of her ass, his cock hardening beneath the cotton of his boxer briefs.

"Again, already? I really *am* impressed, Mr. McCoy."

"It's your fault. You know that lab coat makes me crazy."

She turned around and perched on the dressing table, crossing her legs slowly. Wyatt licked his lips and started stroking her knees.

"Down, boy," Jenna commanded, swatting at his hands. "We have less than an hour before everyone gets here."

"Make them wait."

"I'd rather not risk my dad and Aunt Cheryl seeing us going at it. We may be moving in together, but still... Plus, even though Claudia couldn't get away from FBI training to be here, your mama told me she wrapped up her photo shoot for *More* magazine, so she'll be coming with your abuela. You know they won't be happy if they show up to our housewarming party to find the two of us naked."

"Everyone's going to have to learn boundaries. Now that we finally got my Roughnecks' contract sorted out, I'll be in Latrobe for training camp soon. That means my time with you is going to get very limited. I need to make the most of every minute."

"Oh, stop that. You'll see me when I come to assist the trainers with orthopedic consults."

Although Richard had passed her over for the fellowship this time around, he was emphatic she'd get it next time. He'd been thrilled with her new open-minded and empathetic approach to her patients, after the ordeals of her illness and the public reveal of her relationship with Wyatt. Richard was also thrilled she was the medical head of the after-school program portion of Wyatt's new foundation.

Wyatt had done so much to help her, too, despite her insistence he focus on his career as much as possible. His marketing campaign for the *UPMC* sports medicine department went a long way to healing the group's concerns about her and Wyatt's behavior. And she suspected Wyatt had been encouraging both the team, and its players, to give her a shot whenever they could. It felt like she was finally getting the opportunities and recognition she'd craved for so long.

"Just *seeing* you isn't enough for me, Doc, you know that."

His hands pulled her legs apart and slowly crept up her thighs. Jenna moaned in response. As his rough fingers stroked at her clitoris, still engorged from their recent lovemaking, she gripped at his muscular biceps hard.

Wyatt grunted, but this time in pain. Jenna released him, full of fear that she'd hurt him in some way.

"What is it? Are you okay?"

"I wanted it to be a surprise, but I guess we have no secrets... I've been thinking that my woman can't have more tattoos than me."

"But you don't have any tattoos, Wyatt."

"I do now."

"What?"

Wyatt yanked off the tee shirt he'd managed to keep on during their little game to reveal a tattoo of a brown bird, similar to the one signifying her in the tattoo she, Aubrey, and Tea shared. Situated within the design were the words "Mi Belleza."

"I had them put it near my right shoulder, because jacking

up this part of my body is the best thing that ever happened to me. This injury brought us together."

"Oh. I love it! Does that mean I'm your little brown bird?" Jenna said and kissed the area next to the tattoo softly.

"You are, but I'm never letting you fly away. I love you, belleza. Now you're always with me. And, so that I'll always be with you…"

Wyatt walked around the dressing table and opened the drawer. He searched around inside, then removed his hand — the delicate chain of her locket hanging from it.

"What are you up to, Wyatt?"

"I wanted to put something in your locket."

He walked in front of her again and held up the necklace to her. He let the pendant rest in his palm so she could open it softly. When she registered the picture inside, her brows furrowed in confusion.

"That's the picture Olivia took of us kissing in your driveway. After you ran after me because I was so upset."

"It is. I love that memory. That was a beautiful moment for me — for us. It was when I first realized I needed to have you in my life. I'd been in love with you for a while already, even if I was too dumb to understand it. But that was when the reality of it all hit me. I suddenly got it — I had to make you mine."

"Wyatt's, that's so beautiful, but that article — Olivia…"

"She's gotten what she deserved. Even though I hate what she did, I love that we have this moment captured. Life gave us that gift, and I want to have you wear it next to your heart…and in between your perfect breasts…every day."

"Wow, so poetic."

"It's a gift." Wyatt secured the necklace around her neck and gazed at her happily. Jenna smiled back at him.

"I love that picture in there. You're right. It has to be this picture. You are so precious to me. I love you, Wyatt."

"I love you, too. I'm glad you waited to put something in it. That you waited for us."

Jenna hugged his bare waist and kissed him. Her romantic feelings quickly blazed into something much hotter.

"Um, Wyatt?" she mumbled against his chest.

"Yes, belleza?"

"On second thought, I'd really like to have my way with you again before everyone gets here. Do you think we have time?"

"Oh, yes, we definitely do. We have our very own forever ahead of us."

"And I can't wait to make the most of it," Jenna said, lifting her face to kiss him.

THE END

Keep Reading for a Sneak Peek of
Book Three in the Gateway to Love Series

A STEEL TOWN
(Anticipated Release: Spring 2015)

Claudia McCoy has been told what she *can't* do enough for one lifetime. After a near-fatal childhood battle with juvenile diabetes and having to accept that her dreams of serving the military in combat would never come true, she's thrilled to begin a life on her own terms. Yet, when she finally starts her career in the FBI, Claudia is furious to discover her overbearing big brother, Wyatt, has once again stepped in where he wasn't wanted. His interference has derailed her from her high-profile aspirations of a position in the FBI's D.C. headquarters, planting her instead practically right into his Pittsburgh backyard.

Trey Adler is known for fixing things, but he's also broken just as many — leaving him with regrets that will never go away. He'd be the first to agree he should stay away from a nice girl like Claudia, but he can't deny his friend Jenna Sutherland's request when she asks him to use his position as a temporary FBI consultant to keep Claudia safe — especially because it's clear this little firecracker needs protecting. Far away from all the action she so craves, Claudia is more determined than ever to prove herself in her first major investigation at whatever cost — and those costs are proving to be dangerously high.

Their battle of wills turns quickly into a powerful need for one other, that makes them both rethink everything they ever wanted.

Will Trey be able to keep her alive long enough to give them an opportunity at something real together — a future that can survive the danger in their present, as well as the darkness of his past?

And don't miss out on the Bonus Companion Novella to
A Steel Town —
SHANGHAI WIND
(Anticipated Release: February 2015)

Now, an Excerpt from A Steel Town:

Claudia's boots crunched over a smattering of dried leaves and gravel. The sound was almost thunderous against the silent backdrop of the abandoned steel mill site to which her very first tip had led her, forcing her to pause briefly, as the echoing noise dissipated. The delay was also helpful in allowing her racing heart to slow, if only a small amount.

Shadows overtook the many nooks and crevices of this metallic wasteland, as the ribbons of violet and dusky orange, which had been streaking above the length of the Ohio River, were rapidly surrendering to the much more inky and dark shades of twilight. With a shaky breath, she took out her phone to look at the satellite map images she'd collected before leaving her apartment. Claudia relied on the glow from her phone and made a quick left turn between two small buildings. They appeared to have once been designated for storage, but after years of neglect, the decrepit metal structures had become merely broken-down artifacts of a way of life long since departed from her new home of Pittsburgh. It had been decades since generations of workers reported there every day to craft the metal that formed the backbone of this city's development. Now its only visitors appeared to be graffiti artists, and perhaps the occasional drunk hoping to find a peaceful spot for his escape.

The entire scene was lonesome and anachronistic in a way that made her even more uncomfortable with the task she'd put upon herself. It also seemed like a damn fine place to get tetanus, so Claudia was treading carefully.

She put her phone away and zipped up her light leather jacket with slightly quivering fingers. The nighttime autumn air was crisp, seeping through her thin top, chilling her blood. It seemed to be so much colder down there by the river, the rusted out hulls of dozens of aluminum buildings creating a whistling wind tunnel that buffeted her small body with merciless cutting gusts.

This collapsing metal ghost town seemed a world away from the sparkling high rises of downtown Pittsburgh, and the tree lined brick streets of its historic neighborhoods. The beauty and quaintness of it all didn't make her frustration at her life being derailed by her brother any less suffocating. Yet, this evening jaunt was certainly making her appreciate the city's prettier face.

Calm down, she chastised herself. *I'm the one that wanted to be tough and act like a real agent. That means I need to suck it up, find the box the tipster told me about, and then I'm out of here.*

Her private pep talk seemed to work, steeling her nerves to keep walking with more confidence. With another sure-footed step, she turned sharply to maneuver between two more buildings.

Her feet, and her pulse, stopped short when a shadow flashed across the corner of her vision. At first, she could almost convince herself it was just her imagination, but she whipped her head around and saw a form ducking behind a corner. She caught enough of the view to see it was a man, tall and broad-shouldered beneath his hooded sweatshirt.

Claudia made sure her *Glock* was quickly accessible but she wanted to do all she could to avoid using it. This unwelcome visitor could be a danger, or the person behind her tip, or both.

Seeing as she wasn't even supposed to be there, discharging her FBI-issued weapon was not a good idea. She took advantage of her petite frame and maneuvered forward delicately, venturing toward a more open area of the mill.

When the light was bright enough, she caught his shadow move more closely behind her.

Perfect.

With one quick motion, Claudia spun around with a roundhouse kick to his stomach. The muscles of his abs were firm beneath her blow, but she'd thrown him off balance, and had elicited quite a few expletives from him under his breath. Taking advantage of his distraction, Claudia threw herself on the ground. Supporting herself with her hands, she spun a low kick, taking him off his feet and landing him on his ass.

Worried he'd get back up, Claudia straddled him quickly and pinned his arms to the ground. It stunned her that he didn't fight her at all. *Perhaps he is still winded from my stomach kick?* she wondered.

Securing both his hands in one of hers as best she could, Claudia pushed his hood back from his face. Her breath skipped in her throat. The shadowy figure she'd just taken down was freaking gorgeous.

Dark hair framed his tanned face. He looked vaguely familiar, but she couldn't quite place him. Especially when she was distracted by the way his teasing curve of a smile and his sparkling gray eyes made it clear he was laughing at her. Still not uttering a word, he grinned fully at her and began to move his large torso to sit up and face her.

Aw, hell no, she thought. Moving her hands to his chest, she pushed him hard back to the ground.

"Hey, easy there, little tiger," he grunted out. "I let you have your fun, but this ground is starting to get uncomfortable.

Even for a tough guy like me."

The smoothness of his voice, even through his clear annoyance, was almost hypnotic. His face held a few piercings and she could spy some tattoos peeking out from underneath his hoody, but he didn't look hard or dangerous — so much as intensely sexy. Finding a man this attractive was new to Claudia, and it was really pissing her off. Her eyes were too interested in his strong jaw and chiseled cheekbones, when they should be trying to determine if he was a threat. His face had a couple days of stubble, and she cursed herself for wondering what it would feel like on her fingers. *Would it be prickly, or smooth?*

"Are you done?" he asked.

"Excuse me?"

"Done staring at me?" he teased with a smile that revealed perfectly straight teeth resting behind his distracting lips.

"I-I'm not staring at you. I need to ascertain what kind of danger you are."

"Fine. Play it that way. You don't need to worry about me. I'm on your side."

"What? My side? Did Agent Jacobs figure out I was still going to follow up on this tip? Did he send you?"

"Agent Jacobs? Hell no. That dumb-ass wouldn't recognize a tip in a urinal."

"You're disgusting," Claudia snipped out, but his crass joke made a smile twitch at her lips.

"Besides, I'm not a Fed. Well, not really."

"Then who are you? Tell me who you are right now, or so help me…"

"So help you what? You'll swat at me with those little mitts of yours, again?"

Claudia lifted a fist and went at him hard. She wanted

nothing more than to show him how those tiny paws of hers could do some serious damage, but he grabbed it in one of his large hands before she connected. She shook her hand out of his, fury pumping through her.

"You son of a bitch. Tell me who you are."

"Calm down. I'm Trey," he answered, awkwardly moving his other hand from his supine position to shake hers. "Nice to meet you, Agent McCoy...I think," he added. "I'm one of Jenna's friends." Claudia leaned back, sitting fully on his midsection as she processed this information.

"Wait. Trey? Trey *Adler*? Are you the one that's in love with my brother's live-in *girlfriend*, Jenna?"

"The Adler part is right. But I'm not in love with Jenna. What gave you that idea?"

"That's what Wyatt says."

"What your brother is wrong about is a lot."

"That may be true, but you still haven't told me what you're doing here."

"Um, first, do you mind moving...I know you're just a little thing..."

"I'm not little!"

"If you'd let me finish, I was going to say, no, you aren't that small. But if you don't climb off me we're going to have a situation on our hands. Or in my lap, to put it more accurately."

"You're a pig."

"You're the one that won't climb off me."

Claudia huffed at him, pushing off his chest hard enough to hear him release a satisfying, "oof" sound. Trey lifted a hand to her to help him up, his crooked grin never leaving his face.

She stared down at him for a minute, almost paralyzed.

"What? Aren't you strong enough?" he teased.

With an irritated sigh, she finally grabbed his hand with hers and helped him up from the ground. His hand fully enveloped her much smaller one. It was rough and cool to her touch. As soon as he was standing, Claudia dropped it like she'd been bitten. Now that he was standing fully in front of her, she had to crane her head back fully to meet his eyes.

"Impressive," he said softly. "You really are a pint-sized thing, aren't you? It was quite a pleasure letting you take me down."

"*Letting me?* Screw you." He just laughed gently in return. Claudia tried to bring reason back to her mind. "Why did Jenna ask you to follow me? What did she tell you?"

Shame coated Claudia's throat at the memory of letting herself get so sick in front of her brother's girlfriend — a stunning and confident physician, that knew a diabetic who couldn't handle her shit when she saw one.

Trey looked down at her, his eyes turning warm and reassuring. Claudia decided she preferred his teasing manner to this much more unsettling caring demeanor.

"Jenna didn't tell me anything. She didn't have to. She just asked and I said yes. I'm around the Pittsburgh FBI office a lot with the ongoing investigation into Jack Taylor's murder, so she figured I could keep an eye on you."

"I know that case. I've been trying to get on it. But they keep sticking me on the FBI equivalent of saving a cat stuck up in a tree. That's what..."

"This supposed lead is about? I know. I also know you were told not to follow up on it."

"Yeah. I get told 'no' quite a bit."

"I'm not a fan of being told what to do either, Claudia." It was the first time he'd said her name and it was like he'd poured warm honey down her body. "But that doesn't mean you shouldn't be careful. You were planning to follow up on a shady tip like that all alone?"

"I tried to get support, but they think it's a dumb idea."

"Instead you decided to come out here by yourself — a place that looks like Murder City, population of you? Forget the danger factor for a second, do you know how much trouble that'll get you into with your boss?"

"So? From what I hear about you, all you do is get in trouble."

He stepped so closely to Claudia that he towered completely over her. The heat of his body came over her in waves, almost overwhelming her. Trey stared down at her until she met his eyes fully.

"*You* aren't *me*," he whispered.

"Thank goodness for that," she huffed out, turning to walk away briskly. Claudia raised her chin, desperately trying to remember her original path before this tattooed pain in the ass interfered with her evening, but it seemed like her brain just wouldn't work. A sudden tug at her right arm spun her around, forcing her to look up again, straight into his chiseled features.

"All right, that's it. Your whole feisty thing is cute, and all. But I promised Jenna I'd keep you alive, so I'll tell you right now — this shit's going to get old really quick."

"I'm so sorry to inconvenience you. Here's a solution. How about you leave me alone? Win-win, for both of us."

"Oh no, you don't, little one. Trust me, babysitting a spoiled McCoy sibling is not appealing to me in the slightest, but Jenna is a good friend and I can't say no to her."

"That does a lot for your whole 'I'm not in love with Jenna' thing."

Trey pressed a hand at the small of her back, stilling her.

"Are you scared I'm in love with Jenna, or that I'm not,

and that my heart is available?"

"Oh please. I know your game. You just want to torment me. Thing is, if I don't get going, it'll get too dark to find anything, and this whole night will have been a waste."

"Not a total waste," he answered with a smile, "you got to meet me."

"Ugh, no wonder my brother hates you."

"Trust me, my feelings toward your brother are mutual. That doesn't change why I'm here, or what I promised I would do. If you won't give up, then you're just going to have to get used to me going everywhere you do."

Claudia turned away from him, but her stomach turned when she realized night had almost completely fallen. The mill yard had seemed manageable before, but now all she saw was a vast archipelago of treacherous alleys and easy hiding places. She'd come too far to turn back now, but doubt had crept into her bones, as insidiously as the rust that had slowly overtaken the building in front of her. "What's that they say in the movies?" Claudia muttered to herself. "Oh right. I've got a bad feeling about this."

"Me too. Do you want to leave now?"

"I'm not giving up. I never give up."

"Me neither," he answered.

A loud bang in the distance made her jump. She swallowed hard before choking out, "Fine. If you really want to come, I guess I can't stop you."

"How kind of you, because unfortunately for both of us, you're stuck with me. And I'm not going to let anything happen to you, little one."

TO BE CONTINUED...

CONNECTING WITH CHLOE

Hopefully you enjoyed City of Champions. If you did, please consider leaving a review so that other readers can find it.

Also, be sure to sign up for the Chloe T. Barlow newsletter. It is the best way to catch any deals, giveaways, new releases, or other exciting news about Chloe's creations. You are also welcome to join Chloe's street team, Chloe's Crew, on Facebook.

Newsletter and Blog:
http://chloetbarlow.com/newsletter/

Chloe enjoys nothing more than interacting with her readers, so please keep in touch!

Facebook:
https://www.facebook.com/ChloeTBarlow

Twitter:
https://twitter.com/chloetbarlow

Goodreads:
https://www.goodreads.com/author/show/7376511.Chloe_T_Barlow

Email:
chloe@chloetbarlow.com

Google+:
https://plus.google.com/u/0/116405903319564147007/posts

Chloe's Crew (Chloe Barlow Street Team)
https://www.facebook.com/groups/chloebarlowcrew/

Pinterest:
http://www.pinterest.com/chloetbarlow/

Amazon Author Page:
http://www.amazon.com/Chloe-T.-Barlow/e/B00IXAHC64/ref=ntt_athr_dp_pel_1

Learn more about Chloe, City of Champions,
and the continuation of the Gateway to Love Series at:

Chloe's Website:
http://chloetbarlow.com

ACKNOWLEDGMENTS

The last several months since the release of *Three Rivers* have been nothing short of amazing. I continue to be grateful to every reader, blogger, and reviewer who took a chance on the *Gateway to Love* series.

As always, my husband: Taking this journey with you has been so deeply inspirational and gratifying. Seeing all the time you take to support me during this process is just one more reminder of how very lucky I am to have you in my life. I love you.

My Agent: *Michelle Grajkowski* of *Three Seas Literary Agency* is not only a fabulous advocate for me and my books, but she is also a remarkable person and dear friend. I am thrilled I met her and that she continues to believe in me, and the stories I love to share with the world. I look forward to sharing many more memories with her.

My Team: *Eisley Jacobs* of *Complete Pixels* truly is a magician. She somehow manages to turn all my crazy ideas into a beautiful visual reality.

Marilyn Medina of *Eagle Eye Reads Editing*, thank you for being such an incredible editor, full of tough love and a remarkable eye for story and detail. Working with you is a pleasure I look forward to with bated breath every time.

Kara Hildebrand for being that last set of sharp eyes and warm hand of support that makes the last month before publishing so much less stressful.

Between the Sheets Promotions gets a big round of applause from me for their unending skills and tireless professionalism. They are also incredibly kind and supportive friends that make this journey ever more special.

Joely Bogan of *Book Worms* blog, *Kristina Ohrberg, Ashley Lake, and JoElle R.* for helping me so regularly with all the craziness being an author entails.

Consultants: Thank you to *Deane* and his beautiful mom, *Becky R.* for providing valuable insight into what it means to be a proud Texan. *Tera Lemus* was also a great help on ensuring I presented Wyatt's family and lineage accurately. Wyatt McCoy thanks you all, too. I also thank my wonderful *mother, Julia Kent*, and *Kristina Ohrberg* for their helpful research and commentary on medical points.

My Beta Readers and Author Mentors: Thank you so much to *Kristina Ohrberg, Ashley Lake, Nicole Beckett, Katie Bloch Pettigrew* of *Southern Belle Book Blog, Marissa Vann* of *Smut Book Club, Patricia Booth, Karrie Mellott Puskas* of *Panty Dropping Book Blog,* and authors Helena Newbury, and Julia Kent. Your help through early reading, wonderful input, and general good old pep talks has meant the world to me.

Chloe's Crew: I can't fathom how much my street team has grown since *Three Rivers* released, but what I can believe is the depth of love I have for each of you great Crewbies. Thank you for all you do every day. I am honored you would take time out of your busy lives to be a part of this experience with me.

The City of Pittsburgh: The inspiration this beautiful city provides me is very special to me. I am also thankful to all the Pittsburghers who have been so supportive of this series. I especially want to thank *Lorinda Hayes* for granting my long-held dream of being featured in the *Pittsburgh Post Gazette* newspaper

My Readers: Finally, it is with great pleasure that I thank each of my readers for enjoying the world of Althea, Jenna, Aubrey, and the whole gang with me. You are what make this all possible.

CITY OF CHAMPIONS SOUNDTRACK

- *Time to Say Goodbye – Con Te Partiro* — Sarah Brightman
- *My Silver Lining* — First Aid Kit
- *Luckiest Man* — The Wood Brothers
- *Somebody That I Used To Know* — Gotye
- *Casino (Bad Things)* — Houndmouth
- *Drive* — The Cars
- *Wintersong* — Sarah McLachlan
- *Secret Garden* — Bruce Springsteen
- *Estare En Mi Casa Esta Navidad* — Luis Miguel
- *10,000 Weight In Gold* — The Head and The Heart
- *Stay With Me* — Sam Smith
- *What Are You Doing New Year's Eve?* — Harry Connick Jr.
- *Auld Lang Syne* — John McDermott
- *Dice* — Finley Quaye, Beth Orton
- *Ticking Bomb* — Aloe Blacc
- *The One That Got Away* — The Civil Wars
- *Don't Give Up* — Peter Gabriel
- *Say Something* — A Great Big World
- *High Hopes* — Kodaline
- *Codeine* — Jason Isbell and the 400 Unit
- *I Wish I Was the Moon* — Neko Case
- *With Or Without You* — U2
- *Ledges* — Noah Gunderson
- *Welcome Home, Son* — Radical Face
- *Lost Cause* — Beck
- *Ends of the Earth* — Lord Huron
- *All of Me* — John Legend

Follow Chloe on Spotify to hear this and
other soundtracks from future novels:
http://open.spotify.com/user/chloetbarlow

ABOUT CHLOE T. BARLOW

Chloe is a contemporary romance novelist living in Pittsburgh, Pennsylvania with her husband and their sweet dog. She is a native Washingtonian that graduated *Duke University* with a degree in English and Chinese language. She met her husband at *Duke* and he brought her to Pittsburgh over a decade ago, which she has loved ever since and made her adopted hometown. She also attended the *University of Pittsburgh Law School* where she continued to be a book-loving nerd.

Chloe has always loved writing and cherishes the opportunity to craft her fictional novels and share them with the world. When Chloe isn't writing, she spends her time exploring Pittsburgh with her husband and friends. She also enjoys yoga, jogging, and all Pittsburgh sports, as well as her *Duke Blue Devils*.

She also thoroughly enjoys every opportunity to communicate with her readers. Since the release of her debut novel, *Three Rivers*, she has enjoyed the honor of meeting and talking with numerous fans, and looks forward to getting to know many more.

Made in the USA
Middletown, DE
05 January 2015